ONE OF THE DEATHLESS

Sitting under open sky, the one Jannus had known as a Screamer broke off a brown reed. He studied it in an effort to judge whether the season was early spring or late fall.

He didn't know his kind had come to be called Screamers; had he known, he would not have particularly cared. He was too familiar with his own mind and all its contents, and had outlived too many names, to have much interest in any form of identification beyond *I: myself*.

He was a Tek, one of the Deathless.

His musings drifted imperceptibly into feverish dream. He imagined himself waking in the familiar cylinder whose slick lid, inches above his staring eyes, refused to disengage. His chest pumped for breath; his laboring heart exploded. And at once, it seemed, he was waking yet again in the same opaque case. Fighting free this time, he found himself still enclosed, trapped under a roof with water rising in the chamber without escape for him; and presently he woke yet again, his dreaming mind knowing without thought that the sequence was infinite, before and behind.

He was a Tek, one of the Deathless.

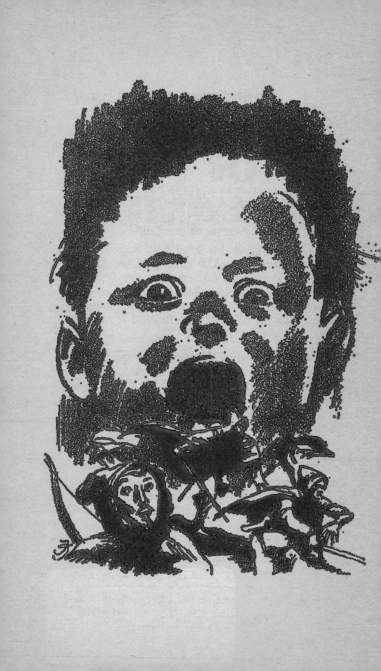

PURSUIT OF THE SCREAMER

Ansen Dibell

DAW BOOKS, INC.

DONALD A. WOLLHEIM, PUBLISHER

1301 Avenue of the Americas
New York, N. Y.   10019

Cover art by Gino D'Achille.

Dedication

The author is ever mindful of the help of Lois Renken and Jerrold Sies: peerless readers, critics, and friends.

FIRST PRINTING, JULY 1978

1 2 3 4 5 6 7 8 9

PRINTED IN U.S.A.

TABLE OF CONTENTS

Book I:

NEWSTOCK

The boy threaded the dark maze of corridors with steps that scarcely rustled the rush matting. In thought he was running—full sleeves flapping, soft-shod feet falling heavily; but in this, as in nearly all else, he maintained a decent control. The seventeen years since he'd been born into this household complex had taught him the approved habits of the Way and he mirrored them perfectly to any eye.

But there were more than eyes to deceive now.

There were the Valde.

Approaching the corridor leading to Southwing, lit by racked torches above the post of the Valde waykeeper, he kept his eyes properly downcast and his attitude free of any but the anxiety normal to a scribe sent on a sudden errand at night when a Screamer was still abroad in the household. His gamble was that the waykeeper would be too upset and distracted by the hunting of the Screamer to take much notice of his own mood, to pierce the surface anxiety and discover the guilty excitement beneath. For he knew a Valde troopmaid could hear only his feeling and not the thought behind it.

In a way, it was a test: if the Valde stopped him he'd know the Screamer had been run down. There'd be no use continuing then anyway. With the Screamer silenced, the duel he meant to spy on would be danced in the Even-hall as usual, not in the secret chamber below Southwing. There'd be no errand he could contrive which would let him past the watchfulness of the troopmaids and into the Even-hall during such a ceremony, though he was a Named man now and free of many of the restrictions that had bound him before. Some lady of the household would be called to pin him with direct questions he could not evade. His walking beyond the Way of custom, and all that lay beneath, secret as a stone at the bottom of the river, would at last be exposed to public view.

That thought deepened his dread, which would be safe enough, blurring subtler attitudes.

He saw only the greenclad knees and shins of the Valde troopmaid as he approached her. He did not look her in the face because it was not the Way for those serving in the household to do so. Doubtless, few wished to. But he, who knew all twenty-two of the Newstock troop, would have felt more secure knowing whether it were Seline or Anshru or Mene before him.

The legs did not move. Her head might be turning to follow him—he couldn't tell. He entered the shadows of the corridor, suppressing relief, knowing darkness to be no protection from a Valde's range of attention.

He remembered a hot doorway, himself a child of about nine watching the troopmaid Poli wet and plait a bowstring from hair drawn from a bundle beside her. "It is wondered . . . how far away you can *hear*." He'd used the general *you* with the suffix of respect (plural): Poli had been a stranger then, a tall adult though only two years his senior.

He could recall the troopmaid's face, intent, inexpressive and impersonal in its perpetual repose—remote but not unfriendly. "How far," she replied, "do you know smoke? It is with the wind, the air . . . if it is mist yet or dry. . . . As with the smoke, do you see, so with the *farioh*, the selfsinging, do you see? Look. A reedhen's *farioh* we know when she is beyond our sight . . . but. . . . It is the difficulty of seeking, do you see, of raveling it out from all *fariohe* of all living things she flies among. . . ." The troopmaid's long-fingered hands separated from the tangle a single silver hair, more comfortable with gesture than speech.

His response was, "I do hear you," the conventional phrase of polite attention and un-argument, though his curiosity remained unsatisfied. He'd wanted precision, distance in rods and spans, not smoke or the vague flight of a bird.

"Why do all Valde have short hair?" he'd asked, on another day

The smell of rain was in the north hallway where four passages converged: where open shutters revealed the greybrown shine of the slow, sliding river, where Poli stood her hours as waykeeper. She'd greeted him as he hurried by toward the minor pages' common room, or he'd not have ventured to look up, recognize her. He could tell her from the others by then, and could pose a question in direct mode without insolence. They were friends.

"The Haffa Valde go shorn," she told him, an answer which clarified nothing.

"I do hear you. . . ."

"The Haffa—"

"There are, perhaps, other words," he suggested politely.

"The Choosing." She hesitated, searching. "We who come to this land. We who serve in Bremner. Haffa: the Choosing."

Surprised, he'd said that he assumed all Valde served in Bremner.

"The Haffa, only."

Later he'd learned the word was related to another meaning *male kin*. A better rendering would have been *the Brotherless*.

No male Valde had been seen in Bremner in living memory. Even in their own country they were rare, it was said: precious enough to be won with blood and long service. The boy had been fourteen before it even occurred to him such beings must exist, that the troopmaids were not as they seemed, self-sufficient and ageless. He'd been older still before he began to try to imagine the implications, to a Valde maid, of living to the age of Choosing without a brother to be witness to her prospect of bearing sons, should she come to mate.

The Hafera Valde were free to seek mates in their season and live out their lives in their distant native forests. The Haffa Valde journied to Bremner in troops of two hundred and served its disputing river towns for ten years, earning then their bride-price to carry back to the Summerfair: those that lived to return.

Passing meat keeps and storage rooms, nurseries and butteries, he came to the second south granary and ducked inside. It was completely dark within the huge room, but he could tell, from the slope of the slippery wheat, the direction of the river door he wanted. The great door was tightly shut against damp but secured only by a thick latch he could lift with his shoulder. He rested then, as much to control his fierce tension as to gather his strength: the Southwing waykeeper might yet notice him. Then he inched the door along its runners until he could slide through onto the unloading ramp.

Twilight still hung in the cool air, but the moon was hidden as yet beyond the escarpment on the other side of the broad river, the cliff of blood-brown rock darkening as the light failed, shutting out nearly half the sky. Having lived under the shadow of the deadly Kantmorie cliff all his life, the boy

tipped his head toward its rim only to check for the moon,
then set to work.

From a length of line sawed from its mooring ring on the
outside of the wharf he fashioned a sling with knotcraft he'd
learned while assigned to the harbormistress, unloading the
barges that came along the smaller streams into the great
river, Erth-rimmon, with the harvests of the men's inland
farmsteads, loading the steam-powered Andran paddlewheel-
ers that carried the bulk of the river traffic. He'd enjoyed that
work and had hoped to train as a counter or lader, so as to remain. But he'd been assigned as under-page and then as page:
the season his voice changed, his mother, the Lady Lillia, had
taken an interest in him and chose to have him about her.
She'd personally selected the mistress to whom he'd been
given—a lady of the third rank, only nine years his senior
and, more important in his view, generally too occupied in intrigue, rank, and her own appearance to supervise him over-
closely. The lady Merleen. That pact was ended now: he was
a Named man, answerable only to Lillia herself.

He was principal Audience Scribe, with quarters of his own.
He was permitted to be abroad in the corridors after sunset.
Since first thaw, he owned a name: Jannus. He was very for-
tunate.

With the sling wrapped over his shoulder Jannus went carefully down the weed-slimed wharf that ran parallel to the
building's outer wall. Peering into the narrow space between
wharf and wall, he found what he was seeking: light shining
from an oblong port half under the surface.

He tied the rope's end to the piling nearest the light, then
retreated to the granary door to wait. At the first appearance
of the moon, the duel would begin.

As the cliff's sheer face darkened he pulled off his clothes,
laying each piece as neatly as he could on the mounded grain.
Though he had a room of his own it was on the third floor, in
Northwing. Traveling back soaking wet was more than he
dared risk. Moreover, his wardrobe had been chosen for him
by the lady Merleen, who'd been of the opinion that his appearance reflected on her among the other ladies of the household. She'd therefore chosen for him clothing of the finest,
least durable materials, with dyes which would be ruined by
wetting. If he went clothed into the water, he'd be piebald
shades of violet for days. That, too, might involve explaining
and so wasn't worth the risk.

Curled into his cloak, Jannus sat shivering, considering the darkening water. Only fifteen days past its thawing, the river was still snow-fat and would bear the taste of snow.

But he would go into it just the same.

There was no way whatever he could prevent the duel.

At the least, he would share it by watching.

He'd watched the Full Moon Dance, when the Newstock troop had been bested. Such duels were public and bloodless: all inmates of the seven households were encouraged to watch, to add their partisanship to the pervading mood-smoke which supported all Valde rites.

Each team of ten, hands linked, curved to attack, trying to find a position whereby the two end Valde might simultaneously touch a member of the opposing team and so eliminate her, without allowing their team to be encircled and defeated. The two lines bowed into crescents and straightened in defense, feinting and retreating.

Eventually the Newstock team was reduced to just Seline spinning with outstretched hands, trying to eliminate one of Slatefen's chain of three without herself being encircled. But the circle was formed, and Seline knelt in token of submission as the cheer went up from the visiting Slatefen contingent who'd come downriver to witness the season's first trade-strife.

But it hadn't ended there.

Occupied with the changes his Naming was working in his life, Jannus was at first too absorbed in his own concerns to do more than note that Poli was absent from her accustomed post in Northwing. He still had enough contact with various pages, unfailing sources of gossip, to know something was afoot; but so many things were continually afoot in the sprawling warren that was the household of Lillia of Newstock that he took no particular notice.

But when five days had passed since his Naming and Poli had neither sought him out nor sent word of congratulation, Jannus became concerned enough to stand outside the Valde troop quarters, up past the jetty, until someone should come out to learn his errand.

It was Aliana Wir, the troopleader, who joined him in the road. "Burn bright, Lillia's son and scribe," she greeted him after the Valde manner, just as if nothing had changed, and stood waiting.

The troopleader had always intimidated him, with her sober, measuring eyes; so he made no objection to her manner of address and responded with full formality, "Burn bright,

Aliana Wir. It is wondered if the troopmaid Poli Wir is ill,
since she has been absent from her place."

Aliana stared at him for a disquieting while. "The troopmaid is well," she said at last, "but assigned other duties. It is
thought you should return to the household and not disturb
her further."

Suddenly cold to the bone and angry to know the whole
troop was aware of his reaction, he turned at once back
toward the household. Because he knew, then.

The Lady Lillia must have called for a single dance, a duel
between the best dancers of the two troops, to decide the issue
between Newstock and Slatefen. And Poli was First Dancer of
the Newstock troop.

The dispute was over the division of river tolls. Newstock
had lowered its rates, bringing more traffic south past Slatefen
without stopping. Slatefen, challenging the change, had called
trade-strife and won, in the public duel. But the Lady Lillia
must have counter-challenged, as was her right under common
custom. There'd be a Quarter Moon Dance, weaponed, between the two First Dancers, and only one would survive it.

Jannus knew such ceremonies were always held in the
Even-hall on the first night of the waning quarter. A complete
moon cycle, from dark to dark, was almost precisely forty
days: so he even knew which night it would be.

He did nothing. He said nothing.

Bremneri women, though lacking the full empathic sensitivity of the Valde, had inherited from a distant intermarriage a
form of the Valde gift, one they called "Truthtell." It enabled
them to detect belief of a speaker in what he said. Through
the centuries, Bremneri women had become shrewd question-
ers, once suspicion was wakened. And, Named or no, a man
had only to allow himself one unguarded action, one careless
word, one visible conscious departure from the Way, to be
questioned bluntly in direct mode and summarily shipped off
to the farmsteads for the rest of his days. Whatever Jannus
felt, he gave no sign.

He reminded himself that it wouldn't be Poli's first duel,
nor her second; he maintained a tense, difficult resignation until the Screamer's eruption into the afternoon's routines gave
him his chance.

About Screamers, Jannus knew rather less than he did
about the proverbial cat, of which it was said, "I know three
things about the Cat; I think I'm none the worst for that."

Jannus knew that Screamers were hated and hunted through the household by the troopmaids—Valde, who asked pardon and consent of even birds they slew in hunting, to whom murder, unconsenting death, was about the greatest horror imaginable. Yet Screamers they hunted into silence with a single-minded ferocity.

He knew Screamers had figured in the nightmares of household children for generations, though none could reliably claim ever to have seen or heard one.

And he knew that asking questions about Screamers produced unpleasant errands, lectures on propriety, or silence.

Among the younger pages there was a legend that Screamers preferred children's faces to gnaw, above all foods less rare and horrible; but they knew no more than he, and their ghastly theories were multitudinous and mutually contradictory.

Eventually Jannus had come to think of Screamers as merely another feature peculiar to this household, like bad chimneys or wet drafts.

The soundless wail only troopmaids could hear might begin at any time, without pattern. Sometimes there'd be no Screamers for a season, sometimes several in a week. Last spring, there'd been a visitation lasting three days without cessation and Fealis, First Dancer before Poli, had gone into hiding to escape the torment. By chance, Jannus knew where she'd gone. She'd been in the basements below Southwing, in the underwater foundations of the household. He'd been disciplining a minor page for lateness and been offered, as excuse, the page's assignment to take meals to a Valde staying in the prohibited basements. The rest, Jannus figured out for himself.

With this newest Screamer still uncaught, the Quarter Moon Dance would be held in that shielded room, where the dancers would find no intrusion on the rite. Therefore Jannus was crouched on the loading ramp, waiting for the moon to rise.

Without warning glow, the round leading edge of the crescent cut into the clear sky. More gradually the downturned talons pulled free of the high black edge of the cliff. Even in its waning the moon was three times larger than the sun and cast hard-edged shadows.

Laying aside his cloak, Jannus descended the wharf to the point where the pale yellow window glowed into the water. He tested his knots again—he could not swim—then lowered himself cautiously into the cold river, finding the loops of the sling with feet already aching toward numbness. The water was level with his chin as he edged sideways to look down through the upper third of the glass.

The room beyond the window was shiny and strange. The walls, opalescent and faintly curved, were neither wood nor cement but something like tile, glazed but without roughness or seam. The surface appeared warm and moist, like slices of a summer river somehow bent and held immobile, or like the interior of a bubble.

No door was visible from his vantage point, no window other than his own, more than head height above the smooth floor.

He was looking down on four women: two moving, two still. Still, seated on cushions on either side of a large enamelled lamp, were the rulers of the disputing cities, dressed formally in their proper colors. Blue, almost black in shadow, her face hidden within the hood of her cloak: Amersiae, Lady of Slatefen. In green that jarred with the rosy walls, chin bent intently onto her fist in a familiar pose, was his mother: Lillia, Lady of Newstock.

And circling lightly in the center of the chamber—sunwise, anti-sunwise—the two Valde: Poli and the First Dancer of the Slatefen troop in leather fighting harness dyed in their troops' colors. In each hand they held a metal crescent, round side outward. The gap between the talons was crossed by a wooden bar the fist gripped. Serving at once as blade and shield, each crescent flashed and turned in measured gestures in the lamp-light.

Poli reached suddenly but the other blocked the stroke with the face of her right crescent. Both dancers then reached out lightly, touching the edges of their instruments—once, twice—without force, only marking some internal measure of their dance.

The circling continued for some while with unhurried feints and counters. There was no pausing, no jagged motion. Then the Slatefen maid struck. As Poli tilted the face of her right disc, the other Valde flashed her second crescent toward Poli's face. Poli barely deflected it upward. A red diagonal line sprang into being across her brow.

Caught by the meaning and the shock of first blood, Jannus called, felt, warning and concern.

Luckily Poli couldn't hear him. The pearly walls protected the Valde from such a fatal distraction just as it insulated her from the Screamer. Unaware of him, she was safe.

The pace quickened. The two Valde swung out with either disc or both, staring raptly into each other's eyes: expressionless, dreaming, their short silver hair clinging wet to their skulls.

At each upstroke of her left arm Poli smeared blood from her forehead to keep from being blinded. Her forearm cast drops on the floor as she moved.

The other Valde had been touched now: along the ribs, and on her right elbow. It became hard to distinguish new cuts from smears. The floor, under their bare feet, must be turning slippery. The flash of the discs from rim, to face, to rim, shielding and striking, became even more swift.

Suddenly both Valde parted their lips: Jannus knew they were singing aloud. There was no pause between strokes at all. The crescents flashed, turned, sliced out level, rounded to gouge up at wrists and arms, in one continuous woven motion.

He didn't see the blow. He only saw the Slatefen maid stoop forward, away from him, and fall loosely on her side, one disc spinning slowly on the piebald floor. As her head leaned to rest, part of the gash in her throat could be seen.

Thrilled, sickened, exultant, Jannus bent his face into the water, choking. After he'd been sick he felt more composed and caught his breath as he paddled clear water toward himself. The port before him was dark and empty.

After two tries he drew himself back up onto the ramp, shivering convulsively. He'd have to leave the rope. His fingers were too cold to manage the knots now. Not much showed. It wouldn't matter. He was bracing himself to stand when he saw something move at the head of the wharf. He remained crouched, squinting to see more clearly in the monochrome light.

Something had slipped through the door he'd left pushed back: a hunched shape too large for one of the granary cats, too small for anything else. It was dragging behind it what he suddenly recognized as his own jerkin.

It saw him. It froze, the moonsilver touching its hairless head—a creature like a skeletal child, narrow pale fingers clutching the cloth. He could hear its breath hissing softly.

Without thought he called, "You can't have that. It's mine." At once he felt incredibly foolish.

The Screamer straightened a little, raked the sky overhead for no visible reason, then jerked its gaze back to the boy. "I need it. I'll die," it said.

"But it's mine," the boy found himself insisting blankly, quite beyond astonishment. "I'm accountable."

The Screamer continued to stare at him, all but its eyes and the outlined curve of its naked skull lost in shadow. "Say I took it."

"No." With sudden inspiration, Jannus added, "Pay me."

"How?" The reply was barely audible.

"Tell me what you are."

"A mind, a body. . . ."

"No."

"Then, an eater of kin. Which is to say, a Tek of the High Plain of Kantmorie."

Irony: evasive, tantalizing. "No," Jannus said again, holding out for more. But the Screamer said nothing. It had begun to shake. Jannus surrendered. "Take it. I . . . . Take it."

The Screamer wriggled into the jerkin, which covered it to the ankles. The intent shine of its eyes reappeared, still fixed on him.

Next, Jannus thought, it would need shelter. "There's a place the Valde seldom go—"

"Price?" murmured the Screamer, but the boy hurried on.

"—upriver, beyond the houses, in the marsh between the joining of Erth-rimmon and the Brownfields. Almost an island. The Valde don't go there."

"Seek me there." With a twisting leap it was gone, striking the water with an audible smack.

Released by the sound, the boy ran to the head of the wharf and stared at the river's dim surface, finding no motion, no sound but the lap of the water against the pilings.

Slowly he stooped for his cloak and retreated into the granary. He heaved the door shut and latched it. Absentmindedly he would have dried himself with the cloak but remembered the dye in time. He set himself to wait, enforcing calm: with the Screamer's escape, he'd have to be even more careful on the way back. The cold was like a second, painful skin but that was all right since Poli was safe. This would be her last duel. She and the rest of the troop would go to the Summerfair and be brided in this, the tenth year of their service.

The freemaid Poli Wir shut her eyes against the warm sunlight to watch the red sparks flash under her lids. It was like floating in bright water after being trapped nearly to drowning among the writhing slimy corpses of trees. She'd been so certain; and yet she was still breathing, and safe.

She felt boneless, weightless. Her contentment spilled into the eddying harmonies of the other Haffa troopmaids, both those in the quarters with her and the rest, bound in the web of alertness woven among Valde troopmaids all up and down the river.

She'd become First Dancer in the long days of summer, the year before. She'd danced five single duels—and yet she was alive. Fealis, First Dancer before her, had been cut down in her fourth dueldance; and Mene, before that, had been lamed and had come to feel too darkhearted for briding. Then there had been the black year, the sixth of their service, when twenty-six had been lost in single and paired duels, and almost as many through the heartsickness of shared and reverberating grief.

So many, so many to have been lost. Of the troop of two hundred who'd set out from the Summerfair, grown maids of eight or nine, less than thirty remained. The flares of the Bremneri trade-strifes had caught them like drifting willow cotton, fewer with each rounding of the moon. First Dancers burned brightest, fueled by desolation, and were the most quickly gone.

She'd utterly believed the death singing in her bones, but had kept it at bay until the long twilights in the too-empty quarters after Fealis had gone to the ground. Then the need had come to fight to establish her will to survive. When the next call came, she had become First Dancer.

The cold tin undertaste of her moods made the continual struggle of the other troopmaids against heartsickness that much more difficult, so closely were their *fariohe* all interwoven. Therefore she began to withdraw and consciously withhold herself from the many-singings of the troop, instead taking for companionship the infinite murmurings and cries of such living things as could not hear her in their turn.

She hunted when she could, west and north, where few people were.

And yet she was still here, and whole.

And soon, in a few days, the new troop would be arriving. The Great Web linking all the stocks up and down the length of Erth-rimmon reported their progress upriver. They'd be here soon. She'd join in the songs of greeting and parting, then stand on a ship and watch Newstock slide away with its Screamers and its incessant trade-strifes, into the marshes behind her.

The vaguely remembered journey would be unspooled:

south to the Sea, then north again along Arant Dunrimmon to Ardun-town, the Andran freeport, and then through the flowering Thornwall into the tree shadows of Valde. At the Summerfair she'd match herself to this or that stranger of her own kin and discover which would fit her singings and her silences, which one she'd hear equally well, far or near; she'd dower that one with her bridestone, that he might warm, with hands and breath, the ten long years' service and let it sleep.

She raised her head so she could see the pearl, the bridestone truly hung on a cord around her neck. On impulse she caught it up in her unbandaged hand and put it in her mouth, to savor it in all ways and keep it utterly safe.

She'd scarcely been aware of the Lady Lillia's bestowal of the jewel: her wounds had been hot, her mind bewildered by the end of the intent intimacy of dueltrance. She fully noticed the stone only on awaking and recognized it as a pledge that no more duels would be hers, that her service had been enough and now was done.

Sitting well clear of the trees, under open sky, the one Jannus had known as a Screamer broke off a brown reed. He studied and turned it in an effort to judge whether the season was early spring or late fall.

He didn't know his kind had come to be called Screamers; had he known, he would not have particularly cared. He was too familiar with his own mind and all its contents, and had outlived too many names, to have much interest in any form of identification beyond *I: myself.*

He was a Tek, one of the Deathless.

If it was fall, he was reflecting, with the whole inert winter before him, he might as well dispose of this body at once and waste as little time and useless effort as possible. But, contrarily, the cold season, with snow available to drink, might well be the only time he could attempt to cross that shelterless furnace, the High Plain . . . provided anybody could touch, much less climb, the deadly cliffside that walled the High Plain from the insurgent lowlands.

Shading his eyes with one hand, he examined the face of the Kantmorie cliff against whose red-ochre stone the Barrier should be invisibly stretched. River birds swung on the updrafts, saffron dots against the expanse of dull orange stone reared far above them; but if any touched the cliff and still lived, he couldn't determine.

The boy would know the season, and perhaps whether the Wall still endured.

He hoped the boy would have the sense to bring food when he came, hoped he'd come before this body died from exposure and neglect.

It was a ludicrous body, he thought: in other times, he would have suspected the joke of an ingenious enemy or an especially mordant colleague. Fish-pale skin, eyes that watered in the slightest breeze, tiny feeble hands. . . . After swimming only a little way upstream he'd had to turn in among the piers and cling to the slimy pilings, panting, half a dozen times before he could go on. It'd been nearly moonset before he got past the crosscurrents of the meeting rivers and dragged himself onto the spongy shore. He was still not really warm.

But it was this spindly container, he reminded himself, which had taken him out of that labyrinthine trap downriver—the unexpected town above and around the base where there should have been only marsh and wind. It had been long, he deduced, since his last memory of waking. There'd been time for a town to be needed and settled and to grow old, himself an unreasoning will fleeing in successive bodies through its foundations, ravening after the sky.

Long enough, maybe, for the Wall to have failed, opening a way somewhere back onto the High Plain.

The boy might know. There was no use planning until he came.

The Tek wished he knew more about the life-cycle of reeds. He balanced the stalk like a light javelin and launched it away into the marsh.

Lightheaded musings drifted imperceptibly into feverish dream. He imagined himself waking in the familiar cylinder whose slick lid, inches above his staring eyes, refused to disengage. His chest pumped for breath; his laboring heart exploded. And at once, it seemed, he was waking yet again in the same opaque case. Fighting free this time, he found himself still enclosed, trapped under a roof with water seeping, rising in the chamber without escape for him from the sense of constricted suffocation; and presently he woke yet again, his dreaming mind knowing without thought that the sequence was infinite, before and behind.

There was a space of time after first light, in the long sunless glow of Newstock mornings beneath the Wall, when no one had a claim on Jannus' time. He used part of it to have some pages' clothing collected on the excuse of laundering and to get a heavy slice of cheese and a heel of bread by an appeal to a scullion with whom he was on good terms. He concealed the bundle where he could collect it later. He hoped to have another break before the daymeal. The marshes would be an eerie place to be wandering, to be looking for a Screamer in the dark.

He left the household on other errands, the first being to locate a rowboat he could borrow without being noticed.

He walked up the broad cobbled way bordering the river, surveying each pier. The wind off the marshes, meeting him near alleys and open courtyards, carried a damp tang; though the day was as yet cloudless, he suspected rain might come after sunappear.

Dodging a loud tangle of fighting cats that unwound suddenly and streaked from underfoot past two children leading a balky goat, Jannus walked out onto the earthen jetty above the piers. A few limbs had been washed up against it during the night. These he tugged free and towed out to the jetty's end, where the current took them.

From the jetty he could see upriver to where ridged water marked the meeting of the Brownfields with Erth-rimmon, with the stubble of reeds and the pendulous cotton willow branches tiered above the scrap of land between. Downstream, southward, he could see the outthrust point where the Innsmiths were encamped with their colorful emblazoned tents. Down there he could see barges scattered half the width of the river and tiny figures, busy, waving at one another. No sound reached him from so far away.

An Andran paddlewheeler was moored at the nearest pier. From the packet's stern trailed two rowboats and a heavy barge loaded with split stove-length wood.

One of those little boats would do, he judged, if he waited till nightfall. . . .

Jannus turned his attention back to the packet itself and watched the dockhands and boatmen shifting cargo bales onto the pier with a block and tackle rigged to the boom. Then he wandered away.

Continuing up the street he came level with a long one-storied building a little distance from its neighbors. He found a seat on the river wall and rested, knocking his heels idly against the stones.

Presently a Valde came out. Ashferia. After a brief glance, Jannus watched a woman checking a series of drop-lines for fish. Ashferia went off down the street, her tabard bright in the diffused morning glow.

Jannus squinted toward the top of the cliff, wondering how long he could wait before he had to return to prepare the Morn-hall. A little while, yet, he decided, and turned back toward the troops' quarters.

Presently another Valde appeared in the doorway. She limped markedly and her forehead and left hand were bandaged. On a cord around her neck hung a smooth white stone, clearly visible against the unadorned green front of the tabard. Though Jannus had never seen one, he knew it to be a bride-stone.

As Poli came slowly across the road Jannus bent his head with unaccustomed formality, aware of a new unease and constraint.

"Burn bright, Hafri," Poli greeted him. It was a friendly use-name she'd given him: it meant *Younger Brother*.

"Burn bright, Freemaid." It was both a greeting and a congratulation. "This is a good place to rest," he suggested.

She settled crookedly on the wall, easing her right leg with visible care.

"It is hoped you mend well. . . ." Jannus inquired; and, when she didn't at once reply, he discovered her looking at him steadily. So she'd known right away, without needing to be told. He'd rather expected that. "Yes," he admitted, "I saw the dance."

"It was not wise."

"Probably not."

"Many things are not wise," remarked Poli, turning casually away. "Yet they are done, and no great harm comes of them, after all. . . ."

Jannus nodded, relieved to know she was not offended at his intrusion on her private concerns and wouldn't report it to the ladies of the household unless she were asked, which was unlikely. "I am Named. . . ." he mentioned.

"I did not know. We were . . . apart, Leani Wir and I—she I danced against, that you saw. And I did not hear of it. So I must not call you Hafri any more . . .? What name have you taken, then?"

"Jannus. . . ."

"From the song, the name?"

Jannus nodded again, hoping his choice would please or at least amuse her—it was not common to present Bremneri usage but was drawn from a ballad of the old times, which she'd taught him.

"And will you stay in the stocks, then, and not go to the farmsteads? That is well. You would not be happy there, they are drawn tight as a stone—" she displayed a closed hand, "—and there is much fighting, contention. . . ."

"And you'll be going," he responded, turning the subject back to what was on his mind. "When will it be?"

She opened the hand, turned it palm-up in a shrug. "When the new troop comes. Soon. . . ."

"I knew I might not hear until you all were already gone, and that seemed—"

"Yes. Better to make the parting than discover it, yes." Her grey-green eyes rested on him, friendly and opaque. "We will make it here, then. It is time for new things, Jannus w' Lillia, no more Hafri to me. Fare well in all your ways."

"Fare well, and happily, Poli Wir," he said, and watched her cross the road and disappear through the doorway.

Jannus' duties required him to act as prolocutor for the Lady Lillia during her daily audiences with inland and outland trade delegations. Such audiences were held at the hour of sunappear in the Morn-hall, whose windowlets of green glass, forming the leaves of a cotton willow painted on the tawny cement of the east wall, spangled the chamber with color at that hour.

The Morn-hall's only furnishings were two chairs, a cabinet, and a screen.

The guest seat, so massive five or six pages were needed to budge it, stood with its attached greenstone cabinet in the center of the floor. The other chair was concealed by the screen, which was worked with designs of safrom lilies and stood against the trunk of the painted tree.

As he was directing the minor pages in the placement of the courtesy foods in the cabinet, his ear caught the faint rustling he'd been awaiting. It signalled that the Lady Lillia was taking her place behind the Stranger Screen, having entered by the private door the screen also hid from view. Jannus quickly surveyed the preparations, found them complete, and with a wave dismissed the pages. After they had withdrawn, the Valde troopmaids posted in the anteroom admitted the first delegate.

The man was a middlesized florid Bremneri with a spade-shaped dark beard, conservatively and plainly dressed. He took his place in the guest seat and tasted at the courtesy foods without unmannerly haste, facing the boy and appearing to take no notice of the screen. He declared his name as Hanthal, serving as factor to Lurbrolestead. He was Newstock-born.

"Have you," Jannus responded, "or any person under your sole control, or any person at your direction or with your consent, had any manner of dealings with the stock of Lisle?"

The obligatory question was posed in direct mode, to prevent evasion.

"My number two clerk I caught discussing it. I thrashed him and he has not spoke of it since, in my hearing. No other has done so, at my will or with my consent. That is full truth."

Jannus waited a moment for a signal that would indicate either that the audience was terminated or that he should pursue the matter; the problem of Lisle, a downriver stock taken thirteen years ago by farmstead men and still held by them, was a precedent no ruling stock Lady treated casually. But no signal came, so Jannus said, "I do hear you. And do you, or any person under your sole control, or any person at your direction or with your consent, plan or contemplate harm to the stock of Newstock, or to Lillia, the Lady thereof?"

"None, by my will or with my consent."

Again the boy paused; but the Stranger Screen maintained its silence. So he proceeded to the factor's business, which involved ordering the year's supply of farm implements and household sundries the stockmen could not fabricate for themselves, the inlands being, like most of the world, metal-poor. The factor also wanted to advise his clients as to the comparative projected prices, per cubic rod, of redbean over early oats so they could plan their crops most profitably.

Discussing the familiar details, the boy studied the factor absently—seeking, from habit, some shadow of himself. The man who'd fathered him would be of the Newstock-born, and early in his service as a page Jannus was certain he must have come close to being dismissed for inept and injudicious attempts to find out which it'd been. Now he knew it didn't matter.

No man, having rejected or been dismissed from the stock at his Naming, was likely to think back to it with any fondness or wonder what'd become of the child, born to his assigned mistress, known to him only by report and by the onset of his Naming. Jannus knew that now from experience. Still he looked, from habit, and found no likeness.

The factor's business was soon concluded and scribed. After the man departed, Jannus set out a fresh cup and a plate of cakes from the supply in the cabinet.

He next interviewed, in succession, three more factors and two outlanders. The first of the outlanders, an Andran, sought permission to display a shipment of horn-shaped lamps, leaving a sample as a gift. Jannus put it into a recessed wall cupboard for the Lady to send for and examine at her leisure. The second outlander was a Smith, chief of the Clan that had been encamped a mile downriver, by permission, as long as the boy could remember. They were chiefly employed as woodworkers and ropers but would often turn their hands to whatever local work was offered them. They had accepted a commission to clear and deepen the river channel around Newstock's landing stages and docks.

The man, Elda Innsmith by name, was short, burly, and red-haired, like all his kin. He wore the same wrinkled cloak to every audience and, genially ignoring the boy, addressed the screened Lady as "Trader." That his freespoken ways never elicited a sign of displeasure or rebuke from behind the screen indicated the tolerance of the Lady Lillia toward a skilled craftsman who'd dealt honestly with the town during many commissions, over many years.

The dredging, the Innsmith reported, had been delayed by the late thaw holding up the wash of the spring floods, as the Trader might have expected, but was now completed. "Four rods, by your measure, to bottom at the shallowest, Trader, fourspan over what you required. Mostly muck, and that an't overhard to shift. Why not do the thing properly, I said, as long's we're about it? But that an't the whole of what I came up for." With an absent "B'yr court'sy," he downed the morn-wine, replaced the cup, wiped his extensive mustaches with a forefinger, and continued, "It's pure neighborliness, I thought, to let you know we're moving on. We were just waiting on this job of work to be finished, and now it is. So don't look to see us beyond a day or two."

"You perhaps lack employment here, Elda Innsmith. . . ."

The question had come from behind the screen.

Seeming to find nothing odd about being interrogated directly, the Innsmith replied, "No, Trader, it an't a matter of that at all. There's things to put a hand to here, I know that. No, it's a purely Clan matter that's of no concern to you or your stock, here. But you've dealt fairly with us, put us under your word—though, Great Wheel, there was no need of that—" he added, chuckling, "and gave our wives good rates on food and suchlike among the other households. So I thought it'd be just common neighborliness, the way I said, to let you know we meant to go on downriver. I'll come by tomorrow to fetch what we were promised for the dredging. We'll be needing it in cash, not in kind, this time, things being how they are."

"It will be seen to. Fare well, Elda Innsmith, and prosperously," came from behind the screen, and the Innsmith clapped hands onto knees and arose.

"And you, Trader, and your boy, here. Scribes a good clear hand, as I've seen many a time."

The Innsmith, thought Jannus, had still not absorbed Newstock ways, after all these years—if he thought to please a ruling stock Lady with praise of a scribe whom she'd borne and then forgotten for the next fourteen years. . . .

The next visitor, the lady of a minor Newstock household, came to request the importation of fifty bolts of woolen cloth of winter-shear weight beyond her usual requirements, due to an infestation of wall-beetle in the principal tailory. She and the Lady discussed the problem without need of a prolocutor; Jannus took an inconspicuous station near the door until he should be needed again.

Tired out by the preparations for the long journey back from exile, Elda Innsmith had retired shortly after dark. He was annoyed to be wakened some time later by the repetition of his name from outside his tent.

"What."

The voice only repeated, "Elda Innsmith, to wake you gives me no joy. . . ."

A Trader's cub, by the mouth on him. Elda shook himself and groped for the tent flap, saying, "Nothing. Go back to sleep," in answer to his wife's inquiring grunt. He poked his head out but couldn't put a name to the high-shouldered waiting shape. "What."

"Elda Innsmith, I . . . need your aid." Not stammering: cautious; deliberate.

More wary in response, Elda retorted, "You need new manners worse. It's the middle of the night!"

"I do hear you. But the need is now."

Elda recognized the voice then, the turn of phrase. "It's Lillia's boy, is it?"

"I am Named. Jannus."

"Fine for you. Should be named Toad: you stink of swamp."

Ignoring Elda's deliberate show of bad temper, the boy went on, with the same tense, stifled stubbornness. "I am Named. I am free to do and be, under my own name. Whatever I have that would buy your help is yours, from the hour that you give it."

No light matter, then. Elda squinted off at the fog-haloed lights of the town for a moment. "Wait." He ducked inside the tent to find trousers and a jacket. Thus protected against the injurious night airs, he towed the boy, Jannus, by one elbow to a spot far enough from the nearer tents to be sure of privacy. "Now," he said, "what's the trouble."

Jannus leaned his narrow back against an upended barge. In a weary monotone he replied, "I want you to hide someone. He's sick. Without shelter, without care, he'll die."

"The outlanders' lodge," Elda suggested.

"No. I thought of it, but . . . he's too much an outlander for that. And Valde come and go freely there. . . . He's a Screamer. A Tek."

Elda shut his eyes and nodded heavily to himself three times. A Tek. The boy had somehow caught a Tek down off the High Plain and was mistakenly trying to bar it from suicide.

Elda had never heard of Screamers. He wondered how a Tek could have escaped the prison of the Kantmorie plateau. He wondered if the Wall had failed.

Sternly he stifled the forbidden speculation and muttered, "No. Let it die."

"That would be murder."

"That would be common sense. They don't die, not the way you will, if this errand's a measure of your wisdom. You won't make old bones, Jannus Lilliasson—not if asking a Smith to shelter a deathless Teklord's your notion of common dealings. If you don't know any more than to do that, you don't know much of Smiths, nor of Teks, either. . . . What makes you think it's a Tek, to begin with?"

"He said so."

"Maybe he lied. Teks an't overfond of truth, if my Grandda's word's to be trusted." Elda shifted from foot to foot, talking to no purpose but unwilling to just turn and go.

"He'll die," the boy insisted flatly.

"You're meat for the Fool-Killer, you are. That Tek is older now than all the years of all the folk in Newstock piled together, and it'll live to see the dust of our grandsons' bones. Supposing it's a Tek at all," Elda added carefully.

"He's a child. A boy half my size."

"What you see is a boy, maybe. It's what you don't see that you propose to cumber me with. But how'd it get past the Wall?" Elda muttered, in spite of himself.

"He escaped from the household. After the daymeal I went to take food and clothing, protection, and found him shaking with fever. . . ."

"A runaway from some other town, most likely—shaved bald for doing something he oughtn't," scoffed Elda, all the while thinking about a Tek, a master-craftsman of the old times, badly bodied, surely dead in a few days. . . . "I'd best see for myself. No, wait: I want a light."

Elda stumped back to his tent for a lantern, which he finally contrived to light with flint and steel from his tinderbox.

"Elda Hildursson, if you *must* bang all over—"

"Hush, woman. I have to see to a boat."

"At this hour?"

"Hush up. An't your concern."

Screwing the wick down until the flame fluttered dimly, Elda rejoined the boy and followed him to the shore, where a small rowboat was drawn up under the overhanging willows. Ducking under, Elda turned up the flame and studied what the boy had fetched him.

It was curled up like a nightworm in the bottom of the boat, having tossed free of a mud-smeared blanket. As Jannus had said, it looked most like a spindly child aged about ten. The back of the hairless skull looked fragile enough for Elda to have crushed between his hands without real effort.

Whatever it might be, it was was surely no runaway Bremneri.

Reaching down slowly, Elda gave the creature's shoulder a rough poke and snatched his hand back. "Wake up."

The mouth moved inaudibly. The eyes did not open.

"He'll die," Jannus, behind him, remarked again. "Without decent care, he will die."

Having seen all he needed to, Elda lowered the flame. He groped for the boat's painter and towed it farther up the shore, out from under the trees: Teks, he'd heard, could not abide a roof. If this one should wake and raise a commotion, they'd all be in the mud together for sure. "An't likely," he remarked quietly, "to live out a week, whatever's done. They don't value a body enough to take the care to keep it long, it's said. And what in the green world made you think I'd be willing to put my neck under your foot, taking such a risk?"

"My neck, as you say, is already under your foot. I freed him and I sheltered him, and you know it. I have a place there." Faintly visible in the first of the moonlight, one hand lifted toward the few town lights, then dropped. "You have only to tell and I'd lose my place. I've been lying to my household for two days. I can keep lying or consent to a death I could prevent—it's too late not to begin, even if I wanted to. All this rests in your hand, now, whether you turn me away or no."

" 'The Fool-Killer visits the trusting,' " commented Elda unkindly.

"You're leaving. You can take him, and no one would know. With you, he'd be safe from the Valde. I can't think of any other way."

"You don't know a thing about it." When the boy made no response, just letting his last flat statement hang there, Elda continued, "You been lying, you say? It's a wonder you an't both in the mud long since, then. You Bremneri don't lie worth warm spit, you got no talent for it. What you been doing is just keeping your mouth shut, an't that so."

"Yes. . . ."

"And you figure that's a lie. It an't. You couldn't keep this quiet a week, not to save your own skin. Much less mine. Somebody'd ask what'd become of the blanket, or the boat, and you'd blurt it all out."

"I've had practice," contradicted the boy reservedly, "in keeping secrets before this."

"Fine for you." There was no sense even talking about it.

Elda swung away and scuffed as far as one of the firepits, still thinking about what he might learn of lost skills and tools from a sick Tek before it died, still with its escape from the High Plain gnawing at the edges of his reluctance. With the Tek safely dead and disposed of, who was to know if he'd had dealings with one of the Deathless? The Ban was like being forbidden to spit on the moon, or walk on the riverbottom: who'd suppose the Ban *could* be broken, so long since the Fall? Who'd think to ask him, or question whatever story he gave?

"And besides, I don't know for sure it's a Tek," Elda muttered to himself. He opened the lantern to blow out the flame. "Come over here. You scribe a fair hand, I said that before. An't that so."

"Yes. . . ."

"What it said, you could take down and keep, supposing there was something worth the keeping. An't that so."

"But you'll be gone."

"Not and leave you open-mouthed in Newstock, I an't. Could be I'd have use for a scribe, going downriver. You're Named, you say. Does that mean you can come and go as you please?"

"Under the word of the Lady Lillia, yes. But—"

"You want to talk to her, or will I do it?"

"Talk about what?"

"It's the only way I'll set hand to the business, if I can keep you under my eye while it lasts, till the secret is cold and you'll find it easy to keep shut, when you get back. When we go, you come with us. That's how it goes, or not at all."

"You speak to her," the boy said finally. "Tomorrow, when you come for your money."

"And you swear me an oath not to speak of this thing, not for any manner of cause, ever—no matter what you stand to gain or lose by telling. You swear that to me by your name." It was all that Elda knew of, that Bremneri put enough value on to swear by.

"All right."

"That won't do. You swear it."

So the boy repeated Elda's words, and swore by his name. Short of bringing in some Valde to be Fair Witness and herself testify to the boy's intention, Elda mused sardonically, this was about all he could hope for. When the boy was through, Elda nodded heavily, accepting it.

So, he thought: *it's done, then.*

Elda, his cousin Sig and Elda's oldest son, Dinnel, stared boredly at the ceiling of the Trader's antechamber waiting for those ahead to get their business done and go. There wasn't much talk, not under the flat fisheyes of the two troopmaids guarding the inner door. Elda had never had too much use for Valde, and today liked them even less. But he supposed Valde were used to that, the way Bremneri men felt about them, if you went by what the farmers said when they came down at harvest season.

When Elda's turn came he went in alone: he'd brought the other two to carry the money chest back. That weight of copper would be quite a load, though he could have managed it himself if he'd had to. He just didn't have to.

He settled himself in the cold stone chair and answered in the usual way to the usual questions about sedition. He studied the boy for any sign he'd already blurted his secret, but the boy looked about the same, except that his wrists were yellow. Elda had no notion what that might mean. Just finding him here, about his usual chores, likely was enough of a good sign.

"Trader," Elda began, swinging toward the carved screen, "a notion came to me after I heard your boy Jannus, here, had come of age, according to your ways and wasn't tied to your house the same as before. See, we're going south quite a distance. . . . Going to the Summerfair, to be plain—south down toward Andras, around across the bay, and then up into Valde." Talking about the Clan's business came hard, hard; Elda made himself do it. "That's a lot of distance on the river. A long way before we come to Quickmoor and get clear of Bremner. We'll have to bargain for fresh supplies, moorage, various things with the Traders in stocks downriver. Myself, I've not had dealing with any farther south than you. So I thought, see, that it might be handy to have somebody like your boy along, who knows their ways and could deal for us. He could catch the packet at Quickmoor and come back upriver. I'd pay him a half ounce piece a day. And food and all, of course," he ended lamely, not liking the odd way the boy was staring at him.

"A lady of my household," said the screened Trader, "would perhaps be more suitable as a prolocutor for you to the Ladies of other stocks. . . ."

"For *them,* maybe. . . ." Elda tried to think of a tactful way to put it, meanwhile scowling at the boy. "She'd come back here most startled and halfway to a babe. Till they're married, our youngsters do mostly what they please in that way. . . . A boy'd get on easier with us, I should think. It'd be us he'd be spending most of his time with, not the Traders."

"I do hear you. . . . Jannus, an offer has been tendered."

The boy looked from Elda to the screen and back again like an idiot. "The Summerfair," he said. "None of the Truthdeaf have seen it that ever I. . . . I'd take no wages. I would serve for nothing, for the chance to see the Summerfair."

"But that's near two seasons' journey," Elda objected quickly, in what he hoped was a reasonable tone, "there and back." He most surely did *not* want to drag an outlander to the Innsmiths' Homecoming, and surely not Jannus, oath or no oath. Carrying your own axe to the headsman, it'd be.

"He's scarce be back before first frost. And how'd he get back, when it comes to that? We wouldn't be bringing him."

"A trade delegation goes from the riverstocks to the Summerfair each year," responded the Trader helpfully. "He could return with them, without great danger or expense. If that were his wish. . . ."

"We don't need him past Quickmoor," Elda declared flatly, tapping the chair arm with his fist and staring the boy straight in the eyes.

"Then you must find another scribe," the boy replied, and smiled.

Boxed. Elda sighed. "Oh, all right," he said sourly.

"Then I accept, if I have leave," said the boy, pleasant and smug as two toads.

"You have my leave," the Trader told him. "It is wondered when you will be setting out. . . ."

"The barges are all but ready now. This afternoon, maybe first light tomorrow."

"A brief while, then. Jannus, after the audiences are done, you are free to make whatever preparations you wish. I will see what you will need is set aside in the second North common room for you, suitable to one of my household."

"Lady, I do hear you."

"Fine for us," remarked Elda, and pushed to his feet. "Be down at the camp as soon as may be," he told Jannus. "There's somewhat to be discussed."

"I do hear you. Your money," the boy mentioned, "is under the seat. . . ."

"Oh, that." Elda caught hold of the box's rope handle and dragged it out the door, where Sig and Dinnel took charge of it.

And after all, Elda thought as he led the way down the hall, the boy might be some use at that, dealing with the downriver Traders. The way Jannus had whipsawed him into agreeing, right there under the Trader's nose, and her none the wiser, was a good sign. And it was a fair distance, he'd been told, to Quickmoor: with just ordinary good luck, he should be free of the company of the Tek and Jannus both, long before that.

The Innsmiths' point was all but deserted when Jannus carefully let down his wicker hamper and sat on it, puffing in the unaccustomed stuffy midafternoon heat. The shallows were full of tents.

Each barge had two thick poles, one rising mastlike at each

end. Between these, the tents were suspended, taking up perhaps a third of the deck area. Innsmith men were lashing great sweep oars against aft poles while yelling children scrambled indiscriminately from barge to barge.

Except for the tents, the barges were the common sort used to move heavy goods with the flow of the current. Raft-bottomed they were, of dressed lumber tarred heavily at the seams, with sides two or three boards higher than the waterline. Jannus hated to think how they'd behave in a strong chop. Or maybe they'd moor and wait out rough weather.

Barges whose tents were painted with like-colored emblems were strung together in chains ranging from three to six or seven. They bumped and rocked as the current nudged them, tugging at the mooring lines which still bound them to the shore.

The emblem for Elda's Family was a black spoked circle, he knew. That string of tents, seven in number, was the farthest from shore. Jannus could count at least ten men working bare-armed aboard them—young men, playfully batting each other with the massive sweep oars. A fellow in a brown sark was shoved and fell backward into the river, hooted at by his nearest kin. Since Elda wasn't visible among these, Jannus preferred to wait in the quiet shade under the willows.

Before long Elda arrived from upriver, occupied with an Andran who was walking virtually backward to face Elda as he talked. Elda came steadily on, making no comment. Something in the set of Elda's shoulders made Jannus suspect him of hoping the Andran would pause or stumble, so Elda could trudge right over him. But the Andran skirted the steaming firepits and the lumped roots as if by intuition, kiting adroitly across Elda's path without actually hindering him.

As they passed, taking no notice of Jannus, he recognized the Andran as Orlengis Ras, master of the packet *Obedient* tied up at pier fifteen, whose boat Jannus had borrowed safely the night before. Orlengis' fair coloring marked him from most other Andrans, who were more often dark as Bremneri. So early in the season, some freckling was already visible across the man's cheeks, above his close-trimmed sandy whiskers. Through the general din, Jannus caught disconnected phrases as Orlengis passed by: "—won't tell you your own business, but—" and "—decent occupation for a Free Clan, no matter—"

They reached the shore's edge. As the Andran hesitated, Elda waded ahead, put his back to the inmost of his Family's barges, and hauled himself to a seat. While the Innsmiths hushed slightly, covertly observing, Elda called, "Tell it to your granddad's aunt."

The Andran's response to this odd insult was equally peculiar. He pulled off his hat and dropped it, freeing his hair which was plaited into one long rope in the fashion of watermen. He sliced off this braid, spat on it, and flung it into the river near Elda's feet. Bending stiffly to retrieve his hat, he stalked back to the path and turned toward town.

Innsmiths were exchanging glances and quiet comments. A man on a red-emblemed barge called to Elda a derisive judgment on fools who kicked trees to see if the hornets were home.

Elda only reached behind to be helped into the barge by the two young men aboard. "You: Jannus," he shouted as he straightened up. "What are you waiting on: frost?"

Jannus thought it best to come without comment. He got his arms around the hamper and carried it to the edge of the shore, then waded out with extreme care until he was near enough for the older of the pair to take the hamper from him with an effortlessness Jannus tried to admire. Elda was already three barges along the chain.

"Was I you, I'd stay clear of—" the man had started to tell Jannus, when Elda called impatiently. The man tucked the hamper under one arm and concluded resignedly, "I'd do as I was bid."

"Who are you, to Elda?" Jannus inquired, as they sidled along the narrow clear spaces and were handed along to the next bobbing barge.

"Dinnel by name, Elda's first-son, now, of those still breathing. Watch the loop, there, or you'll be swimming."

"Not I," replied Jannus, adding absently, "I do hear you.... The Andran rivermaster was—"

"Watch the sweep," Dinnel interrupted flatly, and Jannus accepted the hint that the matter was considered none of his business.

Dinnel set the hamper in the stern of the last barge in the chain, evidently Elda's own, and left Jannus there.

The side of the tent facing the cliff was folded back, leaving most of the barge open to the sky. Looking past Elda, who was spooning fish stew from a steaming kettle set on a brazier, Jannus eventually spotted the Tek curled up in a bundle of quilts—either sleeping, resting, or indifferent, since he didn't turn his head to discover who'd come aboard.

"Expect you missed your midmeal," remarked Elda, equitably enough, as if his earlier bad temper had been dissipated by the encounter with Orlengis. "You had little enough time to get ready."

"Most of it was done for me," Jannus replied, accepting the filled dish Elda offered him, and sat on the creaking hamper to eat. "I didn't realize," he remarked presently, "that you were going to the Summerfair. You didn't tell me."

A grunt was the only response Elda chose to give this oblique apology for the scene in the Morn-hall. "When you're done with that, suppose you talk to your friend awhile. Earn your keep."

Jannus took a few more bites while considering the request. "What is it, that you want to know?"

Elda waved openhanded. "Everything."

"Inaccurate," the Tek put in unexpectedly, without moving.

"What's that supposed to mean? I say, what's that supposed to mean, Grandda?"

When the Tek made no reply, Jannus put down his dish and edged past Elda to settle uncomfortably on his heels, his back braced against the side of the barge.

It was his first view the Tek by daylight. His recollection of pallor and diminuitive fragility was confirmed and intensified. The Tek's eyes were grey as water: lashless, browless, the only living elements in a naked face more alien in its immobility than that of any Valde. Jannus could have covered the whole face, pointed chin to porcelain brow, with one spread hand. Its wrists, protruding from a coarsewoven sark evidently supplied by Elda, were scarcely wider than two of Jannus' fingers. Jannus glanced again at the eyes and knew for certain it was no sort of a child.

Realizing he was thinking of the Tek as "it," the way Elda did, Jannus was annoyed at himself.

"It is wondered," he inquired in formal mode, "what name you took."

"What's yours?"

Jannus told him; the Tek repeated the name to himself with a subtle difference of pronunciation, making it nearer *Jaunosh*. The Tek's accent was odd—most like that of an Andran, but not really like that either. The Tek said, "And what is the name of your shirt?" and pointed at it.

Jannus looked down at himself uncertainly. "It's a common sark," he replied slowly, divining a test but not its nature. "It's cut in the manner of Newstock, without pockets . . . gaudy orange in color though no choice of mine, of summer-shear weight, Valde-woven. . . ." Jannus trailed off inquiringly.

"Those are its qualities—some of them. A description. Not a name."

Jannus began to understand. "Sarks—shirts?—are not named, by our custom. But a living being. . .?"

"A description: a Tek, myself, one of some four or five born in a certain season in a certain year some six centuries before the Rebellion and the fixing of the Barrier. First Tek of Cliffhold Keep, which means nothing any more. A living being, putting on names as you do your shirts, depending on taste, occasion, and proper fit at the time. My last lowlander name that I recall was something like 'Isfelder': I didn't like it."

"How were you known, then, among your own folk?"

"Well enough. There aren't all that many of us—two hundred, five. . . . The Shai keeps count; I never bothered. And only the Shai knows how many of us there are left. . . . Probably most of us. In practice, I was known as *myself*, the myself that wears this body as it's worn others less wretched than the present exhibit." The Tek lifted a hand to inspect it, rippling the fingers like a lady examining a fan offered her for purchase. "We have a means to take and keep an image of this *myself*—all thought, and all memory, and all habits of mind. And this is what is put into each new body, what . . . awakes. . . . The record," the Tek went on briskly after the unexplained pause, "we call a *rede*, and it's the nearest thing to a real name, in your sense of it, that I possess. Unfortunately, it can't be rendered into any human speech. A Valde might warble it for you, perhaps. Are you well and truly answered, Jannus?"

He meant *paid*. Jannus turned up an open palm in a shrug. "I now understand why you cannot answer my question . . . I suppose. Which is less satisfactory to me than an answer: I can't call you 'Grandda'. . . ."

"Oh," said the Tek, as if losing interest, "is that what's at issue. That's simple. Call me whatever you please." He shut his eyes.

Jannus settled more comfortably, clasping his knees, to give the matter the serious thought he felt it required: no Bremneri was inclined to take Naming lightly. He thought back over his impressions of the Tek, seeking the single suitable word. After while, he decided aloud, "*Lur*. That is—"

"I know what it is: *cat*, as a Valde object-name. Are you

satisfied with that, then?" The Tek didn't bother opening his eyes. "All right. In case I'm in doubt which you're addressing among this numerous company, I'll know, if you say *Lur*, that it's myself. The problem with both of you," the Tek added, "is that you want to know too little. I'll have to educate you into a more sophisticated greed or risk becoming dispensable."

"If you're done with that chat," Elda called to Jannus, "come learn how to manage this overgrown bread paddle."

When Jannus straightened, he found Elda standing at the sweep: the mooring lines had been loosed without his noticing. The barge was riding the swift current near the middle of the river. Newstock was already lost behind acres of feathery grasses blurring the west shore like smoke.

Book II:

ERTH-RIMMON

In Lur, Jannus had found for the first time a source more than equal to his appetite for facts. Lur seemed exempt from weariness and impatience, explaining a facet of law, custom, or consequence ten times, if need be, to make it intelligible. Lur talked, theorized, digressed, and linked tales for four days, pausing only to eat and sleep, until his voice wore away to a thin whisper.

All conditions aided and insulated them. The long river hours offered few distractions or interruptions. The banks of grasses, reeds, and early flowering goldmosses slid eventlessly by on the right; the blank ochre face of the escarpment passed as unchangingly on the left.

Occasionally Jannus was called to a turn at the sweep. Then Lur would settle himself near Jannus' feet and continue the seemingly inexhaustible torrent of information. The rest of the time Elda manned the sweep, listening, occasionally arguing this point or that which fell within the Smiths' history or lore.

Lur told them the story of the High Plain, the long becoming of the Empire of Kantmorie: what it had made of itself, done to itself and its colonies during the three thousand years in which it'd been utterly free to amuse itself in any way its diverse imaginations could devise.

Jannus had a picture, now, of the High Plain: flat, yellow and dull brown throughout its surface of scoured or powdered rock where no green thing could survive, with almost no visible water. Teks could have had rivers. Indeed, they could have had an inland sea up there if they'd wanted. But they found the austere landscape agreeable and were content with putting a single immense lake near Down, their seat of power, to nourish that which lived there far underground: the Shai, both a creature and a machine, which the Smiths knew as the Deepfish.

The Teks divided the High Plain among themselves and erected some thirty strongholds and keeps, each occupied by fewer than ten Teks, presiding over extensive desolate hold ings, in an irregular circle toward the edges of the plateau These keeps, isolated by preference, were gathered into a loose confederation ruled by a king chosen from among their num ber.

The king was not selected by inheritance or by general con sensus. Rather, the Shai chose the ruler by informing the con federation whom it would serve: necessarily that individual and no other held supreme power until the Shai withdrew its support and selected another.

For the Teks had ceded that power of arbitration to the Shai almost from the first, to prevent internal strife. They be lieved firmly in what Lur called *the Rule of One*—the notion that stable governance could be achieved only by undivided power held by one pair of hands at a time—and imposed this belief on their agent, the Shai, which executed it faithfully dur ing the three thousand years of empire.

The Shai was Kantmorie's servant, memory, and chief treasure. It was the repository of all the power deriving from all the knowledge Teks had ever possessed, and it could initi ate and pursue investigations of its own with the consent of the king; and a king refused one of the Shai's initiatives at his peril since kings were deposed by enforced ritual suicide.

The Shai wanted only what Teks wanted: order; general properity; freedom for Teks from the visceral details of the processes which maintained them; unbroken continuity of rule; and as much individual liberty and civil justice, both for Teks and for all others, as was consonant with the other aims. The Shai also operated on the assumption that matters were best controlled when they could be manipulated into control ling themselves: as a result, Kantmorie's colonies flourished and the subject peoples were well content.

It was this part of Lur's narrative Jannus found hardest to reconcile with his own knowledge. It was at once too personal to him and too abstract.

That the Bremneri had come from elsewhere, he could ac cept. That they'd been brought to the lands west of Erth-rim mon by the Teks, settled there for the sole purpose of supplying food to the High Plain, he could also accept, though the image of Bremner as some enormous kitchen garden for others' tables wasn't one he especially liked. But that Kant morie was itself a colony, settled in a single day by an immi grant nation after a journey across what Lur named *the Sea of Air and of No Air* from someplace else so distant not even

Teks remembered in what direction it might lie, except up; and that the Valde alone had been here to greet them, profoundly other in feature, custom, and nature than they now were—these things were hard for Jannus to become reconciled to.

It was for Jannus as if Newstock itself, and all his life there, had been set adrift and changed. Without rejecting what Lur had said Jannus stored it, refusing to let it matter yet—the way he'd learned to store other painful knowledge. It was like closing a fist tightly over a cut palm: when it hurt less, he'd be able to open it and find out how serious the wound really was and perhaps let it heal.

The Bremneri had been settled on the land complete with all necessary tools, seed, and living creatures. Some livestock and plants refused to survive, though each had been chosen for almost infinite adaptability; the Teks either bred new strains, adapted native stock, or did without. Lur named and described at least a score of creatures Jannus had never heard of and could scarcely visualize, whose kind had thus disappeared. Some, the Bremneri had replaced by adoption: applying familiar names to creatures strange to them: hawks, for instance, had once been birds instead of the male form of the blacksnake, which wasn't really a snake anyhow, according to Lur. Real snakes had no claws.

That had been Lur's specialty: animals, especially those with backbones that didn't lay eggs. Lur could talk for hours about how bones were connected.

Besides the Bremneri, it seemed, there'd been two other subject peoples to begin with: the Ragdocnir and the Valde. The Ragdocnir were generally called Meks, for the euphony, and were apparently the ancestors of the Smiths. Their function was to farm tools—to grow, tend, and harvest devices of all sorts. The image, Jannus gathered, wasn't all that fanciful, since it seemed many Tek tools and systems were alive after their own fashion and life, Lur contended, was always cheaper to produce than machinery and much more interesting.

Meks were most often householders of one keep or another, but they travelled freely about the continent wherever their work took them. Sometimes Meks became Teks: a Mek with an interesting and complex long-range project could become first in a keep, and even die in that rank if the project still commanded interest and intrigue had turned its lidded stare elsewhere long enough. The Shai had at least twice accepted Meks into the kingship, that Lur was aware of. And the Teks of one keep had gotten so involved in a project, the construction of a wonderful forest, that when it was done they abandoned their keep and spent all their time in the lowlands in the forest they had made, founding the region known as Is in what was now southern Bremner.

The Valde were kept as pets.

During the first thousand years or so, Teks developed wild Valde into household servants and companions, and there were even some pacts; but it was another three hundred years before any children were born of such pairings.

An echo of how the change had come about was still current in Bremner: the ballad of the Lord Gaherin and the Lady Adunna Laer Jannus had learned it from Poli. Its gist was that the two were lovers, childlessness was a sorrow to them both, they nevertheless refused to be parted, and she died. There was no hint Gaherin had been a Tek.

But he was a Tek, and he had a Tek's single-minded assumption that whatever could be imagined could be accomplished if one was only willing to pay the cost in energy and time. He began trying to adapt the Valde, as other native species had been adapted, but with one enormous and seemingly complex difference: he wanted children from pacts between Valde and non-Valde, to make Adunna happy.

The project still occupied him long after Adunna herself was dead of old age, in her forties. The change proceeded through intermediate stages, some more effective than others. In the last decade or two, Gaherin was king. And before he died he had succeeded in changing most of one whole generation of Valde who grew up and had children with partners of either race, and those children did the same in their turn.

The change had a side-effect nobody noticed for some scores of years: of such births, only one in ten was male.

Hearing this, Jannus bent his forehead onto his knees, feeling thoughts and images—the Haffa, the Brotherless, coming into self-imposed exile as troopmaids, season after season, down all the years; the imagined chime of the duelling discs; the shine of a bridestone against the plain green front of a tabard—all falling into newly painful importance. He mourned for high intentions that came, at last, to sorrow.

Toward the end of the second thousand years of the empire, the methods of making and storing redes, the coded records of total mental content, were discovered. When a way was developed to project these redes onto a body grown to maturity without ever waking, immortality had been achieved.

Within a short time it had become the central fact of Kant-morian life.

Suicide became a public art form—even a means of transportation. Murder, unless ingenious, was just a practical joke in dubious taste. Bases in which receptacles for redes—bodies—were grown were established in every keep and the single Tek outpost beyond the High Plain itself. It was in northern Bremner and was called Stock.

The redes were taken, stored, and projected by the Shai, which alone had the means to monitor the multiple comings and goings of its masters. But its administration was limited by five unalterable laws formulated by the Tek confederation: firstly, no rede might be altered in any respect whatsoever—especially, not destroyed; secondly, no rede might be bodied more than once, concurrently; thirdly, only the newest rede might be bodied; fourthly, the maintenance of the bases was to be given absolute priority; fifthly, redes were to be incarnated immediately upon a Tek's death—to the base of choice, if possible: if not, then to the nearest available functional base.

The first of these restrictions prohibited death. It came to be modified. After centuries of personal boredom, a Tek of Cap's Keep put before the confederation a proposal that the king alone be exempted from deathlessness—that when the Shai accepted a king, his redes be destroyed and no new ones stored thereafter. During his tenure, he could be rebodied as often as necessary; but being deposed meant true death. Kings would pay for power with mortality.

This had been in Lur's own lifetime. He remembered registering his approval of the proposal. He'd have been pleased to have done without a human ruler at all, holding the Shai entirely competent to maintain the Rule of One without human interference. He thought the new system might tend to make kings more cautious about meddling since they could well die of the consequences of their actions.

His proposal approved, the Tek of Cap's Keep proposed himself to the Shai for kingship—a novel procedure—and was accepted. His only official act was to order a long-term project to colonize the moon with worms, utilizing the entire present supply; this, of course, ended his tenure in Downbase. In front of a gallery of his household Valde and immediate acquaintances he was executed by a flow of unshielded power and thus became the first Tek to die in about seven hundred years.

Functional immortality had been extended, by the Teks, to some individuals of other nations. This generosity had an unexpected result: the Ragdocnir, the Meks, seceded. One Mek, a man named Smith, was of the opinion that something essential was lost, overlooked, in the taking of redes. He referred to it as "losing his soul," and forbade any of his clan to touch a redecap. Finding this ban ineffective, Smith succeeded in persuading several of the Mek clans to remove themselves and their children from temptation, and led them to a new home in the mountains north and east of the High Plain where they became miners.

"Innsmiths," Elda put in at this point. "That was 'Ironsmiths,' to begin with. We were the iron-working Clan, in the old reckoning, with first claim on all new finds. And now not a breathing soul of us has touched raw iron, to shape it, since I was a lad."

"What happened?"

"There's still a piece of the Clan, back in the mountains, that make it 'Ernsmith,' " Elda went on abstractedly, leaning on the oar. "An't your concern, what happened."

"I do hear you," rejoined Jannus stiffly.

"Oh, I don't suppose it matters. . . . We were exiled. Something my Gandda's brother, him that was Clan leader then, decided to put his hand to. And so we had to come out and do tinkers' work till the time was up. To be plain, I don't know for sure what it was, that he did. That's what the exile was for—to let the memory have time to die out. There's nobody that remembers, now, just how Grandda's brother Tell got the Clan exiled. So I'm telling you no secrets."

"Maybe," suggested Lur blandly, "he found a Tek."

"You shut up. The Wall holds. An't no Teks—at least not to the east of the High Plain."

"How do you know the Wall holds?" countered Lur. "Who's tested it? It could be still holding in one place, and have failed in another. There's a chain of generators buried all around the edge. One could have failed. How do you know?"

"What do I care? What'd I want to go onto the High Plain for, besides the fact that it'd get me outlawed, and the Clan besides? I'd sooner paddle out to sea in a soup bowl when the tidestorm is due. . . . It's all dead up there."

"Not quite. Not yet." But Lur let the matter drop.

The situation of Kantmorie, having been stable for three thousand years, did not easily lose equilibrium. Shifts were gradual. Demands on the subject peoples became heavier and

more frequent. There was less innovation among Teks and no
sense of urgency about much of anything. There was a ten-
dency to drift. The subject nations, by this time five in number, became increasingly restive and were answered by a series
of repressions notable for indiscriminate executions: the High
Plain no longer took either death or life very seriously. Teks
just hated to be disturbed.

The Shai went through a score of kings in a single season,
seeking one who'd stabilize the situation; but things had already slipped too far for minor changes to help and major
changes would have involved the confederation, which resisted
involvement. A Tek of Rork Keep, designated by the Shai to
take the Rule of One, declined in favor of longevity. Lur, too,
was approached. But he was busy producing a biting fly whose
saliva would prevent several contagious diseases in creatures
with spines and that didn't lay eggs. He declined, as did others
afterward. The Shai tried individuals of other nations as kings,
but even the shrewdest and most generous was defeated by the
Teks' absolute refusal to accept any abridgement in their ancient prerogatives. The situation continued to deteriorate.

Oddly enough it was the Valde who first went into active
revolt. Under a former dispensation, they'd been given the
vast forests east of the High Plain to be their own, and allowed to leave the keeps if they wished. Although this grant
had later been revoked, a considerable, if scattered, population
of Valde still ranged the forestlands. Teks occasionally hunted
them for sport.

The Valde had remained slaves for over three thousand
years because, as Jannus knew, they were incapable of murder. They were efficient hunters, the *marenniath*, the empathy-sense, enabling them both to locate prey and to determine
whether it was in "lawful" condition: whether it consented to
its own death as necessary and natural. Unconsenting prey,
beast or human, they could not kill under any circumstances
whatever. So they seemed an unlikely folk to have begun what
became a general war.

But a profound change of attitude had come about. It
wasn't a decision, consciously made, but a change of heart, in-
fectious as love or loathing. Yet there were reasons which
could be put into words.

Firstly, Teks had no fear of death. A slain Tek didn't really
die, certainly not in any sense he himself would acknowledge.
This fact, known by the Valde for a vast time, was suddenly

absorbed, becoming an emotional fact and therefore real. Teks could be hunted.

Secondly, the Valde weren't at all sure that Teks were alive to begin with. In the course of a long, long lifetime, each Tek lost all but the memory of emotion whenever a new rede woke; and, upon waking, the individual became accustomed to suppressing emotion as an unnecessary distraction, regarding it as a trivial facet of the meat rather than the Tek himself who wore the meat. The time came when a Valde could no longer discern within him any inner singing voice. The Valde, as a people, at last had concluded no creature without a *farioh* could be alive in any way meaningful to them. Teks could be hunted.

"The Valde can hear *you*," Jannus interjected then, and told Lur that he knew of the Screamers of Newstock.

"That's different," Lur replied. "That's panic, not subject to will. Shut up, enclosed, any Tek would panic. But that's exceptional. Under sane circumstances I wouldn't let a pet or a couchlet spy on me that way. Your troopmaids didn't chase me beyond the walls, you'll remember." When Jannus had to agree this was so, Lur reflected, "And now they're hunting us because they *can* hear us, instead of the reverse. That must make sense, I suppose, if one is a Valde. . . ."

In any case, all Valde were expelled from the High Plain which then surrounded itself with a field that annihilated any living thing that touched it. Lur explained how the Wall made a man's heart forget to beat and stopped the directions that the mind sent to the rest of the body, causing death from a variety of causes within seconds; Jannus found it easier just to think of it as poison smeared on the cliff.

Teks could pass the Wall safely. The Meks who'd set up the system had also produced tokens of a special crystal that protected against the field. Teks carried these tokens when they wanted to descend into the lowlands.

These tokens had a minor defect: they became useless if wetted. The Meks neglected to give warning of this quality before, by ones and twos, they slipped off to join the free Smiths in the mountains; and it was some time before the Teks discovered it for themselves. Rain seldom fell on the High Plain, and a Tek poisoned by the Wall through a token's failure merely woke in a keep, remembering nothing since his last rede and therefore ignorant of the reason for his most recent death.

Elda grinned through this portion of Lur's recital.

In one of its last unified actions, the confederation of Teks ordered the Shai not to let the Wall fail for any reason whatever, placing it on the same priority as the maintenance of the bases. Then they considered the High Plain secure. They were free to reestablish their waning control over the younger states by force.

Bremner joined Valde in revolt and was devastated by fire. Little food passed the Wall into Kantmorie. The Isles of Andras, once-volcanic mountains in the Bay of Andras where those had settled who wished to pursue abstract speculations and disciplines of meditation, followed their parent state, Is, in defiance. The Smiths hid in their mountains and smiled when it rained.

When the deficiency of the tokens became known, the Teks changed tactics. They decided to wait the younger states out—wait for rebellion to be followed by social collapse and then by fighting among the states, after which one would emerge supreme. Then they'd take control of the victor and things would return to normal. They were the Deathless. They could afford to wait.

It had been a good tactic, Lur thought. He didn't know why it hadn't worked.

Jannus told him.

While the Teks waited, Valde pacted with Bremner. Thousands of Valde with no mates left among their own people pacted with Bremneri men, their allies during several generations of war. Together they healed the burned lands and brought them again to bear and bloom. And the Truthtell came to Bremner. And in those years, too, Valde began the Summerfair, a meeting place for trade and negotiation. Valde supplied Fair Witnesses at request while the Summerfair lasted, guaranteeing the faithful intention of all parties to hold by whatever contracts were made.

The general warfare the Teks expected never came.

The situation on the High Plain became more desperate. The living systems, most fragile, either were neglected and died, or else became a source of food; equipment for repair of nonliving systems became vanishingly scarce. Keeps became physically isolated from each other, separated by unrealized expanses of sand and stone. Redes were shunted randomly from base to base as deaths multiplied beyond the keeps' capacities. Teks attempting to reach Down, claim the Rule of One and die in truth, found themselves faced with an immense journey on foot toward a destination only vaguely known, since Kantmorie had made no maps nor had need of them before.

Many Teks deserted then, using a token to pass the Barrier, and hid among one or another of the lowlander races for a little while, a lifetime; but when they died, they woke in a base in a keep on the High Plain with less means to sustain themselves than before. Bases were damaged or destroyed by Teks in a fury of despair at waking so for the tenth or hundredth time, with no memory of the intervening period of escape, since they usually had no redecaps to keep their redes current after they descended the cliff.

And finally even physical escape was denied them. There were no more tokens. They'd all been lost in the lowlands. Trapped behind its own defenses, the High Plain fell into madness.

"How did you escape it?" Jannus asked Lur then.

"I found a door open."

"No: the madness."

"It's not particularly sane to dread roofs. But I'm quite rational, compared to some. I stopped letting redes be taken. I don't remember anything since—what year is it since Valde's pact with Bremner, by your reckoning?"

While Jannus hesitated, Elda put in, "Eight hundred seventy one years since the Fall of Kantmorie."

"Then it's about two hundred years, and then another . . . perhaps three hundred before that. Something interesting happened two hundred years ago, something I wanted to remember—although that required I also retain the preliminary delights of dying by thirst. . . . I expect your Valde have been hunting me through Newstock basements for the last two hundred years, whenever bodies were available there, but I don't have to recollect it. That helps. It's a smaller suicide," the Tek added meditatively. "Throwing pieces of myself to keep the wolves busy, so I can go on. . . ."

Jannus asked him what a wolf was.

Poli immediately discovered the packet's bow. She spent sunny hours perched on the leading edge of the unrailed deck, enthralled with the sense of motion, of becoming.

In the early morning before sunappear there were cool mists like a second river flowing head-high, when the rivermaster sent the packet on cautiously with lookouts posted aloft. When the day warmed, Poli raptly considered the turning swirls of current in the ship's path as they glided nearer and flexed themselves smoothly in private devices. Then the bow's shadow would suddenly scrape over and roll them flat just below Poli's dangling feet.

Perhaps it was not the water's own dismay, but that of scattering fish, that Poli sensed; she was not interested in making such distinctions. All things blended. A circle of living vibration, voiced and unvoiced, everchanging without progression, extended in every direction: the daysong of Erth-rimmon.

She knew the river gulls' hungry white alertness as they coasted and circled. She knew the choric apprehensions of fish. Insects buzzed with their million anonymous voices. The repetitious selfsingings of reeds and vaguely waving water plants she perceived somewhat as others might the conversation of bees: a ceaseless underhum, scarcely noticed save as it colored all else.

Poli wove *myself-going-first-over-the-becoming-slateblue-river* songs, wordless and only sometimes softly vocalized.

The rivermaster (a stone around which the flowing daysong passed unheard, or perhaps sensed only as a fish would be aware of Poli above the bounds of its world) came again to tell her not to sit there. Booming his impatience threaded with confused skeins of duty, boredom, concern, fear, and contempt, the Andran explained patiently that if the packet brushed a snag or a sand shallow, she'd lurch into the oncoming water and the great paddlewheels would take her. Poli stared at him until he went away to complain to Aliana, who took no notice, inspeaking kind amusement. So Poli stayed where she pleased.

Poli was free. Her own wishes were all she need consider, though she'd have moved if Aliana had wished it, for the sake of the affection and honor due the troopleader.

Aliana Wir, having served two terms in Bremner, was now beginning her old time. The first bridestone she'd earned, she'd given away to a young Haffa she found especially bright of heart, and so exempted her from choosing either troop service in Bremner or becoming *Awiro*, Solitary, on the fields of Lifganin beyond the southern border of Valde. She'd do the same with that bridestone she now wore. For this, all Haffa loved her because she need not have done so: she wasn't too darkhearted to have been brided, had she wished. And their love, in turn, sustained her in the ways she had chosen to go.

Aliana offered to join Poli's *river-becoming* song, which opened hospitable silences for her. Then the twins, Seline and Anshru, the keeneyed, took up the tune aloud. The harmony extended by clusters until all the freemaids were giving themselves to its weaving.

Presently Mene, the lamed, closest of them all to Aliana and the only one who meant not to be brided but to lead a troop back into Bremner next spring, tugged at the melody until she'd gained general attention. Then she guided the waiting hum into the troop selfsinging, the voiced *als'far* joined before contests.

Each, beginning with Poli as First Dancer, blended feeling and voiced harmony to mirror herself, fashioning a complex image to the running litany, *I am myself, no other, this one: know me in this moment.* Each declared herself in turn until it had come round to Aliana, who broadened the song again to *we, ourselves,* in the affirmation of the troop as an entity, a composite of living selfaware voices blended in a strong harmony.

When the moment for silence arrived, each Valde turned contentedly inward or away. Poli could hear the stony *fariohe* of the Andran and Fisher watermen quivering, surprised. Three chaotically whirled *noise, orange/loud/hot/threatening-because strange;* five circled the bright sequence, *warm, yes, the river we know, the very river, magical, strange, perilous, yes;* the last two, more subtle, intoned *beautiful but not ours—do not exist, do not sing where we must hear you, do not be alive in our presence.* . . .

Poli fixed first her eyes, then her *marenntath* on the sliding deeps ahead, where any hostility that existed was clean and impersonal, born of hunger. Her resentment dissipated and blended into the many-motioned present.

The river packets, usually indifferent to day or dark, tied up against the shore on starsdays, the five days at each month's end when the effulgent moon retired to bear her child, leaving the world blind and anxious for the new moon's advent. So the freemaids' journey went slowly. It had been first starsday when they left Newstock; on second starsday, the packet passed the Innsmith barges, still moored in the early morning, with the taste of sleep and the smoke of breakfast fires drifting across the misty water. Third starsday dawned rainy, with a gusty southwest wind too chilly and strong to make it pleasant for Poli to remain on deck. Her half-healed wounds ached and she kept mostly to the cabin the freemaids shared.

Toward evening the wind lulled and the fogs which had been gathering became impenetrable. Joneo Ras, the rivermaster, sent the packet ahead at scarcely more than a walking pace, keeping as close to the west shore as he dared. He sent a man to Aliana to beg, in Joneo's name, the favor of her attendance in the wheelhouse since he was too occupied to come to her. Aliana caught up a hooded cape and summoned Poli and Mene to accompany her.

Up in the wheelhouse, the harried rivermaster greeted them abstractedly with one ear cocked to the deckhands crying soundings. "Next, I'll be relying on echoes off the Wall. . . . But can you tell me, Lady Valde, how far we are from Sithstock? I've been expecting to run onto it this hour and more."

"I cannot give you distances," replied Aliana, "beyond near and far. It is before us, and it is near. They are aware of us. What would you?"

"Lights!"

And the lamps of Sithstock presently bloomed into a diffuse glow, greying the mists above and around the hill on which the stock was set.

Bearing torches, fifty Valde of the Sithstock troop lined a pier to guide the packet to its mooring. Only a year into their service, they welcomed the Newstock freemaids with shy respect. Their troopleader, a Haffa scarcely older than Poli, obtained permission from the Lady of Sithstock to house Aliana and the freemaids with her own troop and led them uphill along the dripping fogbound street.

The Sithstock Valde furnished them with every pleasant and comfortable thing, then kept them up half the night sharing stories. "You're lucky you weren't farther downriver when the fog closed in," observed Serafin, the Sithstock troopleader, at one point. When Anshru wondered why, she was barraged with warnings, dismay, unintelligible dread from the young troopmaids. "Lisle," explained Serafin around a mouthful of nuts. The image behind the word was a closed place, densmelling, where a beast was turned at bay. Curious, Poli reached south with *marenniath*, but either the outlaw stock was too far, or the surrounding chatter too distracting, for her to find it. Having chewed busily and swallowed, the troopleader said, "Like harvest time, when the stockmen come, only more, worse. . . . Do you have henneke nut bushes in Newstock? They grow wild all around here. And we have rabbits—lots!"

The rain fell gently on the barges, at first. Jannus stood at the sweep oar with a cloth around his forehead to keep his hair from streaming into his eyes. By his feet huddled Lur, somewhat protected by a cloak improvised from a square of canvas with a hole cut for his head, fastened with laces at one shoulder. The tent was lashed down on both sides to protect the baggage and Lur couldn't endure the roof thus formed.

"Maybe," Lur was saying to Elda in the hoarse whisper that was all the voice he had, "I'll catch a chill and so die."

"Maybe I'll catch the chill," Elda rejoined in a sour tone, cupping a hand over his mug of hot beer, the last of his breakfast, "and so be free of you."

Lur had been practicing his grin; it now looked more like a spontaneous flash of human expression than like the stiffly bared teeth of some dead animal. He seemed to enjoy baiting Elda. They went on into an argument about the chances of testing the Wall, a subject Elda disliked.

Jannus scarcely listened, returning to his latest preoccupation—brooding about Newstock. He'd been six days on the barge now, but the barge wasn't a place: it moved, and the river moved, and the shore drifted slowly by. And even Newstock was changed in his memory, both smaller and more vivid, perched on top of a cavernous base full of waiting bodies nobody even suspected. Everything was overlaid with Lur's views, Lur's interpretations; so Jannus had turned in his mind to the private things, the ordinary life of the stock neither Lur nor Elda could know. And even in that he found no shelter, no ease.

For everything he thought about made him angrier—the cruelties and petty humiliations of the minor pages by the major, the insolence and perpetual tale-telling of the young girls, the tyranny of the harbormistress, the loveless use of him by the Lady Merleen, the daily caning that punctuated his training as a scribe. The neverending loneliness. The continual sense of being spied upon. All the things which had turned his contemporaries sullen and withdrawn and sent them off to the farmsteads when their Namings came, but from which, until now, he himself had seemed exempt.

Suddenly he found himself angry at Poli, bitterly angry, for the casualness of her leavetaking, for the very aloof sympathy which had enabled them to become, and remain, friends. He recalled his fear, on a hundred occasions, of offending her in the least trifle of word or attitude lest she withdraw and avoid him, recalled it as though it were some injury she'd done him deliberately. The image of himself waiting outside the troop quarters until someone should deign to notice him was like hot water on a scald.

There was no fairness in this resentment. It made him seem disloyal and spiteful to himself, compounding homesickness with shame and confusion, for he knew he'd been well and kindly treated even by his own standards, given more freedom and privilege than any of his contemporaries among the Truthdeaf.

It didn't matter. He couldn't help it.

He was lucky, he thought, to be here with just these outlanders who knew next to nothing about Newstock to begin with and little enough of him. What he felt didn't matter here. He could feel anything he pleased, without consequences.

To get off the subject of the Wall, Elda had started talking about Andrans, who held the mouths of Erth-rimmon and Arant Dunrimmon and controlled all traffic across Andras Bay. Their tolls were high, and they allowed no competition along the bay coasts.

"A naked mountain of rock and ash an't got much to make a man want to live there," Elda was saying, "but as a strong place, a fortress, it's another matter. They don't build or grow scarcely anything themselves—just tax them that do, and that want to move their goods most anywhere by water. . . ."

"Not," Lur observed, "unlike Teks."

"Not damn unlike enough for my stomach, nor for anybody who recalls what became of Amel Tresmith and his whole Family." Finishing the last of the beer, Elda smoothed his mustaches automatically (with rain running down his face) and braced his forearms heavily across his knees. "In my Da's time, the Tresmith, Amel Broksson, contracted to design and build baycraft for Enestro Rey, Duke of the Isle of Camarr. Amel and his whole Family, some forty souls, went to Camarr to undertake the work. They never came back. After three years or so Enestro sent word to the Tresmith Clan that Amel, and all the rest, had been taken in a flash of blackfever and gone to the fire. Died. And they sent a real treasure in trade-metal—copper, and some iron—to show how sad Duke Enestro was about it all. . . ." Elda leaned to spit disgustedly over the side. "And from then on, Camarr baycraft turned deep-chested"—his hand outlined the sweep of a curved keel—"and had a new way of rigging sails, so they could overtake anything else afloat. Camarr turned to taxing the craft of other isles, piracy, to be plain, and got as popular with the other Reyi as he was with everybody else. . . . It's said he stayed out too long at tide-turn and got caught in the storm. At least he was found in a fair-sized tree . . . most of him, anyway." Elda smiled for a moment, grimly. "And now Andran rivermasters start turning up—greeneyed, copper-headed. Tresmith blood, if I've an eye in my head."

"Orlengis," said Jannus, who'd been attending without really listening. A gust of wind caught the side of the tent. He felt the whole barge begin to slip sideways under him and held hard to the sweep, using it as a rudder to straighten the barge's course.

"He's one," Elda was confirming. "He come to me, Orlengis did, that last day in Newstock. He'd heard we were going south, and he was jumping in and out of his skin to get me to go into a contract like Amel Broksson's for his Duke—Ashai, of Ismere. An't heard anything specially against Ashai, but I an't trusting enough to be meat for the Fool-Killer yet, either. Not a Family, this time: a whole Clan, to report dead of the cabbage blight or attacked by starving moles. Not the Inn-smiths! Whatever his grandda did or didn't do, Orlengis serves Andras of his own will, no better than a Fisher, for my money. They—"

Jannus lost the thread again as the barge heeled sharply left a second time, as if mounted on rollers. Before he'd brought it straight he was much closer to the Kantmorie cliff than he'd ever come before—surely much closer than he liked. And ahead, he could see at least two barges that were closer still.

"Elda. I think the tents ought to come down."

"What? Everything would get soaked."

"Just the same, it's—"

The first real blast of wind struck the barge, so that the tentside clapped rigid, straining as it cupped the thrust.

The barge lagged, losing steerage way, and skidded heavily beneath them, so that Elda toppled over backward and Lur caught hold of Jannus' leg to steady himself. Jannus got his right arm over the sweep and locked it against his body, fighting to regain control of the barge's drift.

Elda sprang up, clutching the side, and stood crouched there an instant to assess the state of the other barges. All were adrift, some turned crosswise to the current, making the sweeps of little use. Two barges collided and whacked into a third, smashing its sweep and spilling three or four flailing shapes into the river. Over them all loomed the Wall.

Elda snatched a kettle, a ladle, and a knife. The knife he tossed blindly toward Lur, directing, "Earn your keep," and began hammering on the kettle with the ladle, waking echoes like drowned bells from the Wall. "The tents! Cut the ropes! Cut the ropes!"

Blinking, leaning hard into the stinging rain, Jannus saw Lur scuttle on all fours to the tent's hanging door flaps, check there, then fling himself against the righthand side of the barge to get at the ropes from that awkward angle.

The sweep ground against a hidden stone—they were *that* close to the Wall—and gave Jannus an instant's purchase. He shoved with all his strength, and the barge began to wallow back toward safety while Elda continued to bellow and pound away on the kettle.

Jannus began to work the sweep, pumping with long deep strokes to increase speed so he could steer. The rain made a hissing sound, peppering the surface of the river which began to move in a slow, heaving chop the farther Jannus moved away from the shallows. The tent, finally loosed on one side, billowed and twisted over the peakrope far above Lur's reach. Lur stared up at it, then scrambled across the stacks of baggage to start sawing at the other side as the loose tentside bucked and whacked back and forth above him. Elda threw down the kettle, grabbed the knife, and struck through the peakrope. Still tied on the left, the tent blew over the side into the water and acted like a huge oar on that side, pulling the barge around again toward the Wall. Jannus pulled heavy, uneven strokes, trying to compensate for the drag.

"Sig!" somebody was yelling. "Sig, jump! Sig!" and Elda straightened from hauling fistfuls of the tent back into the boat, hollering, "Sig! Jump clear!"

Two barges, one with a broken sweep, were revolving lazily around each other. Each turn brought them nearer the cliffside. Too far away to see faces, Jannus could see the frantic indecision of those aboard.

A man on the inmost barge wrenched free the bladeless oar, still a formidable pole, and stabbed first at the water, then at the cliff itself, in an attempt to fend the barge away. Except for the wind, silence hung over the river as the barge touched the wet red rock and crunched quietly along it, still revolving. Every standing figure aboard had collapsed.

Just before the second barge collided with the cliff, a woman tossed a kicking child into the river, then sprang outward herself, clutching a three-legged stool.

Those who were able to stay afloat until they could be hauled aboard another barge, and those who were independently able to reach the west bank, were saved—a total of six: two young men, one dragging a drowned infant sister; a chunky girl who shed her clothes to swim unhindered and who at last staggered onto the reedy shore; two small children who managed to hang onto a wooden case flung toward them until they could be reached; and one man who was dragged speechless and shaking onto a barge in midstream and had to be restrained from leaping back into the river to rescue his wife, drifting along shoeless a few rods away.

How many were lost, there was no way of knowing. Everything was too confused for any accounting. Elda, who'd at last relieved Jannus at the sweep, finally brought the barge scraping over the gravel to a place where they could moor. Jannus began to wrestle with the sodden canvas the moment the deck was steady underfoot: trying to fling the canvas, against the wind, over the peakrope he'd retied.

"Leave it be," Elda ordered, as if he bore the tent a personal hatred.

"We need . . . the shelter," Jannus replied, finding each word a labor. Lur came and helped him find enough loose ends of cording to retie the loops. Balanced on a hamper and hanging onto the high rope with one hand, Jannus was finally able to draw the tent over. Working from bow to stern, so the tent was never over him, Lur secured the canvas to the side pegs.

Elda, having set the mooring poles, made no further move and didn't offer to help them. He sat in the stern with his left arm crooked around the pole and his cheek rested against it, staring across the choppy brown river toward the Wall.

"Should have taken that contract with Ashai Rey," he said suddenly, "built the Andrans fifty barges with decorated tents and then let the Fool-Killer come for them all."

Jannus found nothing to say.

The Valde remained in Sithstock the following morning until the weather cleared, then continued south about noon. Tired out from Sithstock hospitality, many of the freemaids went to sleep as soon as the paddlewheels took up a steady rhythm.

Poli slept right through the boarding, though her dream turned dark and anxious: and she jarred awake to find herself, together with Aliana, Mene, Seline, and some six others, trapped in the compartment, at the core of a maelstrom of violent intentions.

Aliana was talking composedly through the shut door to their captors outside: "—enough. You cannot enter save one at a time. We can take you as you come."

"Granted—until the cabin is full. Then what?" replied a man's voice. "We have the boat. We have half a score of your folk. We can take them, and sink this craft."

"With the door barred!" put in another voice.

The first voice said, "Shut up. We can't come in, but you can't come out. Agree, and in five days, maybe less, you can all go on your way no worse."

"On your promise?" queried Aliana skeptically.

"Valde don't need promises: you know I mean what I say. Otherwise, what good are you?"

Somebody inspoke a comment on the excessive faith of Bremneri.

"How do I know," Aliana was saying, "your intent will bind others?"

There was some motion outside, a slight change in the tumultuous hostile expectancy. "There," declared the man, "doesn't that show what I order gets done?"

Somebody—Mene—wondered what'd been done. Poli thought some of the crowd had been waved back: at least the man by the door could be heard now, feeling unprotected. Poli was minded to snatch him in and see what the rest would do.

A summary negation from Aliana. "This one, as hostage, would only free the rest to their own anger and fear."

Poli accepted her judgment.

The man demanded, "Well? Will you come out and talk about it, or not?"

Ashferia abandoned an attempt to distinguish the man's whole *farioh*, to translate the undisciplined welter of fragmentary images and emotions into specific intentions regarding them. There was too much confusion. And, as Aliana noted, he could dislike and distrust them and still subdue himself and others, to his own ends. . . .

"We will come," replied Aliana, meanwhile calling the freemaids to be ready in full harness. When all were ready, she opened the door.

There were men all over the deck, too thickly ranked for any Valde to have pushed through. More men were crowded on top of the high cement riverwall against which the captured packet was tied. Those above held clubs and rough spears. Those below stared and glowered and shifted, a bristly ranksmelling hedge channeling the Valde toward the bow.

Sidling as close to the cabin walls as she could, Poli looked past the men at the angles and faces of Bremneri buildings. *Lisle*, she thought.

The foredeck was also hedged, five or more deep. A clear space had been left in the middle of the deck, where the rest of the troop, bound and leashed, stood with no outward sign of either their chagrin at being caught or their alert hope at the approach of the rest of the freemaids, armed and unbound.

The Bremneri leader was seated on a cask: a lean narrow-shouldered man with clean unpatched clothing, unlike most behind him. His black beard and shaggy hair left unconcealed only his nose, broken at least once long ago, and his eyes, very dark and quick moving, reminding Poli powerfully of Jannus though this man was at least ten years older.

Catching Poli's succession of images, Aliana at once said to the man, "You are Newstock-born," making it a statement rather than a guess. The crowd muttered uneasily, making a peculiar sign with thumb and little finger toward the Valde. Their noise made it impossible to discern the reaction of any one man alone.

"I am called Greyhawk, Trader of Lisle. These," said the man, waving at the shifting hedge of arms and faces, "are my Stranger Screen, my troop, my friends."

The man who called himself Greyhawk paused, studying the Valde for a while. Then he moved one hand, and a boy came to stand at his right, raising three slates bound in wood. Stammering slightly, the boy read in a high clear voice, " 'I, Greyhawk of Lisle, propose this. I need the service of a Fair Witness for the period of perhaps half a week: five days. As none of our women will serve the purpose—' "

The boy colored to the forehead and lost his place. Greyhawk turned as if to take the slates from him but changed his mind and resumed his former pose.

" '—serve the purpose, I will settle for Valde. To take a Valde against her will is perilous, as all men know—' " A burst of laughter interrupted the boy: he looked around angrily until the crowd quieted. He was, Poli thought, very young. Greyhawk had chosen him to entertain the Lislemen, to distract their minds from the encircled Valde, as well as to keep his own words at one remove from himself and so keep his intention wholly private. A shrewd and forethinking man.

" '—as all men know, yet worth the risk when no other way can be found. To you freemaids I offer this choice: to be kept close prisoners in an earthen pit dug for trash and offal and thus copiously supplied with rats, and fed on what you may find there for the next five days, then to be released to pursue your way; or to be housed for a like time in the best we have, while one of your number serves me in the guise of Fair Witness whenever I require. At the end of the five days you will be released, claiming whatever just price you think fit.' "

The boy lowered the slates, looking to Greyhawk for approval. Receiving a nod, the boy escaped back into the anonymity of the crowd. Greyhawk stared at the Valde and waited.

"Either way," he pointed out finally, "you will remain in Lisle and be released unharmed. It is for you to determine the manner of your guesting."

"If you release us," commented Aliana, "what you have done will be known abroad. The stocks will take a price, perhaps as much as you can pay. . . ."

"I think not. If you were harmed or killed, and *that* came to be known—then, perhaps. We are not a numerous stock. Our numbers and power increase slowly." He was, Poli thought, speaking as much to the crowd as to Aliana, warning them, reiterating the dangers of releasing their emotions into open violence. "And what of the Andrans? We would have to silence them too. And without alliance with Andran waterfolk willing to do without trade and harborage anywhere else on the river—without the goodwill of the Reyi and Aiah of Andras, this stock of Lisle would wither and die as surely as an uprooted rosebush. For our lives, we must keep faith with the Andrans. Therefore, for our lives, we must keep faith with *you*," concluded Greyhawk, looking from the crowd directly at Aliana again.

While Greyhawk was speaking, Aliana had been determining the flow of the troop's inclination. A few were terrified. They feared that a hand of days in the hating dread would be like being trapped with a Screamer that couldn't be silenced. They feared the pain might scar them into darkheartedness for seasons to come.

Their wish to lunge into escape was shared by others who wanted to bring the Sithstock troop against Lisle. Aliana and Mene, then others, insisted that the Lady Ultreena would not consent. During Aliana's service as a troopmaid to Sithstock, Ultreena had sent her troop, with that of Highstock, against

Lisle shortly after the town was overrun. All but seven of the troop had been lost, seven remaining to defend Sithstock the last two years of the term. Ultreena would not take such a risk again, not when Greyhawk was pledged to release the Valde in only five days. And if two, or three, escaped, what of the rest?

These obstacles swirled the escaping impulse into confusion and indecision.

A larger group were, or became, warily neutral: they'd endure a brief imprisonment but lend no aid to their captors.

The remainder were single voices. One, infected by the surrounding mood, desired immediate attack on those nearest at hand, regardless of the result: Ashferia. Another still wanted to try Greyhawk as a hostage: Seline. One wanted to know what made the man plan their capture so elaborately, but was herself unwilling to risk to gain the answer: Mene. Another, an innate snatcher of risk, shifted from wanting to call the Sithstock troop to wanting to find out what plans Greyhawk might be hatching to the harm of the other stocks. Certainly no little matter would prompt him to steal a Fair Witness. It would be intolerable to be taken, stupidly held, and then released and never know why. . . .

This latter thought was Poli's.

The mood crystallized quickly around her resolution, as before a single duel. Poli wanted to find out. The rest were more or less willing that she should, predisposed by the habitual deference to the will of a First Dancer.

Having completed his speech, Greyhawk was staring expectantly at Aliana. She said, "The First Dancer will serve as Fair Witness, according to our custom."

Greyhawk apparently found this a surrender, and suspiciously swift. For a few breaths he only leaned back, frowning. Then he said, "I'll send for her when I want her."

If the brazier were moved outside the tent, the rain would put it out. And Lur couldn't go inside. Even wrapped in three damp wool blankets with the canvas square on top, he was utterly miserable and resented the body's perpetual encroachment on the rede—this body in particular. It was becoming difficult for him to restrain his impatience to be rid of it.

Jannus handed out to him a steaming cup of the bitter Innsmith beer. Lur nursed the cup against his chest between sips to eke out every bit of available warmth.

They were alone on the barge. The Innsmith had gone off

downriver on foot, before nightfall, to help collect the scattered barges and tally the missing, the lost, and the found. Jannus had put up the lantern when the fog began closing in; Lur could now scarcely see the lantern.

Jannus ducked out of the tent and began working around Lur, rearranging baggage.

"What," said Lur incuriously.

"Just stay there, it's all right."

Jannus formed two unequal piles of boxes and hampers against the righthand door flap. Then he pulled the flap behind the taller pile and weighted it there. "All right," he directed, "come on."

Lur numbly moved where he was guided, only gradually realizing that Jannus' construction cut off the rain and the wind from the hamper seat in the center. He could look up and see rain slanting past but it didn't touch him at all.

Within the tent, Jannus was shifting the copper brazier carefully with a thick scorched pole kept for that purpose, until he'd slid it to the inside opening of the two piles of baggage. Lur could feel the heat against his face.

Slowly he became less chilled. Jannus added fresh charcoal to the brazier. It hissed awhile, with an unpleasant smell, but finally began to glow. Jannus settled down on the other side of the brazier with a mug of beer. His face was drawn and very tired, with a smear of young beard along the line of his chin. "Elda won't be back tonight," he commented presently.

"Supposing he comes back at all." Lur sipped beer to ease his sore throat.

"Of course he's. . . . What makes you think he might not?"

"It's an excellent chance," replied Lur mildly, "if he should decide to take it. He expected me to be based, dead, by this time and I'm not. And you're nearly as dangerous to him as I am. But perhaps it won't occur to him in time."

The boy made no comment for quite a while. At length, however, he argued, "He'll come back. He contracted with me to go to the Summerfair."

"As he would put it, 'Fine for you.' As I said, maybe it hasn't occurred to him yet. Is there more?" Lur extended his cup, which was returned to him filled, hot. "When he puts me ashore, what will you do?"

Jannus sighed, frowning, and again was slow to answer. "I'd stay with the Innsmiths. I contracted to serve them, and I'm bound by that. And I have business of my own at the Summerfair I won't turn aside from. You don't need me. . . ."

"If not you, then somebody. What I have to do, I can't do alone."

"What are you doing, then?"

"Trying to get to Down and kill the Shai. But what I'll need will be in a keep. Under a keep's roof. I can't get to it myself. But nobody could get it without me, because of the stranger-traps that protect a keep. . . . The only keep I know well enough is Cliffhold. I need somebody to go into Cliffhold for me."

"After the Summerfair," said Jannus slowly, "I'll be going home. I could wait for you in Newstock. If I knew just where the base is, I could let you out again, the way I did before. . . ."

"That's better than nothing. Don't expect me to know you then, though, if it comes to that. I won't remember anything since my last rede, two hundred years ago. It will all be strange to me again."

"I'll remember. . . . Why do you want to kill the Shai?"

"It's the only way to stop this rede from waking. I can't get into Downbase any more than I can go into Cliffhold. I can't claim the Rule of One. So to die, I'll have to take the High Plain with me. It's about time," Lur added aridly.

". . . . I don't know. It's hard for me to judge. But I'll help you if I can. . . ."

There was a shout that reached them faintly. Jannus raised his head, listening and waiting. When the shout was repeated, he answered by striking the kettle, the Innsmith's sometime gong.

"So," said Lur indifferently. "It didn't occur to him, after all. You were right."

The Valde were housed on the upper floor of a house whose tall slit windows overlooked the river. The rooms smelled of recent cleaning, and fresh rushes were strewn on the cold floors. Mismatched bedding, clearly gathered from various places, was crowded into two of the rooms: double the amount needed. The Lislers, it appeared, had been ready for any number of Valde up to fifty.

Meals—cold, as if carried some distance from the kitchens—were delivered by a crowd of sullen men several times a day. No one else visited them; though the town was almost as aware of them as they of the town: the unreasoning dread was as a wet, thick, acrid fog in which the freemaids moved and ate and slept. The more open among them tended to confuse the outside fog with their own fears and become locked in paralyzing echoes from which several freemaids were needed to rouse them. Poli, who had become used to holding herself relatively isolate and closed, was not troubled by these echoes.

The afternoon after their capture, the summons came. Poli took the bandages from her hand and forehead, inspected her attire, then lastly and with reluctance removed her bridestone and handed it to Aliana for safekeeping or disposition, if need be.

The guard of five who'd come for her took her down to the street and along the riverwall with its ill-kept docks. She noted, to her surprise, several women watching her pass, from various doorways and windows. These made odd waving gestures before ducking out of sight. Andran women, perhaps— or some of the few Truthdeaf Bremneri women still born in each generation, who often sought the farmsteads at their time of choosing. Or perhaps they were steadborn of Truthdeaf mothers, and had never seen or been touched by the Valde in their whole lives. Still, it was odd to know that women, of whatever race, lived willingly in this blighted town and hated her equally with their men.

The guards led her across a small courtyard to a carved door and shoved her through, shutting the door solidly behind her.

Two men only were in the large bare hall she found before her: Greyhawk and another, an Andran by dress, both seated at a long table centered in the varied glow of a round west-facing window inset with shards of vermillion and yellow. Of some Lisle Lady's pride, Poli thought, only the window remained.

The Andran, seated nearest the window with his back to the light, was the first truly beautiful man Poli had ever seen. Of middle years, he had noble features and a high quiet brow, above which his smooth silver hair was bound loose under a blue circlet. One hand, brightly ringed, was raised in the act of offering a bit of meat to a hunting-bird, an alver, that balanced with hunched shoulders on the back of his chair. The alver stared ferociously at Poli before taking the meat with a sidewise dip of her head.

Hearing the shutting of the door, the Andran looked around and seemed quietly surprised to find Poli there. He looked to Greyhawk, who was grinning with a fierce satisfaction, for an explanation.

"Now." Greyhawk motioned Poli closer without shifting his duellist's stare from the man opposite. "*Now* tell me this moonshine tale again, before my Witness!"

The man regarded Poli gently, showing no more than mild amusement at what Greyhawk so clearly regarded as a trap. "I am Ashai, Duke of Ismere in Andras Bay, Lady Valde. What I have said here this day is all true."

And as he spoke Poli blankly confirmed the realization that had been growing in her since the door scraped closed: the Andran wasn't really there. She could see him, hear his voice, yet he wasn't there. Unable to control the impulse, Poli reached out and touched his hand: contacting warm flesh, she jerked back two steps.

"Well?" demanded Greyhawk, blazing anger at her, aware only that his trap had gone somehow awry.

With a great effort Poli ignored the unnerving, unliving silence of the smiling man, falling back on the shared alarm of the freemaids to support her in fullfilling her oath. "Greyhawk, I cannot . . . I can't serve you here. This. . . ." She motioned blindly toward the other chair, unwilling to confront its occupant.

Waves of accusation and rage erupted from the Bremneri, so that Poli backed away yet another step. "You slut! I'll see—"

"No! Whatever this . . . this creature is, it is not a living man. Neither living. Nor a man. I do not know what it is," Poli concluded faintly, and felt Greyhawk's rage cool to watchfulness, his attention slide from her.

"It seems, Lady Valde," commented the thing in the chair, the voice musical and gracious, "I must be the Fair Witness here. Whatever pledge she made to you, Lord Trader, she has indeed faithfully kept. She can no more hear behind my words than you can yourself."

"What are you: a Screamer?" asked Greyhawk tensely, and Poli thought again, *Newstock-born.*

The false man appeared to consider, observing the ceiling beams with an expression of interest. "If I understand you, not precisely. But, for your purposes, it will do. And yet I am Ashai, as I have said: duke for some fifteen years of one of the Isles of Andras. Do you doubt me? Would I have a ship, and fivescore watermen—some known to you for years as my servants—under my command, if I were not Ashai himself but another? Moreover, what I have said I can do, I will do. What I propose is possible. Proofs can be given you. This delightful child's revelation changes nothing. You must rely on your own judgment, as any man must."

Sobered, deeply uneasy, Greyhawk was trying to adjust to the new situation. Absently he told Poli, "Get out."

"You swore—"

"Not now. Get out. *Gully!*"

At Greyhawk's shout, one of the guards came in to yank Poli back into the courtyard. The men gathered around and marched her back the way they had come.

That night the freemaids heard Joneo Ras and the nine other captive watermen, housed in a chamber not too far away, being murdered, one by one.

Twenty-seven dead, Elda tallied: eighteen by drowning, nine by the Wall. Almost one whole Family, annihilated in a single morning.

Five more still missing and likely drowned too. Thirty-two, that'd make it. And some of the rest so griefstricken that they were no help to themselves or anybody else and had to be tended like children.

And all because he'd let himself become so occupied with the hope of prying useless secrets from a Tek that the danger of the tents had never even occurred to him.

"Elda!" yelled Solvig from the barge ahead. "Get your head out of the sack!"

Elda found he'd been pushing at the oar so hard he'd nearly overrun the leading boat. Using the increased steerage to veer sharply toward midstream, Elda let the barge drift a little before working back to his former position, last in the string of four. The rest of the Clan he'd sent on ahead to find shelter in Sithstock. There'd been no use in their waiting, moored, until the barges further upstream could join them.

Somebody was jumping and hollering on the shore. The first barge, Kell's, swung toward the shallows and collected the woman: Silla, it was, of Kermot's Family. Kell, moving his barge behind Elda's back out into deeper water, called that she hadn't seen anybody else but he'd keep watch.

Thirty-one.

A disaster, all the same.

Three barges sunk, Elda tallied, and others leaking and needing to be bailed. All the stored meal soaked and bursting sacks. All the hampers of clothes soaked, needing to be unpacked, allowed to dry thoroughly, and packed again to keep rot from setting in. The very hampers smelled musty already.

And it was all his fault, isolating himself with two outlanders instead of concentrating on his Family and his Clan, the way he was supposed to. Nobody had said a word of blame to him out loud except Solvig Torvesson, Sig's younger brother . . . but it didn't need saying. It was his fault because the Clan's welfare was his responsibility.

Solvig was now head of Sig's Family, and Bart's as well, Bart being dead with no grown sons. Solvig's combined Family numbered only three less than Elda's own. Solvig was an aggressive man, barely forty: he'd want more say in Clan affairs, at least at the first, than Elda could afford to surrender. If Elda wasn't careful, Solvig could split the Clan into factions, paralyze Elda's leadership. Elda would have to talk to Solvig and treat him carefully until Solvig'd had a chance to try settling petty quarrels within his own Family and find out how popular that'd make him—until Solvig began learning what was what.

Then maybe Solvig'd be bright enough to sit chatting in a barge and need telling the tents should come down from a Traders' cub never a full day on Erth-rimmon till lately, Elda thought with a surge of bitterness. Maybe he should be letting Jannus run the Clan.

The boy was sprawled half under the side of the tent still tied down—with running loops, this time—leadenly asleep. Lur sat by him in a patch of sun, like the cat he'd been named for, watching the meat-colored cliffs slide by.

"Lur." Elda kept his voice low, mindful of how variably sound carried over water. "I brought you for the sake of what you could tell me. That an't been worth warm spit, so far."

"I don't have what you want," replied the Tek coolly. "You don't want tools, you want the knowledge that first shaped them. That, I can't give you. I know how to use a force-knife, but not how to make it—and to make it, you'd have to make a series of twenty tools and systems first. I can tell you how to cast plarit, but not iron. And you couldn't make furnaces that'd hold molten plarit, even if I knew the composition, which I don't. I'm a Tek. And I never asked to be brought to you, so you have no complaint against me."

That was true, Elda had to admit. The gamble had been his own, and he was accountable for it. It was still his fault, not the Tek's. Fair was fair.

"Look in that round basket, there," Elda directed, "behind you. No, with the zigzag design. There should be some of Dinnel's boy's spare clothes in it. Sort through and see what'll fit better than what you got. Dall an't too much away from your size. . . . We'll be coming up on Sithstock before too long."

Obediently Lur collected a small pile of various clothes. He held up a wrinkled blue shirt to measure its sleeve against his arm, distastefully suspending it from his fingertips.

"That'll do," Elda decided. "Put it on."

"But it's wet," Lur objected, but did as he was told. It was a little too wide for his shoulders, but not so much it'd be noticed. Medd always said children's clothes were always being grown into or out of, never anything in between.

Under Elda's direction Lur dressed himself like a person. In fact, with a knitted cap over his bare scalp, he became much less odd, seen among a pack of red Smiths, than a skinny longlegged Newstocker. Under the cap, Lur's sunburnt face suddenly assumed human proportions; his delicate limbs were fleshed out by the loose-fitting cloth. If he could keep his mouth shut, he might be taken for a child even up close.

In stuffing the remaining clothing back into the basket, Lur tipped it against the boy and woke him up. Scrubbing an arm across his eyes, Jannus paused, staring at the Tek.

"Do I look that peculiar, then?"

Starting slightly, Jannus shook his head. "No, not at all, no. The opposite."

Lur seemed to think about that string of denials, then said, "It's occurred to him, I think. . . . Help me with this." Jannus moved aside and helped shove the basket into its place, as Lur continued, his back still to Elda. "The knowledge isn't lost, just because I don't carry it with me."

"What's that supposed to mean," Elda responded.

"Only that. The knowledge exists."

"Written down?" Elda demanded, eager again in spite of himself.

Lur asked what writing was: impatiently, Elda told him. Though no scribe, Elda knew the general idea well enough. Lur said it seemed a cumbersome idea. "No," he went on, looking around calmly, "it just exists. At Down. The Shai holds it. You're free to do what any Tek would: go and ask for it."

Elda turned away from Lur's cool eyes, suddenly knowing raw bait when he saw it but bait well chosen: and he was afraid. "I told you before, there's nothing could make me set foot on the Dead Shore. Anyhow, the Wall an't failed: didn't you see that plain enough yesterday?" he added bitterly.

"You'll be circling the High Plain on three sides. There are ways the Wall could be tested, each night, and no one the wiser. . . ." Lur had settled back onto the deck, head relaxed against the side of the barge. His face was placid, smooth as lard in a basin.

"May your tongue choke you black," said Elda flatly, "if ever you say another word about this to me. The next word, the next hint, and I land you on the nearest bank. You hear me?"

The corners of Lur's froglike mouth quirked down in the thought of a smile. "I do hear you, Elda Innsmith."

Losing his temper at last, Elda yanked the sweep against his chest, heading in toward the reeds.

"You promised," Jannus objected.

"Didn't promise to do more than nurse him. That's done. Thirty-one dead, three barges sunk, but he's still here, the damned river slippie, healthy and with gall enough to grin at me! . . . You're so choice of him, you can just go too, for all of me. An't too far yet to walk. Maybe your Ma—"

"Get back to midstream," cut in the Tek, soft and curt. "Put me ashore and I'll tell."

Again Elda imagined how fragile that head would be between his hands. "Don't push. I could land you on the Dead Shore as easy. . . .You wouldn't dare tell. Nobody'd let you live long enough to listen, much believe you, if you showed what you are. And we'd be long gone."

"You're slow, Elda: I'll tell *them*." And the Tek nodded toward the other barges.

Solvig. Elda felt sick. With such a thing to charge him with, Solvig would surely split the Clan, break Family from Family in spite of anything Elda could say or do about it.

Elda shoved the sweep away so hard the barge rocked, then steadied and turned. Lur, resting against the side, merely put out a hand to brace himself.

"That other thing," Elda said. "You never speak of it again. Never."

This time Lur neither smiled nor said anything at all.

Having been boosted onto the dock, Jannus took time to compose himself and settle his faintly damp cloak into a decent drape: a Trader would notice such things. Then he passed, with an outlandishly large escort of six troopmaids, through the ranks of Valde on the Sithstock riverwall, the Valde that barred the Innsmiths from landing.

Behind the apron of harbor was a high wall of dressed

stone. Scarred gates were opened a few grudged spans to admit them; beyond, Sithstock was propped on the hillside like a half-opened beanpod.

Two rows of many-balconied houses ascended in tiers, peering over each other's shoulders toward the river. The low stages of the central street were stuffy and dark: the walls cut off the breeze, and the hill before him blocked the westering sun.

Having lived where the Kantmorie cliff supplied a third of the total landscape, Jannus was used to heights—as things to look at. The laced muscles of his knees began to flutter slightly: walking had become climbing.

He paused for breath in a doorway. He'd climbed high enough to overlook the harbor wall and see the Innsmith barges, strung into the current in three jostling bumping lines from the longest pier. Indistinct voices and bursts of shouting still reached him, like the crackling of a fire laid with resinous wood. The Valde troop, of course, were silent. They'd remain so unless the Innsmiths carried out Elda's threat to overrun the harborage, permission or no.

Jannus had never heard so large a troop in full cry: a cool corner of his mind wondered what it would sound like.

He hoped Elda believed the troopmaids would really fight, that an attempt to land in force would be a disaster as great as the storm. True, Valde would not kill without consent, but that consent need not be deliberate: murderous rage would do. And the points of their dagger-darts bore a powerful sleeping salve; if a man slept while flailing in the river, and if the water took him, that was between himself and Erth-rimmon.

Lisle wasn't the only riverstock ever attacked—just the only one successfully taken and held. Valde were not just waykeepers, dancing public mock-combat measures, as Elda's chances to see them might easily have led him to conclude. For all Elda knew, the private dueldances might be fought with knitting needles and won or lost by relative ineptitude. But Jannus knew the troopmaids' ways better, even, than most of the stock-born; and he knew Valde for hunters. He hoped Elda had believed him.

Only in talking might there be a chance.

The way narrowed and became frank steps, passing under arches overgrown with greenstar vines inhabited by swarms of cheeping brown birds. Jannus paused more often, a small hot pain jabbing under his ribs at each breath. He fell gradually behind, resting on each terrace between successive pairs of shut doors.

Half a tier above, the six troopmaids glanced back but continued to climb, behaving more like guides than guards. But they'd know, he supposed, that he wasn't contemplating any desperate act such as charging the hilltop or gnawing through a door and invading some household complex.

Two landings above him they stopped. Discouragingly, they still had breath to hum and trade scraps of words with the doorward who came from the door on the right to meet them. All seven troopmaids turned and stared down at him as he continued to trudge from stage to stage: so he needn't wonder what they were discussing.

"Jan'z Lillia w' hnamm . . .?" the doorkeeper was commenting as he began the last flight.

He didn't like being the subject of half-heard chat when he was a serious errand. "Yes," he called, curt and breathless, "I am Jannus Lillia's . . . son of Newstock: neither . . . an Andran nor an . . . Innsmith, as you may . . . plainly see."

"I do hear you," rejoined the doorkeeper meekly, "guest of the Lady Ultreena." She stood aside for him to pass.

Only four of the escort accompanied him inside. One of those remaining on the landing called suddenly, past the closing door, "Poli w' lef' yes'day, sunappear so!"

Startled, Jannus spun around, but the bar was just falling.

The four troopmaids led him through an intricate series of rush carpeted passages, humming and muttering to each other at a great rate and staring at him every few seconds.

He didn't like it, these troopmaids' casual, familiar way of treating him. It made him feel like an exhibit. Belatedly he began to set himself to suppress both the self-consciousness and the tight, defensive resentment it provoked in him, knowing it would be tainting his *farioh* and they'd be hearing it all.

They were young, he reminded himself—though he'd looked none in the face, he couldn't have helped noticing that. Valde were fullgrown at nine or ten, so age was hard to judge. But these, though as tall as he was, were slender to the point of skinniness; still "with leaves in their hair," as the saying went, the taste of words still new enough to buzz and blur in their mouths. They just hadn't learned the social mercy of full formality which eased one's awareness of being spied upon. A veteran troop like Aliana's would have known—

A troopmaid's mutter dropped Poli's name before him

again like a brick over which his attention and self-discipline stumbled heavily.

"Oh, sorry, sorry," said the troopmaid, patting his arm solicitously until he backed out of her reach.

"Why," he felt impelled to say, "are you all speaking of the freemaid Poli Wir?"

"Oh, only for finding if you're the Bremneri sadhearted so for love of Poli w'," she explained readily, and another nodded brightly, agreeing. "Only finding."

The escort waited around him, attentive, unselfconscious and a little puzzled. Finally he assembled an endurable reply: "Are there that many of us?"

The irony produced an exchange of interrogative looks and hums. "Only you. . . ."

"Then it must be me."

Valde had no sense of humor. Nor had they any native sense of privacy. These didn't understand why he was so upset.

He couldn't control what he felt, but he could control what he did about it: keeping all bitterness out of his voice, at least, he suggested, "Since that is settled, the Lady Ultreena. . . ."

"Oh, sorry, sorry," cried a troopmaid, and hustled them up a stairway, through an arch, and down a hall to the left. Jannus was quite lost.

"Here yes'day," volunteered the nearest troopmaid, still trying to be friendly, "Poli w'."

"Yes. I know."

"Oh, very sad," she commiserated, and the others, stupidly nodding, bundled him through a doorway into a dim little room and shut the door, leaving him with at least the illusion of privacy.

They'd all be outside, he thought savagely, waiting to load him with more poisoned sincere pity on the way back. So he had that to look forward to.

First Aliana's troop, then invading Innsmiths, and then the peculiar spectacle of himself: this must have been a most thrilling time for the Sithstock troopmaids. If the prolocutor started questioning him about Poli in direct—

"You are Jannus," declared a woman's voice, startling him badly, "householder to Lillia, Lady of Newstock."

There was a square hole, he saw now, in the wall opposite. On the far side it was covered by a grate, Sithstock's mistrustful version of a Stranger Screen.

"Lady, that is truth." Answering, next, the usual questions about Lisle, Jannus managed to collect himself; but having an audience in a closet with a female prolocutor did little to put him at his ease.

"And do you, or any person under your sole control," said the woman's voice, "or any person at your direction or with your consent, plan or contemplate harm to Sithstock, or to myself?"

So he was being addressed by the Lady Ultreena herself, without any prolocutor. Prolocutors were partly a concealment for those they spoke for, like a second Stranger Screen, and partly a courtesy to a male guest, neither holding the advantage of Truthtell. In Newstock, this present mode of audience could only be a deliberate insult—but perhaps Sithstock custom differed in this, as well.

When Jannus offered a disclaimer of intended harm, the Lady snapped, "Ha! One of those outlanders threatened to set my underskirt afire and me in it. Another shouted he'd shave me bald and hoped my nose would rot off and improve my face. Don't you consider that contemplating harm?"

By her voice, the Lady was old and extremely angry. Jannus wondered if anything he could say could salvage things. "Lady, there is no excuse for their rudeness except their sorrow and confusion. Many of their kin are dead—"

"None of my doing."

"—and they expected at least common hospitality here and do not understand your refusal of it. So I was sent to speak for them, having slightly more claim on your courtesy than they."

"You mean you can threaten me with trade-strife with Newstock, which has a name for quarreling over a hatful of wheat, and they can't."

That was both blunt and accurate. It was with such an implied threat that he'd extorted this audience. "If the Lady wishes to put it so," he replied moderately.

"When they told me there was a Bremneri boy with that foulmouthed crowd of red Smiths, I expected to find you were a runaway. I learn that isn't the case. Instead, I hear you're off to the Summerfair in pursuit of a Valde freemaid. What in—"

The door behind him opened—a troopmaid with a dagger-dart, brought by his flash of unsuppressed malevolence toward the Lady. The Valde balanced, attending to the grate, then withdrew as quickly as she'd entered.

"What in the world," said the Lady again, in a sterner tone, "made Lillia agree to let you go on such a preposterous errand?"

"Lady. It's none of your concern. I am not answerable to you."

"In my household, in my stock, you are answerable to anything I care to name. Do not try me too far."

"Lady—" Jannus took a deep breath. "I am here to speak for the Innsmiths. If you will not let them land, say *why* you will not and I will report it to them."

There was a silence. Then the Lady said slowly, "Out of compassion, I allowed the first barges to wait for the last. All are now gathered. This is the end of my compassion and the beginning of my duty. They threaten to land, against my ban. They are therefore outlanders indeed and can't be trusted even in my harbor. Lisle was taken by less than fifty men; we profit by that example. This is the word I am sending them by Serafin Wir. This is what you will tell the Lady Lillia when you come before her."

"I do hear you, Lady." Jannus turned to the door: as he'd feared, he found it fastened from the outside.

"You'll be safer up here for the time being. If I'm to have trade-strife with Newstock, it will be for protecting you against your wish, not for letting you walk into the middle of an open battle—and on such an errand! When this is done you'll be sent home to give your account to Lillia." Her voice was receding, withdrawing from the grate. Jannus heard the sound of a door, concluding his audience.

Elda caught just pieces of the refusal, but enough to know Jannus hadn't been any use. The nearest Valde knelt down, reaching toward the mooring lines: Elda pushed her away with the barge pole, just hard enough to let her know to let the lines alone.

"Well?" Solvig was demanding. "Do we sit on our hands, or what? It's getting dark."

"There's more of us," put in Kell. "If we clear the harbor out, we can camp here tonight, anyhow, and—"

"I don't like it," Elda said, looking up past the line of Valde on the pier to judge how much light was left, the chances of finding some moorage before dark on a starsday.

"Nor I don't like it either," snapped his wife Medd, in the next barge over. "But the children must get out of the wet. We need food, someplace to rest, and we need it now. What are you waiting on, then, Elda Hildursson?"

"Grat," called Elda abruptly, "get out of that raincoat. If you go into the river, you'll sink like a brick."

"The darts—"

"The darts are a chance," Elda rejoined. "The river is sure. Take it off, quit holding us up. You: Dan!"

"Here, Da." His youngest son spoke up from behind him somewhere.

"You get Kevel and two or three more, get into the river. Help anybody that goes in. You hear?"

"Right, Da."

Grat finished wrestling his way out of the canvas raincoat. Then Elda said, "Go!" and they all loosed themselves at the piers and the riverwall. Elda crouched down to guard the mooring lines, with people climbing over him and on him to get at the pier.

The attack was more noisy than swift. To reach land everybody had to scramble from barge to barge, waiting turns, stumbling over baggage. When they caught a handhold and pulled themselves up onto a pier, the Valde darts stung many before they'd even found their footing, so that they wavered and stumbled as they advanced, striking about them with poles, iron pots, and whatever darts they could grab, even from their own flesh. The Valde retreated from the docks to stay out of reach.

Elda saw a couple of boys dive off a barge and strike for a pier farther down. Others, following that lead, grabbed at the slimy stones of the riverwall itself. Somebody snatched a Valde by the ankles and yanked her into the river. The line of troopmaids retreated toward the harbor wall, hands flashing as they flung darts. Every once in a while their shriek broke free of the general noise, shrill as a knife honed on a wheel.

Elda stood up to find out how many Innsmiths were still on their feet on the pier above him. A dart struck him by the ear. A second hit the hand he raised to his face. He couldn't see clearly enough to find a target: the few torches became tiny and brilliant.

Somebody lunged past him, under his arm, and was sawing at the mooring ropes. The Tek: trying to set them all adrift, slam them into the Wall! Elda slapped at the Tek with the dart in his hand and flipped him off the barge. Elda reached for the pier but it had moved away, so vague he could scarcely make it out. Then his knees betrayed him too and he collapsed onto a pile of hampers.

Jannus paced around the little room hitting the walls with his fist, unable to keep still and resign himself to how thoroughly he was trapped. High windows, no more than slits. No door except the one barred on the outside and likely guarded. Cement walls.

It just wasn't tolerable that all his caution and self-discipline should be made worthless by a spiteful nosy old woman hiding behind a grill.

Grill.

Against long habit, he went straight up to the grill and peered through. The room beyond was larger, with two full-sized windows beyond which orange sunset was rapidly fading. And the grill itself was carved wood, not metal: a Stranger Screen after all—a concealment, not a real barrier. When pushing at it made no impression he stepped back a pace and kicked until it cracked across. He got his head and right arm through, then, painfully, his other arm and shoulder, and hung a second, head down. Then he fell into the next room.

Without pausing he caught up the chair he'd half landed on and broke out the lattice of the nearer window. A glance slowed him a slate roof some distance below; but it was that or nothing, because he'd never find his way alone out of the household. The Valde would be hunting him like a Screamer as soon as they were done with the Innsmiths. He swung his legs through the window, holding on to the casing. Just as he let go, he saw a Valde's face appear in the square hole in the wall.

He hit the slanting roof sooner than he'd expected and tumbled in an avalanche of dislodged slates down to a gutter where this roof met another, slanting up. That roof proved to support one of the arches, from which he could drop to the stairs.

Glancing back, he found the stairs still empty above him and then began running. He didn't dare take his eyes off his footing again until he reached the level way: then he saw troopmaids coming surefootedly down the stairs behind him, three landings up. And inside the harbor gate, at the street's end, there was another crowd which didn't seem to have noticed him yet, absorbed perhaps in the racket from the harbor. In spite of the Valde on the stairs Jannus forced himself to go more slowly, his eyes searching for a projecting balcony, something to let him over the harbor wall without going near the gate. If the troopmaids near the gate saw him, he was trapped again.

Something hung down the wall to the left of the gate—a rope, with spaced climbing blocks. Jannus ran across the open space beyond the last house, grabbed the rope, and jumped to the highest block he could reach, aware simultaneously that the noise from the harbor had stopped abruptly and that if he slipped or even hesitated a moment, he'd be caught. The rope brought him to a ledge overlooking the harbor, where guards were probably sometimes posted. Taking no time to determine what he might be dropping into, he lay flat on the wall, swung his feet around, and slid off.

He landed sprawling on the harbor stones. There were Valde out here too but they were gathered down beyond the gate, some rods distant. Twisting around, he saw only three Innsmiths standing on the long pier, bending down in some work. As a pair of troopmaids started toward him he got his feet under him and stumbled to the head of the pier. A broad-faced cheerful-looking boy about his own age came and steadied him with an arm around his shoulders, saying, "You're coming, then. I was wondering. Da won't be any too pleased to see you, I expect, but that's his lookout."

"What's happened?" Jannus asked breathlessly, looking back to find that the troopmaids had stopped by the gate.

"Oh, they chased us out. Most of the barges got cut adrift, we're just collecting whoever's left. Watch your feet," advised the boy, handing Jannus to another Innsmith who helped him slide into a barge full of semiconscious groping people. "Best not set down," advised the boy, from above. "You got a collection."

Jannus had no idea what he was talking about. The man nearest him reached down and pulled a dagger-dart out of the skirts of Jannus' cape, displayed it, then tossed it in the river. "There's a couple more," said the man. "You'd best watch out."

Jannus leaned against the stern pole and shut his eyes, trying to begin to catch his breath.

Lur woke to darkness and hands on him. Not a base, then. He held himself still, adding wet clothes to tones of muttered conversation to a slight rocking motion and coming to a conclusion that satisfied him. He was on a barge, among Innsmiths. His head ached, he was shivering, and Elda had tried to kill him. He relaxed.

"It's all right, Lur," whispered a voice he knew, and the hands shifted, easing him to a few spare inches of deck where he could stand. He took the side of Jannus' cloak to wrap about himself and leaned against the boy's hip. The dart and near-drowning had left him dizzy and strengthless. When his shivering eased, he dozed off again.

Motion roused him and he looked ahead to find multiple points of light scattered on the river ahead: fires burning on scores of small islands, perfectly reflected in the still, dark river. At each island was moored one or two of the barges he'd cut loose. There was great shouting back and forth across the broad slow lake into which Erth-rimmon had transformed itself.

Lur stayed close to Jannus, protected by him from the jostling Innsmiths, while several men waded out from an island to help tow the barge to a mooring place. He and the boy splashed, in their turn, to the shore and immediately joined the crowd around the nearest fire. All around them was the racket of Innsmith families sorting themselves and counting heads, passing from hand to hand pieces of burnt-edged fowl and oat cakes with mealy uncooked centers. Lur's hunger didn't prevent him from wondering where a crowd of demoralized Innsmiths could come up with several hundred waterfowl in the middle of the night. He tucked himself closer against Jannus' back, all but his bent head covered by a fold of the voluminous cape.

Lur's suspicion was confirmed soon enough: a Valde came from under the trees with three plucked birds spitted on a stick. She knelt crookedly by the fire to arrange the spit on the rests. Lur was astonished when the boy promptly greeted the Valde, calling her attention to himself: thanking her for the meal, wanting to know what the Newstock troopmaids were doing here. Lur began pinching him fiercely, to make him shut up, but was ignored. And Lur didn't dare do anything really drastic lest the boy's reaction make matters even worse.

In a crowd, in bad light, the Valde might not see him, or notice that she couldn't hear him even if she saw. Valde, in his experience, were fairly stupid and unobservant: *marenniath,* the empathy-sense, was even less selective than ordinary hearing, and Valde lived in a noisy emotional world. Lur still wished Jannus would shut up, so she'd go away.

The Valde, addressed as Mene, was explaining that the troop was joining the Innsmiths on the rest of the journey— acting as hunters, guides, and contacts with the women of towns downriver—because they were unwilling to trust the Andrans any more. Some Andrans, Mene said, were strange, were not-people, *sa'farioh*—without selfsinging a Valde could hear.

Lur began to pay closer attention.

The Valde went on into a long rambling account of the freemaids' capture and imprisonment in a place called Lisle. The one fact of interest to Lur in this recital was that a Valde had encountered this *sa'farioh* in a hall: under a roof. Not a Tek, then, beyond all doubt. So what, Lur speculated intently, was it that was calling itself Ashai Rey?

"—and after the *sa'farioh* had let his own kinsmen be murdered," Mene was continuing, "we knew our safety was in quickness. So we went through the roof this very night, and over across the houses, so," she explained, gesturing, "and then away. And soon we are finding the Innsmiths ahead, known-to-us, in distress, do you see? And Aliana decides they have boats, and are trustworthy, and have need of help, do you see?"

Jannus said he was surprised Elda would accept them, having just met the Sithstock troop so disastrously; Mene, reaching to rotate the spitted birds, implied the freemaids' readiness to feed some three hundred hungry Innsmiths might have had something to do with it. Then Jannus started inquiring about another Valde, Poli—asking if she were out hunting now, or on another island, just tensing his shoulders when Lur pinched him—Mene meanwhile having taken a stick to poke the fire. For a Valde, she looked uncomfortable, fidgety; she finally responded, "She is in Lisle. I told you, she is sworn to be Fair Witness to this Greyhawk a hand of days. This is the night of the second day." She swatted her stick down so sparks bounced. "She was bound to serve her promise, do you see? and he, this Greyhawk, had done us no hurt—"

"Because you got beyond his reach!"

"We were not bound to wait open faith-breaking, do you see?" answered the Valde, with small incomplete motions, leanings, toward retreat. "The way is as open to her as to us, and yet she stays, do you see? She is bound."

The boy's silence gave Lur the temporary hope that Jannus would finally let the Valde go, as she so plainly wanted to; but Jannus said, "How is it, now . . . with her?"

". . . We are too far. . . ."

"You left no one to relay? You left her alone there?"

"Our way is so! The loss of her, she unconsenting—we

could not share that! It would be such a darkness, such a darkness to bear away. . . . No Haffa would have another injured so, for the small comfort of an hour. She knows, do you see? Our way is so."

The Valde's strange anxiety that Jannus be reconciled to a matter Lur couldn't see was any of Jannus' business to begin with was bringing other Valde drifting in, wading up from the shallows, standing silent above the circle around the fire, faces in shadow. Lur kept still as a rabbit under a bush.

"What," said Jannus, in a fairly calm voice, "is the place where she is held?" When there was no answer he said again, "Where is she held? How is she guarded? When will they learn you're gone? Mene?"

But the Valde by the fire had finally been pushed into actual retreat, sliding between two other freemaids, lost among them as they all began dispersing among the flashing crescents cast on the water by the nearer fires.

"Aliana!" Jannus called, a tone of command.

After a moment words drifted from the shallows: "She could not come away before the fifth day, and you would be taken. A Bremneri in Lisle. Even freed, you would be tainted all your days—and who would come to free you, having gone consenting into Lisle? We will not help you to such waste, Hafri. . . ."

The voice retreated into nothing: the boy had driven them all away. With a quick glance right and left, Lur slid out of concealment, saying quickly, "You're going to Lisle, right? I'll come with you. Come on. Is it far?"

"You leave me alone. My whole back—"

"Never mind that now, we have to go. Listen to me. You can buy her free, if that's what you want. Do you hear?"

Jannus looked down at him, frowning vaguely. "What are you talking about? I have nothing that this Greyhawk could want, or would fear."

"Not Greyhawk: the Andran, the *sa'farioh* your Valde met in a hall. *Under a roof.* Didn't you hear her?" demanded Lur, impatient with the boy's slowness. "It can't be a Tek. It's a mobile of the Shai. It has to be! A mobile, with a redecap, and down from the High Plain—the Wall's failed, somewhere!"

"But what could I use to buy her with?"

"Not here: while we're going. Come on. Where is it?"

"Downriver," replied the boy slowly. "Can you walk that far?"

"How far is it?"

"I don't know."

"Then when I can't, you'll carry me, that's all."

By the time Lur came in sight of the first walls of Lisle the lantern was no longer needed to spot the thorny gullies scoring the riverbank. Exhausted, Lur sent the boy ahead to survey and released his body from discipline during the wait. It at once collapsed into sleep, twitching in shallow, fragmented dreams. He resumed awareness with the sense that the boy had been back and talking for some time.

"All right," Lur said rapidly, sitting up, "remember, when your rede is taken, think of Cliffhold. Think of the Isgate Bridge when—"

"Lur, I've never seen it," Jannus replied in a patient voice toneless with weariness. "I can't think of what—"

"Do it. Think of the bridge, blue plarit arch, and the yellow keep tower above it. Cliffhold. I'll do the same. When I find you there I'll give you the outer traps' locations so you can go down and—"

"I'm not going to die for the job of fetching your trinkets out to you."

"You'll die sometime," Lur pointed out baldly. "And when you do, the Shai will still be there, and I'll still need you to bring out to me what I'll need. When the redcap's in your hands, think of Cliffhold. Think of the bridge. If the Barrier, the Wall, is down, we'll have to be quick. . . ." Lucidly Lur explained why, once the lowlanders found out that the High Plain was open to all comers, it was urgent that they snatch and run, before the rest of the looters started arriving, before Cliffhold was dismembered and the tools scattered across half the world. Cliffhold was the only keep he knew thoroughly enough to be able to direct another through the mazes and drowning pits, the stretches of contact poison, the deadfalls. . . .But when the boy said his name and he jerked awake, he couldn't separate what he'd said aloud from the dream-stuff. He rolled his head onto his knees and rubbed the back of his neck. He was thinking only in flashes, with long blank stretches between. He'd have to keep better control, not alarm the boy before the rede was taken. Whatever happened after that wouldn't matter. Waking on the High Plain, the boy wouldn't remember any of it.

"Lur. It's getting light."

Lur jerked his head up to find it was so. There wasn't time, wasn't time. "Can you find him, the mobile?"

"I know something of Lisle now," Jannus replied reservedly, propped against a tree and clasping a low branch like a pillow. "I met a Truthdeaf woman named Bluejay. She herds goats. She took me for a runaway and wanted me to pact with her. Right there, without even the decency of walls. She—"

"Do . . . you . . . know . . . where . . . to find him!"

"Yes! I—yes. I can find him."

Jannus led the way up from the brushy riverbank into roughly furrowed ground where Lur stumbled repeatedly. Hanging onto Jannus' wrist helped.

The boy was chattering some nonsense about fruit trees and wasps, not turning his head toward a figure calling and waving from a hilltop.

"Wave back," directed Lur, "or she'll wonder."

A muddy footpath led them first to a broken place in the outer wall, then to a flattened section of an inner, pole barracade. They were brought to a cobbled weed-clumped street that veered left, toward the river. They walked with care, avoiding piles of refuse active with bold yellow gulls that rattled wings and whistled if they passed too near. Lur trotted along beside the boy, jerking his head around to watch his footing, the paling sky, and each blank window and door. He didn't know if it was the body, poisoning him with its exhaustion, or that dart Elda'd tried to murder him with . . . but if the Shai *had* sent a mobile of itself into the lowlands there'd be a redcap, and a chance of a decent body for himself with full memory—

"Lur," the boy warned, long strides slowing to approach a uniformed man straightening to attention before the carved and painted door of a dark brick house. To the guard, Jannus said, "I have a message for Duke Ashai."

The guard took his club into both hands. "What is it."

"Tell him it is from the one who strung the bridge to the Wood of Fathori," Jannus replied as Lur had directed him to. "The message is urgent and must be given in person, where only the sky can listen. Now repeat it to me."

Jannus' authoritative manner seemed to outweigh his mud-smeared clothes and convince the guard that dismissing them might be unwise. He repeated the request correctly, then, without turning, rapped on the door. "You're not of Greyhawk's guard," he remarked.

"That does not concern you," said Jannus.

The door moved a bit, the request was muttered, and the

door shut again. Lur supported himself against Jannus' side, staring at the insignia disc on the man's harness. Stylized waves, with a gold sun-circle above them. If this was a mobile of the Shai, taking such an emblem was insolence, flaunting the inability of the lowlanders to read it for what it was, an echo of that inlaid on the floor of Downbase. More likely, he thought, it was a tribal sign of the Dukes of Ismere; after all, Andras had been settled by the descendents of the runaway Teks of Debern Keep. . . .

Permission came. The guard searched them both with a series of slaps that would have missed a score of weapons Lur could think of; Jannus surrendered a small sheathed knife, fit to peel fruit. The guard then led them around to the rear of the building, to a ruined walled garden where a man was strolling, the bottom of his blue cape stirring the drifts of dead leaves.

The guard turned back. Jannus went on; and it was all Lur could do to wrench his hand loose before he was pulled under a trellis, covered with thick writhing vines, that roofed the entrance. Belatedly looking up, Jannus showed comprehension and hoisted him over the low wall surrounding the garden. Lur caught his breath, taking fresh control.

The man stood probing at a crack between the flagstones with his staff, which probably housed a fuser tube or a force sword if he was a mobile. Mildly the man said, "What do you want, Teklord?"

"A little Fathori wine," Lur sighed, and let himself down on the stone lip of the dry fountain. The mode of address killed any doubt: the satisfaction was dizzying.

The mobile considered the request with a quizzical expression, then rapped twice with its staff. To the servant who appeared from an inner doorway, it said, "The amber flask, Pero, and three glasses."

When the servant returned, the mobile had the tray set on the fountain rim and itself filled the glasses and served them. Though custom required Lur wait until after the host had drunk, he gulped down the wine as soon as the glass was in his hands.

"Not Dreamwood vintage, of course," the mobile remarked quietly, "but its equal in all but memory. . . ."

Lur brushed away leaves and set his glass down, feeling the flashes of concentration steady into the familiar sense of well-being—so familiar, so sorely missed. . . .

The mobile stood with hands folded over the tall staff, considering Jannus—who, Lur saw, was still holding his glass untasted. "Drink it, drink it," Lur directed. "It's a focuser, not a relaxant. Now," he said to the mobile, "the Wall's down. Where?"

"South. . . . A lowland ally, my lord of Cliffhold?" The mobile moved a ringed forefinger in Jannus' direction.

"He stays. And the name of this child is Lur, for his convenience. Where south? Cliffhold?" When the mobile did not answer at once, Lur snapped, "I am entitled to common information!"

"Of course, Teklord Lur," responded the mobile, still looking toward Jannus. "A dispensible ally, it seems. . . . South from Rork, around the perimeter to Morgan's Hold, the generators were disrupted during a series of earthquakes thirty-four years ago."

Lur calculated, trying to match distances on the High Plain to what he could guess of the river stocks' positions. "From Lisle, all the way around Han Halla, to Morgaard Pass where the Summerfair is held," he translated, for Jannus' benefit. "Is that accurate?"

"Yes. . . .Who is he, the boy?"

Would he be missed, the mobile meant. Lur thought it prudent not to answer that yet. And Jannus, obedient to instructions, did not offer the information. "I would like," said Lur, "to remember. About the Wall."

"I don't doubt it," the mobile rejoined mildly.

"Let's be clear. You have a redecap here."

"Of course."

"And you won't let me use it."

"You do not hold the Rule of One, to command such things. I'm not permitted to destroy your rede, but neither am I required to help you take one. Find a base."

"And enter it how?"

"That," responded the mobile, nodding judiciously, "is a problem not subject to immediate solution. . . . The fact that the Barrier has failed is knowledge I alone can exploit constructively. General looting would rapidly be followed by general warfare among the younger nations—"

"You serve Kantmorie!"

"I serve the Rule of One. Kantmorie is dead, and wants burying. To divert the tidestorm that will follow the looting of the High Plain, I must keep the secret as long as I can."

"Greyhawk—" Lur began.

"Greyhawk has been told I can, by a certain power, open a

way to treasure on the High Plain. So he considers me a
wizard." The mobile shrugged slightly. "I do not contradic
him. I'm told some Fishers consider me a deity of some sort
It's all one, so long as the work goes on, under proper con
trols."

Lur glanced aside at Jannus, calculating with the clearhead
edness the wine had granted him. As he'd expected, there wa
no way to get a rede but to buy it. And he had nothing the
Shai would want, didn't already possess. "Have you gotten a
rede from this Greyhawk?" he asked abruptly.

"It would require imprudent explanation."

"Then you're depending on unreliable reports and limited
observation in your dealings with Bremner. Much less satisfac
tory than an informed contemporary native rede."

The mobile swiveled to survey Jannus in turn. "I see. . . It
is possible," he commented presently. "Who are you, Bremneri?"

"Jannus, Newstock-born, son and scribe to the Lady Lillia
of that place," replied the boy precisely, at Lur's nod.

"Do you know who I am?" inquired the mobile, and Lur
nodded again.

"You're a mobile," Jannus replied, "the rede of a fish brain
that lives under the Lake of Down."

"Well tutored," the mobile remarked to Lur. "Certainly an
improvement over being thought a wizard or some creature
called a Screamer. . . . Though of course in the body of my
birth I was not a fish. A pelagic air-breather, warm-blood-
ed. . . . But no matter. Only Andrans know anything of the
Sea. . . ." The mobile returned its attention to the boy. "Did
you learn that by rote, or can you put it in other words?"

"You're the thought and memory of the Shai, high tool and
treasure of Kantmorie, housed in a human body. And fish or
flint, you won't let Lur die and yet intend to kill both of us."

"Observant, as well," commented the mobile. "To be accurate, I'll have Pero do it. I am constrained from direct murder."

"He knows Bremner," Lur argued, "and how the Valde
serve here, and how to deal with the Innsmiths, a degenerate
Mek clan more suitable than native lowland outlaws for handling the relics of the High Plain."

"Yes, I know the Innsmiths. Perhaps. . . . Jannus, the Teklord offers me a rede of yours in exchange for being allowed
to make one of his own. Do you know what that means?"

"Enough. I told Lur I was willing. But I also have a price."

"A stupid one," Lur muttered.

"That is to be expected," said the mobile ambiguously.

"There is a Valde held here," Jannus went on. "She must be freed."

"I am assuming," remarked the mobile to Lur, "that the other freemaids have escaped, since you are here and asked for me by name."

"Of course."

"But unlike you, they will not draw the obvious conclusion, that the Barrier has failed. That requires a Tek—one who knows the functions and limits of a mobile. And you could not have told them without jeopardizing yourself—"

"I told," said Jannus, startling both Lur and the mobile into sharp attention. "I told Elda Innsmith that the Wall is down somewhere, probably downriver since you claimed to be an Andran. He's a shrewd man. He'll devise a way to test it, if only to be sure."

"Was that your suggestion?" inquired the mobile of Lur, but Jannus answered, without rancor:

"He was too tired; and my life is more valuable to me than either his or mine is to him. If I'm going to trade away everything I've known and seen—if after I die I'll come to fear roofs as Lur does and become what troopmaids hunt into silence with such haste—then I mean to keep in good health, and not die, until I'm very old indeed."

"A Tek, a Bremneri, and an Innsmith," mused the mobile. "Knowledge, precaution, and skill. Perhaps you will be useful to me."

With the staff, the mobile again summoned the servant and directed him to bring the great cask. From this wooden barrel, once the servant had retired, the mobile extracted a yellow plarit redcap from several bushels of cushioning. Laying aside the staff, it directed Jannus to sit by Lur on the fountain's rim, lest the boy drop the cap or try to run off with it.

"Do you agree to my condition?" Jannus demanded.

"That the remaining Valde be freed. I haven't forgotten. Yes, I'll pay the required price, providing it's not necessary to seriously jeopardize my understanding with Greyhawk: he's much more valuable to me, at this point, than you are."

Jannus seemed bothered at such a conditional promise. He looked to Lur for reassurance which Lur quickly gave, anxious to get the redcap into his own hands. "What danger is one Valde to him now that the rest are gone? His secret dealings with a *sa'farioh* are already known all up and down the river. He'll let Duke Ashai have her, to keep his goodwill."

"He's a Bremneri. He'll want a price," argued the boy.

"Sit down," advised the mobile. "The Lord Greyhawk's too ignorant to want a thousandth of what I could lose without missing. I take that into account. It is probability factor—" The mobile paused, rephrased. "It is very likely, nearly certain, that I can buy her for you."

Jannus stood and thought for a minute, as if there were any use in that, or any choice: without this bargain, the mobile would have them both tidily killed. Then, smiling nervously, Jannus sat where he was directed, holding his head very stiffly. "It will remain for three counts of ten," the mobile explained, before setting the cap in place. "You will feel nothing strange. Remain quiet."

"Remember," warned Lur, "what I told you."

For extra safety, the mobile kept its fingers lightly on top of the cap until the proper time was past. Then it lifted the cap and set it on its own head, communing with the Shai itself at Down. When it removed the cap, it remarked to the boy, "So you did tell Elda."

"Bremneri do not tell direct lies. But now, you should know that for yourself." The boy jumped up and slouched away, as if resentful of the mobile's new knowledge of him.

Lur said, "Give me the cap."

"The knowledge," the mobile was commenting to Jannus' back, "takes time for me to sort, having only the resources of this body. . . . I am not, myself, the Shai: only as much of the Shai as can be retained by a—"

Lur snatched the cap. Before settling it he fixed his mind on Cliffhold Keep, as he'd directed Jannus to do. In the same fashion, he'd once fixed his mind on Stock in hopes of escaping the High Plain. While the cap was in place, the mobile kept hold of Lur's arm and retrieved the cap at the first possible moment, using it again to receive a digest of new information. Then it repacked the cap and called the servant to take it indoors, out of danger.

"You," said the mobile to Jannus, "may go free."

"And Lur?"

"He is wearied of the child he wears," replied the mobile obliquely, and the boy looked to Lur in anxious inquiry. Lur rolled one hand in a shrug. The mobile added, "Beware him hereafter, Jannus, if you would continue long in that body. . . ."

"It wants you to mistrust me," Lur put in, firmly, "so you won't help."

"Like Bremneri," snapped the mobile, "I am restrained from direct lies. Be warned, Jannus. If he were not based now, you would not wear that face until sunappear. He wants you as hands, to go where he cannot go himself. Your life is a little thing to him, as against his own death."

By Jannus' face, Lur could tell the boy believed it; but it really didn't matter. Waking, Jannus would remember only up to the moment the redcap had been on his head. Nothing since. "He will come to me," Lur told the mobile. "If not now, soon. Or I to him. And then we will come for you. . . ."

The mobile clasped hands over the staff, facing Lur icily. "You threaten me with death—me, who alone can endure and enjoy immortality, who am greater than you and far more ancient. I guided the crossing, brought you all safely to Down. I remember the centuries of the void and even my oceans of Cetus Mira-Phillipa, which you do not know even as a name. And you, Teklord: if by a wish you could poison this whole world as the High Plain is poisoned, and thereby get the death you want, you wouldn't hesitate. What limits I am bound by, you know; but what limits bind you, save that you cannot endure that anything be over you? Save the limits of your own nature, vision, and desires? If it were in my gift, be sure I would give you what you want!"

Indifferent to rhetoric, Lur requested, "The green, then," and from a pocket or wallet under its cloak the mobile produced a small flask. From it the mobile poured a small measure of liquid, vividly grass-green as tradition required of overt poisons, into the glass Lur had set aside.

The drink was cool and had no taste at all. Like a door closing, the dark came; and, having just lifted the redcap into place, he was suddenly shut closely in a lightless box. A learned reflex jerked his head instantly from under the box's redcap; then he was gasping for breath and blindly trying to force the immovable lid with tiny hands too feeble even to close into fists, breath becoming an involuntary intermittent wail.

Book III:

IS

Jannus was sitting on the riverwall near the white ship of Ashai Rey, paring slices from a lump of cheese he'd bought from a passing woman. He wasn't especially hungry—the odd peace he ascribed to the wine still remained with him. The cheese had just looked good.

Being in proscribed Lisle didn't worry him either, though he expected it would, sometime. Resting in plain sight, watching the Truthdeaf women sweep their doorsteps and toss the contents of nightjars into the river seemed to him quite natural. When the goat-girl, Bluejay, came by selling milk, he greeted her freely and they chatted. He swapped her a slice of cheese for a dipper of milk, though he suspected she traded only from friendliness—a goatherd should have no lack of cheese.

He asked her if the girl-children of Lisle were ever born with Truthtell; she said, "The witches? Oh, we never keep those." Her man, she added inconsequentially, had taken a cough and died before the last great snowstorm. Jannus said that was a pity. She said no, he'd been sickly and not much good for anything anyhow. She'd just decided he was only lazy and pretending, when he'd turned around and died. That just went to show. Jannus supposed it did.

Directly opposite him was a large freestanding building set a little back from the others—Greyhawk's headquarters, he'd been told. A group of men were standing around in its small courtyard: the seven who'd brought Poli. One hailed Bluejay. Sighing, she set on her head the basket holding her goatskin bag of milk and sauntered off across the square. As she reached the man who'd called, the patterns of her large capelike shawl flared into vivid yellows and reds, and the spiky shadow of the ship at Jannus' back was splashed forward across cobblestones: the hour of sunappear, earlier than in Newstock. The fogs had scarcely been warmed when Poli had been brought by.

Presently Bluejay came hurrying back, striding smoothly

93

under the basket. "What do you think! The witches all disappeared in the night!"

"All but one," replied Jannus, and she looked disappointed at not having astonished him.

"She'd be gone too but Greyhawk burned a knotted cord woven of her hair, so she had to serve him."

"Her hair's too short to braid."

"Then why's she still here?" countered Bluejay triumphantly.

"Her bow was strung with braided hair," Jannus admitted, to be fair, gently amused by Bluejay's notions of Valde ways. "Maybe he burned that."

"Mm-huh. . . . What do you know about goats?"

". . . . How to count them, I suppose. . . ."

"That's not much. There's lots to know about goats besides that."

"I do hear you," replied Jannus politely, well aware who'd be delighted to teach him, should he want to know.

"How'd you know what the witch's hair is like?"

Jannus smiled quietly to himself and offered the girl another slice of cheese which she accepted, holding the basket steady with her other hand. "Well, I saw her, for one reason. For another, I've known her half my life. For a third, I love her."

Bluejay stared at him. "The witch?"

"The freemaid Poli Wir."

"You're pacted to her?"

"Hardly."

"But you're a Bremneri!"

"So I am."

"But it's bad luck to even see the witches! Everyone knows that!"

Jannus smiled again, happily, without irony. "I've been told I lack sense. . . ." He was thinking of Elda. "And my luck, of late, has not been good. Maybe that explains it."

Bluejay made an odd gesture, thumb and little finger extended. She did it again, clearly demonstrating it for him. "Catches the bad luck, throws it away. Nobody taught you that? That's a pity. That's where your bad luck is coming from, right there."

"That could be so. I was taught never to look the troopmaids in the face, but I wouldn't do as I was told."

"That just goes to show. You've got yourself lucktied to her, that's what. Jump in the river stark naked on a starsday. That'll cure it."

"Certainly would. I can't swim."

"Oh."

"In Newstock," he explained, "the Wall is closer and the river is strong. Hardly anybody knows how to swim—it's too dangerous."

" 'Tisn't all that hard. I expect you could learn, if you had somebody to teach you right, and you tried hard."

"Your confidence gives me. . . ."

Preceded by one attendant, followed by another, Ashai Rey left the building. The man behind held a leash noosed around the neck of Poli. Her face turned toward the riverwall the moment she stepped into the sunlight—searching for him, knowing he was there. The seven Lislers made the warding gesture as the Valde, hands bound behind her, was led across the courtyard.

"Quick," directed Bluejay, "guard yourself." And she repeated the wardsign, edging off as the procession approached. "Quick!"

"Too late," Jannus murmured as Bluejay bolted away.

Jannus accepted the proffered leash while the mobile advised him. "Keep her so until you're well away from here. The local people have an intense superstitious dread of Valde."

"Yes."

"I can send Pero and Felib with you. . . ."

"No." Jannus started back up the street, aware of Poli pacing just behind him. Briefly he thought how difficult it'd been to adapt his stride to Lur's short legs, especially while he'd wanted to be running, to reach Lisle the sooner. Now there was no urgency in him. He strolled entirely at ease and happy.

People stared from windows and doorways, sometimes throwing wardsigns like threatening fists; but a male Bemneri leading a bound Valde seemed to pacify the more hating and fearful. A few badly aimed stones and hunks of refuse were the worst he had to contend with before he found the muddy path and passed the inner fence.

The gap in the outer wall was too high to be climbed without the use of hands. "Well," he reflected, "at the worst, we could run. . . ." Unsheathing his knife, he found Poli with her back turned, holding her wrists apart to tauten the cords. When the bonds parted, the white weals underneath flushed red, showing the pattern of the braid. Poli clumsily tried to remove the noose but submitted to his help, rubbing her hands together with heavy strokes as though there were still little feeling in them. The moment the noose was lifted Poli sprang to the broken bricks and down on the far side.

From the gap Jannus saw her, already some distance away, running hard across the margin of a field. Watching her diminish with distance, Jannus absently looped the leash into a neat coil and laid it on the crumbling mortar as he went over, following without haste.

Before reaching the thickets of blossoming fruit trees that bordered the plowed land, Poli slowed somewhat and veered to the right, toward the river. Then she was gone in a burst of rebounding leaves and a snow of petals. Jannus circled the neglected orchard because it'd be full of wasps, gnawing buds. No flowering tree could survive anywhere near the river, where the wasps bred, without special care. Untended, this orchard would not endure many more springs.

He edged through a margin of dense brush into the wood. The willows formed a mounded continuous thatch above him. Even at night Lur had refused to come under this canopy, forcing them to scramble along the riverbank. Jannus strolled on a thick, moistly pungent mat of mingled leaves, twigs, and moss, catching at intervals glimpses of the river off to his right shining dully like an overcast sky.

He crossed two gullies with small streams running at their bottoms; the first narrow enough to jump, the second deeper and wider, carrying the recent rain to Erth-rimmon. Above the next streambed a massive willow had cracked, toppling into the water-course one of its trunks—broad slabs of dry, deeply ridged bark shelved with tiers of whitish fungus plates and throwing upward, sheaves of bright new shoots. A pool had formed behind the fallen trunk, too shallow and troubled to hold Poli's image. Tiny beneath the tree, she knelt in the fern; had it not been for the pale motion of her arms as she bathed her wrists and then raised cupped hands to drink, Jannus might not have seen her. The fern-feathers curled almost to her shoulders and the still-living portions of the tree curtained everything with strings of green daggers.

A pair of stoats raised wet blunt muzzles to stare at him. Then they leaped past Poli and popped into a fissure in the trunk. Poli merely continued what she was doing. Her head was tilted, her gaze abstracted, as though she were listening; Jannus looked alertly back the way they'd come.

"No," she said absently: "Anshru."

Another of the Newstock freemaids. Could Poli's *marenniath* be reaching all the way back to the islands?

"Upriver," she said, "maybe two runs, and the rest as far beyond, she tells me. With the . . . the Innsmiths?"

Jannus confirmed it, explaining the agreement while carefully descending the deeply cut bank and finding a place to cross the stream. She made no comment and returned to her inspoken conversation with Anshru, again laving her sore wrists. She hummed phrases in a tuneless, half-audible counterpoint.

Jannus chose a seat in the moss-packed bend of a bare root and considered Poli's back, unaccustomedly free of quiver, bow, and harness straps. Her close-cut hair seemed a cap carved of new ashwood and still bore a sprinkle of round pink petals she was probably unaware of.

"I have a cheese," he mentioned presently. "Do you want some?"

She rocked back and stuck up a dripping cold hand, so he put the remaining cheese in it and placidly watched the willow bannerets stir through multiple shadings of green as the unseen sun came and went.

"I wanted to bring you back your bridestone," he commented, "but Aliana wouldn't trust Lisle, or my chances of delivering it to you."

Poli turned slowly to look up at him, tasting the last fragments of cheese off her fingers. "Oh, what have you done?" she lamented suddenly. "What have you done to yourself, for that *sa'farioh* to buy me free?"

"I sold him something," Jannus replied after a moment, quite carefully. "Something he has use for, and I don't miss."

"You miss it," she contradicted in a brooding tone, still watching him. "You are changed, Hafri."

Jannus pried a fragment of slate out of the bank, smiling gently. "I'm too tired to be afraid, which is a change . . . I'll probably get over it." With precision he tossed the slate into the middle of the pool. "And you have no brother. You are of the Haffa Valde."

Poli swung sharply away, dislodging petals onto the disturbed surface of the pool. She slapped at her hair until the remaining pink dots were all brushed away.

"I no longer care," Jannus continued, lazily separating the layers of a large slate, "if the entire Newstock troop is hearing me or whether the Sithstock troop view me as a pitiful freak. I'm not anxious lest saying the unguarded, the true thing, break the little bond once between us. My folk do not much use the word 'love'. . . ." He dropped a slate, scattering the floating petals. "We have little enough need to. But I love you, and you know it. And you do not love me, and I know that. And I don't care."

"You are changed, changed," she responded in a low, dismayed voice, clasping her arms tightly before her. "You've done something to yourself—paid some great price, you feel. I owe you, you feel. You are glad, believing this."

The list of his sins did not upset him either. "It's a rare thing, you must admit, for a Bremneri like me to have a freemaid beholden to him," he commented wryly.

"You've done something terrible and feel I am the cause. I won't be the cause! I do not consent to your doing an evil to yourself. I did not wish or ask—"

"That's your problem," interrupted Jannus, gently enough. "I wanted to buy your freedom. Be free, then."

"Your words and your selfsinging speak with different voices. The words say, 'Be free,' the *farioh* that I am bound, beholden," she complained.

"Well, Poli, I can't help that. You'll have to find a way to get along with it, I suppose."

"You don't see," she muttered, thumping absently at the surface of the pool, for once visibly agitated. "I don't grudge thanks, I am not so darkhearted as that. But. But the price. I can't consent to what you have done to yourself. It's—what I hear in you is that you feel . . . feel free of consequences because you are sure of dying. . . ." Frowning, she brooded on her preternaturally accurate interpretation, then presently added, "Like a deer pursued beyond his strength, that turns and waits. . . . As if you'd hacked off one arm and proudly display to me the raw stump saying, 'See what I've done, for love of you!'"

"If you were not Valde," Jannus pointed out, "you'd have known nothing of the price from me. I didn't do it for the pleasure of displaying stumps or anything else. And I'm not stupid enough to think I could buy what you don't purposely withhold."

"If I were not Valde, the price would not have been paid," she rejoined flatly. "Is there another you would have ransomed in that manner?"

"You know the answer."

"So. You have done some evil thing to yourself. Accepting the fruits, I would be accepting the roots—as if I wished such a thing on you—"

"You *have* accepted it. You're here."

That stopped her for a time. "So I am," she agreed at last. "I had not thought of it."

"You could go back," mentioned Jannus skeptically.

Her face, as always, was calm—not withholding emotion, merely unused to communicating it by conventions of twitches. "You think I won't, though you do not know why I won't. You think I fear Lisle and you are right. But that isn't why. The fruit, once picked, can't be put back on the bough." Her hands shaped the action, cupping an invisible object for his inspection. "Not that you freed me, but that I took that freedom from your hand and did not ask how it came."

"Don't brood. There wasn't any way——"

"Wasn't there? The instant I stopped being concerned only for myself, I knew. But I did not think or even wonder, before. I did not think of you at all."

He found his serenity could absorb even that. It was no worse, he found, spoken than known and unsaid.

"I heard you come to Lisle," she was continuing. "I was on the roof waiting for the dark to end, for them to come for me with their endless *als'far* of hating, fearing. . . . And I heard you then, calling me so, as you do before the Newstock quarters. . . ."

"I'd hoped you would," he commented quietly, "and feel less lonely. You're not used to it."

"And hearing the kindness, I rejoiced," she accused herself. "I didn't think, he's come to Lisle, which is forbidden him. I didn't think, what will he do, and what will come of it? I only wept with rejoicing, to be known for myself and kindly thought of in the black hour: not wondering if you burned, so long as it kept me from the dark." She lifted her head, giving him a wide, surprised appraisal. "And I have done it before."

"That's all right."

"You knew! Didn't you? You knew!"

"I'd be likely to."

"Then why didn't you tell me? Justly complain of it?"

"Why did none of the Newstock troop complain of me to the Lady Lillia?" he retorted; and, turning away, she made him no answer. "Not because you didn't know: I learned that in Sithstock. I think you all enjoyed having one of the Truth-deaf, at least, who admired and liked you. And I kept my peace, so there was no need to disrupt things. . . . Anyway, you couldn't have helped it," he added more gently and a little sadly. "You're doing it now. Forget a minute what you did and didn't realize: just pay attention to me."

She waited, then understood what he actually expected. She looked toward him, and her eyes slowly filled with tears that made their way down the shadows of her face. "Oh, I am sorry—"

He felt only a distant and kind amusement, reminded of the kitten-sorrow of the little Sithstock troopmaids. It seemed he didn't dread even her pity. He'd become quite impersonal about his feeling for her, as if it'd settled into his bones, too deep for even her to perturb, freeing him for compassion. "So accept the gift and go free."

"I cannot. I won't accept the price. I must *do* something. . . ."

She was quiet a long while; he flipped flakes of slate into the pool and watched them either seesaw to rest on the bottom or be caught by the slight current and toppled over the little fall.

"You will keep my bridestone," she decided, "for me. When it comes time for the briding, I will—Listen!—I will ask you for it again, and you will have the choice to give or withhold. Why not? It's the only choice of—no, listen!—it's the only choice of great value I—"

"No. I won't. No."

"But why?"

Jarred from his remote contentment, he strained to think how he could make clear to her what an agony, how cruel a burden that custodianship would be. He finally said, "I'd sooner carry coals barehanded."

"But why?"

"I'd be jealous. I have been able to live with it till now because there was nothing I could do about it—"

"About what?"

"Your briding, of course. But no, I won't take it. Anyway Aliana wouldn't permit such a disposal—"

"I am a freemaid. I do as I will."

"No, Poli. Worse would come of it: believe me."

"Then we must think of something else." She rested her temples in her hands, appearing discouraged and sad.

The *we*, he knew, meant the other freemaids: another thoughtless stroke revealing what he already knew painfully well. "Poli. Here's what you will do. You'll promise to do me one favor."

"What?"

"Whatever I ask."

She straightened in the nest of fern, thinking a while. "When?"

He smiled slightly at her unsuspicious priorities, at how easy it was for him to follow her clear and selfcentered thoughts. "Soon. When it's needed. And then you will not be beholden to me any more."

"Only one?" She was dubious about such a small penance. "One, then. But it must be needful: I will know," she warned.

"It will be needful. I won't try to invent something."

"Aliana and Seline . . . and Ashferia and Mene and Lerdis," she reported after a moment, "are not content, with this. . . ."

"So?"

"So I am a freemaid, to choose as I will. I bind myself to this, to be free of the sadness of what you have done."

She rose from the fern, brushed the coiled fronds where they were bent from her resting there, and went up under the willow branches. Jannus joined her on the far side of the tree and they walked on, saying little.

Anshru had shot a hare for them. Jannus could smell it cooking long before he could see the fire or Anshru resting beside it.

"Life is smoke," she said in formal greeting. "Burn bright."

"Burn bright," Jannus returned, "Anshru Wir."

After the midmeal they slept, Anshru alert nearby. Jannus woke with the sense that the dreaming time had exhausted him, though he knew that it was only that the sustaining power of the wine was failing. It seemed every inch of his body protested against rising, walking: belatedly remembering every step and stumble of the night journey to Lisle along the riverbank, every bruised scrape collected on the roofs of Sithstock. No caning had ever left him as sore. The two Valde ranged ahead or to the side but never got quite out of sight, so he supposed he should consider them as accompanying him.

He began to wish he'd thought to try bargaining for a flask of that cordial to bring away with him. In memory, its taste and strange virtue seemed almost magical. A *focuser*, Lur had remarked casually, *not a relaxant*.

Jannus realized he was going to miss Lur's cool way of stripping potential glamour from everything. There'd been a kind of freedom in it that Jannus had been able to share. *The rede of a fish brain*, he himself had said, practically to the Shai himself, to Ashai's very face. The bald impertinence of that now frightened him somewhat, though it'd been quite natural, quite objective, at the time. He wondered if the self which would wake someday from his rede would feel that way all the time—alert, analytical, sardonic, fearing nothing—except, in time, roofs. He began to miss Lur.

"Elda says," called Poli, circling back, " 'Are you alone?' "

Jannus spent a moment judging Elda's anxiety, to entrust even so guarded a question to the Valde relay. Aloud, he said only, "Tell him." He waited a few strides, then asked, "What'd he say?"

" 'Good.' And there is word from Newstock, from the Lady Lillia," she continued. "She calls you home, at once. She has heard about Sithstock, and, and is calling trade-strife against the Lady Ultreena. . . . But for Lisle, you are barred from all riverstocks save Newstock, you are called home now to make what defense you will. . . ."

Well, that wasn't as bad as it might have been: at least his mother meant to give him a hearing and had kept him, for the moment, under her word, as her householder. Jannus met Poli's eyes, replying, "Well, I'm not going—not yet. I'm going to the Summerfair."

"That is not wise. You should go home."

"And then how would I call for my favor?" he countered lightly, and saw her abandoning further argument, a mark of how seriously she took the matter of that favor. "Send word, Poli, that I'll write her as soon as I've had a chance to rest. Say . . . no. Just say that, and that I'll go back after the Summerfair."

After a moment Poli looked toward him again, asking diffidently, "Should I tell her why?"

"If the word passes through Sithstock, she'll know. Probably she knows why, already." But it'd been considerate of Poli to have asked him first.

In the twilight they came in sight of the Innsmith encampment. Wading carefully from island to island, Jannus found that all the Innsmiths were assembled on and around a single island, the one farthest from shore.

They had prepared a funeral. On a pyre of heavy limbs piled higher than a man's head were laid those who'd been lost because of the storm. Neither Jannus nor the two Valde were inclined to intrude on that ceremony: instead, they joined the rest of the freemaids on the island they'd taken for themselves.

As evening deepened the pyre was at last kindled. The

circle of Innsmiths tossed their armfuls of faggots and retreated until nothing remained on the island but the enormous
blaze that threw light even as far as the pitted umber face of
the Wall. Standing hip-deep or waist-deep in the shadows beyond the reach of the heat, the Innsmiths blended, into the
stormy roar of the fire, a deep-voiced dirge that echoed from
the cliff in loud and confused counterpoint. What words
Jannus could make out concerned sparks flying upward and
the quick withering of grasses under the sun, calling life, in
sad accepting voices, a shadow and a dream of labor. No
names were named. The dead were committed to the fire
without being remembered in words, which Jannus found
strange and disquieting: in Newstock such partings were
made with a continual calling of names and deeds and ways,
as if in hopes the wandering spirit would hear and be drawn
back into the world of seasons.

Jannus thought of Lur, the death as casual as turning one's
back, and knew the Tek would have felt contemptuous toward
such a display. But Lur had the advantage of complete certainty of what waited, for him at least, on the other side of the
dark. Jannus compromised. He thought about Lur quietly for
a while, remembering the eleven days that had passed since
he'd first seen Lur at the head of the ramp, the long hours on
the river in which it seemed to him he'd come to know Lur
more intimately than anyone else, at any time—remembering
meanwhile that he did this for his own sake, not for Lur's. He
recalled Lur's ways and missed him, knowing Lur would have
found this, too, sentimental and absurd. Considering that the
next time they met Lur would probably be singlemindedly trying to kill him, perhaps it was.

All around him the Valde were humming with the dirge.
That surprised him because the Innsmiths were outlanders
and relative strangers, in spite of their proximity in Newstock.
And Jannus wondered if Valde custom might be similar; he
thought of their customary greeting.

"*Farioh* is the burning," a freemaid, not Poli, replied in his
ear. "We do not do so." She gestured at the immense bonfire,
the Innsmiths' heads silhouetted black against its base now
that the light had altogether failed. "Yet it is a good parting,
this *als'far.* . . ."

It was odd, his being answered so promptly when he'd
asked no question aloud. He studied the intermittently lit faces
around him and presently discerned Poli, a few rods off, doing
something with a lapful of feathers. She again wore her

bridestone, a white dot on the tabard whose green was leeched away by the dark. He only noted the stone, not allowing it to matter.

He wanted to ask her something: and presently she laid aside all but a handful of feathers and came to sit on her heels beside him, saying, "Yes, the troop have always felt kindly toward you, Hafri . . . Jannus," she corrected herself, perhaps more abruptly than was needed. "And there is friendliness, thankfulness, too, because of Lisle. And there is this changing in you, that you shape your *farioh*, selfsinging, differently—with more order, clearness. Clear, almost, as inspeaking. No," she replied, "others do this, at times: the Innsmiths lack the *marenniath*, yet they are shaping a true manysinging. . . ." She tipped the fan of streaked feathers at the bonfire. "And there have been some who could truly speak with the *farioh*, though themselves deaf to it, and again some who are all but silent, singing nothing but 'I am here, myself, alive'. . . ."

She shivered suddenly, and it was easy to guess where her thought had turned. "No," she replied, "not the same. The thing in the shape of an Andran was altogether silent like a black cloud, like the deeps of a poisoned well where no fish are, no waving plants, like. . . ." Her voice trailed off in a half-heard mutter. Then she said clearly, "But the *sa'farioh* seemed fair to you, and admirable."

"That's so."

"Oh, if only you had the *marenniath*—"

Were he a Valde, he thought grimly, many things would be different beside his perception of Ashai Rey. But that edged reflection sent Poli retreating, with her task of feathers, into the gloom among the bushes where he could not see her. He gathered his wet cloak more closely around him and let himself become absorbed in the pyre and the rise and fall of the manysinging of the Innsmiths over their dead.

One breezy afternoon a trio of freemaids returned from Sithstock, where they'd been sent by Elda to trade with the Lady Ultreena for the Innsmiths. Anshru delivered to Jannus a bundle of things he'd asked for, along with a looped string of copper cash: what remained after the purchases. Jannus at once began examining what the bundle contained.

On top were three loose oak-brown sarks of summer-shear weight, and two more of cotton: drab, comfortable, and cool. Of his Newstock finery, only one sark was left both unstained and untorn. It was an unpleasant plum color and he'd been wearing it three days. He pulled it off over his head and put on one of the cotton ones, then swung his arms around over his head, enjoying the new freedom of movement. From Elda's stores he'd taken tan trousers, kneelength in the Innsmith mode; but there'd been no sark to suit his length of arm and torso.

"Mind what you do," warned Medd, Elda's wife, watching his gyrations narrowly as she tested the damp remaining in the skirt hung on a branch.

For there were clothes everywhere, all over the ground and festooning the bushes and trees. Disgorged from hampers, chests, and bundles, they were spread like lichen on every sunny surface. The grass was completely carpeted with freshly-washed fabric ranging from oatmeal white through faded tans and dark muddy browns.

The new sark had pockets; he'd always coveted pockets. He pawed through his hamper for small objects to store in them, then finished unpacking the bundle. There was a goatskin vest, which meant he could store or sell or give away his cumbersome cloak. Next were a felt hat with a brim and a sturdier pair of sandals which, though hog-leather, were so stiff they'd surely wear blisters, at the first. At the bottom he found the real treasure: writing materials and a book of fine ricepaper, all in a red waterproof case.

For all Elda's talk of wanting him as a scribe, Jannus had found the Innsmiths hadn't so much as a sharpened goose quill among them, much less paper or ink. The delay of waiting for these materials had given him the dubious opportunity to compose and discard at least twenty versions of the letter he had to write to the Lady Lillia. The letter had to achieve so many separate purposes, revealing as few of them as possible, that Jannus was convinced only a masterpiece of diplomacy would serve.

With the case tucked under his arm he strolled barefoot through pools where children were trapping fish with clever dams, past the noise of repair work on the barges, where Elda seemed to spend almost all his waking hours. Weaving among patches of sharp stubble where reeds had been cut to mend the Innsmiths' wickerwork, he found a fine flat rock not far from the shore and laid out inkstone, mixing well, paper and pen neatly before him. Having fined the penpoint to his satisfaction, he began writing the salutations. He used a small, spiky script expressive, he hoped, of contrition, tension, and self-control. After the salutations, the letter proceeded:

I have had dealings with Lisle. These consist of speaking with and sharing a cheese with a goatherd called Bluejay. I spoke to no one else of that stock whatever. For this the Lady Ultreena will not give me leave to enter Sithstock any more, as is her right. But she is much perturbed by the nearness of her stock to Lisle, and harsh in her judgments on that account. Also she is old. I would wish no trade-strife called on my account, although the insult was to you through your scribe and householder. But I would hope no troopmaid of either stock would come to hurt through the Lady Ultreena's overcaution.

I went to Lisle to trade for the freedom of the Valde Poli Wir, First Dancer of the last Newstock troop. This I was able to arrange satisfactorily through an Andran, Ashai, Duke of Ismere, who had use for information about Bremneri custom with which I provided him. Since I know little of Bremner that is not common knowledge, I hope you will judge, as I did, that there is nothing blameworthy in this. The Duke consented to be prolocutor for me to the Lisle folk, but did so at my request and the responsibility is mine, I know. But speaking to the Truthdeaf Bluejay was my only direct contact with the folk of Lisle, which is very ill kept and indifferently guarded, save to be hit with a few stones and trash. They have peculiar names there, calling themselves after birds of all sorts, chiefly the raptors.

As to my attitude toward the freemaid Poli herself, it does no one harm. Knowing of it, neither Aliana nor any other troopmaid complained of it to you, as they could easily have done at any time, did it distress any of them. But I desire very much to see the freemaids brided, to see what happiness their bridestones, won in your service, may grant them. I have your word I may go and return, and rest secure in your good faith, that you will make no judgment until you can hear all these things from my own mouth, and ask what you choose, and determine the truth for yourself.

And I have learned of the Screamers, partly from Elda Innsmith, who knows them by a different name. If the troopmaids did not hunt them but rather brought them into the open, for they cannot stand roofs, the Sceamers would not afflict the troopmaids any more. You might learn many interesting and useful things from them if you chose to prevent the troopmaids from killing them at once, as has been their practice. No living stock Lady has ever had speech with such, and they

"What is it?" he inquired of the shadow that had fallen across his page.

"I came to teach you how to swim."

It was a sturdy girl embedded in the river to the knees. Her skirt, gathered between her legs and held, behind, by her sash, hung in looped folds like baggy trousers. A haze of curly copper hair glowed where strands had escaped the broad plait wrapped several times around her head: with the light behind her, Jannus couldn't see her features clearly.

"Kevel," she named herself, "of Sig's Family—Solvig's, now Sig Torvesson's gone to the fire. Kevel Sigsdatter. I can swim."

He recalled seeing her draw herself up onto the riverbank during the storm's confusion, having shed the clothes whose weight would have drowned her. And she'd been a "catcher," like Elda's youngest son Dan, in Sithstock: drawing darted sleepers out of the water alive. Oh, yes: she could swim.

Tapping his pen dry, he inquired, "Do you ward away witches, too?" which of course she'd not understand.

"That's Watertalk of some sort," she commented, inaccurately. "I was told you couldn't swim and wanted to learn here in the quiet water. Is it so, or an't it?"

"I have no immediate desire for instruction," he replied, a statement indeed in the oblique mode sometimes called Watertalk by outlanders, factors, and the like. "Other things occupy me."

"We won't be here past another three days, Solvig says. But please yourself. What's that: accounts?"

"An account, of a sort. . . ."

"What sort?"

"A letter."

"Heard you had the trick of scribing. Is it to your people?"

He couldn't recall ever being subjected to such an unrelenting string of direct questions. But she was an Innsmith, after all. "To the Lady Lillia," he conceded.

"About Lisle, I expect. Do you think she'll let you come home?"

At that, his mild annoyance chilled. "The Lady Lillia can permit or forbid as seems good to her."

"More Watertalk," remarked Kevel, without rancor. "Because you're writing in it, I expect. But I was thinking a while ago . . . how it'd be for you, with no Homecoming and no other Family to take you in, the way Solvig Torvesson did for me. It's bad enough, even at that," she added reflectively.

"I do hear you."

"What'll you do," she persisted, "if the Trader won't—"

"That matter does not concern you, though it gives me no joy to say so."

"No . . . you don't look joyous," she agreed, merely judicious. "What became of your little sisterson, him that was so sick?"

That was the excuse Elda'd given for isolating Lur from the rest of the Clan. Jannus frowned at the top sheet of paper, pretending to read. "He died."

After a startled pause she said, "Could you have caught it, do you think?"

Impassively he replied, "It's possible." That, of course, was a direct and deliberate lie—his first. He couldn't help irrationally waiting to be denounced.

But she merely stopped obstructing his light.

He reconstructed his composure by reviewing what he'd been saying about Screamers. If everything went wrong and the letter failed in all its purposes, the Lady Lillia could forbid him her household and her stock; but she couldn't prevent his waking, some day, in the base under the third south tailory: and he felt it would be well to make what preparations he could against such a time. He added a careful drop of water to the mixing well and took up his pen.

To Kevel, Elda replied, "It was the bonesick. From not eating the proper fruits while the bones were shaping. You can't *catch* the bonesick."

"But the Newstocker said—"

"What's he know about anything?" Elda tossed down his mallet and straightened up, easing his back. "It was the bonesick. And he was up and about, there at the last. What with Medd fetching me salisberry tea to dose him with, he—"

"But it was me grabbed right ahold of him, to get him out of the river, there by Sithstock," the girl stated anxiously.

Elda kept himself from saying she should have left him there, then she'd have no worries. "Look now, it wasn't any sickness that took him off anyhow. He was killed, poisoned, like those Andrans the Valde tell of. And *that* an't catching."

The girl looked for more reassurance to Solvig, working on the barge with Elda and three younger men. Solvig said, "If what that youngster had was catching, Elda'd have gone to the fire long since. Not to speak of the Newstocker himself. Think Elda Hildursson would put his hand to the thing at all, if it was chancy as that? Now quit bothering yourself and us with all this and see what Jessa or Brit wants done."

When the girl had gone and they'd resumed fitting the plank, Solvig remarked, "You made a poor bargain, bringing that Bremneri cub along. Fat lot of use he was in Sithstock. Then he has to run off to Lisle, gets himself banned from all the towns downriver, talking nonsense about the Wall being down, like anybody'd care. . . . Bad bargain. Not to speak of that sick cousin, or whatever he was. . . ."

"Nuisance," Elda agreed, around the two pegs in his mouth. "Though Kevel's got no business hanging around him in the first place."

"She'll not marry your boy Dan, if that's what you're getting at. Watch your fingers, now. . . . Bart, Shoray's second son, will be of an age to marry soon."

And Kevel's dowry would remain in Solvig's Family, and her future children, as well. "Bart," snorted Elda, and handed a peg to Solvig. "That mudhead, and his mother so near-sighted she needs both hands to find herself in the dark. Ought to pair Bart with Jessa's youngest: a mile off, she don't look so bad, even to me."

"Elda Hildursson, you watch how you talk about my sister," warned young Geft.

"And you the ugliest of the bunch. You keep still, you cockeyed newt," rejoined Elda, cuffing water at the boy, who laughed.

"No, Dan's going to wait for the Homecoming," said Geft, who was about Dan's best friend. "See what's offered. He told me so. And about time, too—your Family's been marrying close kin so long you just trade the dowries around for birthday presents."

That was a little too near the bone to be funny: they all sobered, hefting their tools as if surprised to discover them idle in their hands.

"Bad bargain," said Solvig again, a stubborn man when he got started on something, "and not improving that I can tell. Why should we feed him so he can hang around the girls and not turn a hand to help with all this work?"

Following Solvig's glance Elda saw Jannus slide off a rock and weave through the shallows toward the Valde island, meeting on the way two freemaids carrying a pole on which was hung a black wild hog they'd killed. The boy took one end of the pole and waded heavily on, not letting the water take the weight as any sensible man would have done.

"The freemaids," Elda remarked. "Not such a poor bargain there. We'd have been eating fish hash and weeds these last four days except for them."

"So far," Solvig conceded. "Hope we're shut of here before they've hunted the country clean. When's that barge of supplies and all, from Sithstock, supposed to come?"

"By tomorrow sunset, the word was. That boy, he could travel with you awhile," Elda suggested, meeting Solvig's eyes slyly for a moment. "There's little enough barge space to spare. . . ."

Solvig made a noise somewhere between a cough and a laugh. "*Try* to make him feel real welcome. . . ."

"Figured you would. Think I'll tell him."

"Tell Aben about the rope, then, so long's you're headed that way."

On the Valde island were only the boy and four freemaids, the rest still out hunting, Elda supposed. Two were putting up a tripod to hang the hog for butchering. The other pair sat near an open pit gutting and skinning small game. A collection of ducks, ringnecks, great and lesser stilts, peewits, tree-rats, hares, mudchucks, and Elda scarcely knew what-all, were being capably turned into a heap of mixed pale and red meat. Well back from the flies and the mess, the boy was reading something from a paper to one of the pair; the other was humming, paying no visible attention. But with Valde, you never knew. It was as bad as talking to a crosseyed man.

"Burn bright, Elda Innsmith," said the freemaid who wasn't humming, and Elda only grunted in response. The greeting was a poor omen, for an Innsmith.

"The supplies loaded yet?" he asked the freemaid who'd spoken to him.

"Collected," she reported after a moment, "but not yet loaded. They should still meet their pledged time."

"Mm." He spared a glance at the boy. "What are you disguised as?"

The boy returned the glance quizzically. "Myself. A little of this, a little of that. . . ."

"Where'd it come from?"

"Sithstock. No, the Lady Ultreena still won't admit me. But my copper's as good as an Innsmith's, it seems, considering that she doesn't like you either."

"Mm. Finish whatever you're about. I want a word or two."

The boy resumed reading. Elda helped haul the hog up on the tripod, noting that the beast had the stumps of four arrows in it. As soon not have met it, he thought, in a thicket at twilight. The Valde who'd been humming started to sing about arrowood reeds. When dead and rigid, feathered and tipped, they struck down those same birds they'd sheltered as nestlings. The reeds therefore sighed and rattled while waiting in the ice-crusted shallows for the coming of the harvester and her curved knife.

The tune was cheerful and repeated phrases, like some bird-song Elda'd heard some time but couldn't identify. He shook his head, thinking again what a queer folk Valde were. He expected that in a minute the pair near him would start warbling in praise of fresh pig guts.

Finally Jannus finished and came, fastening the straps of a red scribecase, tucking it under his arm. Elda had already decided there was no privacy to be got nearer than shore, so he contented himself with standing in the water on the downwind side of the island, where their voices wouldn't carry back to the Valde.

"What was all that?" he inquired.

"Aliana Witnessed something for me."

"What excuse did you have for scaring Kevel out of her wits, saying he'd died of a catching sickness?"

The boy lifted one palm in a Bremneri shrug. "She was sent to court me and I was not disposed to play. But you didn't come to ask me that."

"You can't marry into the Clan, you'd better get that clear. Kevel's got her free ways, but it's Solvig who says who she marries and that an't any outlander. What's between you and the Traders is for you to settle."

The boy's rather narrow black eyes looked away over Elda's head, which Elda didn't like any too much, being a head shorter. "I've kept out of your way," Jannus commented reservedly, "since that's what you seemed to want. You've scarcely said a score of words together to me, these last days. Now you're snatching pretexts to rough a quarrel with me, and I don't understand why. Is it Sithstock, that's bothering you? I admit I was no help there, though the fiasco in the harbor wasn't my fault—"

"Never said it was. It was him, cutting the ropes."

"Then is it Lur?"

"He's gone, and good riddance. It's that you just have no business upsetting my people—and all this talk about the Wall—"

"Be glad I'm doing it. I liked Ashai, but his purposes aren't mine. If he thought only you and I knew, he might do something drastic to keep the secret. I've sent word all up and down the river by the Valde relay."

"Have your turned herald by trade?" Elda burst out, then forced himself to speak softly again. "Do what you please, then. It's nothing to do with me or mine. The Wall's nothing to me, up or down."

"I do hear you."

"What you ought to do," Elda admonished, "is go home and make your peace with the Trader Lillia before she hardens her heart against you. I hear tell she's sent for you: you should go."

But the boy wasn't misled. "I am going to the Summerfair. You have agreed to take me there."

"In exchange for your help in the downriver stocks you can't even set foot in!"

"That was the excuse. But that wasn't why. Neither of us has forgotten why you brought me. It was Lur. And now that Lur's gone, you want to be rid of me as well. I can understand that. But I'm going, just the same. I'll keep out of your way and I'll be whatever help I can. I'll be polite to whatever Innsmith girls come courting. But I hold you to your word, Elda: you take me to the Summerfair."

"Or else what? Or else you'll tell?"

"I'm not Lur," rejoined Jannus curtly. "I wouldn't use that even as a threat. I swore not to do that for any manner of cause, and I'll abide by it. Only three know: you, myself, and Lur, if he's bodied yet."

"He'll have forgotten."

"No. He had a rede taken, so as to remember about the Wall."

"In Lisle?" Elda responded incredulously.

"Ashai Rey is a mobile of the Shai. He carries the means with him."

Absorbing this news, Elda was struck with a dreadful suspicion. "It's said you bought the Valde free with information about Bremner. You didn't. . . ."

"I let a rede be taken, yes."

"Oh, you damned fool."

Elda swung away and left without another word, too upset to talk or even think clearly. He wasn't angry. A numb sense of oppression muffled him, making him breathe shallowly. From time to time he'd abruptly pull in a long breath and sigh, quite unconscious of the process. When Solvig had asked twice if he'd told the boy, Elda just shook his head and made no explanation. When Solvig asked just how sure he was that it'd been the bonesick, Elda made no answer at all.

He ate scarcely any of the daymeal, alarming Medd, who dosed him with herb tea and put him on his cot with too many quilts. There he lay for blank hours. Long after everyone else was asleep Elda found himself muttering, "The damned fool. The poor damned fool," like a litany; and then the grieving mood broke like a fever and left him free to consider how it all affected him.

And it soon occurred to him that four now knew he'd sheltered a Tek. The Shai, with all Jannus' memories, would have that information too. And so Jannus had broken his oath, though it seemed he'd not yet realized it.

"That ends all bargains," Elda declared to himself and at last was able to sleep.

After the midmeal lame Mene came to ask Jannus to show her how barges should be steered. An Innsmith could have given her better instruction, but most were busy distributing and storing the bushels of meal, flour, dried and salted pork and fish, and preserved fruit which had been floated down from Sithstock. So Jannus gave what help he could, considering that the barges were moored and stationary.

Mene chatted of her home in the Amel-brole Mountains in the north of Valde, a valley not too far distant from the one where Aliana had been born. Indeed, Mene's kin often met or heard Aliana's four sistersons on *fai*. This word was new to Jannus; after disproportionate labor he managed to extract the definition that *fai* was a sort of appreciating/overseeing tour of lands one knew intimately, as opposed to *la'henna*, a deliberate journey, or *faifar,* just hanging around and appreciating in one place. That settled, Jannus asked if Poli, too, was from the north: Mene said Poli was from the eastern fir forest that bordered Arant Dunrimmon, which was too swift and steep for boats. There were rapids in Erth-rimmon, too, she'd been told. What should be done with the oar then?

When Jannus wandered back to Elda's island Medd thrust a wooden-handled crock into his hands, saying Elda'd been up half the night with a flux of some sort—from the slow-moving water, she'd no doubt. "See that bare place on the bank?" She pointed until Jannus nodded. "Go straight on from that and you'll see a spring. Fetch me a canniken of clean water to brew up a tea."

The errand took Jannus longer than he'd expected. Either the spring was farther inland than Medd's brief directions had led him to suppose or else he lost the direct line during an encounter with an angry crested wader which considered him to be after her eggs. Failing to find the spring, he filled the crock instead at a stream that ran over rocks and tasted clean enough to him.

Using the Wall to establish his bearings, he noticed that there remained only a high band of blazing vermillion light, the rest ochre in rising shadow. He might miss the daymeal.

Making such haste as was possible while carrying a crock full of water—which made him think about Bluejay—he reached the river above the landing and followed the bank south. Rounding a tussocky mound he found all the islands but one deserted. And on that one were only three skinny young Sithstock laders, making a night camp. Around the dock-hands moved the highbacked pale shapes of their draft boars, brought to haul the two barges back upriver.

The Innsmiths, reported the laders, had been gone quite a while. They'd not even waited to eat the daymeal but had simply toted the kettles on board and soaked the fires, offering not a scrap to the Sithstockers.

"You're the one as was in Lisle," one of the gangly youngsters exclaimed. "It's wondered what it was like. . . ."

"The orchards are dying for lack of care," replied Jannus absently. "And nobody looked for me, or asked after me?"

"Just cast loose and left. But really, now—tell us about the Lislers. I hear they keep the women in cages and just haul them out with sacks on their heads anytime they want to—"

"Left some stuff behind," interrupted the lader tending the

fire, pointing with a flaming twig. "Could be yours, I'd guess. . . ."

It had been Elda's island. Jannus knew it by the trees. By a rock was a hamper packed with all Jannus owned, including his red scribecase and what remained of his string of copper money. He counted the beads separating groups of ten cash. From the site of the firepit rose acrid steams that blew across him, but he stood juggling the string from hand to hand, coughing absentmindedly.

The hamper he left as he'd found it and returned to the dock-hands, who were occupied in keeping the boars, each as heavy as a pair of men, from rooting in a sack of provisions, driving them away with sharp pointed sticks. When the contentious noise had subsided, Jannus shook the string in the firelight so that the youngsters could see and hear it. "I'll give twenty cash for one of your barges."

"No deal," replied the one who'd pointed out his baggage. "Mistress Rinn would have us skinned bald."

"Twenty coppers for an old hog trough like this?" another scoffed nervously, whacking a barge with his pig goad.

"He's been to Lisle," warned the third; the one so avid, before, for news of that place. "Bad enough we're talking to him, without selling nothing without the Lady's leave."

"And even if the Lady didn't care, Mistress Rinn, she'd have us skinned sure."

Jannus looked from one to another, listening for any willingness to be persuaded. But the formidable Mistress Rinn, apparently harbormistress, had her help too well trained for them to take so much initiative. Else they'd not have been chosen to deliver valuable provisions to unpredictable outlanders, less than a day's walk from Lisle. Jannus knotted the ends of the cord and looped the cash string around his neck, under his sark.

"I'm going to take less than half of what's in that hamper. You can have the rest in exchange for a quarter part of your daymeal."

"You just gave away your bargain," scoffed the second lader, poking a boar casually in the snout as it ducked toward the food sack. "You leave it and we'll have it for nothing."

"No," Jannus contradicted patiently, "I'd weight it with stones and let the fish have it."

"Good clothes?" rejoined that boy, shocked.

So they'd inspected the hamper's contents, but not touched

the string of cash. Either they were honest, or feared direct questioning from the harbormistress. Perhaps both.

"The *Obedient* and the *Ildo Star* were tied up in Sithstock, firstlight today," mentioned the boy who'd gone back to building the cookfire to his liking. "*Ildo Star*'s the upriver packet, *Obedient*'s running down to the bay. Likely they won't be setting out till first light tomorrow, in the thin of the moon and cloudy as it is. . . ."

"I do hear you. That may be useful to know."

"Surely. But about the daymeal. . . . If we share with you we'll all go hungry tomorrow. When you're just a season from your Naming, they don't trouble to invest any too much food in you to carry off to the farmsteads. We've a half loaf apiece and some fatback, to last us two days. And I don't just know what Mistress Rinn'd say about us giving food away, and to you—or even selling it, if it comes to that. She's got to speak to the factors for us, so's we'll get a place when we're Named."

"Can't you stay in Sithstock?"

"Past our Naming? Not hardly. Old Ulseth, who canes the pages, he's a man . . . but he's the only Named man let to live inside the walls. No. We go to the steads before the harvest starts."

"You can come back with us," offered the third boy, diffidently. "I'll take the blame for it, if need be."

"No," said Jannus, "I'm still going downriver. But I'm obliged for the thought. . . ." He caught the eye of the lader who was tending the fire. "You've never asked me about Lisle. That's true."

"That's true," confirmed the boy, faintly wary.

"So it's not your fault if I talk about it to myself and you can't help overhearing. You know how sound carries, over water. . . ."

"I do hear you," replied the boy, now grinning.

So while the Sithstock boys ate their scant daymeal, Jannus told the darkness downriver much of what he'd seen and done in Lisle. And that night he shared their fire.

Poli noticed Jannus' absence in spite of the cacaphony of Innsmith selfsingings, in spite of the fact that the barges were, in the dusk, drifting past Lisle—of which memories were such that just the smell of the streets awoke echoes of despair; in spite, even, of the fact she wasn't thinking about Jannus at all and wasn't at first conscious of what specific lack was fretting her.

She withdrew herself from the web, the watchfulness the freemaids extended over the riverscape and all living things within their range, searching. Having identified the distraction, Poli quickly sifted a great circle to locate Jannus' familiar *farioh*. She did not find it.

Puzzled, she withdrew still further to begin a more intent search, again fruitless. Finally she willed herself into a state near that of dueltrance: systematically eliminating whole classes of things from her awareness until at last only she and the object of her concentration would exist in the silence. To gain true dueltrance would have required many days' preparation. This sudden effort she found like that of trying to search the riverbottom with too little stored breath.

Then she found him. Hungry, he was trying to suppress selfpity, a sense of having been betrayed, abandoned . . . impatience, there was, some fear, and hunger. . . . He was far away, so far that had she known his *farioh* less well she'd never have been able to discern it before she had to surface.

The banished voices blared, loosed again into her mind, but the contact would hold for a while yet—until the distance became too great. Poli leaned back against the supporting arms of the nearest freemaids, who'd kept her from falling into the river while she was occupied.

She roused herself with the intention of collecting darts, firestone, a bow—what she'd need—from the common stock; but the impulse dissipated into lethargy. Her hand lost purpose in the act of reaching, forgetting the task she'd put it to. The web took her back again and she was too drained by the attempt at dueltrance to oppose her own will against the desire of the group that she remain, and rest, and not involve herself in the concerns of outlanders again rashly. Lisle drifted by, and the place where they'd been taken. The web reached, sifted, and weighed. But the tenuous thread binding her to Jannus' distant selfsinging held, without need of effort or conscious intention. She'd hear the summons when it came.

She'd promised him one service and had no doubt it would now be required of her.

The barges found a place to moor for the night some distance beyond Lisle, but no summons had come. As the Innsmiths quieted and the web diminished to the watchfulness of one freemaid alone, Poli woke fully to herself and determined that Jannus too had gone to sleep, still hungry, not having called her.

The new crescent, lagging up through a foam of cloud, cast unreliable shadows, and the slow rhythms of dreams made it hard for her to concentrate, to decide what she should do.

Maybe, she thought, trailing a hand in the water and then rubbing her face slowly, maybe it hadn't occurred to him yet. The pledge weighed more on her mind than his, surely. Or maybe he did not realize in what need of aid he stood. Maybe he imagined he could go on toward the Summerfair alone. . . .

Mene was the only one still watchful. Poli tried to join that alertness, resisting the sleep that lay warm all around them. Mene felt that if no summons came, Poli should not concern herself. But, Poli protested, then she'd never be free of Lisle—she'd still be beholden. Mene couldn't see how that mattered. "When this Summerfair is gone and you are lar Haffa, what is the weather of Newstock to you?"

"It would matter," Poli insisted. "I would still feel beholden."

Mene felt that was silly. Anyhow, the boy had been called home. Probably he'd turn back, and would be safe enough. . . .

That notion, Poli didn't entertain even for an instant. If he'd shifted that great stone, his determination to see her brided, she, Poli, would have known it at once.

"Even so far?" murmured Mene, dubious because she herself couldn't hear Jannus' selfsinging.

Poli hugged her knees unhappily, more at a loss about what to do than at any time she could remember. She finally decided to just wait, remain in range of the call and wait for the thing to become clearer to her. The barges wouldn't go farther in a day than she could run in a day and a night, she thought. Therefore she lay back and determinedly slept until firstlight, then collected harness and gear from the freemaids' supply and took leave of the river, hiking inland until both the Innsmiths and the waking of Lisle dimmed, less vivid than the lazy feeling of a young leopard which had taken a goat before dawn and had dragged it into a thicket of thorn.

Aware of her, the leopard stopped crunching bones, but resumed when she did not approach his kill and made gestures of reassurance. When the sun rose, the leopard strolled out onto the other side of the slate outcrop, above the place Poli had chosen for waiting, to groom after his meal.

Presently he found a comfortable ripple to fit his shoulders and napped with his belly to the sun, both heavy square forepaws lolling relaxed on the rock.

Poli clasped her knees and bent her forehead onto them, dozing while the shadow of the thorn thicket ebbed from the rock and the dull-hued leaves of each bush folded to secure the last of the dew.

Jannus thought of her.

Poli was at once alert though she didn't move, considerate of the cat's repose.

But it wasn't a call, only an unshaped blur of longing and gentleness and well-wishing entangled with his usual association-complex for her, a pattern as clear to her, by now, as her name spoken aloud. This flash of emotion became muted, passing again under the automatic Bremneri self-control. The whole flow of mood, his *farioh*, diminished as his thought turned to some matter considered coldly. Had it not been for the continuing whine of his hunger she would have lost him altogether.

He wasn't going to call her at all.

He didn't know she was near enough to hear.

He didn't know she'd missed him and waited, so he wouldn't call her now or expect her to come. She could, she realized, have known this last night if it had occurred to her to try to think it out from his point of view. It was perfectly plain, she thought with annoyance.

Distant, some freemaid replied with a tart suggestion she come on back, then. Poli shrugged off the interruption. They knew her feeling of obligation, but couldn't understand why it should bother her so, why she had to be free of it. She'd just have to figure the thing out for herself.

He wasn't going to call her, and he nevertheless meant to get to the Summerfair. How could he imagine it was possible?

Poli settled down to an activity alien to her nature. She tried to visualize, not herself in Jannus' place, but Jannus himself—to predict what he, being precisely who he was and no other, would do in this situation.

To ignore the living portion of Jannus that she sensed from moment to moment, to turn from that flow of everchanging mood to an abstract, fixed, and imaginary construction of her own thought—this was more unnatural than to substitute for the present river, memories of ice; more strange because the image she fashioned was of a Jannus she'd never known.

Briefly she wished he were a Valde, so she could have known his intention clearly without sorting through a thousand husks of possibility. Then she sighed, her consciousness of the lives of insects and plants dimming slightly as she applied herself to this dull chore of organization and choice to which she'd set herself.

The Tek called Lur sat on the broken tip of a long arched claw of azure plarit, building-glass: on the remains of the arch of Isgate, the bridge of Cliffhold, his onetime handiwork. The upper pier that anchored the top of the span remained intact and loomed behind the Tek's perch, a pyramid dwarfing the tower of Cliffhold Keep on the plain behind.

From that pier Isgate had sprung out and down to the forest on the west shore of Erth-rimmon far below in an unsupported arch a little bluer than the sky. It had been chiefly a promenade, a vantage point, rather than a thoroughfare. Resting places spaced at intervals had invited Teks and their retinues of Valde companions to pause and overlook the harmonies of river, wood, and sky. A webwork of like-colored threads had rimmed the parapets so nobody would be blown or thrown from the span by mistake. It had quickly become a popular site for artistic suicides and dramatic murders: everyone in Lur's circle of acquaintance had died there at least once.

The pier at the foot of the bridge had opened into the Wood of Fathori. To Fathori, with its seasons of blossoms like luminous moths and of lambent fruit, from which were drawn the opalescent Fathori wines; with its songbirds specially designed and developed by the runaway Teks of Debern Keep to recreate the nightingales of legend, had come most of the folk then alive. But only the Debern Teks remained there, too entangled with their lowland handiwork to leave, founding the region known as Is. . . .

From his perch the Tek could discern the lower pier and the swamp that now extended beyond it, mirroring clouds, as far as he could see. The loss of Fathori and the condition of the bottom pier were matters of indifference to him. What mattered was that he couldn't get down.

He'd thought, with the Barrier gone, it'd be an easy thing to descend to the lowlands. He contemplated his current body, sunburnt, cut and scraped from a day and half scrambling, without water, to dead ends of ledges and fissures in the cliff face: if anything, it was younger than that he'd discarded in Lisle. The hands had no strength to grasp, the arms none to lift or hold.

There was no way he was going to get down the cliff without being better bodied. And he'd begun to suspect there were no adult bodies left in any of the bases of the High Plain. The demand was too frequent and continual for any body to remain unused until it'd ripened into maturity, accelerated though that process was. His hypothesis was supported by the fact that all the skeletons he'd found littering the plain had been child-sized. He suspected his surviving two days in the same body might be something of a record.

He'd crawled out on the bridge to secure an unimpeded fall to the river, a quick death on impact, but was in no haste. He swung his sore feet over the gulf, enjoying the breeze and the respite from attack, reviewing plans and possibilities. And it occurred to him as he rested that though he might not be able to find a body to meet his specifications, he might be able to commission one. Cliffhold Keep was still his, and whatever facilities and capabilities it retained. Though he could not go, himself, into the keep, he might be able to talk to it.

It was worth trying.

He worked his way carefully back along the walkway and circled the saffron and gold tower that was the visible portion of the keep, addressing it at intervals. He was going around a partially devoured corpse when something about the sand near it caught his eye: a stick drawing, all triangles, scratched in the sand, forming the crude outline of a stylized cat's head—the image of the name he'd been given.

His former body had apparently had its head battered in with a nearby stone. So the drawing had been made earlier, before the attack. Standing by the body, he called the keep and found his guess answered. One remote, at least, could hear him and reply.

Having, with some difficulty, identified himself to the keep's satisfaction, Lur found he'd been able to set up the preliminary stages of the project before becoming food. Walking in his own footsteps, as it were, gave him increased confidence in the undertaking and he settled down beside the corpse to finish what he'd begun.

The project was one he'd begun and abandoned over a thousand years before during his interest in lost species. The organic material had long ago ceased to be preserved, but the genetic coding and project plans still remained in the keep's memory. In his former body, he'd even modified them to the keep's present capabilities, which made his present task that much easier, less apt to fatal interruption. But just in case, he scratched the cat's head emblem in three other places, taking his own hint, and instructed the keep to acknowledge and accept him, hereafter, by his name.

The keep, partitioned off by Lur's earlier order from communication with the Shai in regard to this project, was neither intelligent nor well-equipped. It took Lur all night and most of the next day to direct its surviving resources to producing a body to his requirements and reserving it to his own use.

Twice he was attacked by a Tek who had no more wit than to run at him, panting loudly. He defended himself easily enough, suffering no cripping injury, but didn't dare pursue the Tek into the dark and leave his own preparations still incomplete. His own former body proved edible. But it supplied him with little moisture. Before daylight he'd had to bite his own arm to keep his voice audible.

Finally, his eyes shut to keep the dizziness from distracting him, he was able to mutter, "Execute," and it was begun.

It didn't matter that the project had originally been abandoned in failure, that the canine species was still extinct. At the stage he'd given up, he'd produced a promordial carnivore, capable of bounding across twenty-foot gaps in rock trails and of defending itself against all wandering killers that went on two legs.

It would come as a surprise to him, to wake in the body of a beast: he hadn't done so since childhood, and never unexpectedly. But he thought he'd be satisfied with himself.

The panting and scrabbling was coming closer again. Lur leaned back indifferently.

Jannus washed down the last hunk of gritty bread with a swallow of milk and felt considerably less lightheaded and anxious. It'd been a good idea, he thought, to come to Bluejay, though he'd had no idea she had four husbands—three men and a boy—and at least two tiny children strung in hammock-like affairs under a tree. Two of the men were off now in some field, sowing corn; the other pair were by a thorn-walled enclosure minding the herd of goats. The man was named Owl, and the boy was aptly called Crow, being dark, harsh-voiced, and unsmiling.

Bluejay herself, seated on a stool before the doorway of

her sod hut, rhythmically milked a succession of goats into a clay pitcher locked between her bare feet. At her signal, Crow would come to tether the next goat and release the last back into the herd.

"Owl!" she cried. "Can't you keep them out of the nettles? Get them out of there!" She pointed with a leafy switch, and the man called Owl moved to do as he was told. "You see that patch is grubbed out before tomorrow, you hear? And I wonder," she added to Jannus, surveying the goats and Owl, her newest pactmate, with equal dispassion, "why the milk won't sell. Sithstock-born: none of them with the wit of a witherbush."

From what Jannus had seen, they'd little chance to use whatever wit they might have; but he didn't want to start discussing Bluejay's choice in husbands and attended silently to retying his bundle—what he'd chosen to carry with him.

Bluejay loosed the final goat herself and emptied the pitcher into a leather sack supported by the familiar wicker basket, visibly careful to let no milk spill on the red Newstock cloak folded on the grass by her feet: the price of his meal. "A lordly-looking cloak," she commented softly. "Thought so when first I saw it. Think maybe I'll lend it to Owl, come the first of the cold weather. . . . He's not a bad old lad, that one. Ran from a duel over in Darkwaterstead country. See how quick he moves, even though he hasn't the ghost of a notion what he's about? . . . Crow, you waiting for me to milk them twice over?" she called sharply. "Take the stretch past the burned land today, past the ditch—but don't let them get into the knotweed, mind!" Again looking around at Jannus, she said, "You're bound to follow that witch still, are you?"

"Seems so."

"Should have done what I said." Vaguely her hand moved in the wardsign. "Next best, get a cord of her hair, tie three knots in it, spit on it, and then burn it. That'd bind her to your bidding, don't you see. That's how I come by Crow."

"But I mean to have her go free."

"Then the more fool you, because nobody walks free. It's one thing, or it's another. . . ." She turned her face toward the man called Owl, who was tending the children as the scattering goats passed by; her hand still rested on the soiled red cloak. "Crow, that all the faster you can go? At that rate, they won't be past the ditch before I get back. And you watch out for that wolverine pack Sparrowhawk spotted yesterday, lest they've ranged north, and for the grass-cats."

"Don't see you running," called young Crow, in return. "Don't want to find no hay-burrs on your back, neither. Four's enough."

"Go on with you!" Grinning, Bluejay took the cloak into the hut and returned fastening a string of cheeses to her sash, where they hung like great pale beads. "I'm way past my time today. Come on and I'll point you a place where the packets put in, sometimes, to cut wood."

They followed a trail that wound among little crooked vallies and through fields of hip-high grasses mixed with tall wildflowers of pale blue, lavender, and white set on slender canes—spikeweed, she called it. She broke off a cane and tasted at it, showing him how to put a thumbnail between the joints to get at the sweet juice. The flowers, she said, would make you break all out in spots; so he tossed these aside.

They came over the top of a hill from which the river was visible, and the dun roofs of Lisle. Bluejay began telling him how he should go, to reach a place where a packet could put in near shore, then broke off, frowning. "Something behind," she said, reaching into her sash. "Could be a grass-cat or even a shadow-cat, though they'd sooner hunt high, from a tree or a rock. . . . Cats are bad this season nor don't give tongue while they're hunting, like wolverines. . . ."

As she spoke she was pulling out an odd device, a bone box set on a handle. It made an astonishing clatter as she swung it in a vigorous circle. Still whirling the box, she turned to look back up the path. "You never took that cord of hair, like I said?" she inquired, letting the box's circle lapse into forcelessness.

Jannus, who'd been uneasily watching the bobbing weeds on either side, jerked around. He saw a Valde in Newstock colors descending toward them. "No. . . . I have a cord, of sorts, but I . . . I decided not to use it. . . ."

It was indeed Poli, very trim and competent-seeming in full cross-strapped harness, the rows of feathered dagger-darts concealing the bridestone. The curved bone tip of a slung bow showed diagonally behind her left shoulder. One hand held the midstrap of a long bundle rolled in canvas; the other swung free with her stride.

"You mustn't try," Poli called while still twenty paces off, "to cross the Murderlands, the place above—"

"I didn't call you, Poli. Did it seem as if I called you?"

"I know that. But you mustn't—"

"Then what are you—"

"To warn you not to try to climb the Wall," she replied impatiently. "It is—"

"But I had no notion of trying to cross the High Plains. For one thing, it's across the river and I have no boat. . . ." With increasing diffidence and embarrassment, Jannus felt he was mentioning the obvious.

Poli stood a moment as if puzzled. "Then you're going to Lisle? You mustn't do that either because—"

"He's going to hail the downstream packet," stated Bluejay tartly, startling Jannus, who'd assumed she had run off as she had before. Bluejay went on, "He hasn't been to Lisle today, he's not going now, and what's it to you, anyway, what he does?"

Facing Bluejay, who stood resolutely staring off to one side, Poli was outwardly placid but showed small hesitations, matters of stance and tension, that Jannus could read: and he judged her almost as uncomfortable, in this cross-purposed meeting, as himself. "He has been," she said to Bluejay, "as a younger brother to me; and I am beholden to him and would be free of it. I offer help also from affection, as you have done."

"That's neither here nor there," snapped Bluejay. "I've been paid. What you should do is, go off and let him be."

"Poli," interjected Jannus hastily, "I make known to you Mistress Bluejay of Lisle-stock. Bluejay, this is Poli Wir, freemaid and First Dancer to the last Newstock troop."

"Burn bright, Mistress Bluejay," said Poli. "You have no cause to fear me. I mean you no harm."

"That's as may be. But I mean what I said. Bad enough he's bound to follow you, without your making it worse. And if you don't like my saying so, that's too bad." Grimly braced, Bluejay turned to Jannus. "I'm behind in my time. Do you want to see that place, or not?"

"I am obliged to you, Mistress—but no. I can find it."

"And so it goes," she rejoined disapprovingly, and continued down the path at an awkward gait that showed the effort of not running and not looking behind her, the hanging rattle stick punctuating her march as with minute drums.

"I do not understand," Poli remarked softly. "I was so certain you meant to go into the Murderlands. . . ."

Jannus hesitated, choosing words. "Maybe it was my thought of my friend who died in Lisle. . . ."

"No, it was nothing from your *farioh*. I was trying to . . . to think myself as you, and it came to me then, the sureness that you meant to go into that place. And yet I was mistaken."

Somehow she'd gotten hold of the connection between himself and the High Plain—Jannus couldn't imagine how. She'd misapplied it, but she knew the link was there. Finding the subject too dangerous, Jannus said only, "I'm going downriver. I know Orlengis Ras, the master of the *Obedient*—"

"Yes. He is known to me."

"He's Ashai's man, and he has a grudge against Elda. I thought I might talk him into letting me take passage at least to Is, or to Quickmoor—either to spite Elda, or thinking it would please Duke Ashai."

"The *sa'farioh*," she said coldly.

"I can use his name without having to claim kin, can't I?"

"Can't you buy passage?" she asked after a moment.

"I haven't the cash. What I have, I'll need to eat."

They had begun walking, following the path merely because it was there, to be moving rather than standing stiffly, uncomfortable. Working up the joints of a spikeweed cane, Jannus went on, "I'll manage without calling for the favor. I wouldn't have you turn aside for . . . for this. It's my concern. With the Innsmiths, you'd be sure to get home safe, and in time. Can you catch up with them?"

"We have free passage on Andran craft," she reminded him, "because we give them leave to hold Ardun, beyond the Thornwall."

"I know that. But would you trust any Andran—"

"Orlengis, you say, is Ashai's man," responded Poli meditatively. "I fear no harm from Ashai. No," she continued, answering his confusion, "because he could have kept me in Lisle, had he wished. So why would he wish hurt to me now? Enough talk of the *sa'farioh*. Where would you leave the river?"

"If I left at Quickmoor," he replied slowly, thinking aloud, "I could follow the Innsmiths through Han Halla: they'd leave a track even I couldn't miss."

"Not in Han Halla. You have not seen it."

"And you could join the Innsmiths at Quickmoor," Jannus continued, unheeding, "if you'd rather not stay with the *Obedient* all the way across the bay and up to Ardun. The Clan stops there, at Quickmoor, to sell the barges. I heard Elda—"

"You cannot find your way through Han Halla, unguided. Believe me. I say what I know. Could you not make your peace with Elda, whatever is between you?"

Jannus tried to consider it fairly. "I tried once, but he made it plain he wanted me back in Newstock, or Lisle, or on the moon. Anywhere else. I didn't think he'd just leave me, though. . . . I thought he'd keep his word. He must be more frightened than. . . . But no. No." Poli looked at him inquiringly but, as he volunteered no explanation, asked no more.

"Then I will guide you across Han Halla, and I will be free of the memory of Lisle."

"I didn't say that."

"How else? You are pleased, to be companied so. . . ."

"Never mind whether I'm pleased," he retorted, "I can't help that. This is my concern. I just don't think it's a thing that should be required of you—"

"It is the proper favor. It is needful. I must be free of Lisle, and you must cross Han Halla."

"It's not that simple. I don't want—"

"I did not consent to what you did in Lisle, yet I took the fruits,' Poli interrupted coolly. "Take this. Or don't, as you please," she added with a change of tone, a hint of baiting. "I will hail the *Obedient* myself, and cross Han Halla alone without waiting for the troop or the Innsmiths. And you will do as you please."

"That's just stubborn," admonished Jannus, suspicious of the change in manner. "And I don't believe you'd do it, either."

"You'd never know, because you would never come alive out of Han Halla."

"I do hear you."

"But we will travel together as far as Quickmoor, in any case. And far enough into Han Halla for us to see how you fare."

"I haven't said I agree to any of this," he objected.

"No, you have not said so," she assured him, faintly emphasizing *said*.

"Well, I haven't. Just listen to what I say and leave the rest alone."

"I do hear you," she replied smugly.

He'd never seen her in this sort of teasing mood before and wasn't sure what to make of it. "What does Aliana say to this?" he demanded, his farthest reach for discouragement.

"She's too far away now. And I am a freemaid," Poli replied promptly.

For once. For once, no unseen audience, judging each word before it was past his teeth. It was astonishing. He found himself smiling. "Would you promise not to send any more women to court me?"

Poli considered the grass, swinging a spikeweed cane pensively. "I heard your thought of me so plainly. . . . It is sometimes hard to attend to necessary things, so distracted. . . . I thought, if one came. . . . But you were unkind," she added abruptly, "to the girl Kevel."

Beneath the disapproval, the teasing note was back; and Jannus responded to it. "But I was polite to Mene, you must admit. Her going on about barges, with threescore Innsmiths wandering around for her to have asked, each knowing fifty times what I do . . .! Did you think I wouldn't notice?"

"The ship is coming," Poli announced, "but there's a quicker way—"

She set off toward the river at an easy jog and Jannus was drawn into motion without particularly thinking about it, cheerful and slightly breathless.

Whenever Elda wasn't occupied with the tricks of current, formation, and weather, either standing at the sweep or supervising his youngest son Dan in his turn; whenever he wasn't involved with details of disputes, plans for after the Homecoming, or moorage in this or that river stock, to be secured by the freemaids; whenever he wasn't absorbed with being hungry or roused or tired; whenever his mind drifted, undirected by his will or his duties, he watched the Wall.

Often now there was rubble, flung by the quake: visible quite far out into the river, creating hazards and sometimes rapids. Often, too, there were narrow jumbled strips of beach above the reach of the spring floods, where sometimes there were bones in unbroken mounds that took hours to pass.

They would crunch like twigs, Elda mused, under the foot of the first man to walk the Dead Shore.

One morning, while idly watching a golden gull soar in and out of the sunlight not yet slanting down to touch the foggy river, Elda saw the gull drop to a nest on a ledge halfway up the escarpment. Faintly he heard the cries of its chicks as it disgorged fish into their stretched gawping mouths; and he watched that spot until nest and gull were only a guess, until that stretch of cliff was blocked by another outward ripple in the dull folded stone, pushing the river into a swifter westward swing. Elda lay awake most of that night and was irritable for days afterward for no reason he would say.

The *Obedient*, Jannus had learned, usually made the run to Quickmoor in fourteen days, including the usual stopovers for passengers, cargo, and fuel. On the thirteenth morning Jannus woke believing he must have missed breakfast, seeing shadows so sharp and clear. And that confused him, since part of the chores he did in lieu of fare was serving the passengers and doing all the cleaning up afterward. Scrabbling into his clothes, he went out on deck and discovered that the cliff had vanished. Level marsh stretched out on both sides, east and west. Jannus just stood and stared.

After a while he asked a crewman splicing rope if they'd passed the Broken Bridge. Without looking up the man replied, "Dunno, ask 'Kalas."

"But you—Oh, forget it." He spotted Perkalas, the Fisher steersman, alone up in the wheelhouse. Balancing on the ladder, Jannus asked permission to come up and, when it was granted, put the same question to the small man, meanwhile staring in unaltered fascination at the bare, flat vista revealed, from this higher vantage point, to the eastward where the orange sun floated.

"Passed Cliffsend last night, where the bridge is. Must be you were asleep," replied Perkalas readily enough.

"Did she run all night?" From the crew, Jannus had caught the senseless habit of referring to the packet as feminine.

"Oh, it's all clear water, once you're past Cliffsend. Nice full moon up, and all. . . . Even stopped once—for wood. But that was past midnight, I expect you were asleep." Perkalas smiled, his knobby lined face in profile, still attending to the river. Under his longbilled cap, his hair was chopped off raggedly just below his ears, as the rivermaster's was, though Perkalas hadn't ever spoken of Elda in Jannus' hearing. "Down here," the steersman went on, "you start to get the tide lifts and it an't safe to moor. We just run right along, except for starsdays."

"If I'd known that, I'd have stayed up. I wanted to see that bridge." Jannus noted the petulance in his voice, suppressed it. "I'd heard about it—an arch all of . . . of blue glass, where there was a forest once. . . ."

"Fathori. Time was, Fathori was there, the Fishers' woods

. . . but that's all done now. Should have said something if you wanted to be called. It's nothing much to see by night, anyhow. Just—"

"What's this?" The sharp question was the rivermaster's, as Orlengis climbed the last few rungs.

"Boy missed seeing the bridge," replied Perkalas, surrendering the wheel, and both men smiled: Orlengis taking stock of the river ahead, Perkalas stretching as though he were stiff. Knowing smiles, without friendliness—excluding Jannus from some shared private amusement.

Jannus was on civil enough terms with the rivermaster, considering they'd exchanged barely a score of words since Jannus had come aboard. Orlengis had let his steersman make all the arrangements, seemingly indifferent whether Jannus came, or paid, or not; but Jannus believed he owed his passage to Orlengis' dislike of Elda, who'd left Jannus behind, just as he suspected he'd been put to scrubbing decks and pots, despite his years as a lader, on Orlengis' order.

The rivermaster grunted softly. "There's that Valde in the bow again. Get her out, 'Kalas. We hit a snag and she'll be dumped right under the wheels."

"She pays no mind, you know that," replied the little steersman in a resigned tone. "Will she mind you?" he asked Jannus, alert, not friendly.

Jannus let the dare pass unremarked. "I'll see what the cook wants done, by your leave. . . ."

"Sure, go ahead," replied Perkalas, when Orlengis ignored the polite leavetaking. "And call your Valde out of there, why don't you?"

Jannus just went on down the ladder. It wasn't the first time somebody aboard had tried to egg him into claiming or asserting control over the Valde—they of course all knew about his having brought her out of Lisle—in an effort, perhaps, to determine the relationship between them. Many of the attempts were less subtle than Perkalas', and there'd been obscene suggestions and speculations made, carefully within his hearing, which he'd likewise ignored. He suspected there was money bet on it. If he'd had an acceptable confederate aboard, he might have made himself some copper if he'd known which way to bet.

He helped clear the crew's dishes away and laid out places for the passengers, who arrived in indolent twos and threes. When their meal was at last finished and the pans scoured to the cook's satisfaction and put away, Jannus collected two bowls of oatmeal peppered with raisins he'd put aside, set two mugs of tea on the tray, and carried it all to the foredeck directly below the wheelhouse, out of its sight. Settling himself crosslegged on a coil of rope, he wordlessly invited Poli to join him.

"A river-slippie came to me and offered three wishes," he announced to her, nervously cheerful. "The first was for breakfast, the second for your company." When it didn't occur to her to offer the expected prompting, he finished. "And the third I have yet to use. What should it be, do you think?"

He'd recently discovered the delight of telling involved and preposterous lies, especially to the cook.

Poli only smiled vaguely, attending to her food. "It is most joyous, hearing the life all around, so." She gestured with her spoon at the eastern shore.

"I miss the Wall," Jannus confessed. "I'm so used to it, I guess. . . ." He thought about being protected, sheltered, having a known dependable object to rest his eyes on though all the rest should alter around him: consciously choosing these images to clarify the vague words.

Poli nodded slightly. "The open. I dreamed of it last night. Even sleeping, I knew we had come free of the Murderlands."

"Can you hear Quickmoor yet?"

". . . .No," she reported.

"We come to it tomorrow, they say. Poli. . . . Are you sure you don't want to wait for the rest of the troop? Or just stay aboard, go on to Ardun?" Five of the passengers were a trade delegation from Overwater: she could travel safely with them.

"Will you call for this, as your favor?" she rejoined at once, and he was briefly angry to think she'd imagine he would ask her to abandon him, as a favor. Then he realized she was teasing him again: she bent, smiling, over her bowl, remarking, "You do not wish me to remain behind or go off alone. So why do you keep talking as if it were otherwise?"

"What I want, and what I think, don't necessarily agree," he replied, rather tartly.

"That's what I said." Looking out over the east shore, Poli told him, "We are within the arms of Han Halla: look at it.'

What he saw was swamp—water fenced crazily with clumps of reed and bushwillow—with no visible merit to prompt Poli's fond regard.

When they were done he collected the crockery and returned it to the galley; and noted, when he stepped out on deck again, that she had returned to her favorite perch. He wondered how the betting ran now.

After Overwater and Aftaban, the barges passed no more towns. The low hills flattened again slowly into fens hidden behind screens of arrowstalk reeds pushing toward their summer height of eight or ten feet among the clicking broken stalks of last year's growth. There was no true shore to be seen. The Innsmiths moored the barges with anchors, out in the slow current, to escape the clouds of misery flies that spun anywhere the arrowstalk grew. Breezes out of the west smelled like rotted lightning.

Yet this ugly country had its people. Once Dan pointed out daymeal smokes intertwining above some inland settlement, likely Newthaven on the Yellowfields River that fed the swamp that fed Erth-rimmon. But the smokes Elda noted were solitary, rising in the middle distance or far away, so only the plume's wind-scratched top showed over the green flags of arrowstalk. Never was more than one seen at a time; but there weren't many times, either, when the horizon was altogether clean.

"Corpse-eaters," muttered Elda, and spat.

"But this here's still Bremner, an't it?" asked Dan, at the oar.

"Long's you see *that*," Elda replied, jerking a thumb at the Wall, to which his back was turned, "we're in Bremner. And a bit beyond, besides. Corpse-eaters claim it too, for all the good it does them. . . . Time was, the Yellowfields was called Iswater, Isrimmon, in the Valde style. Time was, this was Is, and the Fishers don't forget it. Look at it." Elda scowled at the faraway scarf of smoke. "Fishers. Maggots on the corpse of their old lands, beggers at doorways built of stone stolen from the ruin of their roads, letting Andras pirates steal their sons any time they're of a mind to, snatching their food dripping from the mud between their grand-das' bones. . . .

It wouldn't happen, Elda was thinking grimly, to the Innsmiths. They'd have their Homecoming. Rights to the Clan diggings would come back into their hands. And when those diggings were at last scraped clean, then new mines would be started, even if the finding tools, the Tek tools needed, had to be begged from Deepfish itself at Down, up on the High Plain. . . .

Elda watched the Wall flow by for a moment, just long enough to remind himself how much he hated it and how glad he'd be to come to the end of it, out of reach at last.

Through the slow days Elda kept looking ahead, and so was among the first to spot, on the clifftop, a small spot of color like a lake seen from a mountain, a spot that peered above intervening folds of the cliff during the whole of a long morning's travel; then a yellow finger, lower by half, flashing as clouds came and went overhead; finally the ruined span itself, a talon that jutted from the cliff and ended high in the air, slightly past midstream. And beyond, through the angle of cliff and bridge, the level land called Han Halla lay steaming under the sun.

Just ahead, the fallen piece of walkway stood crookedly on end like a tower on the west shore, with the river curling around it, propped by the lower pier hidden, for half its height, by the arrowstalk and the river's advance over its groundings. Nothing moved but a few drifting gulls.

The barges approached the Broken Bridge well away from shore, where the swiftest currents would carry them quickly past: for the Valde freemaids had sent warning of a crowd lying hidden among the reeds and high sawgrass.

A shout from the leading barges cried confusedly of some obstruction. Elda's barge bumped into Tib's as Tib snatched his sweep clear just in time. Elda jerked his own oar to an angle as his barge was banged from behind. The sudden jolts of stopping and of collision flung more than a few people into the water and Elda, hopping heavily from barge to barge, had trouble placing his feet because of families crowded to the sides to drag somebody out of danger from the narrow shifting slits of water open among the packed craft.

The barges finally sorted themselves into a line about five deep, stretching from midstream to the half-submerged pier, all stopped dead in the water. In a barge in the front rank, Elda was kneeling and groping in the water. His hand touched something smooth and slippery: a cable about the thickness of two fingers, just under the surface. Though he peered intently, however, he couldn't see it.

"Some piece of the walkway," Solvig declared, behind him. "Must be: blue, like the rest up there. Drifted along, must be, till that rock slide caught it. Over yonder."

Peering under his hand, Elda could see what seemed to be
a tangle of blue threads that came out of the river and were
held by a heap of rocky rubbish at the foot of the cliff.

"Can't have been there long," Solvig was going on, "or the
packets would have got together, towed it loose or something.
Can't go neither upriver nor down, like it is now."

Between the sunken pier and the first thicket of arrowstalk,
the river was hardly knee-deep, Elda judged: too shallow for
the barges to pass. Unless the webwork could be cut, they'd
have to unload and tote the barges around. So they tried cutting it. Kell went after the slippery cording with a hatchet
where the web seamlessly joined the fallen length of walkway. Then he tried a knife. His hammer just rebounded with
a musical sound that hummed and reechoed long after the
blow was struck. "Leave off," Elda advised wearily, but Kell
wanted to try burning it and Elda had to let him go on and
try, though there was no sense in it, the stuff was plarit.
Sooner cut ice, he thought, with a hot feather. "You want to
try biting it?" he demanded caustically, when Kell reported
the cable not even warm.

"No, that's my turn, I suppose," admitted Kell reluctantly,
handing the firepot full of coals back down.

The jeweled shadow of the upended walkway cast a purple
glow over all the nearby barges, making the faces turned
toward him seem like great bruises. Elda declared, "Then
there's nothing for it but to unload and drag the barges
through the shallows. Can't take more than a day. Cheer up!"

"Elda Innsmith," said a soft voice—one of the Valde
freemaids, touching his shoulder to direct his attention downstream, where a small round boat made of bundles of rushes
had bobbed out into open water and was being paddled
toward them along the margins of the arrowstalk screens.

In the coracle was a white-haired ancient with a forked
beard covering most of his ribs, each fork tied with red cloth
strips crosslaced from chin to wabbling tip. His only visible
clothing was a cape that seemed to be made of speckled
feathers. His look was birdlike enough, for he was gaunt and
long of nose.

Having come nearly to the pier, the old Fisher hooked one
knoblike elbow around a sheaf of canes and called in a high-
pitched voice, "You pay us. Then go."

"Toll?" remarked young Edald, to nobody in particular.

"Why not?" rejoined Kell, with a cynical shrug. "Andrans
do it."

"Andrans hold the Sea. Corpse-eaters," quoted Dan, ceremoniously spitting, "hold only the mud."

"Right now they got the best toll gate *you'll* ever see," put in Elda. "You mind where you spit till we're past this. Grandda," he called to the old Fisher, "what pay do you want, then?"

"Pay us all metal. Then go."

"Don't want much, does he? How many," Elda muttered to the Valde at his side, "does that old stilt have hid?"

"Many," was the calm, vague reply.

"Fine for him! How many, then? As many as us?"

"No children. No women. Many men . . . at least a score. Perhaps twice, three times a score."

In the farmsteads there was a saying, "To get Valde count": it meant to be short weighted, cheated of the full amount. It was also said a Valde couldn't hit eleven with her sandals on. Elda now appreciated these sayings. "Who're you, then."

"Aliana Wir."

"Then get your girls into the barges closest to shore and tell—"

"It is already done, Elda Innsmith," replied the Valde composedly, giving him a better opinion of her again.

The Fisher was meanwhile shouting, "All metal here, owed to us! Pay us all metal!"

" 'Then go,' " chorused half a dozen Innsmiths in unison with the old man bobbing in the coracle. Elda shouted, "Grandda! Just suppose we don't feel like beggering ourselves on such a fine afternoon. What then?"

The Fisher raised his paddle. From the nearest screen of arrowstalk a ball of dried mud with reed stems rayed out all round arched, flaming, into a barge on Elda's left. The mud cracked when it hit, releasing a blob of foul-smelling oil that instantly began spreading flames across the deck. The small fire was stamped out before any hampers caught, but the point was plain. The Fishers could have any number of such simple firebombs. They could toss them from cover in perfect safety.

"All right," Elda muttered rapidly, "the barges nearest midstream get pulled toward the Dead Shore as close as is safe. No yelling. Go." Lightly he punched seven of the young men squatting around him. They moved off, to spread the word. "Your troop," Elda continued to the Valde, "get into the reeds. Knock out as many as you can, circle off downstream on foot. We'll pick you up as soon's we get clear. Go. Wait! Throw first at anything near a fire, put the fire out. All right? Then go on."

Elda straightened up, trying to see how far the midstream barges had moved without actually looking at them; they seemed as tightly packed as ever.

"Grandda," he called, "we an't done any harm to the Co—to the Fishers. We're Smiths, out of the north, not Andrans. We—"

"Know you: Meks." The Fisher passed a spread hand over his stiff white mop of hair to show how he'd known them. "Closed the high to us. Stole our trees with fire, leave water only. Steal hills, planted ground, leave water only. Steal—"

"Not us, Grandda. Somebody's been lying to you. What trees? How can anybody steal a hill?"

The Fisher whacked the water with his paddle, jabbed it at the Kantmorie cliff. "Steal Isget, make to fall. Owed to us, for that we hold to our land, plant rice where is water only, plant again Fathori, our Dreamwood, in the—"

There was room, open water, on the left side of Elda's barge. He and Solvig grabbed the web and began hauling the barge along, letting the others aboard tend to the fireballs that began falling from shore.

More bowl boats spun out of the reeds upstream. Reeled out on long grass tethers, the coracles were kept from drifting into reach while each Fisher busied himself with a firepot and a supply of mud missiles. Still other Fishers began scaling the walkway and soon were bombarding the nearer barges with fireballs and shrewdly slung stones.

There were fewer missiles leaping from the marsh, now: the Valde darts, Elda reckoned, taking their toll. First one, then another, of the braided tethers was cut, each loosing a hovering coracle and its frantically back-paddling Fisher into the outstretched hands of the Innsmiths, who dealt with each levelheadedly. The flimsy craft, they simply tore into chunks and discarded; the firepots, they doused; the unarmed kicking Fishers were chucked over the web into the powerful midstream current, which ought to carry them a fair distance before they could regain the shore. But only seven thus came their way.

Across the web, at least ten coracles were coming upstream but, so far, had cast no missiles. The water would have swept them away if paddling stopped for a minute. Elda couldn't guess what mischief they might be up to, and said so.

"I'll go into the river, Da," proposed Dan breathlessly, opping up on Elda's right. "Cut the ribs right out of those oats, tip the—"

"Stay put. Get that fire, 'fore the tent catches. Do what I ay!"

A missile descended; Inetta, Sig and Solvig's dour mother nd the sister of Elda's wife, neatly caught it in a long-andled pan, where it flared harmlessly, and flung it down-iver with a flick of her wrist. The trick was cheered by those vho'd seen it and was widely imitated, so that few of those ireballs hurled from shore touched the barges at all. Dan be-an calling out as they fell, claiming those in his reach for his and alone.

Nearer shore a tent was alight, a danger to its neighbors. When Elda had gotten help and put out the fire, he stood wiping his smoke-stung eyes, thinking it was plain that the barges had to get off the web. So far nobody had been seri-ously hurt on either side, as far as he knew; but in an hour the sun would be gone and he had a dread of what might happen in the dark, with the moon hardly more than a nail-paring. Fishers could swim right up to the barges unseen. And with people moving around so, nobody could keep track of the children—they could fall between barges or be swept downstream in midriver. If nobody chanced to see them, they'd be gone. Elda could hear more than one name being called, over the general din, even now. And after night had come. . . .

He looked around for Solvig but couldn't find him, though they'd been together at the blazing tent. Elda started working his way from barge to barge, beginning to hurry, snatching hands offered him, stumbling over and through piles of bag-gage. From the last barge out he spotted Solvig already in the water—partly swimming, partly pulling himself along on the top strand of the web. Solvig was halfway to the Kantmorie shore.

Solvig had been expecting him, because he glanced back and paused, one arm over the web. They understood each other perfectly.

Solvig wasn't waiting for Elda's permission: first choice, first chance at all unpleasant duties, rightly belonged to the Clan leader. But if Elda declined to walk the Dead Shore to pry the net loose, Solvig would. And Solvig would thereby ir-revocably outlaw himself and his closest kin, likely his whole Family. He'd lose the Homecoming, the Innsmith diggings,

everything they'd worked and waited for so long. Or else
Elda would, and the Clan leadership would pass from his
Family to Solvig's.

Elda met the younger man's gaze for what seemed to him
quite a slow while. What finally settled the choice was that he
wouldn't let anybody else to be the first to set foot on that
shore. If it had to be someone, it would be himself, whatever
came of it. Elda struck the water awkwardly, making a great
splash.

The current pressed him close against the web, forcing him
to use the same stroke-and-grab method Solvig had. Saying
nothing to the younger man, Elda pushed by and continued
until his feet found slimy rubble.

The beach stank. Besides the usual bones, there were piles
of child-sized corpses broken among the boulders, partly
shrouded by clouds of whining flies. Elda began breathing
through his mouth; but that was worse. The smell was so
thick he could taste it. That image he instantly stifled and set
all his attention on finding places to set his feet.

In spite of the gull he'd seen and all common sense, he still
halfway believed some sudden force would strike him down
at the next advancing step. Not until his hand touched the
hot orange cliffside did he truly accept that the Wall had
failed, that he faced only dead stone.

Had there been more time, he'd have had his Family sign
painted there.

He began attacking the pile of rough rock within which the
web was embedded, dislodging three or four boulders before
he reached one he had to stop and shove back and forth. It
passed the balance point and toppled, landing with an unpleasant noise he didn't investigate. Where it'd rested he
found a trimmed pole, broken off short, that'd been used to
lever the rock on the pile in the first place. Elda hefted the
pole a moment. Then he hurled it against the cliff.

He was so angry to realize the Fishers had been there before him, that they'd set the web themselves and had not just
seized a chance-brought opportunity, that he didn't much
care that Solvig was wading up from the river and setting his
hands to the next stone.

Freed, the web whipped from the lower rubble, scattering
melon-sized rocks like gravel under the tension of the barges
moving downstream. Both men went down, coughing and
groaning. Elda thought his left thumb was broken—maybe

his whole hand. It was bad, thinking of broken bones in this place.

With eyes squeezed shut, he burst out, "You're meat for the Fool-Killer, you are, Solvig Torvesson. Should have stayed where you were. Just waste, the both of us, where only one was needed."

"Thought about it," Solvig admitted, after a burst of coughing. Gravel gritted as he regained his feet.

"With me here, you held responsibility for the whole Clan. Now you brought your Family into it too, for nothing—half the Clan—and nobody but Fatface Grat to lead what's left. You ought—"

"Said I thought about it." Solvig had retrieved the piece of pole and was sighting along it to judge its trueness of line. "Look at this. . . . Branches haggled off with a hunk of slate, looks like. Nor a sharp one, neither. A born fool can crack a slate so's to give it a fair cutting edge. Corpse-eaters. . . ." Solvig flicked the nubs of branches disapprovingly for a moment more, then tossed the pole aside, looking toward the river. "They're clear, now. . . . No Corpse-eater," he continued levelly, "is going to set foot where I don't dare, to lay traps for my Family. Not after Sig. That, I just will not abide."

"Should have thought first of the Clan—"

"Don't nag me, it's done with. Caught your hand, did it?"

Dan came hop-skipping over the debris at the edge of the water. "Come on, Da, 'Vig. We brought one barge in a little way—a little way down—Whish! What a stink! It's awful, I—"

Dan jumped sideways and dove, to free himself of the appalling smell.

"Won't be that easy," Elda muttered darkly, stepping to avoid a nearly naked skull buried in the gravel.

Book IV:

HAN HALLA

Quickmoor, as Elda had been told, was a freeport. Bremner claimed it, and a certain Lady Baillen held nominal rule. But outside its walls, an international mercantile district spread down the skirts of the two hills all the way down to the long, long piers. Another lady, a former bead girl called Rayneth, held court here in the outer crescent: rule enforced by hired axemen paid by levies on Crescent merchants who generally then gave them "a little something extra" to keep away on a regular basis. Private quarrels, as Elda saw, were settled by a version of the duelling code of the Bremneri farmsteads. Following the other heads of Families, Elda sidled around one such duel—an old Bremneri steadholder and a brown-uniformed Fisher, circling each other with whip-knives in a circle of noisy wagering onlookers.

Elda had never seen such a town. It was a smaller counterpart, he'd heard, of the Andran freeport across Han Halla—Ardun on Arant Dunrimmon, the great river of Valde. But the Clan hadn't been even this far south in Elda's time, or in his father's. He only knew that the Crescent was a place where a man could easily be lost.

Along its haphazard passages roamed Andrans, Fishers—slave, hired, and savage—Bremneri men of both stocks and steads, and ambling harlots of three races. These included Truthdeaf Bremneri women whose custom was to plait, into the black ropes of their hair, laquered wooden beads in the number of their fee. A decent lady of the inner households, by contrast, went by heavily veiled, boxed by eight Valde in red and saffron tabards, the foremost swinging a clapper to clear a path.

Women were held in common in some places, men in others; but nowhere else that Elda'd ever heard about were there free women who sold themselves in a short peculiar slavery for their own profit.

Looking at the crowds and the shouting merchants, dodging

143

push-carts and quarrels, Elda fell gradually behind and scarcely noticed when it was that Grat and the rest became lost to sight.

It didn't matter any more if he fell behind. Grat was leading the Clan now. He'd let Elda finish the agreed sale of the barges, so as not to parade their private differences in front of strangers. But once they'd reached the street again, Grat had divided the other heads of Families into porters and guards, to transport the cashboxes back across the Crescent to their camp at the edge of the marsh. In neither group did he include Elda. So Elda wandered along more or less in the same direction, taking abrupt intense interests in things he basically cared nothing about at all.

Though many days' journey from Andras Bay, Quickmoor was a seaport in all but name. The lift of the tides raised the river ten feet or more, then sucked the water away again rapidly, leaving the long slanting piers on their high stilts naked for half their length, as they were now, with all the boats moored away out at the ends, and the laders trudging heavily uphill with their bundles and bales, toward the warehouses on shore.

Elda found himself entangled in a buzzing crowd of Valde in various costumes, shorn nearly as bald as Teks—new troopmaids, plainly, awaiting passage to some upriver stock or other. Elda tried to ask where they were bound, but either he couldn't make himself understood or else the smell of his mood repelled them. They darted away like fish schooling, regrouping behind as he passed.

It was too bad, he thought, that he couldn't have brought Jannus this far at least before setting him down. The boy would have enjoyed the man with the ten-pound rat he offered to match against any cat brought against it. Elda waited a while but nobody brought a cat; the rat man looked resigned and moved off, his scarred tailless fighter perched alertly on his shoulder. Since folk in the Crescent seemed willing to bet on a spitting contest, or on which way the loser of a duel would fall, the rat man was likely suffering from success.

Turning away, Elda found the passage blocked, as wasn't uncommon. Since a bump could easily flash into a duel—a stupid proceeding—Elda moved aside toward the niche vacated by the rat man. But the Andran moved too, still in the way, with Elda in a corner. It was Orlengis, and he looked happy. Elda thought hard of Aliana Wir, wanting her to send one or two of his boys, or somebody, with no faith she'd hear him in all this crowd or do what he wanted if she did hear: she was Grat's left hand now, not his own.

"My master bids me greet you," Orlengis was saying, "in the name of Lisle and in the name of Isgate Bridge. He bids me to renew to you the offer made in Newstock, adding the rank of Ai, Administrator, to his former proposal. If you again reject it, my master gives me the pleasure of denouncing you at the Summerfair for having set foot on the Dead Shore."

"Fine for you. Now get out of my way."

"Duke Ashai would be answered," refused Orlengis, polite as a page.

They were about of a height, but Orlengis was thirty years younger. Elda weighed the chance of successfully breaking the halfbreed's arm against that of being found by his own people with Orlengis sitting on his head. He glared at the ground, unobtrusively looking for a fair-sized rock. "And if the answer's the same, do you just run back and weep on his sandals, or what?"

"I'd like," said Orlengis, shoving him lightly against the warehouse bricks behind, "to see you outlawed. I would. I'd like to find out how long you keep your smug talk about 'free people' when strangers cheat you on a contract and there's not a damn thing you dare to do about it, and your children hungry and hanging around them that eat and offer scraps." Another bump, scarcely more rough than a pointing finger between ungentle men. Nevertheless, three passing Fisher servants paused to watch. "I'd like to see that, Cousin," declared Orlengis.

"*Cousin*, you say. Well, Enestro, may his bones rot and pollute Camarr so that the rats run mad through the passages—Enestro took your grandda, no fault to him at least, and it was a black shame, too. So you can claim kin, for all of me. But it's all the more reason nobody but a fool would take such a contract as the one that swallowed the Tresmiths, of his own free will. Does Ashai think I'm a fool, then?"

"He thinks you have noplace else to go. And he's right. But don't you put Duke Ashai's name in the same breath Enestro's, who held Camarr before Ashai married into the house and took the rule when Enestro was put out of the way. Because I recall how things were, before, under that ugly toad. Ashai Rey, he's the greatest man living in the world," declared Orlengis, with a certain solemnity; and when

Elda made a derisive noise, Orlengis flushed from throat to brow. "It's true. When Turteo cut my father's throat to get the *Obedient*, Duke Ashai only let him keep half the profits and made him take me on as mate and then steersman, to learn the river. From Duke Ashai's own share he set aside a quarter to be my wages, until I'd earned the price of the ship as it'd stood under my Da's hand. And then Duke Ashai made Turteo Ras sell to me. That was six years ago. There was no blood feud, only three of my sisters had to be sold, and I am Ras, Rivermaster, as my Da was. Ashai Rey is a wise, shrewd, and just man, and he's put Ismere first among all the Isles of Andras. I was lucky the day Camarr came into his hand. But you're stupid, Cousin. Stupid not to follow a good master when one makes you fair offers. You—"

The crowd now numbered ten or more. "I'd serve Kenni-ath Rey before I'd serve *him*," rejoined Elda roughly, naming one of the more currently infamous of the Islemasters. "And I'd strip naked and dance off into the reeds with the Fisher folk before I'd bend my neck to Ken—"

Orlengis was truly a servant. An insult to his master broke his temper. In an instant the two men were wrestling about, Elda at some disadvantage with a sprained thumb. Seeing no weapons, the crowd drifted away until only two Fishers and a bead girl remained. Before Orlengis could pin Elda decisively, a pair of axemen arrived with a summons for Elda from the "Lady Rayneth"; that Orlengis grunted and stood clear was a mark of how unwilling people were to cross any of the Crescent guard.

Elda went with them, chiefly glad to be clear of Orlengis and made cautious by his continual awareness of being amputated from the protection of the Clan. His mind was full of the failure of his summons to bring him any help. He vowed to have it out with Grat what was to become of his Family and Solvig's—whether the Clan would stand to the Summerfair judgment together, or whether Grat meant to weasel out with the other nine Families, clean-handed and smug, and leave the other half of the Clan to fend for themselves as outlaws hereafter.

Occupied with such thoughts, Elda paid little attention to the novelty of speaking to a ruling stock Lady—in all but name—alone and face to face, and indeed absentmindedly addressed her as "Trader" more than once.

She was not a bad-looking woman, though skinny in his opinion and over-elaborately dressed—embroidery stiff on every inch of cloth, two and three rings to a finger, hair jewelled as well and puffed up like a jackdaw's nest. It seemed she was gathering information about old words and phrases still in use among Smiths—such phrases as *by the Wheel, seal and spit, damned, the Fool-Killer,* and a score besides. What he said was taken down by the woman herself, the quill scritching busily.

Explaining how river-slippies lived in the fogs that twirled over the water and, some said, would drink your soul if you passed through them without saying the proper charm, Elda decided this occupation of hers was no sillier than those of other Ladies he'd met or heard tell of. They were all peculiar in one way or another, as was only to be expected since they busied themselves with everything under the sun but their proper work.

When he'd been closeted with her in the enameled box of a room for a quarter hour or more, a tall fairhaired man in Andran dress strolled in, swinging a knob-handled cane, and stood inspecting the top written sheet over the woman's shoulder. She finished her line, then lifted her face, smiiing, saying to the man, "Thank you for indulging me—"

"One does not 'indulge' a scholar," he chided in reply. "Producing the first written dictionary is a great work in its own right. And he is the man who could devise and construct you a printing press, if he were so minded."

Then for a moment they were both looking at him like two civil cats, and Elda was terrified. He'd realized who it was that'd had him brought here.

"Would you prefer I retire, my lord Duke?" the woman was inquiring, already capping the mixing well and gathering up the written sheets.

"Thank you, my dear." Ashai Rey waited until a painted panel had closed behind her before settling himself in the cushioned wing chair she'd occupied, his long legs stretched out at ease, the stick extended like a third limb. "Well, Elda. It's time we talked, I think."

Elda sat perfectly still, making no reply.

"Oh, don't let's start this way," observed the mobile genially. "You swapped enough words with Lur, and no lightning has struck. . . . And there's no need, now, that your association with Lur should ever become known, unless you choose to tell it yourself. Nobody but a sanctimonious Smith would ever reproach you for the Dead Shore, for rescuing your own people under such circumstances. As a man in my service, you'll be received with honor wherever you go."

Elda fisted his right hand, damned Ashai for thinking of saving Elda's pride when he need not have: when, with Jannus' knowledge, he could have outlawed Elda ten times over at the Summerfair without having that net set and so bringing all Solvig's folk into it too.

"Well," remarked Ashai, "if you were certain of not being persuaded, you'd not hide in silence, I suppose. . . ."

"Think what you like," Elda snapped, and then leaned back in his chair and sighed. "You might as well let me go, Deepfish. Since the bridge, Grat Davitsson's been Clan leader. So even if I agreed, it wouldn't mean a thing." Elda would have let Orlengis break his arm before admitting that: now he volunteered it with a certain weary relief. It wasn't as if the Shai was a man, like other men, after all.

"I don't need the Clan," replied the Andran calmly. "I have all the ignorant hands I could possibly need or use. You, and your Family, would be enough. I'll put you in sole charge of the salvage of the High Plain, under my seal." Removing a carved ring, he tossed it on the inlaid scribe table, continuing, "It has to be done, and done now."

Presently Elda remembered to shut his mouth. "Why?"

The Andran surveyed him, a friendly appraisal. "I know you as well as is possible without a rede—no, don't worry, I won't insist on that. Whatever 'soul' you believe a rede omits, you may keep, for all of me. And I hope to make an end to redes, altogether. . . . No, as I say, I know you as . . . shall we say, a good workman? And, simply, I have a work that needs such."

"Whose idea is this—Lur's? It would be!" muttered Elda, at the Andran's quizzical nod.

"But you'll recall I've been courting your Clan's help since first thaw. And you may not know that I heard of the exile of the Innsmiths, and its term, eleven years ago. I've been waiting all this time to approach you directly. I didn't expect to be rushed, as I am now, though that was always a possibility. . . . I sent Orlengis Ras in Newstock, thinking it might help that he was close kin—by an outsider's standards, at least."

Elda snorted and the Andran shrugged ruefully, saying, "I know better now. No outsider can play politics with a family feud without getting his hands burned. So I arranged that someone set foot on the east shore of Erth-rimmon, to help clarify your alternatives. You, I'm told, and another: Solvig?"

The shrewd question startled Elda. He'd agreed before he realized it.

"That must be about half the Clan," mused Ashai.

"He should have stayed put!"

"He couldn't, any more than you could, knowing that the Wall had failed. You can't unknow what you know. . . . And now the Clan is split. That must be painful to you, having held it together for so long, waiting for your Homecoming. . . ."

"Don't talk butter," rejoined Elda roughly. "If you were all that sorry, you could have made the Corpse-eaters leave the web where it was."

"Perhaps." Ashai Rey picked up his signet again, turning it idly around one thumb. There was a small close-lamp on the table by his hand. He flipped a shutter aside and touched the wick with his ring: in a minute jolt of flame, the lamp was alight. "Perhaps," he said again, casual as though he hadn't just performed a great wonder, "it's time to stop, as you say, talking butter. Would you have taken service with Rayneth, had she asked you?"

"Might have done, for some specific chore, maybe," conceded Elda slowly.

"I thought as much, yet I didn't approach you through her. Can you guess why?"

"Because what you need done, Rayneth couldn't even pretend to know, I'd suppose. . . ."

"Exactly. Not even a Tek could direct you on the High Plain in what needs to be done. You'd have guessed—not in a month, or a season, but eventually—that it was the Shai of Down you were working for and none other, mortal or Tek. And then you'd have quit and brought your Family away, with such a knowledge of the keeps and the uses of what they contain, that nobody in the lowlands must have. Isn't that so."

". . . .Suppose so."

"You believe I have no soul, and therefore refuse to serve me. At least that's the usual Smith stand. I believe you have none either, nor anybody else, but I won't argue about it. Will you serve my son?"

Elda found himself gaping again. ". . . .What?"

"This mobile has a son. He's now twelve, born in the usual fashion, with whatever equipment your own son Dan has.

He's as yet too young to take the Rule of One into his own hand, as I mean him to do as soon as he is able—"

"You're going to make a child of that body the king of the High Plain?" asked Elda incredulously, and Ashai frowned and shook his head.

"No. That's done with. The actual title will be the Master of Andras, but he will hold the Rule of One as it can exist in these later days. The name doesn't matter. The Rule of One is always served. The Master will have in his charge all that is left of use on the High Plain. He must: otherwise there will be war, such a tidestorm of war as the lowlands have never seen, not even in the Rebellion. Can you imagine it? Eliminate the Valde, who care nothing for such tools. Eliminate the Smiths, who won't touch them, on pain of outlawry. Eliminate the Bremneri, so occupied with their little feuds that they've forgotten whatever they formerly knew of Teks, knowing no device more complicated than a steam motor. Eliminate the Fishers, disorganized and demoralized. Who, then, will be left to strip the High Plain, now that, thanks to Jannus, everybody knows there is no Barrier to prevent them?"

"Andrans. . . ." supplied Elda, seeing the sense of it.

"And what is Andras? An ambitious and adventuresome people, caged by the tidestorms to the coastal waters and the rivers, turning their energies instead to murderous intrigues against one another, each jealous and suspicious of any new power held by his neighbor, his enemy, or his ally. Arm such a people with fusers that could turn Quickmoor into ashes in the time it would take a man to walk the Crescent road from end to end; with beams like the Barrier; with contact poison and blindness. . . . Whoever takes these tools and weapons will learn enough of their uses to destroy the nearest set of reaching hands. Can you imagine, Elda, what it will be like? No sea trade, nothing crossing the bay at all. Bremner isolated, with no troopmaids to hold the stocks. Civil war, within three seasons. Smiths cut off, with nobody to buy their work or send food to maintain them. Social collapse, about seven seasons, and the first raids into Valde within ten. Andras slashing out, isle against isle, until some one faction dismembers the others and gathers all power to itself. And then that one will look toward the forests of Valde, the mines and works of the Smiths, the fields of Bremner, each in isolated confusion. Can you imagine it?"

With a certain humility, Elda replied, "I've never seen a war. Nor want to," he added, more forcefully.

"If I hold the tools, the tidestorm will never come. The tools are there, and they will be used: power doesn't just disappear because its painful; the Rule of One doesn't cease to exist merely because no one hand is chosen to hold it wisely. Better that these tools be held by the Master of Andras, controlling all the isles, than by, say, Kenniath Rey and his folk, or such as Enestro, whom I had removed. Under a united Andras, each land can follow its own ways, interrelated through Andras and its stable and enlightened trade as they are now interrelated haphazardly through Valde and the sentimental habit of its Summerfair. The tools are there, Elda. The looting is already beginnning. Who shall have the tools: the Master of Andras, or another?"

Elda shoved to his feet and swung to the painted panels concealing the door. The nearest showed a naked girl who appeared to be turning into a tree—either that or her feet and hair were badly drawn—being chased with a net by three dwarfs. Or maybe the men were supposed to be farther away. They all looked deformed.

But the adjoining panels, where they'd caught her, were worse.

"What you're saying is that the High Plain, and the way it was before, will come into the lowlands, no matter what I do or you do. It's just a question of how, an't that so."

"Not exactly. Andrans aren't Teks. There will be no deathlessness among them. And no Andran would spend a lifetime on developing a fly whose bite cures disease or on growing a forest from seed."

"That boy of yours—what's his name? You never said," inquired Elda, looking around.

"Pedross. Why do you ask?"

"Doesn't matter. So it'd be the High Plain all over again, with Pedross a king in all but name, and some new mobile at his right hand, just like before, an't that so?"

"You're avoiding the issue, Elda," commented the Andran patiently. "It's the tools. Who shall have the Tek tools? On that, the tidestorm rests. You've longed for such tools, were hungry enough for them to risk losing the Homecoming to shelter a Tek. And the power of the idea of them is nothing to the power of the tools themselves. I know you for a pragmatic man, one who can walk the Dead Shore when the need comes. Take the ring, Elda."

Elda had the notion that Ashai kept using his name partly to remind himself who he was talking to. "The boy—Pedross. Do you care anything about him?"

"Certainly," replied Ashai coldly, yet a little puzzled.

"Come a choice between your precious Rule of One, say, and the boy. . . . Suppose he didn't like being king, once he'd tried it, say. What then?"

"Then I'd have to find and train another to be Master of Andras. He'd be no use, actively, consciously, resisting me."

"And what'd become of him, then?"

"Why, I have no idea. What difference would it make?"

"I don't know. 'Tan't likely anyhow. . . ." Elda tried to think, believing the case had been put to him fairly, trying to imagine the whole world as he knew it tearing its own throat out. The pain of believing it could happen was almost too great to be borne. It ran right through him, making his eyes feel hot and dry and his cheeks stiff as wood. He found himself thinking again of that poor child Pedross, born, bred, and even conceived, by the Wheel, to a purpose beyond himself like a goat, but without even a goat's moment of hot pleasure at his kindling for an excuse. . . .

"You send that skinny whore before the Clan," he said abruptly, "and let her tell how you tided her into the rule of a Bremneri freeport. Let them choose. Send them Orlengis, to tell what a fine master you make—how you only let the man who murdered his da for the boat keep *half* the boat and then let Orlengis *work* for him to buy it back. Great Wheel! And he's *proud* of that!"

"It satisfied his custom, which was all that was needed."

No words would say it. Elda reached past the proffered ring to grab the searing glass of the lamp and flung it across the room, where it burst in a flash of igniting oil that pooled and blazed on the tiles.

"I'd sooner go to the fire myself. I'd sooner the Clan was split, or all gone to the fire, then have them or their children come to be grateful for such justice as Orlengis got because I bent my neck to the Deepfish or handfasted myself to a boy too young to know what's been set going in his name. No. The Rule of One an't all there is. There's right, and there's wrong. If the Empire comes back, it comes—but not through me. We were spared in the fall of Kantmorie. Maybe we'll be spared your tidestorm too."

The room reeked with smoke. The fire flickered only in the channels between the tiles now, outlining them with hic-

uping round-topped flames. The room, and everything in it,
eemed to be twitching.

Ashai warned, "You'll be outlawed. And when you are,
ou'll be any man's meat: to take, or kill, or use any way he
leases."

"That just may be," Elda replied, cradling his scorched
and. "But I recall hearing you expected the tidestorm once
efore, and it never came. Maybe you don't know everything
ou think you do."

Elda swung around and shoved blindly against panels until
he hit one that gave, and passed by unmoving sentries again
nto the open and the clean smell of the river.

Jannus was led circumspectly into Han Halla. Poli relied
for her bearings, she'd told him, on those plants that were
aware of the invisible sun. She avoided the sinkponds partly
by knowing what sort of flowers preferred them; though twice
in the first few days she'd stood quite still and unslung her
bow, for him to hold to, to help her ease free of the deadly
footing. Jannus followed, as far as was possible, precisely in
her footsteps except when crossing the broad spongy mats of
entangled lily stems, roots, and float bladders. These sometimes were broad enough to take most of a day to cross; he
and Poli always found one to camp on when the light began
to fail and the Powers could no longer guide them.

There were some plants that felt the tide; but he and Poli
had to stay beyond reach of the tideflow, so by night they
rested, with nothing to mark the passing of one hour into the
next until finally the light began to seep back and they could
go on.

North became simply where the water lay sweeter and
south, where it turned strongly brackish twice a day. And
only the flowers and Poli knew east or west. Thus, she guided
him.

There was no such place as far away, except in the mind.
Han Halla was like a land in a cloud or the deep floor of a
sea of air. The sun was visible only one day in five, and then
at midday only, as a golden directionless glow overhead. The
moon was not to be seen at all, or the stars Jannus was accustomed to view as sentries holding the sky secure in the
days of the moon's absence.

When there was no rain, there was mist to make all distances equal. No chill breeze stirred, no hot sun baked. The
chains of high lilies and low lilies, the multihued mosses and

ferns spread like mosaic isles of feathers, the unfamiliar open-mouthed flowers with ribbonlike tongues trailing along the surface, all bloomed and rested according to their own rhythms, as though Han Halla kept a perpetual high summer. Impartial lilies floated on sinkpools and shallows and every flower rested with its image.

The first morning he'd been conscious of the danger, for a little while. An hour after they entered the mists, he'd been utterly lost. The folly of his plan to cross the fens alone chastened him. But soon, with wariness undimmed, he absorbed the tranced airs of the place and willingly surrendered accounts of days, thoughts of before and behind.

Once, while Poli was off hunting and he waited on the knees of an immense, almost leafless tree dripping with hairlike mosses, Jannus tried to compare his present mood with that brought by the wine of Ashai Rey; but it wasn't really like that at all. It was different. Then he forgot about it in watching a dipper bird poking among the grasses, bobbing its body in a way he found comical.

And when Poli came back with a large fish spitted on an arrow and a bundle of dry wood to add to the stock they collected and carried, she was humming cheerfully, willing to stay or continue. Jannus used his own knife, it having the better blade, to scale and clean the fish. Poli folded their daymeal in a lily pad and they drifted on without a word said or needed.

"Don't split the Clan," Elda pleaded, standing apart with Solvig as his cousin put out the last of the night's watchfires.

For answer, Solvig tipped his head toward the two separate groups of laden Families that stared at each other in the pallid light from beyond the border mists of Han Halla; behind Solvig's Family was the paved way and the wet slatey roofs of Quickmoor, seeming to hover over dim emptiness. The Clan was split already, the gesture meant; and on Solvig's right thumb was the seal ring of Ashai Rey.

"At least let the Smith Council hear the thing, make its judgment," Elda argued. "You can go contract with the Deepfish after, if you must. But—"

"I'm contracted to the boy, and an't a breathing soul can claim different." Solvig finished wetting the fire and began stirring the steaming chips morosely with a stick. He looked sick, hopeless; Elda blamed Ashai, who'd sent axemen to fetch Solvig while still cajoling Elda in that stinking jewel-box of a chamber. That, thought Elda, won the year's prize for all-round gall.

"An't the boy's ring you're wearing."

"You want to see the tidestorm come, then? 'Maybe it won't,' with nothing to hold it up—that an't no answer." Solvig faced off toward Han Halla. "Look at that, Elda. You expect I'll put my Family through that bog for nothing? It an't the same with us as with you. You had reason but I walked the Dead Shore for pride. The Council'd outlaw us sure. You know it too. There's just no use in it. '

"An't it worth the chance?"

Solvig just let the stick drop and turned stoop-shouldered back among his own Family, gathered on the outer stones of the Crescent. While Elda continued to argue, Solvig bent down by his allotted pile of bundles and began looping their cords over his arms and neck.

Alis, his wife, helped him arrange the load; she said to Elda, "Let him be! We been all through this with Grat, and with Inetta, twenty times over. It's sealed, settled. Anyhow 'tan't yours to decide no more, Elda Hildursson—"

"Shut your mouth, 'Liz," said Solvig.

"Forget Grat putting you from the Clan," urged Elda. "My Family'll stand with you in this. Just come to the Summerfair, try! Grat and his piddling Families of two granddas and a lackwit cousin—Deepfish didn't even trouble to have *him* fetched—'

"Grat never touched the Dead Shore. We're the ones that carry that stink—just your Family and mine. Chances are, you'll be outlawed too, with Orlengis there to speak against you, and afterward, just meat to whoever can get at you quickest. At least I got Ashai's hand over me and mine, and that's some better than nothing. . . . I don't see what good you see in going."

"They have to lift the Ban. Somebody has to tell them so, tell them why!" Elda had been thinking about it all night, and decided it was the only way.

"Let Grat do it," rejoined Solvig listlessly.

"Grat couldn't talk a fish into eating flies. Grat don't know what I know, and he an't got at stake what I do. Somebody's got to try and make the Council see plain sense, 'Vig—come that far with us. Don't split the Clan!"

"An't no use in it," Solvig said again, standing crooked under his load. "Grat's put me and mine out of the Clan, and the Council will hold him right in it and outlaw us, and that'll be the way of it. We been among strangers all my life, and Torve's and Hildur's before that. There's worse things. If worse comes to worst, you come to us. We'll make a new Clan between us—"

"With our necks bent to the Deepfish? Man, are you in such a rush to make Fishers of all your near kin?"

Solvig started toward the dark roofs, saying, "An't such a Fisher as to go back on a sealed contract. You try, if you have to. But if worse comes to worst, you come to us."

While Solvig and his Family grew gradually more indistinct, Grat's confederation began moving toward the dim sunrise with the Valde ranging along the edges of the crowd like herders. Two hung back until Elda was ready to turn from the empty road and, with his Family, step down from the last paving stones into the mud.

Poli said. "You still don't know how to swim," finding him to blame for it though it was her first mention of the subject. "Going round everything deeper than a duckpond takes twice as long."

He blinked, not quite awake yet but happy, saying, "I'm in no rush to get to the Summerfair." Teasing, but without the usual bitter undertaste of earlier days.

"You should be able to take more care of yourself, do some of your own watching." After all, there would come an end to this drifting. He should be getting ready for that instead of behaving as though they'd gone on *fai* together.

"I'm wet enough to start," he commented, still untroubled, wringing a few drops from a sleeve.

"It rains nearly all the time here," Poli informed him. "You're not used to it."

"On the contrary, I was raised underwater in a large pearl-colored cave. Two of my brothers were fish: one was a—"

She had no intrest in such chat. She chose out that pool where there seemed to be the fewest yellow snakes (the brown ones fled any approach, and could be ignored) and began his instruction.

Much sooner than she'd expected, he was stroking about with confidence and enthusiasm, almost quietly. The way the water helped him, as long as he kept his back straight, especially delighted him. But he refused to open his eyes underwater, claiming it was too murky to see anything anyway—which was likely true, after all the flailing around he'd done.

When she decided he was only playing, she gathered up their bundles and hurried him on, circling only those pools that stretched out into the mist without visible shore or resting place.

She began commenting, every evening, on how much farther they were going in each day's travel, though she wasn't at all sure: one mere was so like the next, and the one before. Nevertheless she had decided it was so, and was continually expecting to tread unexpectedly into the first patch of Lifganin sunlight or strike the first dry ground or catch the daysong of the open plains beyond the eastern margin of the marsh. She was perpetually disappointed. He, still on *fai*, accepted without argument her claims that the sun was really up, or really hadn't quite set, though it stretched their day of journey beyond dark and dark.

But one morning—if such skyless, frog-resonant shadow could have been honestly mistaken for morning by anyone— he refused to budge, cheerfully claiming it was the first day of summer, a holiday. He had no more idea of the day, or the week, than she did. But that didn't prevent him from steadfastly maintaining today was a holiday.

"Not even Fishers have to work on Summerday," he invented brightly. "That's the day they come from all around to stare at a knife and fork laid on a rock in the exact center of the Is marshes. They—"

"Then do as you will. I'll hunt."

He didn't mention the darkness, or the half-duck remaining, already cooked, from the day before. He thought she was lonely for the rest of the troopmaids, or was wearying of his uninterrupted company, or feared to be late for the Summerfair. . . .

She only knew she had to get away.

She set out east as soon as the plants could discern the sun, at a pace too swift for hunting. From a sense of responsibility she kept a bit of her attention on Jannus, though as the sun ascended, she'd have been too far away to have been of any help, if help was needed. By the time the sun was overhead (requiring a grudged stop until it canted west) she should have been a great distance away. She was sure she'd followed almost a straight path, without rest or pause. Yet the mutter of his moods reached her as clearly as though he were beside her. Indeed, she had to concentrate to focus the always-faint vegetable sun-awareness that guided her.

And still she'd seen no clear patch of sky nor any stretch of land not balanced on a basket of roots and stems, with water beneath.

The sun moved, and she went on.

He was beginning to worry about her. That irritated her. She forgot or put aside the memory of the two sink-ponds, of the quiet yellow snakes that crushed large prey and stored it underwater until it was reduced to manageable chunks. Nevertheless she turned back.

Still later he began to be afraid for both of them, which made her push to regain her morning's pace, following the fading light.

For a while something stalked her. The birds were aware of it, and started up in alarm at the limits of her hearing, but the stalker itself somehow eluded her seeking *marenniath*. Eventually she outdistanced it, or it lost interest, or else she simply forgot about it in the sense of what a long useless run she'd had.

As she was going cautiously, with the nightly percussions of frogs peeping and booming, rebounding like echoes from all dark sides, she caught the tang of woodsmoke. Eventually she spotted the fire and wearily threaded the meres between.

He tried to tease her about her emptyhandedness after such a long hunt, but soon fell silent—outwardly composed, inwardly resentful of her abrupt return without apology or explanation, hoping for explanations, at least.

Making an effort, she responded, "I needed to find out how far it was to Lifganin, to the other side."

He listened, ready to find out. Finally he asked out loud, "Well, how far—"

"I don't know."

"I was worried about you," he next said diffidently, serving up a bowl of duck mixed with rice. It seemed she'd taken the pouch of salt with her, not noticing. She seasoned her food, then set the pouch where he could reach it.

"Poli, are you angry at me, or what?"

"Angry?" She examined the question in some surprise. "I've no reason to be angry with you."

"I do not hear that as an answer."

"Then, no: I'm not angry at you." She tried to attend only to her food, so conscious of his bewilderment and resentful anxiety that she found it more difficult than usual to be sure which feelings were his, and which were her own.

Afterward she busied herself with oiling her harness, taking the spare bowstrings from their watertight case to rub them with wax, putting salve on fresh blisters. All that while her *marenniath* was lunging outward for a trace of the dry grasslands: though in the dark she could not have told swamp from hill, were the hill only beyond the rim of the firelight. She could not rid herself of the oppressive pulsing of the frogs.

Finally, with a kind of ferocity, she let her hands fall idle and made a serious attempt to enter dueltrace, seeking Lifganin as though it were a person.

What she chiefly heard was Jannus. She couldn't block him out. Her immobility alarmed him, which made it that much harder to block his *farioh* and made her that much more frantic. A cycle of echoes and re-echoes of increasing intensity was linked that spun her into panic and engulfed her.

She came to herself lying on one of the canvas groundcovers. The fire was out. Jannus was awake, terribly upset, somewhere close by. Controlling her own answering panic as best she could, Poli got her elbows under her, discovering at once that she had a violent headache and felt sick and disoriented.

"I'm all right," she announced rapidly, "I swear I'm all right. Stop—try to stop being frightened, it makes it worse. Please, I'm—"

The impact of his reaction, the white-hot relief/dread/love bursting like visible light, again shattered her self-possession.

The mists were pale yellow when she emerged from nightmares of random flight. Her head and shoulders were cradled against Jannus' chest. He was half-dozing, stroking the side of her face mechanically as if he'd been doing so for hours.

When she stirred, he woke fully and put his hand down to steady himself; but his *farioh* remained cool. Poli thought of it as green, stirring cautiously around her like cool green smoke. While the light increased neither of them moved, sharing exhaustion and caution.

"I should have warned you," she muttered, able to be calm because he was so. "I was trying to force dueltrance, to reach Lifganin. Your concern started a mood echo. I was locked in."

"I don't understand." Cool, green, undemanding.

She tried to explain dueltrance to him—the rapt closeness that gradually excluded all else. As she spoke she was aware of his withdrawal to pursue a separate line of thought. And that succession of attitudes, as clear to her as speech, made her fall silent.

For it was true. She'd been in something like dueltrance for days. That was why she'd had so little energy to set up a rival, conscious focus. That was why the echo had been so devastating.

"Are we duelling, then?" Jannus asked in a light tone, his *farioh* damped rigidly to life-sounds alone—like the impersonal sound of the frogs, or of breathing.

"The troopmaids learn to call it dueltrance," she said, the words dull in her mouth. "That is what we use it for. But it . . . it has other uses. . . ."

After a while he said again, "Are we duelling, Poli? Or what?"

"I don't know. Too tired to think in words any more—"

He understood the appeal, and outwardly complied. But there was a kind of ruthlessness rising in him that wouldn't let either of them rest, though he'd retreated to the far side of the lumpy floating mat and said nothing. A few paces made no difference at all. It was as if he were breathing in her ear and, some minute soon, might shout.

At the same time it seemed to her that she was being watched: that her smallest action was being observed and minutely examined, and it was therefore of incalculable importance that she do nothing, disappear.

There was a jarring, regular pain in the back of her neck, spilling into an unsuspected crevice behind her eyes. Squinting against the distraction, she found footing on the ropy surface of the mat and started away. *Away* was a secret direction, known only to herself.

Her arm was caught and she stood passively, balancing. He was close again. It made no difference. Short-tempered, stiff, tired, frightened and impatient, he inquired patiently whether it was light enough for her to hear the flowers, to know what pools were safe. She shook her head, recalling that as the proper gesture. She was free to go away, having made the proper sign.

But he was still close, still holding her in place, which surprised her. But there was no difference, close or far. The breathing was there, regardless: personal, his own.

He wanted to know was it an echo again, what he should do to help, or stop, or do, how—

And he was still there, once more doing no more than

breathe and hold her arm. His face was averted so he'd not see her and so react to her distress.

Somehow he was telling himself a story. His cheek was like plaster, but, inside, he was telling himself some story with quiet things in it, images of patience, mild curious seeking, green. . . . It was the story of the moon lost in the water, the one he'd made up on the paddlewheeler. The details of words were gone from her but the images linked steadily, predictably.

Her stifled feeling withdrew.

Like one fetching a stone out of a deep well, or climbing a narrow railless stair, she slowly emerged from the echo, holding steady whenever the story faltered, then balancing on his renewed painful calm to rouse her awareness of the crooked fibres underfoot, the nearer pools, the lilies and fish of different sorts, the nine distinct birds stirring within her range. Thus supported she reconstructed the world around her until it was whole.

And she found he was still there, exactly the same. He didn't know she'd come back.

But of course. He couldn't know.

She had to pinch him to recall him from the story, his final strong place—like a windowless room with thick cool walls. He eventually risked meeting her eyes, wanting certainty that it was safe now to come out, let go, stop.

Reaching to her neck to unfasten the bridestone, she idly thought of the Summerfair, wondering what sort of man she might otherwise have been drawn to choose.

There were no proper cups, so she stooped to dip water into her palm; and, still uncomprehending, he did likewise when she told him to. She turned their two hands, palm to palm, saying, "Water into water," and watched the drops fall. Then she gave him their bridestone.

Once off the High Plain Lur almost starved before he gained enough coordination to hunt. It wasn't that the body was defective: his mind simply lacked the experience to operate it efficiently. So much of the sense data was different, so much unintelligible to him at first. Odors, especially, were incredibly varied and pungent, yet had no meaning at all. It was as if he'd acquired an entirely new sense. It took him four days even to realize that prey downwind could smell *him*, whereas prey upwind could not.

The distortion in hearing was less marked, but still confusing. He'd never been a studier of living animals. A rattle in the grass was merely a rattle in the grass until a spear-billed wader erupted into his face, defending her nest; he nearly lost an eye. Even sounds familiar to him in former bodyings were magnified and sharp and so turned strange, perplexing.

Colors, conversely, had ceased to exist. He saw everything in shades of grey that merely darkened somewhat after nightfall. His night vision was quite good. But he had to learn to judge distances all over again. His eyes were nearer the ground, unless he reared up on his hind legs—awkward and conspicuous in that position. And with only moderate effort the beast he wore could spring thirty feet. He often judged things as effectively farther than they were and overleaped them.

This disorientation led him to prefer easy prey, such as Fishers. He could smell their stores of sun-dried fish at vast distances and call the Fishers from their fires out into the dark. For the beast he wore could speak in a human voice. That had been well done, in his opinion. His articulation sounded normal even to his newly-acute hearing, yet the requisite alterations in the beast's mouth and throat didn't interfere with his eating.

He'd stay with a kill for about a day, alternately dozing and acquiring greater skill in handling the beast's enormous strength and flexibility of response. Though he often had to range widely in his hunting he always returned within sight of the cliff by daylight. It was his own reliable bearing in the increasing sameness of marshlands.

Since Cliffhold had still been functional when he left, with no sign yet of looters, he had some idea of how much time had passed since Lisle. The Innsmiths and Jannus would be far ahead. Therefore he travelled across the precipitous canyons and rock-choked ravines aproning the cliff's southern face, only descending into the slow lowland mists to forage and drink.

The farther he went from Erth-rimmon, the scarcer became prey he could catch. For almost a week he subsisted on mouthfuls of marsh hens—eating them in their feathers he found disagreeable—and one rabbit in twenty he'd bound after.

Han Halla seemed totally unpeopled, at least within the range of his hunting forays. As the beast he wore had no natural enemies, being unique, it had no natural prey. The rare wild hog he'd find far enough from its pack to be safely taken only gave him strength to go on, without satisfying him. He began to pay for the beast's size and power with unending violent hunger.

It was fortunate, he thought in an objective moment, that he hadn't found the Innsmiths. If in fact they'd pursued their intended route through Han Halla, they were apparently following a longer circle farther south, deeper in the swamp than he dared go. Lur knew he couldn't have taken an Innsmith here without risking being hunted in turn by the Newstock freemaids. And though he was no longer bodied as a child, he'd be reluctant to face such pursuit again, especially on ground so treacherous to swift retreat, ground that would speak to Valde with so many living voices, surrounding and defining his own silence. A disciplined troop of Valde was probably the only force capable of hunting him to the death; it was probably as well that he wouldn't be tempted to make trial of it before the grass plains of Lifganin gave him a clear uncomplicated chance at Jannus. After that, he didn't care.

One twilight, beginning his hunting sweep, he heard the regular splashing that meant a runner and drifted closer to investigate. He couldn't discern colors but the tabard itself identified the runner as a Valde who'd served in Bremner. Probably, he thought, she'd be an advance scout for the Innsmiths and in link with the rest of the troop. Reluctantly he let her pass.

Munching a frog somewhat later, he took sardonic consolation in the fact that at least there was no lack of water.

Two or three days after that, in the forenoon, he came upon a uniformed Fisher quite by surprise. The Fisher was concealed in the high sawgrass and Lur, waking right into him, lashed out reflexively and broke his back.

Lur regretted the kill. He'd have preferred to have asked a few questions first.

Just before nightfall, as he lay dozing lethargically, a trampling and splashing brought him alert. The noise was converging on him from all sides. Rolling to his feet, he thrust into the sawgrass field where the man had lain hidden. Taking care with each step, he passed between two of the advancing ring. They too were Fishers, apparently in search of the man he'd taken, cautiously calling a sibillant name. Lur circled around behind them, listening and watching.

They found his kill and at least one of his tracks. All he overheard were frightened exclamations and a quarrel over whether to disobey orders by lighting a lantern—whose orders, they didn't say. Discipline prevailed. The swamp darkened at its own pace.

One man began tooting on a sort of flute, playing only a few short passages. The call was echoed both to the north and to the south, from far away. Lur had heard that noise before, but had assumed it to be the call of one of the thousands of birds he didn't know. He became even more interested.

The whole crowd moved into an outward-facing circle. Lur caught the shine of several broadknives with metal edges. The Fishers stood whispering dull things like, "What was that!" and Lur dropped his chin onto crossed forepaws; nothing else happened for quite a while.

At last, out of the south, a complicated passage reached the tense huddle, within which a muffled quarrel erupted over who was going to stay behind. Blows were struck, though apparently not with the broadknives for there was no scent of blood; eventually the luckless one took the flute and the rest retreated in a scampering rush. Presently there was the glow of a lantern, tiny with distance.

The remaining Fisher, having pushed through the tall grass to open water, swam to one of the rafts of stems and roots to take up his vigil.

When Lur could scarcely discern the raft, and judged it would be pitch black by human standards, he slid into the water and began paddling out. The beast wasn't well adapted for swimming but could function well enough at need.

He'd forgotten that the mat would tilt under his weight. The Fisher had had more foresight than he. Screeching, the man leaped headlong into the lake, threshing frantically. Lur, panting, was about to go after him when sounds indicated the Fisher's noisy haste had attracted the attentions of one of those middle-sized constrictors.

Lur sighed and, with great care, paddled indirectly back to the grass.

The crowd, he discovered, had taken the rest of his kill, which he considered spiteful of them. Nevertheless he settled down to see if still another would come to replace the one taken by the constrictor. When he'd waited quite a while, and heard distant flutings several times in two directions, and still nothing had happened, he lost patience and interest together and jogged east where the dawn was gathering. When the sun edged into view, it was over hills.

Thoroughly delighted, Lur bounded into the grasslands. He'd hated the enternal mists of the fens: they were too nearly a roof for his comfort.

His morning redeemed his frustrating night when he encountered a grazing herd of large animals—some sort of outsized goats or antelope—and pulled down a yearling. The rest of the herd attacked but he kept them at bay long enough to drag his kill into a dead tree, feeding then at leisure and humming to himself.

Elda, with his Family about him, was just finishing his meal of cold oat gruel and plant stems the Valde claimed were decent fodder for humans, when Grat came over from his Families' fire: plunging, sliding, falling chest-deep, as they all did in this unholy muck.

Elda'd never had much use for Grat. Grat's habit was to squeeze up his wizened fat-nosed face and find objections to anybody else's ideas; and his only son, Frid, was misfortunate in his bones, always breaking one or the other, so nobody wanted Frid for their daughters or marriagable kin. Grat had a standing grievance with the other Family heads on that account. Now he was Clan leader.

Settling on the raft of roots, Grat opened a bandanna full of some sort of seed pods. Dan took one, reporting it was good: "Tastes like rye bread, more or less." The boy offered some to his mother. Medd likewise said they were good, the tastiest thing she'd had since the boughten bread went bad. Then, politely, she and the boy sloshed off and settled with Dinnel's family, to leave the men alone.

After some aimless trade of talk about the damp-foot and Frid's sprained knee, from falling with his leg jammed between two roots, Grat scowled at his fists a moment before coming to his real business: "We been within spitting distance of dry land for a week, did you know that?"

"How'd I know? All this bog looks alike."

"An't you going to ask why we an't out of it, then?"

Elda reached for one of the pods. Chiefly, it tasted dry: a fine taste. "Figure you came to tell me that."

"There's Andrans on the grass!" Grat burst out, as though he'd found worms in his supper. "Andrans and Fishers besides, out of Ardun-town, the Valde say. They're just waiting for us to come out where they can grab us! We went north, but they can go faster on grass than us in this muck, with so many half-lamed. . . . We doubled back south, but they turned with us. They're there now, just a mile or two off. Hear that?"

Elda listened, shook his head.

"Listen: there. That hoot."

Elda heard it, a hollow musical note that rose clear of the endless shrilling and booming of the frogs, the whine of bugs. It seemed to echo more faintly, far away.

"That's their sentries," Grat stated. "They're spread along every mile of the edge of this swamp. Took one, day before yesterday, but they knew by the quiet he was gone. We didn't know their signals, and they whistled and piped for hours, so there was nothing gained, they knew we were here, so we turned the fellow loose again. We can't fight 'em, and we can't stay here beyond another day or two—with the food gone, and the Valde. . . . The Valde, they're gone now. All but two. They left, for fear they won't come to the Summerfair before the husbands run out, green daughters of snakes that they are."

"Two: Aliana, that'd be," said Elda soberly. "And who else?"

"Who knows? But two an't no help. Can't hunt for all of us, nor help against those stinking Andrans. Just up and left us, the rest did, about an hour ago. . . . So what'd you do, if you was me?"

Elda thought Grat seemed to have tried all the sensible things, though he didn't say so. Likely he'd done what Aliana told him to, anyhow. "From Ardun, the freeport, you said? That's Domal Ai, that's Master there. What's he want with us, do you think?"

Grat spat to one side. "What do Andrans ever want?"

"I suppose. It an't seemly, the way they been courting Innsmiths, this spring. . . . Well, you can't stay or go back, and you can't go around and get past them. So what do you expect me to say?"

"Well," said Grat, blinking uncomfortably, "there's this chance. . . . If they had my folk, or yours, they might be satisfied and go home."

"And you think it should be mine. That stinks."

"Now, hold up. I think it should be mine. The Clan. We done nothing. We got a right to the Homecoming. So it could be that the Council would make the Master of Ardun give us up. But your folk, they could be lost, like the Tresmiths. . . . So I figure it should be us, to go out on the grass."

Elda took another pod and was silent awhile. "Grat Davitsson, you always been a squint-eyed whiner and a nuisance," he remarked softly and with affection. "Can you see my Family begging favors of the Council, us with the stink of the Dead Shore on us, saying we're what's left of the Innsmith Clan? They wouldn't even give us a hearing. They'd outlaw us, first thing. And then who'd speak for you, tied to work tables down in Ardun?"

"Maybe so, maybe no," replied Grat, in the dubious, faintly insulting tone Elda had learned to dislike in thirty years of Clan meetings. Now, Elda was scarcely aware of it. "Nor you nor I know what the Council will do," Grat went on. "But somebody has to stay, and I'd sooner it was us. We got the best chance of getting free again."

"A chance you could put in your eye and not blink."

"Better than all of us taken, and nobody left to speak for us! Seems to me you walked the Dead Shore, when you were Clan leader, because it was needful. Seems like this is needful now, in my turn."

They sat a while. Then Elda said, "What'd your Families say, to this?"

"One thing and another. You know."

"Surely."

"Damn: here comes the rain again," remarked Grat casually, and made the mistake of looking up. After a bit of coughing, he went on, "You led us twenty-seven years, come first frost. They'd see you put out of the Clan so long as you'd get your say before the Council, fair and square. But not like this. You know. . . . I just come to tell you, so you wouldn't follow along behind us and then wonder where all the pikemen come from. You stay here. The Valde will stay to show you a way out, once everybody's gone. Me, I wouldn't trust myself to find my nose with both hands in all this, without a Valde to hang onto."

"No. No: it can't go that way," Elda said, bitterly, reluctantly. "You earned your Homecoming. You'd be heard. You and yours stay here, then speak for us before the Council. You got the best chance. At the worst, the Clan wouldn't be lost."

"A Clan of seventy-two souls?" Grat broke in. "What are we, a troop of Valde, to come to the Summerfair with a fifth of what we started with and count ourselves lucky?"

Shushing him with one hand, Elda continued, "And it'd be better to be under Domal Ai than handfasted to the Deepfish, like Solvig. You and yours stay here. Look at the thing plain: it's the best chance, an't it?"

"My Families won't stand for it. . . ."

"Then don't tell 'em till we're gone. I didn't ask advice before I walked the Dead Shore to loose that web. By the time they've missed us, they'll think again."

Elda had hoped to speak to the Council from what he'd learned of the High Plain and of Ashai Rey, to warn them about the tidestorm of sudden change and war ready to break over their heads if they stubbornly held to the old ways; he looked sadly at Grat and said nothing of this, knowing Grat would ruin about any cause with pleading it. Elda didn't even trust Grat to talk the Council into making Domal Ai let them go—and that was an ordinary matter of decency and general common sense, compared to telling the Smiths they had to lift the Ban on the High Plain after the better part of two thousand years. . . .

As if aware of the thought, Grat said, "I'll do what I can. The Council has the say to outlaw you or no, not Domal Ai. He can't just steal you, before the Council has had its say. There's the matter of Amel Tresmith's folk, that were taken, and the Council never said *boo*. That was a black shame on them, and I figure to tell them why."

Elda tried to picture that—Grat, with his whiny voice and his red screwed-up face, like a babe ready to scream, hopping up and down and hollering "Shame!" at the Council. He just nodded.

Near the margins of Han Halla Jannus woke from troubled dreams to find the country in expectation of the dawn.

First the mists stirred, folding like pale silk; the frogs' creaking faltered gradually into total silence. Poli's slow breath came warm against his neck.

By degrees the three layers of vegetation acquired color, as though it were a liquid they drew out of the earth; light seemed to shine through these colors rather than upon them: the sky was still dark. On every side birds were waking.

An edge of the sky became streaked with pink and fallow gold, reflected perfectly on the stillness of the nearest broad mere. Poli stirred then and they loved unhurriedly until after the sun's enormous rim lifted above the fog-guarded flatlands.

This sun was vast and mild, effulgent as it drew itself from the shining waters; Jannus found that two hands, extended in a long stretch, were too small to eclipse it. Gathering its ponlerous glory about itself, it changed from an oblong to a round that diminished to the size of a copper and, a hard white disc, shielded itself at last in cloud.

Sight of the sun roused in them again a hunger for solid ground and distances, so they decided to travel today rather than spending the morning fishing and swimming idly, as they often did: for they were no longer journeying but wandering in what Poli called *larfai*, with no purpose save their own contentment from moment to moment.

As they strolled along the edge of a mere, Jannus considered their reflections. He had the respectable beginnings of a beard which seemed to intend to be curly, though his hair was so straight he'd improvised a headband from a bowstring to keep it from continually falling over his eyes. Poli's hair, perpetually wet like his own, had grown into a dense crest of shaded bone-yellow. But then, it hadn't been cut since she'd won the bridestone, whereas he'd been neatly barbered by Medd a day or so before Elda had abandoned him. And Jannus had no idea how long ago that'd been.

Thought of the bridestone made him seek its reflection. It'd gotten inside his sark again, as it had a habit of doing: he fished it out and looked back to the image. But the mere, jarred minutely by their footfalls along its rim, was too poor a mirror for fine detail.

Grasses ahead stirred, and Jannus lifted a hand to the loops of the dart-strap he wore: but Poli said, "Weasel," and he let the hand fall. She had no weapon ready to hand. The straps of her harness had begun rubbing red weals on her shoulders, so she now carried her quiver and bowcase rolled into her bedding. Jannus carried the strap with its pads of darts, having a good eye for a mark.

Jannus drifted into thoughts of the grasslands, the forests beyond, and the Summerfair.

"Why?" said Poli after a while, and one hand moved slightly, implying she didn't see any sense in continuing that journey now.

Well, they had to go somewhere. . . . "No, what I really mean is, why not?" Her sidewise glance was quite pointed, and he laughed. "But I'd like to see the Summerfair just the same. No Bremneri—no man, anyhow—has seen it that I've ever heard of. There's more than the bridings, after all. There's the Choosings and the Troopcalling, and there's the Innsmiths, too—their Homecoming."

He'd like to reach the Summerfair before them, to greet Elda with Poli beside him and watch Elda's face.

"If you want to," responded Poli indifferently. Shifting her bundle to the other hand, she said, "Not so different as you, from your women."

He looked over at her dubiously. "Whose women?"

"Of Bremner. Valde men are not unlike us, to look at. . . . They do not grow hair on their faces, or elsewhere, except on their heads. They do not use the breathtalk much," she listed, with obvious care to be precise. "You asked me," she added, puzzled by his reaction.

He didn't realize he'd been wondering about that, not specifically. But that wouldn't prevent Poli from catching a flash of something, just enough for her to glimpse the rest. Sometimes he found her new unwilled sensitivity preturnatural and rather disquieting.

"I don't know," she said, again an answer. "About what other Valde will feel about us. I don't know."

"Well, pretend you're a Hafera Valde," he suggested, "wedded these ten years, with two crops of children, and you meet a Valde freemaid—"

"I'm not a freemaid."

"All right, a lar Haffa who's served her term in Newstock only to marry a deaf Bremneri, getting into love-trance with him partly out of isolation. What would you make of her?"

Poli shook her head, unwilling to pretend so involved a thing. He was bothering her, he could tell, but he was bothered himself and didn't care. He was entitled to be bothered, had a right to feel whatever he felt—as long as there was no danger of starting one of those agonizing echoes.

She'd assured him that as soon as he stopped trying to block and deny that part of herself that was him—which he still didn't altogether understand—but as soon as she'd stopped, the chance of such a cycle building was all but gone. Only if they both panicked at the same time was there any risk. Knowing himself not prone to panic, Jannus wasn't worried about that any more. He'd even gained some liking for the smaller mood-echoes. In touch-loving, for instance, they were especially nice although of course he could appreciate only the result, not the process itself.

Touch-loving. That was what Poli named it. Merleen, his assigned mistress, had referred to it as pact-renewal, a recollection that made him grin wryly.

Poli had relaxed: so she'd caught that last sequence too.

Just the same, he wondered how she felt about meeting her kin, so brided. She certainly wasn't eager to return to Valde. . . .

"I can't hear when you do that," she complained.

Hear anything else, she meant. Jannus was becoming used to translating. "I worry about your being hurt," he rejoined, just as crossly. "Is that so strange?"

"Jannus 1'," she replied, suddenly gentle, "all things come when they come. I can't treat these may-be mists as real, now. *Now* is all there is. I'm not good at supposing."

He knew that, as a fact. But knowing her ways emotionally, he was discovering, was a different matter entirely. He kept expecting her reactions to be like his own, which he considered stupid of him but which he continued to do just the same. Whereas her way was not to expect at all, applying the energy instead to the moving present in a manner he found difficult to visualize.

And yet, that she kept defying his expectations was less distressing to him than the discovery that he could no longer predict himself. He was prey to inexplicable intense moods arising for no reasons he could identify, which drove him to say and do things that later often puzzled and disturbed him. Bluejay would have thought it a spell, witchery of some sort; but he knew that though Poli might have waked something, she had no power to put it there. The perpetual sense of motion, the sudden upwellings, were all from his own nature.

Nor was Poli responsible for the dreams, in which she seldom even appeared. Yet nightmares had lately begun erupting into his sleep, often waking Poli with their ferocity. The instant he woke, the terror plunged beyond his mind's reach; but he could reconstruct images of loss and change, and feelings of smothering enclosure, tinting ordinary things with a dread unavailable to his waking mind. Poli could name to him what she heard in his *farioh* at such times; but she could make no interpretations, lacking that special skill, she said.

Along with these changes, Jannus sometimes recognized in himself a weariness like that of a swimmer on the skin of swift turbulent deeps. Sometimes he got tired of *feeling* all the time and wanted just to rest on the surface, drift, in spite of the danger.

Valde weren't like that. If she'd married a Valde, their moods would be flowing in easy harmony unvexed by expectations, confusions, words, or shameful tiredness.

"If you wanted to," he inquired, believing himself only

curious, "could you still choose a man of your own kin, at the Summerfair?"

Poli whirled around, visibly angry. He thought she meant to hit him. But the striking hand grabbed the bridestone and yanked, breaking the cord. Before he could stop her she'd hurled the stone as hard as she could away into the lake.

"There," she snapped, "do you believe it now, that we are bound and I will not leave you?"

But he'd treasured the bridestone, it'd been important to him—

"A trinket," she responded, "a thing, a nothing! You think, as it was given, it could be taken. You think, it's so small, you could lose it. You look at it twenty times a day, fearing the cord could break, and it be lost. There. It's gone. Is the pact broken?"

He reached out but she avoided him and sat on her heels next to a tree, still fixing him with that demanding, accusing stare. "Trinkets," she spat, holding up the hand he'd tried to grasp. "The hand could be cut off. The hand is not the bond. Two streams meet: can you afterward separate them? Water into water. So it is done at the Summerfair, and so it is. While we live, the bond remains. But your doubt of it can turn it to our hurt: there are more bonds than one."

Jannus accepted the distance, settling down where he was. "What I feel," he said at length, "I feel. If I could believe in order, feel to order, I'd be master of pages or some such in Newstock right now. Maybe. . . ."

The sheet of water beside them was pierced by the first raindrops. Janus looked up automatically, though there was nothing to see, and had to blink. Rain in Han Halla fell straight down, without breeze or force but thick enough to choke you if you forgot to keep your head down.

For a moment they were both listening for any warning mutter of thunder—lightning, on the flat marshes, was a deadly danger— but, finding only the steady plittering, they relaxed again into their dispute.

" 'Water,' " quoted Jannus, surveying the rain with tired humor, " 'into water.' So it is done in Han Halla. . . . Maybe I'll come to believe it—the bond. But I can't, yet. The differences are so sharp to me, just now. . . ."

"You look for them."

"Maybe. I don't know. But I fear the differences could make you regret that . . . that you chose as you did—"

"The bond would still endure," she put in, inflexibly serene.

"Fine for us! Much joy we'd have, of such a bond as that! But I could stand that," he decided, realized. "I could even stand knowing that. But I don't know what I'd do if I couldn't reach you at all. It's come to be like trying to imagine starving, or dying—"

"I know it." Having made him say it out loud, she relented and came close. The contact was reassurance, comfort. They bent their heads, each against the other's shoulder, against the warm rain. "You just have to have faith in what you can't believe," she murmured presently. "There's no other way."

Jannus entertained himself for a while in trying to get his mind around that statement, chasing *faith* and *belief* down endless spirals, at last dismissing it.

"I still wish," he remarked, "you hadn't thrown away the bridestone. I liked it, just for itself."

"I liked it too. But we kept tripping over it, and it wasn't worth that."

"Next time you want to throw away something of mine, ask me first?"

But she refused to make such an open-ended promise. She would commit herself only to such concrete things as lifelong bonds; actions tomorrow or next week were too vague for promisings. Jannus found that funny but, predictably, she didn't see why, either before or after he'd explained it.

In some ways, he knew her very well. That reflection reassured him more than anything she'd said.

In Ardun, the Innsmiths were moved from their first prison, a great ugly shed of a warehouse, to a brick building near the harbor. They were assigned ten rooms opening off a broad central dining hall; the eleventh room housed the guards who stood, day and night, on both sides of the only door to the outside. Over each room's window was a freshly mortared grate.

From his window, Elda could see masts and fixed loading booms swinging and dipping and hear faint calls and shouts from the harbor. He couldn't see the river, Arant Dunrimmon, itself: the roofs of the long lines of warehouses, probably stuffed full of Summerfair goods, were in the way.

He was thinking that Grat must have passed through the Thornwall by now and be safe in Valde, following Arant Dunrimmon north to the Summerfair and all that. . . . And

Solvig, he'd be on the High Plain someplace looting a keep, sending the stuff down to Lisle for the pleasure of Ashai who'd killed his brother Sig, split the Clan and seen to it that all but a scraping of it would be outlawed, meat to such as Domal Ai, Master of Ardun. Elda hoped Solvig didn't think of it that way, though, or he didn't know how Solvig would get through the days.

In a settled, almost absent-minded way, Elda hated the Deepfish. The hatred had grown in the long forced march across Lifganin, his Family herded along by Domal's pikemen. Since Elda was now quite sure that they'd never get free of Ardun, that the Homecoming was irretrievably lost, he found himself reviewing memories, scenes. For instance, he regretted throwing the lamp across the room, in Quickmoor, rather than into Duke Ashai's face. He'd just been gentle and peaceable too long, he'd decided since, to have recognized the time for violence quickly enough. He'd mised his chance, and now regretted it keenly.

And it was too bad he'd been in such a rush to get shut of Lur and Jannus. With all the useless forbidden things he'd had to listen to, he might have at least found out what ways the Deepfish could be directly hurt; if there were such ways, Lur would be the one to know them. Maybe Jannus would know too. But Elda had shut his ears to all of it, greedy for the Homecoming he'd now lost anyhow. It wouldn't have hurt to have such things to store next to the fact that there were probably fewer Teks than Innsmiths. It wouldn't have hurt to know what a man could have done, or could do, besides toss a lamp. . . .

Elda pulled at a grate over the window, thinking that the reason they'd spent the first night in the warehouse was probably that the mortar on the bars hadn't fully dried. It wouldn't have suited for fresh-caught Innsmiths to have torn out the bars and walked away. No danger of that. There was noplace to go. Ardun was built on a long fishhook spur of land between Arant Dunrimmon and the Morimmon, with the Thornwall closing it off on the top. But had Ardun been flat and unwalled as Newstock, Elda reflected, there still would have been noplace to go for him and his Family.

He hadn't yet gone to visit the sick. His son Dinnel, according to Medd, was mending but Medd's own sister Inetta was worse. He'd have to see her, he thought, and take her inevitable tongue-lashing for leading his Family into such a state. Better to go to the fire, according to her way of think-

g. But Elda felt that there was always time enough to go to
~~~~e fire; he'd as soon wait and find out what his choices
~~ere. Inetta, though, would most likely be too stubborn to
~~ait. And with both her sons, Sig and Solvig, lost to her, she
~~as entitled to be as stubborn and bitter as she pleased.

Some stranger's voice calling from the dining hall brought
Elda out of these glum reflections. It was a scribish-looking
pindling man, plainly dressed, wearing clear glass circles in a
wooden frame over his nose: a steward of some sort, Elda
supposed. The man was attended by two hulking guards
armed with swords—metal from hilt to point, a great rarity.

"Everyone over the age of nine will come with me," the
man announced, and walked out through the door at the end
of the hall, which the guards opened smartly before he got
here. Elda gestured to the others and followed.

They didn't go far: down a set of stone stairs, still within
the building's walls, into a workroom that took the entire
space under their rooms and dining hall, then through that to
a yet larger storeroom. There the man stopped, and everyone
stopped. For the storeroom was packed, floor to ceiling, with
wooden bins holding every kind of object, all unmistakably of
Kantmorian workmanship. Plarit, metals, crystal, glass, stone,
shaped in rounds, cubes, tubes, rods, like sorted with like. The
rich bright colors, wakened by lamps, made the bins seem to
contain an immense harvest of glowing strange fruit.

The man went around behind a high bench on which a
variety of objects were neatly laid out. Lefthanded, he took
up a carrot-shaped green tube. "This," he commented, displaying it, "seems to be some sort of knife." He moved the
tube against a stick fastened upright to the bench. The stick's
end clattered on the cement floor; otherwise, the operation
made no sound at all. "But the odd thing is this," the man
continued, and quite calmly reversed the tube and moved its
end across his own throat. Somebody's breath hissed. But
nothing happened. The man blinked at them, quite unharmed, remarking, "It ignores anything alive. Useless, of
course, as a weapon."

As the man was setting the knife down to proceed to the
next demonstration, Elda said, "Will that thing cut plarit?"

The man's eyeglasses flashed as he turned to identify who'd
asked. From a bin he selected a turquoise plarit globe about
the size of an apple, tossed it underhand, again lefthanded, to
Elda and then tossed the little green knife-tube. Elda held the
tube, smaller end down, a cautious distance from the globe

and moved it as he'd seen the man do. The globe remained unmarked.

"About a thumb's breadth," offered the man neutrally, when Elda glanced up, "seems to be the proper distance. . . ."

Elda held the tube slightly closer and a hair-fine line was scored in the globe without cutting its surface quite through. He was recalling the web under the Broken Bridge, how they'd tried to cut it and been forced at last onto the Dead Shore, which in turn had brought them here. . . . He moved the tube closer yet, and the ball squirted a jet of pink dust all over his chest before he could fling it down. The dust smelled like daisies and sand and, somehow, too, like early morning—a complicated smell that clung wherever the dust touched, still squirting and pooling in layers above the globe as it rolled lopsidedly to a stop.

To rid himself of the scent, which he disliked not because it was unpleasant but because it had frightened him, Elda brushed one hand with the other, forgetting he still held the knife: his left sleeve dropped off, sliced right off his arm. For an instant, ice seemed to have formed under his cheekbones: he took deep breaths and held the tube rigidly at arm's length until he could trust himself again.

After a moment Elda bent to retrieve the emptied globe and with care and deliberation he cut it all the way through until it lay, two hollow halves, in his hand.

"The knife," said the man, and waited until it was returned to him, "it only cuts to a shallow depth. Now look at this." He held up a thing like a long-necked squash, creamy yellow in color and glowing faintly. "It's a light. It shines all the time, but more brightly the darker its surroundings. There was a man who cut one of these with a . . . a deeper knife, four days ago. He burned both his hands off."

Setting the light down, the man pushed his cloak back over his right shoulder. His right arm was tied down, attached to a belt of plarit cording. Having fumbled a knot free, he lifted the arm and turned back the loose sleeve with his other hand. The arm had what looked precisely like a woody vine growing from the shoulder: a single coarse-grained stalk descending to the elbow, then branches of increasing fineness encircling the forearm, hand, and fingers, the fingers being completely encased in wiry fibres. He held the arm up as though it were fragile or not really his own, or like somebody balancing a pole in the air. Taking one of the small plarit scent-globes in his left hand, he passed it to the balanced right hand which exploded it in one sharp squeeze. Waving absently at the cloud of scented smoke, he put the tips of rigid fingers above the bench's surface and, exactly like a man testing scalding water, poked through. The fingers left four separate holes in the thick wood.

"Don't step on any of the globe shards," he advised. "They'll cut your foot in two almost before you feel it. This splint," he continued, again displaying hand and arm in their woody sheath, "also has its dangers. If one moves too quickly, it can break his arm. So I take precautions." He started to tie the dangerous arm down again. "There are four more like this, but each is almost three yards long and has ten or more fingers. This was the only one sized to human proportions. What sort of a creature—"

"Where," said Elda, and swallowed to wet his mouth, "where did Domal Ai come by all this?"

"I am Domal," mentioned the man, still busy with his knots. "This is the first part of the contents of a place beyond the mountains north of Lifganin. In Kantmorie. It's cost me one hundred seventy nine men to find all the traps—or all the traps we yet know about—inside the first room and part of the second, that adjoins it. A path that is safe, and actions that are safe, become deadly a quarter hour later, with no warning and no sign. It's a miracle of ingenious execution. . . . And it's cost me over eighty to learn what things are safe to touch even after they're brought out, and which are not. More: even the safe things, like the light, have their perils. Come this way now."

The Master of Ardun led them through a series of narrow aisles between rows of as yet empty bins to the doorway of a chamber where five children in coarse smocks were manacled, hand and foot, to a wall. Their heads showed the first down of hair, eyebrows: the faces were lax and stupid, but lifted eyes glittered. Even knowing they must be Teks, Elda found it an ugly sight.

As if aware of this, Domal Ai remarked, "When I left them loose, they devoured each other. Unless they're bound, they kill each other or themselves with incredible quickness. I started with twenty-three. Twenty-three, of fifty I had collected to begin with and sent, heavily guarded, across Lifganin: less than half survived to reach the Sunset Bridge. Now I have five. They are shrewd, cunning, malicious, and stupid, by turns. You cannot rely on anything they say—but they

have been my only key to unlock the treasure back there."
Turning toward Elda, Domal added, "These are the
Deathless, that were your masters in the old time."

"Our masters. Your fathers."

"Many-times grandfathers, rather," rejoined Domal Ai, accurate and indifferent. "An honor we share with the Fishers."

"An't there someplace outside, open, that you could keep
them? You'd get more sense out of them that way," suggested
Elda uncomfortably, half expecting some sign of recognition
from one or another of the Teks. But none even looked at
him.

"No. There's nowhere more secure than this. That's why
you're here," snapped Domal Ai, turning to make a path for
himself back through the Innsmiths, who took each a peek
into the chamber and then edged off with some gesture or expression of distaste.

Well, Elda thought, he'd learned one thing—that Domal
didn't know beans about Teks. It would be funny if Domal
should be the one to start the tidestorm going, as seemed
likely. . . .

When the group had reassembled in the work area, Domal
Ai gestured to one of the waiting guards. The third exhibit of
the day was produced: a bound captive who stumbled, then
regained his balance and stood fixing Elda with a blind green
hating stare. Orlengis. Gagged, bound, on a leash.

"I have an enemy," the Master of Ardun was saying:
"Ashai, of Ismere. He's called that. But he holds Camarr by
marriage, and the Twin Isles by invasion, just above two
weeks ago. He's not the first of the Reyi to want to bring
back the old ways—one Master over all isles and the Isles of
Andras over all other peoples—and always the Aiah and the
Reyi have joined to bring such a one down before his
strength was great enough to resist us. We of Andras have always kept freshest the memory of the Kantmorie that was,
and of the Rule of One. It's a disease that takes one or two in
every generation; we know its signs. But Ashai has moved
both too slow and too fast—too slow, so that no one took
warning from any one thing, and too fast, in that he readied
himself and took the Twin Isles from that fool Kenniath
without alerting a single one of my spies. But by this act, he
has moved into the open. He is stealing, from the corpse of
Kentmorie, weapons to put the rest of us under his will. So I
must take new ways to protect the honor of the City of the
Rose, and the safety of its bride and spouse, Valde beyond the

Thornwall, before Ashai's hold over Kenniath's people is secure enough to let him turn elsewhere. I must make of myself
a slaver, to whom Fishers used to flee for protection and employment, so that Ardun is the most populous settlement in
the world; make a troop-leader and scavenger of myself, or
else give over to him Ardun and the gates of Valde.

"But not for this alone is Ashai my enemy. He has done a
thing for which there can never be any forgiveness: he has
broken the faith of Andras with the Valde. In Lisle of Bremner he allowed Valde to be taken and put in fear of unconsenting death. That he took Joneo, my servant, and all his
crew, and let them be killed—that's a little thing, though I'll
take my accounting for that too. . . . But to do such harm
to Haffa freemaids, and on their way to their bridings, so that
Valde do not come any more into Ardun, which has never
before been empty of their voices—"

The Master had begun to pace, in his plain agitation,
within the space between one broad table and the next; the
Innsmiths exchanged glances, extending to their captor the
courtesy only of silence. Elda had a notion that the captive
Screamers had as much to do with the Valde's avoiding
Ardun as anything that'd happened in Lisle; but Elda wasn't
about to tell the Master that what he hated so was his own
fault. Anybody fool enough to volunteer that sort of news
deserved what he got.

"Ardun," Domal Ai was continuing, "isn't tied to Valde by
blood, as is Bremner. Yet we are tied. The Summerfair, and
the Summerfair peace, are Valde's gift to us all, as freely
given as snow-water in spring. It's of no profit to them, for
they have no interest in making or storing, in twice-done
things. And the Thornwall is Ardun's reply: not as a shrewd
bid for favor, dying flowers in a suitor's greedy hand, but as
a living token of ancient love and protection—stronger and
greater as the seasons pass over it. I will not have that love
put at hazard, or consent that the long faith between Ardun
and the People of the Trees be broken by some hobbling
abortion of an upstart Islemaster—"

He sounded most, Elda thought, like a man whose wife
had been the butt of some joke at meeting. But the notion did
little to lighten the growing dark tension Domal's passionate
anger roused in Elda's heart. Elda kept looking past the Master to Orlengis, whose rigid expression Elda had begun to in-
terpret not as hate, but as terror.

And it was of Orlengis the master was now speaking. He

said Orlengis was the first of Ashai's servants to come within his reach since word about Lisle had reached him. "I'm going to have this one skinned, and the skin tanned and stuffed. Then it will be returned to Ashai as a reply to his offer of damage payment for the deaths of Joneo and the rest. . . . Damage! Much he knows of damage, when the Valde abandon Ardun of the Rose!" The Master recollected the Innsmiths again, and the peculiarly windowed eyes found Elda. "From the steersman I extracted the information you'd refused to serve Ashai, and that this man bears you a spite on that account. That's good. I will therefore give permission for you to observe the skinning. I've been saving him for you."

Elda folded his arms and sighed. "He's distant kin to us. Let him go."

The Master seemed unprepared for such a notion. "But I've already said what I mean to do," he replied, as if that settled it.

"Your folk were at least killed clean. . . ." But that wasn't the point. "Look, now. Suppose I knew a way to get the Valde back into Ardun." The Master scowled, started to reply, but Elda went on, "Never mind how. Suppose I could do it. Would that be worth your letting that misborn toad go his ways—to the Summerfair or wherever he pleases? It an't a fit thing, to skin a man. . . ."

Domal Ai settled on a bench, crookedly because of his bound-down arm, and everybody stood around while he thought about it. "But he's your enemy too," he remarked at last, perplexedly.

"That's as may be. The day a Valde comes through the Thornwall, or across the bridge, you turn him loose. Will you contract to it, or no?"

"Agreed," responded Domal Ai with finality; and, queer man though he was, he'd abide by it, Elda had no doubt.

"And another thing, now. You want us to work with that scrapwork of Tek tools in there. You can make us do it, I suppose. But you'll get such work you deserve from folk shut in a box like so many rabbits. An't a threat. It's a fact. Or you can use your wit and contract with us, free and open, to learn of that stuff what we can. Give us the run of the city. Let us out of this box."

"You'd contract to handle things of Kantmorie, though everyone knows no Smith—"

"An't your concern. You say you an't a slaver by choice: state terms, then, like a free man."

Quite abruptly, the Master decided. "I'll contract with you," he said, rising, holding Elda's eyes intently, "if and when you learn how to free me of *this*." And with a rough gesture he yanked up the sleeve, exposing the arm in its growth of dark vine.

Elda pushed his eyes uncomfortably away. "Done," he said.

"Done." Again concealing the diseased arm, the Master went off up the stairs at a measured pace echoed precisely by his swordsmen, with only Orlengis breaking the rhythm.

"Well," remarked Elda's cousin Tildur, "you set your hand to the Wheel at last, an't you."

"In it, more likely," put in Tildur's wife tartly, but without anger. "If we an't to have the show of a public skinning to enjoy, might as well turn what profit we can."

"There's that," admitted Tildur, and sighed.

Book V:
LIFGANIN

Hunting on the rolling grasslands of Lifganin, Poli glanced up. A monstrous sand-colored cat twice the size of a panther was regarding her from a rock outcrop. Palming a dart, she threw, then dropped flat to have a chance of avoiding its spring. She'd had no warning at all, couldn't hear it even now—

Having jabbed arrow-notch to string, she pivoted on one knee, hoping the cat would be slowed by the dart so she might be able to loose before it was upon her.

Quite empty, the tufted hillside below her undulated in the breeze.

Poli looked behind her just as the cat lifted its head. Both ducked: Poli below the ledge, the cat above. Its thick cable of tail thumped into Poli's shoulder, startling her so badly that she lost her footing and slid sideways into the open. She grabbed a second dart as she fell, hurling blind and off-balance.

"Stop that," said the cat.

Poli got her feet under her carefully, staring. Her hand automatically moved to straighten the arrow against the bow. The cat's forepaws showed unsheathed claws as long as her fingers; two fangs bulged the cleft upper lip out like pockets and dropped, bone daggers, to at least a hand's span below the broad, box-like chin. She could smell it now, a strong musky scent not unlike a leopard's; but no selfsinging came from it. It was silent as the stone on which it lay flattened. She began to bring the bow around.

"Stop that," the cat said again, flexing its claws against the rock with a grating noise.

Poli stopped, watching its shoulders for the first signal of its spring.

"I'm not hunting you," said the *sa'farioh* cat. "Go away. Back to Jannus."

Poli retreated one step, two. The cat sat up, looking off

185

toward Han Halla, where the sun was turning red and flat as it entered the mists. The cat raised a paw, to groom unconcernedly the pads and the sickle-curved claws.

Having sidled perhaps twenty slow paces downhill, where a single leap could no longer reach her, she pulled the lowered bow, levelled, and loosed, all in a sudden motion. But the stone partially shielded the cat, leaving for targets only head and neck: the cat yeowled and disappeared, so she couldn't be sure she'd struck it at all.

She turned and fled.

Sore-footed on grass after weeks of spongy mats, mud, and wading, she made herself settle to a trail-jog. Cats could charge like avalanches, over short distances, but given a head start Poli believed she could outrun it. She threw the focus of her *marenniath* before, behind. In her wake, the small life among the grasses took alarm and remained still and fearful longer than she liked.

Perhaps the cat was following. She couldn't be certain.

Ahead, she could catch the manysingings of three distinct bands of Awiro Valde—the Solitary, Haffa who'd refused the Troop-calling at their time of Choosing—and sent a silent cry of warning and of appeal for aid. But each band continued in its separate harmony. They hadn't heard her, though she could hear them plainly and even distinguish individual *fariohe* here and there.

She reached Lifganin-stream, chief water of this land, and slid down the gorge, plunged through the shadowed water, and scrambled up the other side. Cats hunted chiefly by sight, and she meant to lead it north until the twilight was deep enough to cover her doubling back. Pausing briefly for breath, she sifted the life behind her but still found no certainty of pursuit. She cased her bow and jogged on through the wind-troubled grasses.

Jannus had cut turves to bare a circle and placed them, dirt side up, around the circle's rim. He had the cookfire laid but unlit, although the light was ebbing: Poli would need no light to find her way back to him. He sat in the deeper shade of the grove of tall pale-skinned trees that bordered Lifganin-stream. He was recalling that other time in Han Halla, the time Poli had been so long returning and the pact between them had been made. Knowing she'd be hearing him, knowing she always heard him now, he carried on a one-sided dialogue complaining of her lateness. It reflected, he declared, on her supposed hunting skills and therefore on his choice of her as his guide and companion. And beneath this teasing stirred the unease that woke whenever she was parted from him and out of his sight.

The coin-sized leaves high overhead flickered. The stream ran down below its deep-cut banks. A few frogs began to pipe.

There was a splash upstream. Then she was with him, before he'd time to do more than come to his feet: holding on as if she'd fled to him from something that ran behind. Warned, Jannus at once cast his thoughts back to Erth-rimmon, imagining the river-bottom and light sifting down like slow dust. This image he held as she jammed words into the measured exhalations of runners' breath:

"Met a cat. *Sa'farioh* cat. Bigger—twice as big . . . as a grass cat. Couldn't kill it. Tried to outrun—"

"Did it follow you?"

"Don't know! *Sa'farioh*!" She paused two full breaths, leaning her forehead against his neck so he felt the pulse of her long run still pushing her. "Never saw such a beast. Said it was not hunting me . . . but cannot trust such—"

"It talked? Spoke to you?" The green image vanished, replaced by a profound and unwilled calm that spiraled steadily out from a still center. Lur. Lur, for certain.

Jannus surveyed the branches far overhead, evaluating the diffuse leaf-cover as a roof. He drew Poli a few steps into the grove—only five trees thick, at its widest—amazed to realize he hadn't thought about Lur once since going into Han Halla: as if Lur and his purposes had ceased to exist merely because Jannus had forgotten them for the time, unreflective and self-absorbed as any Valde. . . .

"I have called the Awiro Valde," Poli was continuing hoarsely, "and they will come to me here, the mara-folk—"

Jannus embraced her lightly, releasing himself, and said, "Stay here. Listen for him: listen for the silence around him." From his belt he took a pair of dagger-darts and laid them on the raw turf-bottoms as he knelt with striker and firestone.

"What is it to you," she whispered, having followed him from the grove, "this *sa'farioh?* How does it know your name?"

Jannus wanted her back under the trees, but she wouldn't go. So he chipped at the firestone with greater haste. "I think he is the friend I lost in Lisle. Lur." He smiled coldly. "I named him so . . . and he's taken me at my word, it seems. He's a Tek—one of the Deathless."

While he spilled the sparked grass into the tinder and blew it into a tiny flame, Poli remained silent at his back. "It will see the fire," she remarked neutrally.

"If he's followed you, he won't need the fire. I'd like to see him, if he comes. . . . He'll like being a cat; he hated the child so, the child he wore before. . . ." The fire had begun to burn. Laying a few heavier sticks in place, Jannus said, "Can you climb one of those trees?"

"From there, I could not put arrow to bow."

"You still have that pad of darts. The trees, and not knowing where you may be, might keep him off. I'll come under the trees if I have to."

Poli stood heavily, staring at the dark grasses. "What is between you at this *sa'farioh?*"

"It's part," Jannus answered slowly, searching a good simple way to put it, "of the price I paid in Lisle. I am bound, for myself and for him, to help him in a certain task. If I refuse, or if we fail, I will be *sa'farioh* on the High Plain when it comes time that I die. He believes that *sa'farioh*, I would be of better aid to him. So he hunts me now."

Poli appeared to think about this. "You sold your death," she formulated, "to buy me free."

Jannus considered this way of looking at it, meanwhile noting a stronger stir in the high grasses, moving from right to left. "In a way," Jannus said, "that's so."

"And the other *sa'farioh*, the Andran Ashai, holds it."

"In a way. . . . The deaths of all Teks, all the Deathless, are gathered in a certain place on the High Plain, the Murderlands. Lur wants his back, and to do that he must loose all the other deaths as well." Seeking ways to explain, Jannus found himself imagining black pigeons freed from a cage, each turning into the shadow of a man as it reached its owner and fastening itself to his heels, moving behind him as he moved. "If I was to die right now I'd wake on the High Plain by morning," he went on. "And I'm not much afraid of that. But I'd wake having . . . having forgotten everything I've known and done since Lisle. It would all be gone. And I would neither know nor care what I'd lost. . . ."

As he spoke the nightmare-dread rose in him, attaching itself openly for the first time to its proper object. So some part of him, he thought, hadn't forgotten about Lur at all. Something had realized the utter loss hanging over what, against all expectation, he'd found.

Poli went two smooth paces, facing the dark with the fire at her back. "Deathless! What do you want with us?"

Two lambent green circles flashed and were gone, to Jannus' left. Jannus picked up the two darts he'd laid aside and rose, facing outward as Poli had done: the fire between them, the grove guarding their backs. "Are you glad," he called, "to be rid of the child?"

Poli said, "How can his death be ransomed, O Deathless?"

Jannus said, "What makes you suppose I'd wake at Cliffhold, Lur? I'd never seen it, I thought about Newstock instead. I'd be based in Newstock, my own place—and how would you come to me there?" That lie, Jannus thought, should make Lur hesitate.

"I don't believe you." The voice was a startling bass, blurring the *b* sound, coming from nowhere in particular. It was an inhumanly large voice, subtly jarring because, in spite of himself, Jannus had still been visualizing the child—grotesquely hidden, somehow, in an animal pelt, but still Lur as he remembered him.

"He would be lost to you, Deathless," said Poli, unexpectedly supporting him in the lie. "But we would ransom his death, for him to hold. To do this we would help you claim yours, willingly."

"So," said Lur's new voice, "the Valde was properly grateful for her rescue. I assume it's the same one? If you prefer she survive, come away from her."

"Tell me what it is you want done, and maybe I'll come."

"Talk is wasted. You won't remember any of it. Nor will I. The Valde may enjoy whatever pleasures she finds in revenge, and dispose of the cat. Your rede will call you to Cliffhold, and you'll remember all the directions I gave you before Lisle. You'll bring out the blue ball and the rest to me—"

"From Newstock?" interrupted Jannus. "That may take some time."

"Deathless," said Poli, "you are stupid to cast away such aid as we both could give. Silenced, what would Jannus care for you or your plans? We will loose the deaths for you, we two."

After a moment Lur moved into the edge of the firelight: between them and the grove. Though Jannus should have been warned by the voice, he was appalled by the size of the beast Lur now wore. Though the grasses were hip-high, the cat's head and dun shoulders rose above them, casting back the firelight from eyes each as large as a fist.

Poli turned but did not hurl a dart. Nor did Lur spring. Presently Lur said, "Valde do not make reliable allies."

"The Bremneri stocks find us so," she retorted.

"Yes: you hunt Teks through Newstock basements."

"What we hunt, we take. You have need of such. Consider this choice while you hide. and you must hide, Deathless, and quickly. Go into the stream, for the mara come. You have no selfsinging but they are beasts too and will scent you and pound the body you wear into the earth. Quick! They are close, now!"

Even Jannus could distinguish a hustling thumping noise now; the cat's head lifted uneasily, facing north.

"I heard their feet long and long ago," commented Poli, "while you, the beast, heard nothing. You need my aid, Deathless. You must spring now or else flee—"

Her arm snapped forward. The missile struck the cat in the neck. Yeowling, he bounded at Poli before Jannus even had time to turn his head: and by the time he'd turned, Poli was flat on the far side of the fire and the cat was gone.

Jannus had time for one step before a pale shape, moving too fast to be seen distinctly, burst out of the darkness, all but running into him. Then two more, one leaping over the fire and scattering it so the creatures rushing behind, veering and wheeling, seemed to float through patches of moonlit grass to disappear into the shadow of the grove and suddenly loom inches away and hurl themselves past.

"What stoats' nest?" bellowed a voice, rousing other cries on every side. "Here! Here, children, here!" the voice howled, the others clamored, "Har, haro, chern haro!" while Jannus tried to reach Poli but met a barrier of strong-smelling longhaired living hide that lunged against him and knocked him over.

Tall pale legs struck and leaped all around him, but he was not touched. He lifted his head slowly to find the beasts ranging into a flickering wheel, turning with the fire, himself, and Poli at its center. The wheel slowed, stopped: there was silence, except for great gusts of breathing.

Poli came slowly to her feet, taking no notice of him. Having shed her harness, bow, and darts, she stood emptyhanded. A beast came cautiously forward and bent its head to smell her shoulder, then retreated. Another advanced and did likewise, then two together. Then five. The circle began to shift and move randomly. But none of the beasts came near Jannus.

Thinking he'd seen the outline of a lifted arm, he looked harder. As his eyes adjusted to the moonlight he distinguished heads set on ordinary shoulders, arms. . . . But legs—there were too many legs, and—

What he saw suddenly resolved itself into normal-sized people perched on the backs of large four-footed beasts. Some beasts were thus oddly companied, and some not. Without apparent distinction they came forward in their turn to inspect Poli.

Their strongest sense appeared to be that of smell. They approached delicately, so close that the tips of their projecting spearlike horns were behind Poli and useless as a defense, leaving each bending neck unprotected. He was watching, not an inspection, but a ceremony—a mutual surrendering of defenses.

With some reluctance he let drop the lone dart he'd managed to hold onto in the confusion.

A soft nose whuffed just under his ear. Rigidly controlled, he made himself turn slowly to stare into one large dark eye which had a dubious rim of white all around. The pupil was slit horizontally, like a goat's. Hoping he was right, Jannus reached up and grasped one of the whorled horns. With a steady, gentle pull he drew its point level with his chest. And for five heavy heartbeats, he waited. The beast flicked spoon-shaped ears and breathed at him, then turned and trotted away, flicking its long paintbrush tail.

These, he concluded, were mara. It would never have occurred to him to connect imported wool at twenty coppers a skein, delivered, with beasts so large and formidable. He was more genuinely afraid of their physical nearness than he'd been of the cat.

His wariness seemed to make them shy, but he couldn't help it. He spoke respectfully to the hooded Valde that companied the beasts but none answered him, which made him no more comfortable and further delayed the ceremony of greeting. He still had a crowd of mara, ridden and partnerless, around him when Poli's greetings were done. She bent to rebuild the cookfire, another Valde standing beside her as if in conversation. But Jannus held himself still until the last mara had met him and wandered off to graze.

"Haro, Jannus l'Poli," called the strange Valde by Poli, the loud voice he'd first heard. She tossed back her hood and waved him nearer, slapping him resoundingly on the back he came in reach, exclaiming, "Didn't know what we run onto,

us! Frightened the air so, stink of the cat, smoke, out
lander—"

"This is Morgala Wir," Poli interposed into the other'
hearty, fluent confusion, "freemaid of the Aftaban troop
troopleader to Overwater—"

Jannus lost the rest of it because Morgala hadn't ever
paused. "Said she was lar Haffa," she was saying, *"larfai* in
the briding—didn't say Bremner boy, name-choosers. Ei
I heard no Bremner *fariohe* a hand of years and more. Ei
what a way to waking the old Third Kindred, briding in the
swamp so! What need? At . . . at the—"

Morgala met Jannus' angry eyes and her babble stopped
Abruptly she walked off through the grass, clasped the neck of
a grazing mara and began to weep.

"Be sorry for that," Poli told him shutting her teeth on the
final word.

"Our pact is not her concern."

"They came to our need, out of her memory of the river-
link. We have no claim on the mara-folk. Morgala is not
Kevel Innsmith, that you can be cruel at whim."

Jannus didn't like it, but accepted the reprimand and the
implied duty to mend matters. He sorted through his mind for
something he was sincerely sorry about and, thus armed, went
after Morgala and patted her wildly tangled hair. "I'm a
stranger," he said, keeping his regret firmly in place. "We have
met no Valde since . . . since we began the *larfai*, and I fear
for Poli being hurt through me. I ask your pardon."

He felt a little silly, as if he'd tried to pet Aliana Wir. But it
was hard for him to imagine Morgala as a troopleader, hard to
conceive of the reserved Aliana bursting into open tears because her feelings had been hurt.

Morgala looked around after scrubbing her cheeks on the
mara's shaggy neck hair. "To serve ten years and be brided to
a Newstock boy in a swamp, and nobody to be glad with her?
You do well, fearing hurt so. It will come. Spare me the
Watertalk regrets of you."

Jannus held his temper. "Fearing this meeting, I have made
it badly. I ask your pardon, and your help in mending it."

Morgala sniffed pensively, then shook herself. "My fault
also. My fault of me, to think of Bremner. Does not joy me,
Bremner." She slapped the mara's side; it whuffed at her comfortably and dipped its head again into the grass. Morgala returned to the fire, where some of the Awiro seemed to be
starting preparations for a daymeal.

It was hard to tell just how many Awiro there were. They were dressed all alike, in knee-length flowing gowns of interwoven brown and green over darker trousers, with soft shoes or boots laced at the side. Their faces, too, were alike: calm, blank, and unlined as though age touched them only as wind touches water. Jannus found himself searching firelit profiles for a peculiar nose, an odd-colored eye, for freckles or an idiot chin to reassure him. He looked at Poli. The only differences his eye found were her faded Newstock colors and her shorter hair. If she took Awiro garb and went hooded, he wasn't sure he could have picked her from the rest. This unlikely speculation bothered him disproportionately.

And he was worried, too, about Lur. The cat could not have gotten far before the dart sleep took him. The mara, with their wise, wicked goats' eyes, were scattering, apparently calm; but what would happen when they found the cat, Jannus wasn't sure.

He wanted Poli to come away, talk in words he could hear, but felt too self-conscious even to call her. Likely this sudden company, after the weeks of Han Halla, was welcome to her. He could only intrude, couldn't help but intrude: they were Valde.

He stepped into the grove and sat against a tree, wishing there was a door he could shut, somewhere he could go.

The Awiro, Morgala was telling Poli, hadn't met any *sa'farioh* before: only the other kind, with the ugly, hating suffering. Around them there was a wincing in the surrounding *als'far* like the first prickle of lightning or the wet chill breeze running before a storm—a wincing, a turning away, from Awiro and the mood-sensitive mara alike. "From the high, they come," said Morgala in the breathtalk, to make herself heard. "We do not go, any more, to our summergrass places, the cool steep. Do no go any more, either, to the Rosetown, you know it? for salt—"

The vague unease sharpened into chorusing images of flight—flight of the Deathless themselves, flight of the Awiro from the pain and horror of such, present flight from such memories, demands that she and Morgala not hold to such things, that they all turn away to the pleasures of night, and food, and rest. . . .

And Poli, infected by the ache of Jannus' antipathy, snapping back that she was lar Haffa of the Newstock troop and had endured Screamers hours at a time and the mere thought

of them was nothing, nothing to get so agitated about; they re
plying that they, the Haffa Awiro, had chosen long life and
peace and were not obliged to endure such pain. . . .

Aloud, against this chaotic counterpoint, Morgala was say
ing, "You have two ways to go, you-both. Into Valde, the one
Shelter behind the Rosewall, stay there. No Deathless is pass
ing very far, you know? It would soon be hunted, killed. And
you-both could live so."

Most Bremneri, she went on, inspeaking as the surrounding
protest eased, lived to huge ages, often spending six, seven
hands of years just being old instead of a hand of seasons;
Morgala herself had been old since the leaves went quiet and
fell, and felt that to be more than enough. Almost surely Poli's
seasons under the sun would be done before the Bremneri
even began his old time. "And what matter to you then? If he
lives or is lost, if he wakes again and goes not to the ground,
what matter? You will not know it."

It would matter, Poli insisted. That he'd forget themselves-
together, that was a great dread even now, between them. And
the dread would work its changes. It could not be put aside,
forgotten.

"Even on *larfai*?" To Morgala, that was ruining a good hot
afternoon with brooding on snow.

"Yet the winter comes," rejoined Poli sharply, "and those
without shelter prepared are astonished while they freeze."

Morgala wasn't interested in arguing about it. "Or, you
know, you can go to the cat and find how these deaths are to
be loosed." She didn't think it'd be all that pleasant, either, to
have for company on one's *larfai* just a Bremneri and a
sa'farioh cat. But then, she'd never brided in a swamp, or any-
place else. . . .

Poli accepted the gibe and the group's gentle breath of
amusement, letting it be her own. And at the same time she
thought, soberly, that if these were their only two choices,
then there was no choice at all. Jannus' *farioh* told her they
could never live contentedly among Valde.

As she had accepted the Awiro's amusement, so now they
accepted her sadness, merely sharing it, without the distance
of pity or judgment. Some things, they knew, could not be and
one turned quietly away and was reconciled to what remained.
The Awiro, who'd turned from the Troop-calling, knew that
well, without bitterness.

And among the mara two males, finding them all so melan-
choly, began a bowing mock battle, squealing and rearing,

inting with their horns, to deflect their Valde companions
to laughter and memories of the season that was past, when
e midwinter fierceness had been upon them. A few Awiro
n to the two, joyously wrestling and encumbering the pair
ith their arms and their weight. The mock battle spun out
to an elaborate game of tag chased in the moonlight through
e rest of the scattered, peaceful herd.

Poli went to Jannus' retreat under the trees, relaxing into
is relief, and leaned to rest against his side. Sleepiness settled
pon her, so that even her wrists felt heavy.

"Whatever made you throw that dart at Lur?" he asked
ddenly, choosing this to be angry about. "He might have
greed—"

"Wasn't a dart. It was a stone. But it could have been a
art, and he knew it," she explained with drowsy precision.
So he knocked me over. With his claws sheathed. So I'd un-
erstand he could have reached me, even if it'd been a dart.
ut it wasn't. It was a stone."

Lur waited until he was sure he recognized Jannus before
howing himself on the rock where he'd first encountered the
Valde. And recognizing the boy wasn't all that easy since,
eside the Valde, Jannus had acquired wispily untidy black
whiskers and a floppy armless circular cape identical to that
he Valde wore. Lacking color sense, Lur couldn't be sure, but
e imagined the capes would be some hideous shade—bright
ink, or the traditional green of overt poisons.

The pair ascended the hill rather in the fashion of cranes,
urveying him quite blankly.

His allies.

And it was beginning to smell like rain.

"What is this blue ball?" demanded the Valde, without
reamble, "that you want?"

"Hunt for me," Lur countered, watching to see what their
reaction would be. "This beast hasn't been fed since yesterday
morning."

"I will hunt for us all, Deathless, when you say what you
mean to do to loose the deaths."

As Lur had expected, the boy had done nothing to properly
discipline his companion. The prospect of training her himself
bored Lur enormously. Not even bothering to reply, he
bounced down the far side of the rock and started north,
where the best hunting usually was at this time of day. Within
a minute the pair had caught up with him: the Valde's pace

adapting to the rolling jog that was the beast's habitual tra
gait, so that she ran easily at his shoulder. The boy hung ba
slightly, carrying the Valde's bundle as well as his own b
also moving without visible effort.

When the Valde veered a little more west, toward H
Halla, Lur turned to her without comment.

"Pig," she remarked, after awhile. "Five together. Take t
one I strike."

She waved him toward one side of an irregular patch of ta
wildflowers whose scent mingled mint and some sort of frui
With the breeze behind him, Lur bounded into the flowe
with a loud snarling cough. Unseen, the pigs erupted on th
far side of the patch. The Valde flung a dart. Lur reached th
staggering sow as its tusks slashed at grass stems near th
Valde's knees. Almost casually Lur broke its back as h
turned to face the remainder of the pack, which grunted an
muttered a moment before diving, pigs and piglets, into hidin
again. Then the Valde motioned him aside and began butche
ing the kill in what seemed a competent fashion, with Jannus
assistance.

Having removed perhaps a quarter of the carcass, she said
"The rest is yours."

"I'd like it cooked."

"It will take two hours to gather enough wood. Twice tha
again, to cook it. Does the beast insist on cooked food?" re
joined the Valde coolly.

Lur ate the pig as it was, turning his head sideways to crack
the bones.

The pair shared out a loaf from a leather wallet Jannus un
slung.

When he'd finished cleaning his forepaws and face, Lu
rose heavily and continued north at a walk. Having fed, the
beast was lethargic, wanting to drink and rest. But Lur kep
it moving until they came to one of the hundreds of streams
that crosshatched the uplands—most running southwest and
emptying into Han Halla. There he drank his fill while the
pair collected dead boughs among nearby trees.

When Lur hauled himself over the bank, he found Jannus
weighting with stones the bottom of a sheet of canvas he'd tied
between trees, like half a tent.

"It'll rain from the south, I expect," the boy remarked, as
Lur approached.

The Valde glanced up briefly, then went on constructing a
square tiered cookfire above a small flame already burning be

low. The smoke, Lur noticed, was indeed blowing toward the north in irregular gusts.

Lur surveyed the trees for overhanging branches, but they were high up and diffusely leafed—less solid than the dark plane of clouds. Tolerable. He found space to stretch out between the canvas and the fire, and let the beast sleep.

He woke suddenly, as usual, and looked all around him before resting his chin again on crossed forepaws. The fire, a thick mound of coals, was hissing and flaring intermittently as it was struck by raindrops and by grease from the skewered pork propped above it. Beyond, the rain fell steadily. With their backs to him, Jannus and the Valde sat cutting and eating what looked like carrots, a piece at a time.

"The problem," said Lur—and noted he'd startled them— "on the High Plain is water. There is scarcely any. If I needed it in quantity, I had it brought in as ice, to the holding pits prepared for it. But for ordinary use there were waterballs: blue plarit balls, each with a handle, a button, and a spout. Press the button and water comes out the spout. They form water from the residual moisture in the air—even on the High Plain air has *some* water vapor in it. . . . Most of the ball is casing, armor protecting the part that extracts and condenses the vapor. But for practical purposes it's just a blue plarit ball a little larger than a head, with a handle, a button, and a spout. Push the button and the water comes."

Jannus shifted so he and the Valde served each other as backrests, with the boy facing Lur. "The waterballs wouldn't be anywhere but a keep, on the High Plain?"

"No. On the lowlands, there's no need. It rains. And a ball can't supply large amounts of water—"

"And would any keep have them, or only Cliffhold? Any keep? Good. Because Teks have begun coming down out of the mountains, according to the Awiro Valde, who've had to abandon their usual summer pastures in the hills. That means there's a base, a keep, not too far from the rim—"

"And the Barrier isn't there to stop them," finished Lur "Yes. That would be Cap's Keep."

"There's more. Screamers are being held in Ardun. That's an Andran freeport just south of Valde, on the river—four, maybe five days' walk southeast. So if Cap's Keep is being stripped, it probably isn't by Ashai. Domal Ai knows the Wall has failed too."

"And when you get this ball," the Valde put in, looking around, "what then?"

"Without a portable water supply, no one could reach Down on foot from the edge of the cliff, from the lowlands. I'd need to carry such a weight of water that another person would be needed to help bear the load, who in turn would need more water, and so on; and killing your bearers isn't practical, after the first few." Lur had tried that. "Down was placed so as to be inaccessible by—"

"You could plant water," said the Valde, "a day's walk apart."

"Stored in what?" snapped Lur, not liking being interrupted.

"Fired clay pots. Sealed."

"It'd take months to set such caches, months on the High Plain. We'd be killed and eaten three times over, and forget where the caches were set. No." Waterballs had another use which made them necessary: when the casing was breached, they exploded and left a considerable crater; but Lur had no intention of sharing that information yet.

"And when we come to this place," rejoined the Valde, taking another approach, "how will we buy back his death, and yours? What is the price?"

"Can you buy sunlight today," Lur countered, "to fall on just us here? Why not?"

"The sun is farther than the clouds. The clouds have power here now."

One could always depend on Valde, Lur reflected sourly, to know where the power was—generally the strongest thing nearby. "Forget the clouds. Could you pay the sun itself to hold to one place in the sky, and never move, for a whole season?"

"So there would be no night? All the plants would die and the—"

"But *could* you?"

"But the water streams would bake away," the Valde persisted stubbornly, "and all life perish for the lack of—"

"But suppose you wanted to! Could you do it!"

"I can't suppose myself wanting such a thing," replied the Valde firmly.

Thus balked, Lur looked to Jannus, who was carving up his wretched carrot and refusing to be any help at all. "Here's a more direct analogy," Lur said, rather grimly. "The sun obeys laws and has no choice but to obey them. Likewise, the Shai. It can buy deaths, but not sell them. Can you see that?"

"To get dark for yourself," she formulated, "you mean us to kill the sun."

It was much too literal, but Lur was sick of the subject. "Yes."

"Oh." Apparently satisfied, the Valde leaned aside to rotate the skewers.

Finally taking a part in the conversation, Jannus asked, "Couldn't you just claim the kingship?"

"Downbase is roofed."

The boy nodded meditatively; then, casually, he mentioned the obvious: "That wouldn't bother me. . . ."

"No," agreed Lur tightly.

"Did you try, before the roof-fear came on you?"

"I don't know. Probably. It doesn't matter now."

"To you."

". . . Yes. . . ."

Seeming to ignore the tension, Jannus scraped his lank hair back with a spread hand and continued to whet the carrot like a dagger. "Would the Shai accept me to hold the Rule of One, do you think?"

"He accepts everybody: for terms varying from several centuries to about the time required to sneeze."

"It's your sarcasm I've chiefly missed," commented the boy, glancing up pleasantly. "That and your dependable clarity of purpose. Don't worry, Lur. I'd never go into Downbase unless I was sure of coming out again."

Lur just looked at him balefully, and the boy sat up straighter, appearing surprised.

"Lur, I'm no Tek. I want to live, and not forget—don't you know that? Can't you believe somebody else might not be in such an indecent hurry to dive into the dark?" The boy sat blinking at him, between incredulity and amusement. "Truly, Lur, you needn't be anxious on that account. I don't think the Shai would tolerate any king not of his choosing very long. And I'm not even a Tek. I don't know anything, really, about the Rule of One, and I don't care to. I wouldn't last as long as a candle."

Unconvinced, Lur began grooming the underside of a paw, unsheathing the claws. If Jannus claimed the kingship, nobody else could do so until he was disposed of. But then again, Lur thought, he didn't mean to go into Downbase himself anyway. He meant to break the lake dome and starve the Shai of energy, power. If Jannus was inside when the dome was cracked, then Downbase would make an imposing tomb. Relaxing, Lur began using the moist paw to smooth the side of his jaw and the fur behind his ear, thinking about what might be stolen from the looting of Cap's Keep, if they were quick enough.

The cat, most agile on the loose rubble that floored this narrow mountain valley, sprang over the hedge of brown bones and disappeared from Poli's view. She hauled skeletons loose as she would fallen branches, to clear a path. But until Jannus overcame his awed repugnance to the scope and nature of the barrier, she made no move to pass through the opening. His will to go on drew her forward, rather than any impulse of her own. Each advancing step brought her nearer the insupportable raging of the Screamers.

"This," Jannus was remarking, "is where the Wall was."

Poli made no response, but moved when he moved.

She'd entered the outer edges of the Screamers' torment in the mountain meadows below the snow line, the pleasant fields that remembered the Awiro and their herds. Each winding stony canyon had intensified the babbling roar, as though it were a cloudburst river ravening down toward her along the naked folds of the rock. Sleepless till dawn, she'd kept from being swept away by a retreat into something like dueltrance: she held to Jannus, but was aware of him only vaguely, as through a fever haze.

The rift became a crooked balcony overlooking a scene that seemed the outward image and confirmation of her inner state. Beyond ramps of slatey spillage the land was a glittering yellow-white, featureless, undulating queasily beneath layers of ascending heat waves. The wind that scraped up past the rift mouth baked her face dry in a moment. The opening had been scoured smooth. The edges were so hot that she jerked her arm tight against her as if scorched.

Jannus was pointing. Lur had found a way down, was a writhing amorphous pale streak emerging from the shadow of the inner cliff on the slope of ashen spillage. Jannus was marking aloud the series of ledges and cracks that would give access to the ramp—his *farioh* cool, curious, wary: like a fish regarding her shadow on the stream. . . .

He knew she'd been wakened by a Screamer, but had no idea of the torrent against which she'd been forcing her way. He didn't know because she hadn't told him. His lack of anxiety for her was necessary for her to hold to. Yet it was monstrous that he should not know, without need of telling.

Images of flight flashed upon her, so mingled in the dreadful cry from beyond the rift that for a time she had no realization that it was she, herself, in flight. She merely found herself standing in a warm meadow, with nothing disturbing the inner or outer silence but the rush of a cataract plummeting in headlong bounds to the valley floor. She made her way the few paces to the cataract's pool before she was overcome by convulsive shivering and nausea.

Presently Jannus was there, helping her to clean and steady herself. It was strange to be touching him and yet feel he was very far away, his *farioh* so faint. She wondered what could be wrong with him.

All at once it came to her that she'd run away. She'd abandoned him like a wide-eyed hare racing before a brush fire. The shame of it roused her to tears. She knelt shaking her head, repeating aloud, "You don't know. You don't know," sadly to his questions.

She saw Lur lounging toward her and cried, "Get away from me!" The cat checked abruptly and edged off a little distance, then flopped down, panting.

By degrees the meadow became real to her, as colors become real during sunrise. Her awareness of the plants and the small life among them increased. Poli dipped the back of a hand in the pool—the water clear and icy—and wiped her forehead slowly.

"Poli, you——" Jannus was beginning.

"Let her alone," directed Lur, from across the space.

"But I have to know what——"

"*I* know what," replied the cat. "For me, it is roofs. Let her alone."

And Poli blinked at the cat, surprised that it neither mocked nor accused her. Then she looked past him, up at the barrens below the snows, the way she'd come. Faintly, now, she could again hear the crying of the Deathless: faint as the sound of wasps, circling.

"I am shamed. I ask your pardon."

"Granted," said Lur. "Let's eat before we do anything more."

While Lur and Jannus—principally Lur—were eating, Poli began explaining what she'd heard. "And there are many of them, many. . . ."

"Then they have a source of water," remarked Lur promptly, "and they're in the open. Or you couldn't hear them. And only water would permit a crowd. . . . But by tomorrow, half should have killed the other half, and it may take a few hours for the redes to be rebodied, with such a number as that. We'll start at first light, before . . . or could you try again tonight? The dark could be an advantage. And it will be cooler."

"We'll go tonight," agreed Poli.

Jannus, unsure of the best course, made no objection.

Poli rested, even slept a little. In the twilight she followed the cat across the meadows almost eagerly, determined not to shame herself by repeating her morning's flight. And she did not. But neither did she reach the wall of bones. There came a point where she was utterly unable to proceed, her concentration weakened by Jannus' solicitous watchfulness.

The following morning she insisted on trying yet again, declaring that she was rested now and well prepared. Jannus doubted it, but consented to try. She found, however, that though her body was rested and well, her *marenniath* shrank as if scalded at the least touch of the terrible cry and she had no power to block the pain for even an instant.

She could manage, she thought, except for Jannus' constant scrutiny of her for visible sign of her state. The danger of becoming locked in a mood echo was growing, beyond her power to control it. She wanted to leave Jannus behind and make the attempt with Lur alone: she disliked the cat intensely, but at least he was no distraction. But Jannus was flatly opposed.

"Think," she encouraged, "as if I am only away hunting, as—"

"I can't pretend that," he replied.

The cat showed his fangs in a wordless disgusted snarl and bounded away up the cleft alone.

The looting force had shunted the Teks, fifteen or twenty of them, off into a funnel-shaped pen whose point touched the wall of the keep. At least Lur assumed they were all Teks. Such a menagerie would be most unlikely otherwise, since scarcely half the captives wore human shape.

Three were birdforms of a hawk sort, with wingspans so broad the mere narrowness of the enclosure kept them penned. Two were pale long-necked birds of almost equal size, one of which had been struck down and was a mounded lump against the pen stakes. One of the hawkforms was standing on it, intent on keeping the other two at bay with wordless hisses and half-raised wings. The other hawkforms hunched and tramped, tailfeathers dragging, seeking a good angle of attack.

Lur could have predicted birds, had he thought about it: while he'd been going in for lost animals, Cap's Keep had been absorbed in such frivolity as beastforms specifically intended to house redes but lacking usable hands or vocal modifications—mere dress for sightseeing. To produce what he saw below him, they'd overrun Cliffhold for the better part of a century, interfering with his own projects.

Were he a hawk, now, he could reach Down in a day. And then stare at the tunnel of Downbase, he reminded himself, no better off than before. It was better to be a cat.

The remaining beastforms were reptilian: shell-encased, thick-limbed. Developed as a water-conserving form, most probably. These rested, heads retracted, at intervals down the length of the pen. The manforms, children and adolescents, climbed and bounded on the shells in apparently random motion. A head shot out, beak clapping shut: the shellform had acquired a meal. Presently a port in the keep wall irised open, letting an additional manform into the enclosure: the meal, rebodied. The speed of the reincarnation and the variety of beastforms proved Cap's Keep remained in better condition than Lur would have expected.

Past the pen and its menagerie passed workers in small groups, entering or leaving the keep from another irised port nearer Lur's vantage point at the foot of one of the long spills of sharp-edged rubble. He saw a work gang of six—little men, not Bremneri, stripped to sandals, kilts, and broad-brimmed hats—appear from this second port guiding and dragging a many-wheeled cart heaped with large ratio-arms, probably from the keep's external handling systems—chopped off, by the look of them: wasted, dying. The cart, with the ratio-arms piled like so much timber, was maneuvered into place beside two others at the side of a pavilion-sized tent—or at least the roof of such a tent, for the sides were rolled up as if in hopes of a breeze. In this roof's shade, three men moved around a table as if inspecting and tallying the loot. Against the white glare of the plain, the shadow was intense: the men underneath were featureless dark shapes that bent, turned, and gestured against a blazing ground.

The work gang trudged from the cart to a shallow sloping trough whose upper end was outside the Tek pen. At once, the lower end of the pen became a scrambling, flailing mass of assorted Teks fighting for space at the trough. Undisturbed, each of the gang in turn went through the motions of drinking and scooping their floppy hats full of water they then sluiced over their heads and shoulders.

While the keep's domed shadow shortened, Lur watched the work gangs move between keep, pavilion, and trough. Seldom was there a moment when there was no one either just approaching the trough or just turning away. But Lur thought he could creep unseen along the far side of the pen and get in springing distance of the trough's upper end—near enough to snap at the handle of the waterball that must be there—in the first unguarded instant.

With gliding controlled strides, Lur moved across the expanse of open ground between the spill and the keep. For a moment he paused, panting in the keep's skirt of shadow, then circled around its blind right side toward the pen.

"Break the poles and let me out." Lur whirled: the voice'd been practically in his ear. A manform, adolescent, moved beside him on the inside of the pen, stopping when he stopped. Long oozing scratches were gouged from the crown of his head and across one eye, which was swollen and sightless. "Levitation, theorist," the Tek identified himself, "based in Murfez Keep until it was broken. Can't reserve a beastform here. No standing. I'll carry the water. I have hands and you don't. I have to carry the—"

Lur swiped at the whispering Tek through the bars but only scraped his hip, so quickly did the other spring away. Lur crept on to the corner: a clamor on his left announced that somebody was drawing water and letting some run down the trough. Lur lay flat.

"Don't think because you can get a tiger and I can't," said the other Tek loudly, "you'll steal the water and keep me from getting to Down. Let me out, or I'll see you based—"

"Shut up."

"The cat!" the Tek began screaming. "The cat! The cat!"

Lur tried again to get at him through the bars. He could only hope the looters would take no notice. But as he crept hurriedly nearer the end of the pen, a crowd of the little workers came bounding toward him, brandishing painted clubs with curved metal teeth. They checked when they got a clear view of him; then the edged clubs began to arc toward him. Lur turned tail and ran.

On the rock spill he began to outdistance them, his broad pads sinking only slightly while they had to scramble and slide. But Lur had to ascend the entire three-mile ramp and squeeze among the rocks of the mountainside before the pursuers turned and began trudging down again.

Lur, by this time, was terribly thirsty. So he headed toward the nearest water: the cataract in the valley, some miles away. When he arrived he found nobody there, but his nose, and a pile of firewood gathered since the morning, informed him his capricious allies had not been absent long. Lur waded right into the fall pool, and drank until the baked feeling receded. Then, without waiting for the pair to return, he again took the twisting way leading up and out to the inner face of the mountains. He did not descend the ledges to the spillramp but instead found a shadow to nap in until dark. Then, in the sudden cool, he ambled down the still-searing rubble and again crept out toward the pen.

"Are you going to let me out?" said his nemesis, the instant Lur approached the stakes.

"Yes. Now shut up."

The Tek only chuckled, while Lur took a moment to survey the scene. Work was proceeding by torchlight; and from the open port, white light spilled from the keep's interior. By the head of the trough, three workers were drinking and talking in tired voices.

Lur circled back around the keep to approach from the side nearest the pavilion, where the loosed Teks would create the most confusion. He leaned against the poles and they creaked. He tested until he found one more shallowly set than its neighbors and reared up, digging foreclaws into its top. Inside, one of the turtleforms leaned the edge of its shell on the stakes, which creaked again. A hand snatched at Lur, tearing fur from his shoulder; he flinched but made no sound, putting all the cat's weight and strength against the post. Instead of pulling free of the ground the post snapped suddenly about halfway down, leaving Lur rolling with his claws deeply embedded in a thick pole about five feet long. The manforms, narrow enough to shove through the gap, sprang onto his shoulders and side, tearing and biting.

Lur couldn't run, couldn't defend himself except with fangs and hind feet. Frantically he bit at the pole, freeing first one foot, then the other, meanwhile rolling and kicking out with his hind feet, his nose filled with the stink of blood and festering wounds.

The looters came running. They swept away the remainder of the manforms that tried to scamper away, then ringed Lur—some carrying torches, some with those wicked toothed

clubs or long pikes. He turned at bay against the side of the
pen, roaring, left forefoot raised to strike out at any who'd
dare come within reach, protected by the poles behind him
from the thumping strikes of the birdforms dancing and
screaming inside the pen.

As a looter poked toward him with a pike, and a thrown
firebrand bounced sparks at his flank, Lur turned and jammed
his shoulders through the gap he'd made and burst into the
pen, slamming at the head of the closest hawkform as he
bounded onto the shell nearest him. Gathering himself even in
the instant of landing, he leaped the high barrier of stakes on
the other side.

Striking the ground, he doubled and raced to the top of the
trough, easily batting aside the few startled looters between
him and his goal.

In the moment before the mob arrived he saw the plarit
cord that, passing through the handle of the waterball, was
fused to the ground on either side of the trough. The ball was
locked in place.

Lur beat the mob to the spillramp and labored up it, eventually leaving the torches and the shouting behind. He'd been
very lucky it hadn't occurred yet to any of the looters that a
fuser beam could be used as a weapon.

Elda was told in the morning that a Valde had come across
the bridge, to Ardun's noisy and protracted delight; but he
didn't hear about the cat until later. He hadn't expected any
Valde to return so soon, because there was still one Screamer
left. Elda hadn't had to do anything. As he'd expected, he'd
just had to wait until the Screamers saw to the matter themselves, each in its own ingenious fashion. None hung onto
breathing with anything like Lur's perverse determination.

So he hadn't thought any Valde would start coming back
for another week or so, till the last Tek was gone.

But he was called up from the workroom and into the yard,
enclosed between two wings of the building and a high wall on
the street side, where the children were let run while their
parents were down below. He found Orlengis waiting for him
with the news about the Valde.

"So I owe you my hide, that's plain," remarked Orlengis,
glumly enough. "And I'm obliged to you. I still have to go to
the Summerfair, and tell about the Broken Bridge, and
all. . . . I have to do that, you see that. . . . But I'll tell

about what Domal here's done, maybe get you clear of Ardun, at any rate. . . ."

"Don't trouble yourself," said Elda. What with all the tools in the storage bins, and what they'd already smuggled up into the living quarters in spite of frequent searches, the Innsmiths could slice the whole building up like a cheese any time they pleased. Domal Ai didn't make much of a jailer, Elda thought: he hadn't the practice.

"Whatever you please, then," Orlengis rejoined dubiously, and with a certain relief. "They got my ship," he added, and kicked morosely at a clump of grass in the courtyard's packed dirt. "The *Obedient*. And they won't release her to me. And little 'Kalas, do you recall Perkalas, my steersman? They killed him, in a really shameful way . . . and he was with my Da. . . ."

"Likely Ashai will get you a new ship."

"Likely. But it won't be the same. You know."

"He don't—Ashai. He'll figure everything's fixed—"

"Let it be," directed Orlengis, without energy. "Well. Time I was gone." He wandered back to the big iron gate, where the guards let him out.

The cat, Elda didn't hear about until noontime, and didn't think much about it at the time. He'd just finished watching the last Tek demonstrate how to drink a powder that eventually ate a large ragged smoky hole in the flooring. It being time for the meal, Elda ate; but his thoughts were elsewhere.

Near sunset the grown Innsmiths were again searched and permitted to trudge upstairs for the daymeal. Elda and Tildur and Tildur's wife Fren—a shrewd woman, careful with tools—were discussing whether to leave the big purple globes until they'd found another way of learning what was inside: it was a little purple globe that'd eaten through the Tek and the floor. It was a problem like having to break eggs to see if there were chicks in them.

Similar sorts of talk moved ahead and behind on the stairs: everybody seemed to find a separate satisfaction in working with the Tek tools, in considering problems of ways and means. Of course there was the tidestorm, already building, still unresolved. They could, of course, ruin all the stuff they now had—but that didn't help the stuff that'd come from the second chamber of the keep, that Ashai's men had just lately gotten into. A huge act of sabotage couldn't be hidden: they'd only get one chance at it. In the meantime Elda thought about the tidestorm only when he couldn't help it. It was like the warning twinges of some sickness he'd die of, sometime.

After the meal they were served slabs of strawberry pie—prisoned or not, they were excellently fed—while the children clambered into the deep windowsills, where it was coolest.

"There it is! There's the cat!" one boy burst out, and children balanced on furniture and on each other to peer through those grills not denied them by adults' curiosity.

"I swear, Elda," called Medd, "that's the boy you left behind on the river, the Newstocker. Come and see if it an't. Got a Valde with him and the biggest cat I ever seen. Elda? Come here and see."

It wasn't all that hard to see them: folk on the road had moved well clear, even into the gutters, as the two and the sand-colored cat approached in a leisurely way, surveying the buildings they passed.

Chiefly, Elda recognized Jannus by his walk. The boy was got up in a fantastic costume of full-sleeved collarless grey overshirt and dark green pants—Newstock colors, Elda recollected—with a triple string of coppers hung across his chest like a Quickmoor whore. Black bearded and braided of hair, the boy was made more of a spectacle by the fact that the Valde with him was dressed just the same—Orlengis' passage ticket through the Thornwall, Elda didn't doubt. Neither showed a weapon, or needed to: surely the biggest cat in the world padded on a loose leash between them. They were about three houses away.

Retreating to the dining hall, Elda shouted for everybody to come away from the windows. When only a few budged, and those unwillingly, Elda started from room to room shoving them away from the windows. But, emptyhanded, the Innsmiths were bored and unhappy, the children most of all; the windows drew them back again the second he moved on.

"Elda Hildursson," exclaimed Medd, "what in the green world do you think you're doing? Leave me be! 'Tan't no harm to look at a cat."

Elda wavered, then gave up. His Family'd be seen, then, like a cage of squirrels. He didn't have to be seen too, gawking like a fish: he resumed his place at the table and poked at his pie.

"Why," Medd was saying cordially, balanced on a chair to look down through the grate, "I never expected to see *you* east of the swamp. . . . She is? Well, an't that a thing! And how'd you come by such a cat as that? Surely, where else would he be? Elda?" she called, turning. "It's that Newstocker, just like I said. What? Yes: Jannus, the Trader's boy. Elda, he wants to see you—"

"An't giving audiences today," muttered Elda, but he pushed to his feet, all the same. Medd's climbing down gave him room to fold his arms on the windowsill. "What."

"Elda?" The boy backed a few paces into the street, until they could see each other. "This is Poli lar-Jannus, my pact-mate, that I brought out of Lisle. And Lur," he said, waving at the cat, "you already know. . . ."

The cat reared up against the window: the room went dark and children at near windows screeched and scrambled back into the dining hall. "Where's the equipment from Cap's Keep?" the cat muttered at him and flexed its claws in the top of the grate. "Did they bring waterballs out? Force knives? Fusers?"

"Lur, get down from there," came the boy's annoyed voice. "Now there're guards coming."

"Where is it?" the cat was demanding, looking fiercely past Elda, searching even while the leash hauled at him. Reluctantly, the cat dropped to all fours and paced back to the Valde, facing the approaching guards.

The day doorkeeper had called archers from the yard gate and another pair from the nearest warehouse to support him. "Freeborn," he called persuasively to Jannus, "come away, show your marvelous beast at our barracks in Coiners' Street. . . . Oh: I see you're not registered. Then you must entertain us another time. It's too near the horning. Come, I'll show you the quickest way to the ferry landing. . . ."

And while the doorkeeper chattered diplomatically, the cat was settling into a crouch, tail stirring slightly. The doorkeeper lifted a finger, which brought the archers' bows up, and exclaimed how it grieved him to insist they come away but they knew all unregistered strangers had to be out of Ardun by the third horning. Meanwhile, inside, one of the stewards ordered Elda, with less politeness and a fair-sized truncheon, to get away from the window and back to the table. Elda would have lost his temper if Medd hadn't started complaining about the furniture. She yanked a leg off a chair and waved it in the steward's face to show him, with several men sitting on the table and calling encouragement.

Elda turned again to the window.

Jannus and the cat were being herded toward the ferry slip by the cautious archers. But the Valde was still here, ignoring the coaxing that was all the doorkeeper dared use on such as her.

"We have seen Orlengis," she told Elda, just as if the doorkeeper were ten streets off and Medd and the steward weren't still whacking wood on wood in the doorway. "We know what you do here. To kill the Shai we have need of a waterball: blue plarit, about the size of a pumpkin. Push the button and the water comes. . . . Good. You have seen such. And a force knife, we need: cuts with no blade . . .? Good."

From him, though he hadn't opened his mouth, she'd taken all the answer she cared about. He'd no more say about it than an apple tree. As she strolled away, Elda grabbed the grate and pulled with all his strength just to give his anger someplace to go, then swung around. "Medd! Let the poor man be!"

They couldn't take the Dungate ferry in the morning: without the pressure of a pair of archers, the ferryman refused to have such a mischancy looking creature as Lur on his craft. Not, he said, if each of the cat's hairs was a finger, and every and each finger jammed with fine rings from nail to knuckle.

Arduners seemed to talk like that.

Though it meant walking all the way up to the Sunset Bridge, Jannus parted with the ferryman cordially, having bought one of the man's carved trinkets for friendliness' sake. The ornament was ivory, fashioned in the shape of the Blooming Rose, emblem of Ardun. Jannus strung it on a cash cord for Poli to wear, but she didn't want it. So he wore it himself.

The detour meant it was long past the third horn of the morning, at which time the gates were opened to unregistered strangers, when they crossed over Arant Dunrimmon into Ardun. The bridge led them into the district called Whiteflats, where yesterday they had met such an astonishing welcome, with Poli all but dragged off to be welcomed by the Master's chief steward and pelted with rosepetals while Jannus, and even Lur, were scarcely noticed in the commotion. She'd reported afterward that she'd even been apologized to for Lisle, on behalf of the Master, though nobody in the crowd had the least idea she herself had been among the captured freemaids—they seemed to take her for an Awiro. She'd liked being surrounded by all the joyousness but had found her tolerance for such celebration dimmed by the realization that nobody had any real notion of who she was. Refusing an invitation to take the daymeal at the Aihall, with the Master, she'd come away and rejoined them as soon as she could.

They'd spent the rest of the afternoon making money, showing Lur in different parts of the city, charging people for the opportunity to touch him. After investing some of this odd income in new clothes for himself and Poli, Jannus had found an understeward and set up for today several matches for Lur in the duelling pit in the Aihall Square, where Jannus hoped the Master could be drawn into wagering some small items brought out of Cap's Keep.

Lur had been willing enough, until they'd met Orlengis in the Aihall Squire and talked to Elda. Now, Lur wanted to forget the original plan and concentrate on forcing Elda to smuggle out what they needed. He lagged against the leash, which Poli held since that seemed to reassure the passers-by: so they went slowly.

"But Orlengis said Elda didn't care about being freed," Jannus argued softly. "He's got the tools he wanted in the first place, and the protection of Domal Ai against Duke Ashai. Why should he help us?"

Lur stopped entirely, sat on his haunches and dropped both forepaws on Jannus' shoulders—which in itself was enough to make people stop and watch, from a safe distance—to covertly mutter in Jannus' ear, "Get him to cut a waterball. Blow the place up. Then we can snatch and run."

Jannus tried to budge the paws, laying like sacks of mud. Lur grinned into his face. "We work through the Master. You can't slaughter half a town to steal their rings afterward. Now get off me. There's a man bringing a cage of wild boars at noon, and we'll be late and forfeit the bond."

For just a moment Jannus wasn't sure Lur wouldn't kill him and ignore Poli's dart, as he'd meant to do in Lifganin; but Lur decided not to force the issue after all, and sullenly dropped back to all fours. Lur never had liked the notion of getting the beast involved in duels. Jannus suspected he was just looking for an excuse to drop the plan.

Ardun, Jannus thought as they turned into a cross street, was immense beyond his expectations: Quickmoor could have served it as little more than a minor enclave, Newstock as a district. It would take a month just to learn the names of all the streets and a season, at least, to explore them all. "Here's Bakers' Street," he remarked to Poli. "Do you want some jam tarts?" He ducked into the crowd that made no way for him alone and bought a net sack of ten tarts for the outrageous price of two coppers, or twenty 'bones,' as the ivory coinage of Ardun was commonly called. But Jannus didn't mind the price. He had a whole hundred-string, all metal, an equally absurd amount, from yesterday's meanderings.

He offered a tart to Lur, eternally hungry: Lur approved. So Jannus shared out the remaining tarts equally and they strolled, in their circle of conspicuous privacy, into the open square.

On three sides were the connected buildings of the Aihall, pierced at intervals by arched passageways for the street traffic. These buildings were chiefly of the brownish-red stone of northern Lifganin, with balconies above, roofed terraces below, and hundreds of broad windows. On the many lattices and shutters, all of ivory, were carved versions of the Blooming Rose emblem of the town and the town's Masters.

Enclosing the square on the fourth side were the true roses: the Thornwall, border of the land of Valde. Infinitely entangled and impenetrably green, the rose hedge stood at equal height with the Masters' Tower and sifted its pungency in the slow enclosed airs within the square. Its blooming signalled the start of the Summerfair, visible around the whole southern border of Valde. Across the acres of square, each rose appeared tiny and gemlike on the broad unbroken face of the hedge.

A path marked by straight strips of plantings—chiefly beds of neatly trimmed and probably overtended rosebushes—led from the gateless hedge to the door of the Masters' Tower. It was, Jannus had learned, known reasonably enough as the Rose Way. People passed along the Rose Way and came at last to the hedge; but what became of them there, or how they entered, Jannus could never quite discern. Yesterday he'd been too busy avoiding being pushed, by the crowd that'd welcomed Poli, either into a fountain or into the round tiered pit to the left of the Rose Way.

The duelling pit had originally been used to settle quarrels among men, under the Master's eye, as was still common in both Quickmoor and the farmsteads of Bremner. But the Master before Domal Ai had outlawed public duelling and substituted the equally edifying spectacle of the public whipping of those who violated his prohibition. Now the pit was rented by the hour from the square's steward for various contests, with seats rented in turn from the contests' organizers.

Under a notice board with the nature of scheduled contests printed in large letters, Jannus spotted the man who'd agreed to bring pigs. Jannus opened his red scribecase, ready to enter the agreed wager customary between himself and the man— fifty coppers, or the equivalent in bones, at four-to-one odds—when it developed that the man wanted Lur to fight all three pigs simultaneously instead of in succession, as had been agreed before. Jannus didn't have to look to Lur to know the cat would never put up with that. He eventually talked the man around, on the grounds that the longer the contest, the more people would be drawn to watch it and hire good viewing space in the tiered seats. Already the circle was filled from top to middle tier as people saw Lur, studied the notice board, and decided to remain to watch. Probably more than a few had seen Lur, and heard about the match, yesterday, and had come to the square just to watch.

The man and Poli went off to collect the seating fees, leaving Lur tied to the notice board. Jannus dragged the box that served as a scribe table a few rods away from the cat and settled down to tally the bets offered him, writing names and figures in neat columns.

Noon, or the fifth hour as they called it here, was announced from the Masters' Tower by a horn much higher in pitch than that marking the opening or closing of the town; Jannus hoped the hornblower, from his high perch, would have noticed the crowd by the pit and Lur's formidable bored shape sprawled on the grass, and would report to the Master that there was something worth his interest down here. The present Master was reputed to be a betting man, and from the Awiro, Poli had learned he had often, in past seasons, been accustomed to hunt in Lifganin. Such a man would take an interest in unusual animals and good contests. Or at least it seemed reasonable that he should. Or Jannus hoped he did. . . .

Finally the line of bettors was reduced to two. Writing the last name, Jannus closed his book and capped his ink. Poli, having strung their share of the seat fees, came to untie Lur and lead him down into the pit by means of a ramp she lowered with a pulley. The three boars were already down there in boxes with doors the man could raise, with a jerk on a rope, by leaning over the wall that protected the bottom tier of seats. As Poli hauled the ramp back up, the first pig was loosed.

All black prickly edges, the boar looked like something ineptly assembled out of shavings. Generally a match for a grass cat, the pig was probably at least twice Jannus' weight, but the distance and the angle diminished it, whereas Lur looked almost normal as he walked uneasy figures at the opposite side of the pit.

The boar trotted a few steps before spotting Lur, then charged. Lur sprang straight up in the air, so high that the pig had whirled and was coming back at him before Lur's feet touched the dust. He bounded sideways but the boar turned with him, so he clouted it to give himself time and room to move. The boar may have staggered a step, but its momentum was greater than the force of Lur's blow and it struck the cat head-on. Instead of raking and retreating awhile, as he and Jannus had planned, Lur closed his jaws on the pig's back and held that grip until the animal was still.

The hair along Lur's spine seemed as spiky as the boar's had been, showing his disquiet at finding the pig so quick-moving. Paying no visible attention to the crowd's noise above him, Lur dragged the pig against a wall and tore free a few mouthfuls before the pig man could reach a second rope. Even then, Lur pretended no interest in the next boar, but proceeded with his untidy meal until the boar actually charged him. Crouching over his kill, Lur hit the boar with a spread forepaw—this time, hard enough to knock it rolling. Its shoulder bleeding, the pig became more cautious, dancing on its tiny sticklike legs to approach from an angle rather than directly. Snarling around the current mouthful, Lur threatened with a raised paw but didn't budge as long as the pig kept its distance, treating it as though it were a fellow predator after his kill.

The pretense failed when the pig, having circled to the right, feinted right and lunged left, scoring Lur's flank with a swipe of its tusks. Lur slapped it into the wall and apparently broke its spine with that one furious blow, for it didn't move.

The third bout was somewhat anticlimactic, since it was increasingly plain that Lur could slaughter the pigs practically at will. Lur was a false cat, but a true killer; the illusion of combat was hard for him to remember and maintain.

Nevertheless, with wagers and bench hire (though no spectators had consented to sit nearer the pit than five tiers up), Jannus had strung and knotted over two hundred cash in metal and bone when the match was over. The peculiar thing was that, although half the crowd drifted away, to shade and cool drinks, perhaps, more continued to arrive and pay for seating. Jannus discovered that people were willing to spend money even to watch Lur gorge himself on raw pig and irritably lick his flank.

The second match never materialized. The brothers with the swamp snake failed to appear. Lur ate what was left of the pig and made threatening gestures at the scattered observers whenever it occurred to him, then eventually wandered to the shaded rim of the pit and flopped on his side, panting. And people paid to watch that too.

When Jannus next looked, Poli was down in the pit fastening collar and leash. She faced quietly up the aisle she meant to walk, and people on that side hastily vacated their seats. She led Lur onto the ramp she'd lowered, up the aisle, and to a fountain by the Rose Way (where people could watch him as close as they pleased for nothing, and did). Jannus felt he should have thought about getting Lur up from the pit himself, but he'd been keeping his spare attention on the balcony of the Masters' Tower, to know the moment Domal Ai should show himself. Having declined his invitation, Poli didn't know the man and therefore couldn't judge his mood or interest.

Lur hauled Poli, at leash's end, into the shadow of the nearest rosebush. Having looped the strings of cash around his neck, Jannus joined them there.

"And what's it accomplished," Lur was muttering, "all the dancing around in—" He shut up as a man and three children, all richly dressed, passed by up the Rose Way.

"Do you want something to eat?" Jannus asked Poli. "There's a man selling fish and rice from a cart, over by the third arch, there. . . ."

The food, he discovered, could be served in a long handled gourd, but that would cost extra. And it could have salt and seasonings added, but that would be extra too. And it happened that the vendor also had a skin of wine, but. . . . The vendor was very apologetic and very polite and had probably dismembered somebody's mother to get this prize place, right by the Rose Way.

When Jannus went back he found Poli with her eyes shut and the heels of her hands laid over her ears: it was plain she found the inward clatter of Ardun both distracting and tiring. It was one reason they hadn't paid the registration fee that would have let them stay after the third horning; the other reason, of course, was Lur—who, having eaten and drunk, was now asleep. Their plan to catch the notice of Domal Ai seemed to be going awry. Jannus touched Poli's arm and they dipped into the seasoned food in the gourd. He hadn't bought any wine, so they drank from the fountain.

There was to be, at the ninth hour, a simple but showy match involving Lur with the passage of assorted fire hazards—more a display than a contest. The pit had been rented for the entire afternoon. Seeing a man approaching whom he recognized as the steward in charge of the square, Jannus assumed the steward wanted to know if they still wished to reserve the pit, which had been vacant now some while.

But the steward presented the compliments of the Master and inquired whether Jannus would engage his beast for a further match. He addressed Jannus as *Freeborn,* apparently a local use-title.

Jannus licked his fingers clean and expressed himself most gratified by the Master's notice, adding that agreement would depend on the nature of the match and the stakes involved, since one did not risk such an unusual and valuable beast lightly.

"Surely not," concurred the steward. "The Master has a particular interest in cats, using them to hunt in the wilderlands west of Arant Dunrimmon. He would match two of these against yours, to judge the quality of all."

"It is wondered what stakes the Master would find interest in," responded Jannus, casting the inquiry in the politest mode.

"You are Bremneri," said the steward, apparently noticing the phrasing. "Are you yourself the trainer of this cat?"

Jannus considered. "No. One called Lur, after his profession, taught this cat his skills."

"A pity: the Master wished to take the trainer into his service."

"It is known that the Master appreciates skilled hands," rejoined Jannus drily, thinking of the Innsmiths. "But it is possible the Master might find another wager I might propose equally suitable. . . ."

"Your courtesy, Freeborn, brightens an otherwise undistinguished afternoon. . . ."

"I have some small knowledge concerning the High Plain, to which purpose I have already met with Duke Ashai, of Ismere. I would like to view Master Domal's collection of artifacts, that I might inform myself of any not already familiar to me. . . ."

Not surprisingly, the steward seemed taken aback. He stared at Jannus as if suspicious of a joke—Jannus looking blandly back—and then said to Poli, "Lady Valde, is this Bremneri known to you?"

"He is."

"Will you serve as a Fair Witness in this?"

"I will not," she replied. "Yet I myself say both his knowledge and interest are real. And he has met with Ashai, as he says."

"I came to Ardun," Jannus put in, more and more pleased with the effect of his bait, "chiefly on the chance of acquiring some small items of interest from among the Master's collection. The wager would thus be happily arranged."

The steward handled his mouth uncertainly. "I am not authorized to make such a wager. Will you kindly wait until I can consult the Master's wishes in the matter?"

"The Rose Way must make all travelers eager to linger," Jannus replied, and grinned at the steward's back.

The steward didn't return. Instead came a spindling elderly man with framed glass circles over his eyes. Jannus, quite sure this was the Master himself, was mildly disappointed: he'd expected someone more prepossessing, who looked more like Duke Ashai.

Poli nudged Lur, who woke up with an inquiring grunt; the old man glanced aside sharply at the noise, then paid the cat no further attention—staring instead at Jannus, as though he were the more outlandish creature. "You know things of the High Plain, do you?" he said, for greeting. "Who taught you to call it that?"

"Why it is called so, in Bremner," lied Jannus, quite calmly.

"Is it. And what are these, then?" He pointed at the frames over his nose.

Jannus could see Poli without having to turn or look aside. He caught the slight motion of her hand, relaying Lur's warning. "Clearly," he replied, "they are intended to aid your vision in some fashion. But I've never seen such. They are of modern workmanship."

"What makes you think so?" challenged the Master.

"Kantmorie seldom worked in wood, firstly. They preferred crystal lattice and ceramic and, of course, plarit." Jannus was quite confident. All the way across Lifganin, he'd had Lur drilling him in what was likely to have been found in the outer chambers of Cap's Keep—what each thing looked like and could be used for. "Second, no Tek would tolerate a body with poor vision long enough to need to devise such a tool for it."

The Master seemed to make up his mind. Pulling off a glove, he bared his right arm to the elbow, revealing a network of fibrous filaments. "The controlling arm," observed Jannus, in a tone of pleasant discovery, "of a radio handler. Have you taken the larger arms, the remote handlers, from the keep's inner wall?"

"Yes."

"That's a pity. They'll all be dead now . . . unless you've kept them in salt water . . .? That's too bad. They're all dead, then."

"How do you get it off again?" demanded the Master tensely, as if there were some trick in the question—like the one about the eye glasses.

Jannus checked with Poli, found no warning. "Could I see where it roots, at your shoulder?" he requested, delaying, and fingered the calloused lump at the thick part of the stem. "You've been wearing it a long while, haven't you? I'd think that would be uncomfortable—"

"It is."

Jannus' fingers found a spongy bubble, a node on the stem, and drew his hand quickly back. "You *have* been wearing it a long time—it's getting ready to spore. That's a bit dangerous: I'd take it off, if I were you."

Poli told him quietly, "He can't."

"Ah. I see. Then we have a basis to trade from, I think. I would like at least one variable force knife—a tube, usually green, about as long as my hand, cutter adjustable from zero to about five rods, Bremneri measure—and at least two waterballs. They're blue plarit, a little larger than a melon, with a button and a spout that water comes out of. They're common enough, you should have several. . . . And in return, I'll tell you how to remove the control arm before it fruits and spreads all over you."

"You're no Deathless—you're too old," reflected the Master abruptly. "What are you, then: an agent of Ashai Rey?"

Jannus found himself recalling Lur's answer: *a mind, a body.* . . . He said, "I'm the man with the cat who knows how to rid you of that vine." When Domal Ai looked to the file of archers waiting at the head of the Rose Way, Jannus decided it would be better to answer the question. "I serve no man. Yet I have met Duke Ashai, and seen Tek work in his hands. I bargained with him for the sight of it, as I meant to do in Ardun."

"Why did you set your cat to kill my soldiers in Han alla?"

Lur made a slight shrug of admission and looked away, cking his whiskers meditatively. At a loss, Jannus had no ady excuse to serve as a plank over this suddenly dangerous asm; Poli intervened, saying "Han Halla and Lifganin are ilderland, Domal: free to all hunters."

That was pointed enough, considering the Innsmiths. Domal garded Poli perplexedly. "Are you of the Awiro, Lady alde? I was told you were. . . ."

"I am lar Haffa. And you must take the bargain or else alk away. You cannot have him, Domal: we are on *larfai*, e and I."

"Oh! I didn't know, never thought," stammered the Master, d from brow to throat. "He wears no stone, and, and he's a remneri!"

"We are of the Third Kindred," said Poli firmly.

Clearly, Domal was suddenly unsure how to proceed. The reats and the actions suitable for coercing a Bremneri no-ody were abominations if they included a Valde. Domal asped his hands together thoughtlessly and winced as the ontrol arm magnified the force of the grip painfully. He oved his right arm carefully away from him again. "I must ave time to consider the proposed wager properly," he told annus, becoming very formal. "Until the twelfth hour? But o: I see you are not registered. Will you and your lar guest ith me tonight, then?"

Jannus invented a proverb, replying, "Cats and Valde are est content beyond walls. Your graciousness honors us, but o."

"Then as soon as may be after the third hour, tomorrow. nd we well settle the nature and the amount of the wager hen."

"I do hear you."

"That's Watertalk, isn't it? My acquaintance with the Brem-eri Way is slight: does that mean I may expect you?"

"The wager is of some small interest to me, as well. We will ome."

"Good," said the Master, and went back down the Rose Vay, his right arm held stiffly at his side.

Lur muttered, "What's proposed?"

"You," replied Poli, "against two trained hunting leopards."

"We're away past that, now," said Jannus. "That vine has a pore case the size of a plum on it."

"Hard, to touch," asked Lur, "or soft and spongy?"

"More leathery."

"It won't spore until the case is hard and brittle. It will b safe to be around him for a few days yet."

"Sour things," recited Jannus, fishing for the memory "make the control arms return to dormant phase. Is that right Vinegar would do, wouldn't it?"

"Any weak acid. Don't be near him if it spores, though. I you breathe the spores you'll be on the High Plain sooner tha you expect."

With that unpleasant thought, Jannus went off to the foun tain to duck his head. As he wiped his hair back out of hi eyes, he noticed the fire hazards being set up in the pit.

"Leopards," Lur breathed, slouching behind Poli toward th pit. "And this beast with a belly full of pig and agile as mud Leopards. Your confidence is excessively touching."

"Shut up. We're past that now. Jump a few fires and you're through. Unless you mean to come into the Aihall with us to morrow. . . ."

Mechanically, predictably, Lur glanced up lest a roof creep upon him unaware.

Elda was sitting with his son Dinnel, whom he'd just fetched back from the sickrooms, when noise from the stairs and a sudden inrush of people marked his Family's being released from the workrooms. For a while the room was crowded, everybody wanting to touch Dinnel and hear his assurances that his head was fine, and he'd been treated fine. Finally the rattle of the daymeal being wheeled in drew them back into the hall, leaving just Elda, Medd, Dinnel, and Dinnel's wife Letty, who nudged and edged until Elda surrendered his space at the bedside to her and went over to stand by the window.

"Bett lost that greenstone box of hers," said Medd, untying her coil of braids, "after they searched the last time. You'd best see about it before you go, Elda, she's real choice of that box, carried it clear across Lifganin, you recall. . . ."

"I'll talk to her. If one of the stewards took it, an't much I can do, though."

"Talk to her, anyhow. And how was Inetta?"

Dinnel said, "Inetta's gone, Ma. When I woke up this morning, she'd died. When Da came, he saw that what was needful was done. Here, seems like they just put them out with the tide."

"Now, an't that a thing!" Medd began undoing one braid, exposing a narrow black tube stuck into the braid where it was thickest. "Pity," she was saying, "there's no way of sending word to Solvig. He'd want to know." Freeing the smuggled tube, she set it on the windowsill by Elda's arm. "That what you wanted?"

Elda scraped the concealing paint off the knife with his thumbnail, so the tube shone green as new grass. A luminous bead was stuck on the narrow end: Elda tapped it, but it was solidly attached. "What's this?"

" 'Twas with the other knives, in the same bin. . . ."

Elda pointed the tool away from him and twisted the apparently seamless handle in the way he'd learned. The bead moved smoothly outward on the end of a stalk of gold-shining filament. " 'Tan't a knife," he remarked.

" 'Twas with the others," Medd said again. "What is it, if it an't a knife?" She reached to touch the stalk, then froze, turning up her palm in slow surprise. "It cut me! It an't supposed to do that! Look here, Elda—I never even touched it, and it cut me!" She showed him her hand, with a thin line of blood scored across three fingers.

"Stand clear, hear me?" Rotating the barrel as far as it would go put the bead halfway across the room, marking the end of the weightless stalk. Elda screwed it down again, to about a knife's length, and brought it toward the wooden arm of the nearest chair. The stalk never touched the wood: nevertheless, while it was still two fingers' span distant, a groove appeared on the wood and deepened as Elda tilted the tool. There was no force, no effort, but the wood was sliced completely through.

"You watch out for that, Elda," advised Medd, wrapping a bit of cloth around her hand. "That one *would* take your arm off, not just the sleeve."

"But what *is* it?" demanded Dinnel, propped on both elbows to see.

"Call it a sword, I expect. . . ." Elda screwed the bead, which he'd guessed was a marker to show the end of the invisible blade, tightly against the top of the tube. The stalk, maybe, served the same use—so a man using the sword wouldn't cut both his own legs off by mistake. Elda bounced the sword lightly in his palm, thinking that this was just the sort of tool Domal would have loved: a weapon, pure and simple. It was almost too bad he'd never get the chance to see one.

Medd finished binding her fingers and she and Letty got

Dinnel on his feet, helping him out to the place saved for him at the table. Their second boy, Ed, came and stood in the doorway, blocking it, while Elda used the sword to cut a good-sized hole in the floor nearest the outside wall, laying each board carefully aside without noise. Then Ed came in and quickly slid down into the hole until his feet found the top of a bin and he could climb down the rest of the way. In a minute he started handing up the things Elda'd had put aside in one pile as useful, which Elda put on the far side of the bed, out of sight. Then Ed used the bin as a ladder again and reached, so Elda could yank him back into the room. They put the boards back crosswise and set a chair over the place.

"See nobody sets in that," Elda remarked.

"Don't worry," replied his son, going back to the door to check on the two stewards.

"An't worried. And you see to it Domal don't miss me."

"It's all set. You'll have a beautiful funeral, right out in the yard, before he knows you're ailing."

"And don't let him bring any more Screamers here, whatever you do, or the Valde will keep off and there's no telling what he'd do then. You tell Dinnel."

"Soon as he's fit," agreed Ed, moving aside to let Medd pass carrying a bundle concealed in the folds of her skirts. From it she took several unbroken loaves of bread and most of a ham. She did these up in a shirt and tied the arms together through the handle of one of the waterballs. Elda meanwhile was using the sword to cut out bricks at the bottom of the outer wall, behind the chair, until he had a space big enough to crawl through. Medd was busy binding the collection of Tek tools into a second pack, but was having trouble covering the light so it wouldn't shine.

"Wrap the tentcloth around it," Ed advised.

Though there was some risk, Elda visited the hall to make his farewells, remembering to cough every now and again because he was supposed to be ailing and the stewards might remember. Everybody save the youngest children knew he was going to move against the Deepfish openly, on the High Plain itself. Elda could see the difference in their faces: they no longer felt trapped, though only he was going. "Sorry," one would say, "sorry about Inetta," looking up with a sly, knowing face, touching him on wrist or arm as he moved. "Sorry," they said, "Inetta an't here to know. . . ."

Passing Bett, Tildur's daughter, Elda spoke to her as he'd promised about the greenstone box; after a minute she shook er head and said it didn't matter, he should just take care. And Irwen, Edald's wife, expecting her fourth, clutched Elda's wrist, saying finally, "You be careful, Da. . . ." Reluctantly he let him free himself—pale, likely sick with overexcitement: it'd taken her that way the last time, Elda recalled.

By Dinnel, his eldest, Elda also paused and cupped the bandaged side of his son's head, where the Fisher pikeman had hit him in Lifganin.

"Old men like you," commented Dinnel severely, "belong to be gumming leather and saying as how it's going to storm. They'll send your ears back by bird, and serve—"

"Hush up. You keep track of your Ma. Don't let her nag Irwen overmuch. And remember Ed's got say about when you're fit to take charge of the Family—"

"When I can wrestle him down two falls out of three, first thing tomorrow morning," replied Dinnel. "Letty, make your manners."

"You take care, Da," said Dinnel's wife sourly enough—she and Elda had never got on, and it was plain she liked Dinnel heading the Family.

"You enjoy the funeral," Elda told her cheerfully, then remembered to cough as the stewards moved in to clear the tables.

When he'd finished his leavetaking, Elda went back into his room, where Medd and young Dan were waiting for him. Medd had made him a Family pouch stuffed with a snippit of hair from each of their kin, according to the old custom. Elda bent his head and waited patiently until she'd got the pouch tied to her satisfaction, then worked at getting his boots off so he could tie them fast to his belt. On his nod Dan poked his head through the hole in the bricks to look, then pulled himself through. Elda, less lithe, lay down and then hitched forward on his elbows, dragging the bundles behind him.

Cautiously barefoot, alert for the nightwatch, the two Innsmiths went up the road past busy torchlit docks. The tide was low, and the boats were away out at the piers' ends, so Elda and Dan could pass without being seen. When they reached a dock that was empty they dropped down into the heavy mud of the shore and waded out along the pilings until they reached the river.

Arant Dunrimmon proved to be a faster stream than Erthrimmon. Even in midsummer, above its joining with the Morimmon it was cold as a cave spring. Before they were even halfway across, they'd been carried past the gravel spit at the tip of the peninsula and entered the turbulent cross-currents of the meeting rivers, with warm waters layered unexpectedly under or across the cool.

Whenever Elda became tired he walked water, with Dan beside him, letting the dim shore flow by as it would. Once in the shallows he heard a Fisher outposter's piping, like that he'd heard at the edge of Han Halla; but the water carried them silently past.

With the river so low, and the current so fast, they had quite a time hauling themselves up through the mud on the far shore. Dan went first, still carrying the bundles, offering a hand to Elda whenever his father became bogged down, until they reached solid ground at last.

The lights of Ardun were just visible, only two of three of them, tiny as fireflies. They circled a little way from the river, to be clear of wandering outposters, before stopping to rest.

"Where are they, then?" Dan whispered, meaning Jannus and the Valde and the cat.

"Someplace. Just keep still. They got to find us."

Though it was warm, Elda pulled off his clothes and twisted out of them all the water he could: Han Halla had taught him to hate being wet. If the High Plain was as dry as all that, he thought, this could be his last soaking for a while.

The stir and shift of the high grasses in open country was an odd noise; when Elda tried consciously to listen to it, it became lost in the whine of his own blood behind his ears, as if listening itself made a sound.

Jannus was roused from a dream of waking, an unpleasant series of nightmares in which he'd repeatedly believed himself to have escaped from delusion only to find each sunlit landscape beginning to twist and leer around him. Therefore he would not at first trust the quiet dark or the setting moon, watchful for changes.

Tensely alert, he shook off a touch on his back, saying curtly, "No. I have to watch the grass." The words seemed to roll and circle in his mind, and he suddenly felt what a peculiar thing he'd said. Rather than reassuring him, it made him feel the newest dream shift was to be within himself: a terrifying suspicion.

He was grabbed and held hard. The breath against his rigid cheek was Poli's. Slowly he leaned into her support, neverthe-less haunted by the fear she'd turn, unseen, into something horrible. A part of him waited frozenly for that to happen, even while the rest groped for her comfort.

His shoulderblades were rubbed, and then the cords in the back of his neck. This touch-loving had its effect. The waiting part of him either retreated, or else he ceased to be aware of it: the habit of trusting the apparent surfaces of things was able to reassert itself.

"I woke you," he said to her softly. "I'm sorry."

"In your dream, you didn't call to me. It would have waked me sooner, if you'd called."

"You weren't there. In the dream, you weren't there and I didn't want you there. I was afraid you'd turn into something too, if you came. . . ."

"Hush. . . ."

Presently he wondered what the dream had sounded like, to her. He wondered if he sounded like a Screamer.

She made a negative shift. "Not to me. But the Awiro," she added slowly, "they. . . . You'd be in danger of them if you were to sleep in Lifganin alone, and dream so." She laid her face against his shoulder, perhaps inspeaking to the Awiro who'd been troubled by his nightmares. At least she seemed distant. "Elda," she remarked suddenly, "is in Lifganin."

"What?"

"I hear Awiro who hear him. No: I hear him now, myself. . . ." After a brief listening, she added, "He's waiting for us, annoyed we are so long in coming, afraid a little we will not come. . . ."

Jannus freed himself and groped forward until he touched fur. Determining which way the hairs lay, he found Lur's shoulder and bumped it as he would a man's. Lur rolled over with a grunt, his eyes wide as sudden moons.

"Elda's in Lifganin, looking for us."

"Did he bring a waterball with him?" Lur asked at once.

When Poli said nothing, rolling up their blanket, Jannus replied, "We don't know."

"Hurry up," said Lur to Poli, roving around her, visible only when the moon rebounded from his eyes. "Come on. Which way?"

She tied a cord. "That way, along the river, not too near—"

Lur waited for no more instructions, but was gone. By the time Poli guided Jannus to where Elda was waiting, Lur was there already, scrabbling at something in the grass.

"Jannus?" called Elda, hearing them approach. When Jannus replied, Elda asked, "Is it safe to show a light?"

Poli made a small affirmative sound, so Jannus said, "Keep it down in the grass. . . ."

Fireless, barely casting a shadow, a pale yellow globe outlined Elda's hands holding it. Elda swung it toward Lur so quickly Jannus thought he'd barely resisted doing it before, safe or not.

"Four!" said Lur, swinging around his fanged grin. "He's brought our four waterballs, and a fuser, and a—no, two force knives, and—"

"Whatever seemed like it might be useful," Elda interrupted, stiffly getting to his feet, leaving the globe on the ground. "It's really you, an't it," he remarked to the cat in a deliberate tone, but received no reply. "You: Dan—come on back!"

Lur's head disappeared below the grasstops; perhaps, like Jannus, he was surprised to find Elda companied. Looking off to the side where the cat'd been, Dan came up beside Elda and waited. "Now," said Elda, "tell Dan how to get that vine off Domal Ai, that's stuck to his arm."

Jannus hesitated because that was their chief trading point. Then it occurred to him it wasn't needed anymore, that they wouldn't have to chance the dangerous hospitality of the Aihall this morning after all.

"Myself," Elda was saying, "I'd as soon leave the thing to choke him, or whatever it does. . . . But we can manage Domal, and who knows who'd come after him? And it's the price of a free contract with Ardun for my Family, and I need to know, to get my people out of that box."

"Soak cloths in vinegar," Jannus replied then, "and wrap the arm in the cloths, especially at the shoulder. Keep them wet until the roots retract and the vine starts to curl. But *tell* him, Dan—don't *do* it. Lur says it's getting ready to throw out spores, and if you breathed them a thing like that would start growing inside you. Don't let him come near anybody—"

"And after it rolls itself up," Lur put in, showing himself again, "don't burn it: plant it in the ground."

Jannus looked around sharply. "Lur, are you sure of that?"

"Heat will release the spores. Don't burn it."

"All right," Elda said to his son, "now tell me." And Dan repeated the directions, was corrected once, and repeated them a second time to Elda's satisfaction. "Tell Edald I said, don't wait for the funeral: see to it first thing. Now go on."

Having reminded Elda to take care, the boy jogged away, back toward Ardun.

"It'd be handy," Elda stated briskly, "to have a cart. And

we'll need more food than this, things that will keep in the heat. Jannus, you go into Ardun first thing and buy what I tell you: last time I seen you, you had enough copper on you to drown a goat. You'll walk lighter for the lack of it. Lur, how long do you figure it'll take us to get there, at the longest?"

"I don't know," said Lur finally. "I don't recall ever walking to Down."

"Well, figure it out! What's it level with? Lisle? Sithstock? Newstock? What?"

"East of Debern, west of Morgan's Hold," snapped the cat.

"Fine for us! What'd Debern close to, then"

"It would be near Lisle," Lur replied slowly, apparently deciding to accept that organizing journies was Elda's special competence. "Level with Lisle, I would guess, but far from the rim."

Elda was silent a moment, calculating. "A month, that'd be, at the outside—forty days for the whole trip, to Down and back off the High Plain again. Now you tell me just precisely what you mean to do when you get there, to Down."

"Break the lake dome. Starve the Shai of power to maintain the bases," Lur said, as if grudging every word. And Jannus realized he himself had never thought to ask Lur that obvious question. A result, he thought lightly, of too much association with Valde.

If Teks were few and gathered, for the most part, around the widely-spaced keeps, Poli should have no such trouble going onto the High Plain as she'd had before. All they had to do was pass wide of Cap's Keep and any others they found on their way north. And Elda was already deep in organizing everything else. Jannus felt relieved and more pleased than he'd expected to find Elda was going too.

The moon was down and the dawn not yet begun—almost like a starsday, with Elda's globe the only light. While Elda and Lur went on planning, Poli and Jannus settled comfortably back to back and listened to the flinchbugs and the shrill peeping of the night-flying gnatcatchers that wove and turned just overhead. Jannus found himself willing to risk sleep again after all. If the dreams returned he'd just call Poli who would come to him there and guide him back to reliable grass that would remain itself and not change. He remembered he'd been afraid to do that, before; but he couldn't remember why.

Book VI:

THE HIGH PLAIN

By day, the High Plain was an incandescent blur wherein the only motion was the rippling heat waves that shifted and flowed in mockery of water, pooling in illusory sheets across sand pockets. Poli suspected a lake had been slain unconsenting in this place, and that it was the memory of its spirit that lay thus uneasily over its glittering onetime bed.

Having waited out another day, they would go onward at night, the coarse sand cooling slowly underfoot, across an unchanging scoured flat of grey-blue and utter black. Lur led them, according to certain stars he knew, during the first long nights when the moon had retired to bear her child; there was nothing by which Poli could have guided herself.

At first light Elda would cut, with the Tek knife, two holes in some flat rock to receive the tent poles and, from these to the corners of the wicker cart, he'd stretch the tentcloth of diaphonous white fabric, a roof without walls. They'd drink and lave baked faces, then sleep by turns through the worst of the heat.

Poli savored her turns to wake: she'd stare for hours at Jannus' shirt or Elda's hair to slake her eyes' growing thirst for color. As her turn she took the hours from midafternoon to evening, when there seemed no air to breathe, just for the sake of the bright shadows on the plain as the sun dropped low. Once she quietly took the bead-sword and touched a thin, unfelt line above her knee, just to enjoy the living red.

In those waking times her mood would gradually tune itself to Jannus' dreaming without her becoming aware of it. Some evil dreams thus occupied them both for longer than she would have chosen, until he'd call out to her and rouse her attention. But he seemed not to know whether the dream had held him long or briefly and continued to trust in her vigilance and protection.

She battened upon his selfsinging and Elda's as urgently as her eyes drank color, open to all their moods, for the High

Plain seemed leeched of life. The daysinging and nightsinging
of the High Plain was an unchanging and utter silence. The
occasional distant Screamer became more a relief than a dis-
comfort; she searched for the sound of them continually for
the sake of the cat. "That way," she'd say, pointing, and the
cat would go. Presently the faroff voice would be gulped by
the silence, and eventually the cat would rejoin them and lie
panting while somebody filled basin after slow basin, so Lur
could drink.

Lur drank so much because he'd taken for his watch the
time before hers, the noon hours when the sun's angle denied
him even the shadow of the tent. Poli would sometimes wake
from a stifling nap to hear his steady panting while he waited
for the sun to cant west far enough to grant him a strip of
dark to rest his head in. Such sounds were loud, in the great
silence.

At each rest, a cache of food and water was buried to serve
their journey back, when the waterballs would be useless. In
eight night's travel, some thirty caches were laid, each marked
with a stake Elda fused fast in the sand.

On the ninth night, the empty cart was left to mark the final
cache. Elda shouldered the pack holding his third and strung
the light globe to his belt, just for the light's company. A blind
man, he thought, could walk the High Plain and never trip.

Trudging away from the cart, Elda hitched at the pack to
make its weight more comfortable. None of the Tek tools
weighed more than a handful of wet leaves; it was the other
supplies, the things they'd need when knife and sword and
waterball failed, that were so cumbersome. But after Deepfish
went, nothing but the tent would remain of use: Lur had told
him that whatever had no life of its own, whatever drew
power from the Lake of Down, would all fail.

Deepfish itself couldn't be touched: even mining down to it,
through layers of sand and crisp brittle rock, through strata of
obsidian and shift pumice that flowed like dry syrup, would be
a labor of generations—even supposing the Shai would do
nothing in its own defense, which wasn't likely. But the whole
High Plain was fed by light on the lake, sunlight on the leaves
of strange water plants that required air around them that
wasn't the world's air, as the water they floated on wasn't
water but something else. If the lake dome was cracked, Lur
had said, the special air would boil away all in a moment. The

plants would wither and die. And, no longer linked to the sun with leaf and stem, Deepfish would starve.

Elda thought about Domal Ai, how the Master would fume to discover his perilous treasures dead as mud. And Ashai Rey, braced for a tidestorm that'd have the force of a good wet sneeze without the fusers and knives and swords, all the entrancing trash. . . .

"And Ashai Rey, now," said Elda meditatively to the cat, who was pacing off to Elda's right. "Will he just fall over, or what, when Deepfish goes?"

"What does that matter? Draw me a drink."

"Matters to me." Elda shrugged the pack straps off to get at the basin. "The sun will stay on its tether whether you're here to see it or not. A good piece of the Clan is bound to that boy of Ashai's, and I want to know if he'll be inheriting sooner than Ashai expected."

"The world," rejoined Lur, in his burring mutter, "goes around the sun. Not the reverse."

"An't what I asked you. Else you can call Jannus to draw your drink. He an't anxious that Deepfish go."

"He doesn't have to be. He can walk onto the Sun Circle of Downbase and be free." Lur's head turned toward where the boy and the Valde should be walking, past where the globe showed anything to Elda's eyes. ". . . .No. The mobile would become a separate self, like any other Tek. As the Shai itself was, in the beginning. It would just lose the interconnected memories the Shai holds . . . and the Shai's immortality. Eventually, Ashai would die."

"Sooner he fell over, and was done with it." Elda held the basin under the thin steady stream from a waterball. He had just set the basin down when first the Valde, then the boy, wandered into faint visibility, the boy saying to her, "What is it? A Screamer? Poli, is it a Screamer?"

The Valde gestured with one arm, a wave covering half the world, making no answer.

"Stand clear," warned Elda, grabbing in a pocket for the sword, and wrung the tube to project the gold thread marking the blade. He had the blade about half extended when the attack came: a huge bird that was just abruptly *there*, sweeping over Lur's back into the Valde and enclosing her in its wings so she and it looked like a Fisher feather cloak blown rolling over the ground.

"Keep away," Jannus ordered them, already diving, and thumped at the feathered body—likely with a dagger-dart in his fist, for in two breaths the bird quivered and slumped. Grabbing a wing, Jannus hauled the bird over but as he bent to finish it the Valde twisted to her feet and sprang away into the dark. Only an instant slower, the boy pivoted and was likewise gone.

"Stop waving that around," said Lur, and waited until Elda had screwed the bead tight against the tube before passing by Elda to crunch the bird's neck. Lur was in that position when a second bird swept into him, flashing into sight out of the mouth of the dark just like the other.

Elda stood balancing the closed sword, afraid to use or even extend the blade again in such dim confusion. Thinking it'd been the light calling the things, like moths, Elda unhitched the net holding the globe and stuffed it into his pack with tentcloth over it, though that meant he couldn't see a blink of what was going on.

Some motion in the air warned him. He flopped on the pack and heard the thing sweep by just above him. Its wings made a loud clopping noise as it began to climb again.

Elda hauled one of the tent poles free of the pack straps in blind haste and stood with the blunt end braced in the crook of his arm, trying to guess from which direction the bird would come this time. Any way, he hoped, but from directly behind him! It was all he could do to stand still and not spin around to defend his own back.

"Careful." It was Lur's bass mutter, off to his right.

"I put it away—the sword. An't safe."

On that assurance, Lur came and sat at Elda's back: sat, to leave his forepaws free. Elda knew because he patted the air behind him until he hit fur, to be certain.

They waited.

"You: Poli!" Getting no reply to the soft call, Elda whispered to Lur, "Where'd they go to?"

"Keep still."

"What'd they run off for?"

"She ran and he hit her with a dart," replied the cat cooly. "They're about twenty yards off. He's got the sense to keep still. Now shut up: there must be ten or fifteen Teks—"

Lur's voice stopped, and Elda braced himself, but no monstrous bird collided with the pole. Instead Elda heard feet, running. The sound was neither near nor far, and there was something peculiar about it. The footfalls were too far apart: that was it. Just slightly too long for a human gait, as if an intant of floating slowed each descending strike, or else the legs were abnormally long.

The unnatural bounding continued for a long time without either approaching or diminishing. It just hung in the dark. Then, between one leap and the next, it stopped.

"Birdform," commented Lur.

So a bird had taken the runner, without sound, off in the night somewhere. Elda didn't like to think about it. "Can you till see Jannus and—"

"Yes. Shut up."

By inches that inadequate paring, the new moon, rose to occupy a rift in the distant mountain wall.

From standing tense and unmoving for so long, Elda's left leg was invaded by cramp. He tried to rub it without putting down the pole, found that useless, and had to sit down before the knot would ease even a bit. Except for the breath whistling through his teeth, he risked no other sound.

The cramp slowly relaxed, leaving behind a warning tingle that made him reluctant to put weight on the leg before he absolutely had to. Accordingly he sat and listened and waited with the pole under his hand.

The moon's sliver provided just enough light to make him strain to see and not enough for him to distinguish anything: he kept testing by wiggling fingers before his face, imagining each time that he could see the motion. But unless he stuck the hand right in front of the moon, the fact was that he couldn't see a thing.

Somebody began drawing water into a mug. The first splash startled Elda badly, and he whispered, "Leave off!" since the sound of water would call dryland creatures, most likely, even quicker than light. But the boy or the Valde, whichever it was, continued to let the waterball flow until the mug sounded full. That was stupid: Lur, the only one of them who could see, hadn't even chanced lapping at the basin Elda'd filled for him.

After awhile Elda could hear the two of them muttering together—just muted voice-sounds. Lur's voice adding a comment made Elda realize his back was unguarded—the cat had just gone off silently without warning. Angry, Elda pushed to his feet, leaning on the tent pole, and hobbled nearer the soft voices.

"—have to, then we have to," Lur was saying.

"No," Jannus replied. "We'll wait till they've all gone past."

"What do you mean," Elda interposed, thumping what he thought was Lur's side with the pole, "going off like that?"

Ignoring him, Lur said, "There's three, anyway, gone back to the base. They'll be behind us now. They'll never stop passing."

Jannus argued, "But there's no base nearer than Sith Keep, you—"

"The birdforms are from Cap's Keep. I saw them there. Where the rest are based, I don't know. But they're all around us. We can't avoid them. Go on with us, or else turn back. You decide. Personally, I'd send the Valde back, if you're concerned about her: she's no use as a guide anyway."

"No," said the boy in an expressionless voice.

"Then do what you want." Lur's voice retreated: after a minute, sounds indicated he'd begun a meal on one of the giant birds.

Elda settled carefully to ease his leg, hearing meanwhile a scampering sound from off in the night. When at length that faded he chanced a whispered question: "The Valde hurt, or what?"

"There are Teks," replied Jannus, "all around us—mostly Screamers, but some *sa'farioh*."

"Hunting us?"

"Hunting whatever moves. Passing us, going toward Down. Screamers are . . . are very painful to Valde."

She'd run, Lur had reported, and the boy'd had to catch her with a dart to stop her, keep her still. A hard thing. A hard thing, to find needful. Elda chewed gently on the inside of his cheek, where he'd bitten it earlier. "So. What's to be done?"

"I don't know. I thought we could avoid the keeps and not come near any large numbers of Screamers. I thought we could manage that way. There's only three hundred or so, alive on the whole of the High Plain!"

"I can bear it," put in the Valde's voice, quiet against the frantic control in the boy's. "It is the silence, that makes me reach too far. I can close off the silence and hear you alone—"

"You can't stay in trance whole days and nights."

"If I must, I can," she contradicted. "I endured Lisle. I can bear this too."

"Lisle—" The boy drew a deep, gasping breath. "Lisle is comparable to the High Plain, is it? And pigs grow wings and fly away into the sun."

"You must accept this, Jannus 1'. Or you make it harder for me."

Uncomfortable at the intimate dispute, Elda said, "Well,

ou tell me anything I could do to help and I'll try. Or maybe
ur's right, and you two ought to go back. What's to be done,
e'll do."

"How do you know."

"Well," Elda rejoined mildly, "Lur says so. . . ." That
eeded no comment, and got none. Elda sighed. "Before, he
n't had help," he argued, "nor tools. And he wants Deepfish
rought down as much as I do. It's—"

"No. He's hunting his own death. Just that."

"Same difference."

Jannus said nothing.

The smacking, crunching noise of Lur's meal paused; the
at said, "We'll go on a while tonight, but after this, we'll
move by day for the next five or six days—until the moon
ounds more. We're too vulnerable in the dark."

Elda limped back to where he'd dropped his pack and
craped at the ground with his stick until he found it, making
ure everything was secure. After Lur'd had his drink, Elda
ollected the basin and they moved on, slowly, and with no
onversation, hearing occasional cries and signals of the un-
een migration passing around them.

In spite of the fact that the Valde was no help, Lur found
he hunting disquietingly easy—easier with each day's travel.
There was never a time when at least one partially gnawed
carcass was not in sight between the twin flat plates of plain
and sky. Seldom were they four the only moving creatures vis-
ble in the vertically undulating air.

Lur had an impression of haste and desperation. Carcasses
vere posed in running sprawls, reaching north. Generally Teks
aung around the bases, where the freshly bodied were a source
of meat and moisture, and the keep's shadow provided a shield
against the sun. That Teks in such numbers should suddenly
lesert this marginal security and trek across the barren flats
vas perplexing, strange, and perhaps dangerous. Lur couldn't
understand it at all. Nevertheless he could see that the whole
High Plain was in motion, with all bodied Teks singlemindedly
converging on Down.

The birdforms passed first, nearly all within a day's time.
The next morning Lur spotted one, and, a little later, another—rebodied at Cap's Keep and hurrying past. After that,
e saw no more at all.

Behind the birdforms moved the swiftest bipeds, chiefly

Adapted out of Sith Keep not too far distant now off by th
foot of the Morbrole Mountains. The tall Adapted stalke
across the gravel flats in their mincing, chickenfooted wa
balanced upright by the weight of their tails. These Adapte
were relics of an attempt to produce an amphibious sul
strain capable of being settled on other continents not mod
fied for human use, beyond the tidewracked ocean. Lur foun
no use in asking them for news: they'd turn their outsize
scaled heads and look down at him, breathing harshly ove
thick black tongues, each lipless mouth set in a perpetua
grin around rows of needle teeth—all unmodified for cor
versation.

To the outspoken relief of Elda, none of the Adapted wa
interested in turning aside from the chosen line of march an
farther than the nearest carcass: they, too, found meat eas
to come by and saw no need to risk a fight.

Brooding in the twilight, Lur tried to reason what purpos
could make so many Teks suddenly start adopting beastform
what could have changed. . . .

Jannus asked him something about redes and Lur respond
ed, "I don't know," without listening. Presently the boy set
filled basin of water before him, and Lur noticed that the ca
was actively suffering from thirst.

"I know a rede isn't a tangible thing," the boy said, sittin
on his heels while Lur drank, "but neither is a word. Could ;
rede be written?"

"I don't—"

"Look: like this." Jannus held out the ivory rose, the trin
ket he'd bought in Ardun. When the boy pointed with ;
thumbnail, Lur could see carved scratchings around the out
sides of the petals.

"What do you say," Elda wanted to know, "to traveling by
dark again? This heat—"

"I don't care," Lur replied. "Just don't use the light." Th
next wave, he was thinking, would probably be manform, by
default, and therefore capable of speech.

"Might as well leave it here, then. No use toting anything
we don't have to."

"Lur," persisted the boy, still holding the pendant.

"Get me some more water." While the pan was filling, Lu
made up his mind. "Elda, take the watch until I get back
Keep the force sword extended—stick it in the ground, cu
off anything that moves. I'll call when I get back." Lu
crouched over the pan, lapping.

"Where are you going?" Jannus asked. "There's no need to
~~~nt. . . ."

"I've never seen the High Plain full of Teks, or so many in
~~~astform. . . . Something's happened. Something's changed.
~~~don't know what, and I need to know. Again," he added,
~~~dging the pan.

When he'd drunk as much as he possibly could, Lur
~~~nged east, toward the mountains that separated the High
~~~ain from Valde. All the keeps were toward the edge of the
~~~ateau, radiating from Down, alone in the interior; Lur
~~~ought his best chance of encountering a Tek that could talk
~~~ him would be in that direction.

As the heat underfoot dimmed, Lur was able to catch the
~~~ent of scattered carcasses. Rock held scent poorly, and the
~~~at wasn't designed for locating prey in that fashion. But Lur
~~~ought a man moving unshod through the day would have
~~~oody feet by evening, and blood was an odor that didn't
~~~de easily.

He found two such tracks, but the blood of each was al-
~~~eady crusted and he passed on. The third track was fresh,
~~~nd led him finally to a carcass with most of the torso miss-
~~~g and an Adapted's acrid body smell still hot in the air. Lur
~~~acked off with care, for he had no interest in testing the
~~~at's strength against the talons and the leathery hide of any
~~~dapted.

Lur sprawled awhile, resting. The moon was well up, half
~~~und: to his eyes, the surrounding plain was daylit, lacking
~~~nly day's unremitting glare. His advantage over a man-
~~~orm would be considerable. Yet he wanted no needless risks.
~~~ spite of the abundance of food and water, the relatively
~~~ow pace, he was tired—as tired as he could recall having
~~~een since before Lisle. Unless he took care he might do
~~~omething stupid and be granted no time to regret it.

A wisp of sound brought his head up. He waited until he
~~~as certain from what quarter the sound of footsteps was
~~~oming before he moved. He paralleled the walker for a
~~~hile, judging the Tek's condition from the lag and uncer-
~~~ainty of his steps, and veered in until he could see the figure
~~~nd was moving practically at its heels. With a sudden rush
~~~e sprang at the Tek's back without, however, unsheathing
~~~is claws, remembering the Fisher he'd taken prematurely in
~~~an Halla, and stood with his forefeet on the Tek's spine to
~~~old him in place.

"Cliffhold," he identified himself, "mammals, genetic surgeon, third aptitude; structuralist, seventh aptitude, built gate."

"Rork," gasped the other, "optics, theorist, based in Ror oh not now, not when it's so bright in Down—"

Lur tried to get the Tek to rank himself either in kee ranking or by aptitude level—there'd been several opti specialists in Rork—but could only get one or two words connected sense from several minutes' babbling about lig and Down. And all the while the Tek's back jerked ar humped in a ceaseless effort to escape.

"What's changed?" Lur demanded finally, abandoning a tempts to make contact. "What's happened in Down?"

"Down! Down, Down the light," crooned the Tek, the screamed, "Get off!"

Lur cuffed him. "Quiet. What's happened in Down?"

"Off! You can't expect me to be civil when—"

Lur raked the Tek's arm with deliberate care. "I'll give yo civility, you'll wake in Rork tomorrow unless you tell m what's calling everyone to Down!"

"You've been too long in that body. Base yourself. The you'll know. I'm not a convenience like the Shai—Aaal Downbase, open to the light! Open, open, open—" panted th Tek.

That instant one of Lur's hind legs was seized, clamped the toothless beak of one of the turtleforms. He screeche and twisted, forgetful of everything but the pain and the fea of being based now, thrown far from Down—open, unroofec Lur struck with both forepaws for the eyes, doublin wrenching head and shoulders clear of the ground, reachin again for the head, roaring—

Self-awareness, seeping back to fill the blank void, connect ed him with his body's steady motion. He still wore the ca and it was walking in a procession of Teks under a sky grey ing with dawn. He'd almost caught up with one of the Adapt ed.

Resuming control of the cat, he veered aside and sat down He hadn't been based, as he'd first feared: he'd just lost him self temporarily, as though he'd fallen into a roofed pit. Satis fied he knew where and what he was, he inspected the cat' condition. The right rear leg had been badly lacerated but though stiff and nearly immobile, the bones seemed intact. By an awkward contortion he could manage to lick the gashe banding the leg below the joint and smooth the spiky blood matted hair around the wounds.

He wondered if he'd travelled all night. The thought occurred to him only in connection to how far away Down remained, how long he'd have to rely on the lamed leg before the cat could be discarded. If Downbase was unroofed, nothing mattered in the least except his ability to reach it.

An unfamiliar sort of beastform was coming up behind him on multiple stilted legs. Taking no chances, Lur moved aside and limped on, maintaining a prudent distance between himself and the nearest Teks, so that they formed a sort of loose and shifting constellation, each solitary and intent.

From an intolerable dream of utter silence Jannus was wakened, not by Poli, but by Elda. With one arm numb to the fingers, Jannus tried to determine if the cord binding his wrist to Poli's was still tied, for his first thought was that she was gone—that the enclosure of trance had failed and she'd fled the blare of the Screamers.

But the arm was numb because Poli was sleeping on it.

"Quick," Elda was whispering, "one of the grey-hided dragons—"

Jannus' voiceless call did not wake her either, and there was no time now to do what his suspicion wanted. He hauled her bodily to her feet and dragged her after Elda, following the bright line of the force sword.

"One good thing," came Elda's mutter, "they don't seem to look left nor right. . . ."

Jannus, fumbling the loop of the cord over his knuckles, made no outward reply. Inwardly he flung cries, questions, anger, dread at Poli, who seemed both to stand quiet beside him and to recede, becoming tiny and unreachable as a star.

The sound of the dragon paced nearer; one of their packs was crunched underfoot. The light of the sword flashed for an instant against the curve of a gleaming black eye, unpleasantly shrewd. Then the dragon's course curved just enough to take it past beyond reach of a sword blow. Steady and unhurried, the footfalls faded.

Elda led them back, holding the sword carefully away from him until he sheathed its light in the sand. Rummaging in the damaged pack, he uncovered the globe whose light splashed upward from the pack's mouth onto his face and chest. "Made a mess of this," he muttered. "Flatbread, they call it: well, it's flat now, for a fact. And the winterfruit—want some?"

Passive, Jannus accepted a double handful of the dried

fruit, from which Poli's fingers dipped a piece or two. "Here," he said, "you take it," and thrust it all into her hands. He didn't want to talk to her, or be near her, until he could stand to know what he'd discovered.

It didn't matter what he felt. She couldn't hear him.

He found one of the waterballs and drew enough to wash his face, using a cupped palm to catch the stream. His eyes felt gritty and raw from constantly squinting into the glare.

"And the cat isn't back yet," Poli's soft voice was observing.

"An't seen foot nor feather of him. And it's past midnight, away past. Jannus, fetch that ball here."

"There should be one by you."

"Um. All right, I got it." Splashing and blowing showed Elda was wetting his head. "This listening an't my notion of fun."

"I'll watch," offered Jannus at once: he was most unwilling to sleep any time soon, to fall into dream again with no defense.

"You sure? You an't slept more'n a couple hours. . . ."

"I'll watch."

"Whyn't you watch, Poli? You're most rested, and it don't seem—" Elda amended his thought tactfully. "Jannus, don't it seem she could take the watch, better than you or me, Screamers or no?"

Poli said, "They don't bother me now—the Screamers."

Jannus laid his forehead against his bent knees, his back to Elda's light globe.

Elda waited, then repeated, "Don't it seem—" and Jannus made himself reply, "Go on, then. It doesn't matter."

Elda was a minute telling Poli where the force sword was, then moved over to scrape a new hip-hollow in the sand. Jannus pulled the cord back and forth and around—striking the carved rose and returning the cord in the other direction. There'd be no need for it, to warn him if Poli broke trance. The Screamers didn't bother her any more.

"You're not resting," she whispered. As if she knew.

"No."

"Share backs, then."

Thinking of no good reason to refuse, he slid over and did as she'd asked. The contact gave him no ease. He leaned on her as on a door shut against him.

It was monstrous, that a Valde should have been brought

› this—bereft of what separated her from such as Bluejay, Lillia, Merleen. . . . And he'd brought her to it.

Across the plain, past the black mountains of the Mor-aard, would be the Summerfair. If he'd stayed in Newstock he'd be there now at her briding, with no thought of him, in-stead of in this dead, deaf place. That a Haffa should be so maimed, closed, changed. . . .

And Elda too, Jannus thought suddenly: Elda would have had his Homecoming except for being presented, one night, with a Tek bodied as a bony child.

"Elda. Elda. . . ." Jannus reached out a foot and nudged him.

"What." Elda sounded set to jump in any direction.

"I'm sorry I ever brought Lur to you. You'd have had your Homecoming, with your Family and all. You wanted and worked for it so long. I'm sorry."

"Fine for you! Couldn't you wait till morning to tell me that?"

"No."

Elda rolled over to look at him. "Don't take it so to heart, lad," he said presently. "And don't take too much credit on yourself, neither. You an't the one sent Orlengis, or set the net under the Broken Bridge. That net was enough to catch me and draw me here, just by itself. . . . And I took Lur in of my own will, too. You an't to blame for it. And what would you have done, tell me, if you hadn't fetched him: watched him die?" Elda grunted derisively. "It an't in you to do that, no more'n I could see Orlengis skinned for a public treat. There's things that just an't fit to let be. Talk of Lur—he back yet?"

"No," said Poli, reminding Jannus she was there, listening.

"Hope he an't met a brace of dragons. . . ." Resettling himself, Elda again fell silent.

"Jannus'l, what's the trouble in you?" The merest breath of words.

"I was thinking about Elda—being solitary, away from his Family." Part was true. It didn't matter.

And she seemed satisfied with it, for she merely shifted, leaning her back more solidly against his. "Tie the cord," she said after a while, "and rest, while it's cool."

Without having to think about it, Jannus unlaid the two strands of that attempt at subtlety: she wanted to find out if he knew; and whether, if he knew, he could trust her enough to risk what waited in sleep. A little curtly he replied, "Not yet."

The pause that followed then was very odd—expectant, teetering continually on the edge of speech without anything being said.

Maybe, he thought, she was unwilling as he to confront the thing directly. He knew of himself that he could bear sadness—even a great deal of sadness—but not publicly. Not if he had to share it, admit it. Privacy alone made it endurable. Perhaps, maimed, she'd come to feel the same way.

She pinched him, hard.

He jerked, astonished, barely restraining a dangerously loud noise.

"That hurt, didn't it," she remarked. And she reached around and pinched him again.

"Stop it!" he hissed, rubbing his arm.

"I thought it did," she mentioned. "So I have sold something of myself, to buy you something you're not sure you want at the price. Now you know how I felt, after Lisle."

Jannus leaned forward clasping his knees, not altogether sure she wouldn't pinch him a third time. She'd succeeded in startling him out of isolation, but the grieving mood could not be touched by such play. "I never pinched your arm purple."

"No. Perhaps it's different, then."

"No. . . . And I don't consent to it—to what you've been brought to."

"It is worth it to us," she replied coolly. "If you had not sold your death, the memory of my spirit would be staining Lisle. What comes of that, comes."

"No. I won't abide it."

"You will. And I will require of you a favor."

Almost, he laughed. He ended with his teeth clenched and his head leaned back against hers. "What favor would you have, then? That we go down through the Morgaard Pass to the Summerfair, so the Haffa can admire your choice in men?"

"Go to sleep," she said, "and let me watch. I'll keep my hand on your neck. When you dream, the blood changes. I'll know it."

There was an awkward, dragging pause. He was recalling how he'd waked, in past days, with her relaxed hand under his chin or curved against his shoulder while she slept. But she'd be awake now, watching. . . .

"I don't know," he admitted finally, "if I can. But I'll try, if that's what you want. . . ."

"Tell a story to yourself," she suggested.

Without argument Jannus stretched out and composed himself as best he could, sharply conscious of the touch of her fingers against his throat. He wasn't in any mood for constructing lies, pleasant or unpleasant, for any purpose whatever. Instead, slowly, he began pursuing his earlier thought about redes and names.

Turning the cord about his hands again, he came to the rose carved of mara horn, on whose six outer petals he'd inscribed in cursive script Poli's name and his own. Working at that with the Tek knife, he'd wondered, as he often did, what his rede might look like, written down. And then the thought had come to him of Poli's bridestone: existing still but lost to any human purpose.

If his rede were written here, and here only—dropped from the Shai's memory, inscribed on this one bit of ivory— how could it then wake in a base? Would his rede not then be lost to the Shai as the bridestone was lost to Jannus? Could the redes, the names, the shadows of all the Teks be written on one huge page and rolled up and carried out of Downbase beyond the Shai's responsibility? And would the Shai permit it?

Lur, indifferent to the weight of names and ignorant of writing, hadn't even listened to the idea. And his judgment probably wouldn't have been worth much anyhow. It would rest, finally, on the Shai's intention toward Teks.

The only way to find out would be to go into Downbase and ask the Shai.

The thought of Downbase, which he visualized as a black, toothed trap, faded into a recollection of Ashai Rey pacing across the withered garden, turning a face courteous, beautiful, impersonally shrewd. . . . Jannus imagined Ashai incongruously whirling a rattlestick to frighten off the cat, making a wardsign as protection against Valde. But what sort of a sign, Jannus wondered, could one make against an Innsmith?

Jannus imagined himself writing his own name in enormous letters on a wall covered with red cloth. The black script began to blur and flow through the weave of the cloth. Surrounding shadows crawled up the wall to engulf the letters; all light failed.

He lurched awake, rigid and terrified.

"See?" whispered Poli cheerfully. "I knew."

He groped, found a foot of hers to pat in consciously am-
biguous reply. He had to get away. Topaz light was sliding
up from behind the mountains; he went that way, swinging
his arms and stretching, yawning to unclench the locked
muscles of his jaw. When he became calmer he scuffed back
across the ash-colored flat, wondering how many days he
could manage not to sleep at all.

"You sure?" Elda leaned to squint over Poli's shoulder at
the mark she claimed to have found in the sand. He didn't
need to see the mark. Seeing it, he was none the wiser—it
looked like what it was, a wrinkled stretch of sand. Just the
same, he knew it was a cat track. He'd insisted Lur had been
taken by some dragon or other, and the recollected words
were sour in his mouth as bile.

Resting in a balanced crouch, the Valde touched the sand
delicately with her fingertips, removing distortions and loose
grains until even Elda could tell there was a track there—a
large depression behind, four smaller ones in front. If a cat
track looked like that, then it was a cat track.

"He decided he didn't need us after all," commented Jannus indifferently, though he'd been the first to decide Lur had
deserted them. Elda would have expected the boy to take
some satisfaction, at least, in having been right.

In the four days Lur had been gone, and since finding out
about the Valde, the boy had turned very quiet and seemed
to have trouble sleeping. He'd have tried to walk all night
and most of the day, if Elda hadn't pushed him into better
sense; as it was, their journey had lost discipline and pattern.
They just walked until somebody, generally Elda, sat down
and insisted on a rest that might end up stretching out for
hours, or they'd pause to drink, with the same result. But
Jannus wanted to keep moving and the Valde of course
wouldn't cross him, so Elda put up with the fits and starts of
travelling and kept patience with the boy's moods. Elda
couldn't mend things and so considered it best to let them be.

The Valde brushed out the mark in a tidy way, then rose
and moved on along the broad trampled stretch of sand, with
its grisly markers every few hundred paces, that pointed the
shortest path to Down.

They'd passed through the stumplegged turtles two days
ago. The wavering black dots some distance ahead were men;
Elda knew because every now and again they'd circle one the
sun was claiming. These sometimes stared and made wordless

noises, but only twice did Elda have to bat one aside with the pole. If a Tek could move enough to be dangerous, he'd be moving along the path, not lying on it.

Elda noticed one corpse away off to the left, visible as a toad on a tabletop. What made Elda curious enough to turn aside was seeing that it had clothes on. He snapped his fingers and pointed where he was going to bring the other two after him.

Stretched on its back, the corpse was so baked there was no smell to speak of, and it was intact and seemly enough, arms neatly folded. The clothes were homespun, brown in the creases, otherwise bleached almost white—trousers and a crudely stitched sleeveless shirt. There was hair, brittle looking and so coated with dust it was hard to be sure of the color.

"No Tek," decided Elda hoarsely, and watched while Jannus wet a thumb and smoothed a strand of the corpse's hair, a delicate gesture. The hair was black. "Lisler?" Elda conjectured.

Jannus waved for Elda to move. When Elda's shadow fell across the face, Jannus leaned to study it. At length he looked up and asked for the fuser. "Think he was called Crow."

"Lisler?"

Straightening away from the body, Jannus dipped his head once in confirmation.

Elda got out the fuser and set the three controlling rings. While Jannus stood somberly out of the way, Elda brushed the heat beam across the Bremneri who might have been called Crow. Presently there was only a waxy patch of melted sand.

"They came this way," called Poli, pointing to the west.

It was a track even Elda couldn't mistake; a shallow trough four or five arms' span across, running west across the glittering flat and heading east roughly parallel to the Tek's line of march. Something big had been dragged past here, toward Down.

"They laid . . . laid down a wood road," the Valde was reporting, studying the corrugated sand, "for something heavy, laying the wood down before, taking it up behind. . . . Then they walked back the way they'd come." She pointed out the marks of feet, still to be seen clearly in this windless place.

They kept to the drag track, following it east. Elda watched the ground, collecting and then tossing away the small debris of the work gang in hopes of finding some hint of what sort of thing Deepfish might have contracted to have the Lislers deliver. From the track he already knew it was heavy and the size of a young house.

There was no news in a bit of broken rope or a cracked sandal sole. But the oval piece of wood he found stuck at an angle in the sand, he kept and dusted carefully, turning it in his hands as he trudged. It was one plate of a knife hilt. The blade, likely broken, had been thriftily pried out for reforging and the hilt discarded. At each end of the plate was a groove where a band had been fastened: two bands of twisted copper wire. Elda knew because he'd seen the tool whole. It'd belonged to Davit Ventersson, of Solvig's Family.

The sun was well clear of the mountains and false water seemed to quiver on the sand just ahead, never reached, never absent. Time, Elda decided, for another rest. He unslung the pack to get at the tent stakes. The thump made the other two look around, Jannus turning by degrees like a creaky two-wheeled cart.

"No," he argued hoarsely, beckoning with a loose-armed wave.

Elda took no notice, but let the faint sound of water dropping into a cup be his argument.

When they'd all drunk what they could, Elda finished propping up the tent to give some shade as noon approached. Thus protected from sunstroke, Poli discarded her hat and poured several cups of water over the back of her head and then sat motionless, her cottony hair dripping onto her shoulders and back. Elda went by her to where Jannus was sitting, to show him the hilt plate. Hit only chest-high by the tent shadow and too stubborn or too tired to move, Jannus turned the plate disinterestedly and then handed it back.

"Belongs to Davit, of Solvig's Family," explained Elda, settling down prudently within the shade. "So whatever they were hauling was something Deepfish don't trust the Lislers to manage alone. What do you make of it?"

"He's opened Downbase."

Elda checked his first incredulous reaction and said instead, "How do you figure that?"

"Made it accessible to Teks. So Lur decided he didn't need hands or help any more. It has to be that."

"Lur said that wasn't possible. . . ."

"There's a tidiness to it," Jannus remarked, not listening. "His opening Downbase draws Lur off. It brings Teks from all over, and that provides a hedge of Screamers around Down no Valde could endure. That should have eliminated Poli and me."

"I'm here too, you'll recall," put in Elda, rather acidly.

Under the shadow of his hatbrim, Jannus' black eyes squinted against the glare and became less vague. "Oh, he'll have made provision. He'll be watching for us. . . ." His sweat-streaked face lifted until he was gazing meditatively straight at the sun.

Elda yanked him sideways under the tent, thinking that'd be all they'd need: the Valde deaf and the boy blinded. Jannus moved convulsively against him: Elda had just warning enough to catch Jannus' wrist and stop the dagger-dart an inch from his knee. Elda might be no match for Orlengis, but he could hold such as Jannus still all day, if need be. "An't hurting him," he said quietly, very mindful of the Valde at his back, and levered the dart carefully out of the boy's fist. "Got half a mind to stick you with this," he told Jannus, keeping his grip, "to have you asleep for awhile. You're getting too strange to be safe."

Poli asked, "What is it?" just noticing something was odd. Elda let himself relax a bit and ease his hold. He'd been expecting she might come at him from behind, himself without a chance even to turn. But now, he supposed, she knew only what she could see, just like a regular person.

"You'd best let me alone," the boy advised reasonably, as if speaking about two different people altogether, "or it'll change. It's on the edge of changing now."

With that cryptic announcement he finished freeing himself and started on down the track, paying no attention to Elda calling him to come back, wait. The Valde hastily caught up the two packs, his and her own, and was off after him, trotting in bursts of three of four steps in an attempt to catch up, trying to get her hat back on with both hands full. And that left Elda to pull the tent down again and fold it small—his mouth too dry for proper commentary—to get the poles fastened under his pack straps and his waterball, in the string net, slung at his side: the pair by that time far enough ahead to flicker like Teks, wading knee-deep in the phantom water.

Before shutting his pack, Elda took out Lur's drinking dish, stepped on it, and scuffed sand over the pieces. At least he wouldn't be lugging *that* any more.

It was several hundred paces before Poli could get the boy to hold still. Elda had a shrewd notion his catching up would jar the boy into motion again. So he stopped where he was, feeling mildly guilty to have the shade of the tent roof to himself while they were up ahead unprotected from the full heat of the day; but all they had to do was come back, after all. And his guess had been good: he woke from an unplanned nap to find the pair just where they'd been and the sun beginning to tilt toward evening. Elda drank, washed his face and his feet, and slowly reassembled his gear.

It was a wonder they hadn't both been taken with sunstroke, but they hadn't. The boy lifted his head as Elda came toward him, and spoke to Poli, whose head and shoulders were pillowed on his legs. As she stirred he twisted around to dislodge the two packs, wedged with sand and serving him as a backrest. Pushing to his feet, Jannus commented in a husky whisper, "They've all gone past."

Elda swung around, and it was true. As far as he could see, nothing was moving in any direction except the flickering, twitching air itself. Whatever Teks had survived to get this far had passed beyond his view.

"Poli," the boy was saying, "can you hear me now?" Letting the packs drop, he reached out to touch her side, then slowly turned away and bent again to his task.

It was too difficult to look at anything steadily. Elda squinted hard a few times to ease his eyes. "How many got this far, do you suppose?"

"The birds. The . . . ah, the dragons." Jannus shrugged into his pack, one arm at a time. "Maybe a few turtles. I don't recall seeing a man since. . . ." He fell silent, as if trying to sort through the times, then finished, "Since we found Crow. I wonder. . . ."

Poli said, "You will not come this way again, Jannus'l. We will have your shadow back. You will be free of the dreaming."

The boy nodded and then sighed, as if a full breath was a luxury he was allowing himself.

Walking on, Elda was calculating that all the Teks wouldn't have passed in his lifetime or Jannus'. The first fast goers had been able to prey on their companions; those just bodied, just setting out now, would find sunbleached bones and sparse company. Even if Jannus was right and Downbase had been opened, nothing much had changed as far as Elda was concerned. The tidestorm was still gathering as surely as it had been doing since the Wall failed. As long as one Tek remained, the bases and the tools would be maintained. The lake would have to be destroyed, Deepfish ended. He hitched one strap of his pack higher on his shoulder.

Something moved.

They all saw it, dropping instantly from their separate thoughts to wary inspection of the ground off to the right.

The sun had dropped low enough to catch each roughness in the land and throw little parings of dark beyond each bit of raised crust. The plain had become a dull orange sea rippled with innumerable flecks of intense purple. The very colors hurt. And all was overlaid by the eternally twitching shivering air, blurring even short distances into feverish unreliability.

Elda had yet to find any single thing to focus on when Poli said, "It's the cat."

Unable to spit, Elda grunted instead and started walking on. But they weren't coming. Jannus stood like a man waiting for a signal, the Valde watching him to discover what it'd be.

"Let him alone," Elda called angrily, "this once!"

The boy decided then and left the drag track, trailed by the Valde and, finally, by Elda. As they got nearer, the cat lunged, on the second try, to a sort of sitting position. Neither Lur nor the boy wasted breath on greetings or complaints or excuses. Jannus knelt down by Lur's flank, pulling his waterball around in front of him.

"I busted his bowl," mentioned Elda, with a certain satisfaction, but Jannus was using his hat to catch the flow. Lur lapped with his forelegs braced before him like props. They quivered at the strained position. Presently he let himself slide, with an ungainly jolt, to his former position.

"Can you walk on it?" Jannus was inquiring.

The cat shut his eyes, elbowing nearer the hat to drink again. One hind leg, Elda could see now, was a mass of caked scabs and dirt. That accounted for this reunion, then.

Poli wet a pad of cloth and touched Lur's leg, but the cat flinched away with a faint snarl. "The beast will do," he said, and dropped his muzzle back to the hat, but Poli pulled it from under his nose and shook the remaining water out.

"Later," she advised. "You'll founder yourself."

The cat glared, panting. Every rib showed under his dun hide. Then he heaved himself upright, weaving slightly. With his shoulder braced against Jannus' hip he managed to straighten the sound hind leg under him and was standing, after a fashion; but so much of his weight was leaned against Jannus that the boy had to take a step to keep from being

pushed over. The cat swayed but kept his balance. His head
hung, and his panting was like short bass coughs or growls.
He edged a foreleg ahead, then the hind. Despite Elda's anger, he was impressed. There was a fascination to watching
like that of seeing a fine wild fire that happened to be burning your house down.

When Lur had lurched a few steps without falling, Jannus
took his hat back from Poli and walked slowly level with the
cat's shoulder, asking, "How far do we have to go yet?"

"See the cloud?" the cat responded.

Elda stared past them and, above the layer of heat flux, he
could make out something orange against the yellow sky,
something that still caught high sunlight. Anywhere else, he
would have taken it for a cloud alone on the far horizon.

"Lake dome," said the cat briefly, attending to his footing.

Between one step and the next, the moonlit landscape
changed before Poli's eyes. She found herself beside a glade
on a lush midafternoon meadow cupped within low hills.
Ahead of her a pear tree, bearing both flowers and fruit,
overhung a rock-rimmed pool. There were coolness and
color, and a wonderful smell drifting from the tree on a
moist breeze. Each leaf, each hair of grass, seemed perfectly
formed and distinct, as in the clarity of some pleasant dream.

The loveliness called her to reach out with *marenniath*—
forgetting, in astonished eagerness, the past days of unre-
lieved silence; she touched horror.

Dimly, as from birds passing above clouds, she heard the
anguished self-absorption of Screamers and recoiled into
night before the door of Down.

Ahead, Jannus stood turned half toward her, his face
relaxed into an expression of wonder—bemusement overlaid
upon caution and doubt. His head turned, following nothing
she could see, and he went two steps farther into the zone of
illusion.

She and Jannus had been walking ahead; Lur was slowed
by his lacerated leg and Elda, shut sword in hand, was their
rearguard.

"Quicksand! Stand still!" she cried, as though they all were
in Han Halla. Without waiting to find if she were heeded, she
shut her eyes to hold clearly the images of Jannus and the
distance between them, and advanced five measured paces.

She was back in Morimmon-vale, in sun-flecked green un-
affected by her memory of having closed her eyes. Single-

minded, she clasped with a firm grip the nothing before her, receiving no answering sense of contact or weight, and tried to retreat.

A cat, mouth writhed back into a snarl, leaped into view. Spread talons jabbed toward her eyes. She stopped her almost automatic gesture of defense and instead bowed her head and hung on to whatever she held. The blow glanced off her shoulder, so that she staggered aside onto the crumbling edge of a deep gully. A squat tree proffered a bare limb at just the proper height to be grasped but she put no trust in that either and did not reach for its support.

She fell, not into a gully, but from the side of the High Plain itself: first wet clouds, then Erth-rimmon, a twisting blue-brown serpent, spun through her tumbling view. She struck what seemed to be a ledge, falling hard on her left shoulder. Then she could feel herself begin to slide. There was a stone she could have held to, and indeed, she saw her hand go out and grip it. But the pain in her shoulder prevented a sure hold. Both hands were needed. She rejected the hand she saw, disavowed it as her own, and fell backward.

With no sense of impact, she opened her eyes.

The moon hung round and serene over the luminous lake dome. The High Plain was around her again, all things in their former places—the crouched or stilted outlines of Deathless roving nearer the irised door set aslant in a tall mound—but Poli didn't trust it. She took no notice of the questions Jannus, lying beside her, was asking. He lay on her right though her clasped arms were still locked before her, empty. She tried to think of some way to test the scene, to be certain; meanwhile, she did not let go.

And all at once there *was* weight in her arms. Not Jannus but a decomposing corpse lay upon her and she could feel it stirring. Poli turned her head aside but she didn't let go.

She tried to reach out to Jannus' *farioh*, but heard nothing—not even Screamers. Though that sense could not be fooled, neither would it wake to her demand. But the certainty appeared within her that though the trickery was strong, it could warp and change only what news her senses brought her; it could not touch will, memory, thought—those powers in her that were least Valde. She had not let go, and therefore what she had caught, she still held; the boundary lay behind her as she had fallen, and not off to one side, as it now appeared.

With this conviction she hitched herself backward in spite of all appearances, all senses.

The continuing pain in her shoulder increased, became intense and immediate. She saw the curve of Lur's claws, sunk partly into the strap of her pack and partly into flesh. It was now Jannus she held, his hand halted in the act of bringing down a dagger-dart. Elda grabbed her under both arms and dragged her and Jannus farther back, then let go.

Pale and plainly shaken, Jannus flung the dart away with sudden ferocity. "You . . . turned into something." He sounded as though he half suspected her of having done it on purpose. Poli felt it was safe, then, to let go. Climbing to his feet, Jannus stared in one direction, then another. "I was in Ardun—"

"Whyn't you warn us about this?" Elda was demanding of Lur.

"There was never such a trap set about Down," replied the cat. "Illusion. Hearing, seeing, everything?"

So this was what the *sa'farioh*, the Andran, had bargained for in Lisle, Poli was musing. At last, she had found out.

"I was in Ardun," Jannus was exclaiming. "I was *there*, clear, clearer than this. . . ." He waved a general hand, looking to her for confirmation. "Wasn't it?"

"I was elsewhere," she told him.

"But you were *there*. With me."

"No. Only a seeming."

Elda put in, "But what is it?"

"Debern's projector," said Lur. "The Shai has had Debern's projector moved into Downbase. So—"

"Make it plain," Elda interrupted. "What is it?"

The cat was gazing off toward the mound that held the door, head held low and tail flicking as though he were thinking of stalking one of the wandering Deathless. When Elda repeated his question, the cat said absently, "There was a Debern Tek who became curious about creating experience: sensory composites that could be projected on a bodied rede, Illusions. She—Debern Teks had a habit of being bodied as women—she developed a projector and had a First Showing. So it must have worked. I didn't go—I didn't want anybody tinkering with my rede. Apparently others felt the same because she was given the choice of taking on herself the Rule of One, to be responsible for the development of the process, or else abandoning it. She abandoned it. It was after that, that the Debern Teks began work on Fathori, deserting their keep. . . . And now the Shai is using it to give the impression that Downbase is unroofed. It isn't, is it. I can't see past the mound."

Jannus, the tallest, stared off toward the mound. "No. I'm sorry, Lur."

The cat swung his baleful gaze toward Poli. "Except for you, I'd have the protection of the illusion, like the rest."

"Let it take you, then," she replied, indifferent. "It is strong."

"But the roof's there. I know it. No illusion. . . ." Muttering, Lur was turning away. He moved forward: into the zone.

"Get—!" began Elda, too late, breaking off as he realized Lur was already gone, separated by more than distance.

Replying to Jannus' plain concern, Poli said, "It is very strong. Even warned, I saw only what my eyes brought me. I was in Morimmon-vale, or its seeming. It speaks to each according to his own wish."

Elda was still dissatisfied. "An't proper, to just walk off and leave us, with it all yet to do."

"What," rejoined Jannus coldly, "did you expect? He doesn't care about anything else. He never has. He is what he is."

Having moved steadily toward the mound, Lur had begun to veer. His hitching three-legged gait slowed as he approached the other Deathless and passed among them, none of the dark shapes touching or meeting another, weaving separate paths.

The plates of the door opened, retracting around an immense hole—Poli thought first of a cave, then of an eye, opening. The cat's course altered as though the opening had called to him. He moved into the cave and the door's overlapping plates spun shut, again reflecting the moon.

"Very tidy," Jannus remarked. "Much tidier than actually digging through sand and rock, actually opening the base. . . . Maybe Lur was right. Maybe the tools for that don't even exist any more. But this way was even better—a bait, a trap, and a defense, all in one. The Shai always takes the easiest way. Gives a careful push and then lets matters arrange themselves without him. Or that's what Lur told me once. The chief tool and treasure of the High Plain. He uses what's already at hand." Jannus' face was still and remote as he continued to stare past her at the door. "In Ardun, the Ardun I saw, you were with me, no longer maimed. You were explaining how I might come to have the *marenniath* too. And then you . . . changed. The Shai took my secrets, as the handiest thing to bind me with. What I want. What I fear. The dream, moved into the waking world. . . ."

He was, Poli decided, enormously angry—a Bremneri altogether, knowing himself to have been spied upon, invaded, tricked. Some things, she could know even without the *marenniath*.

For Lur, very little changed. The hot smell of the sand underfoot, the two shadows given him by the lake dome and the moon, the faint undertone of dead meat on the still air, all continued. But as he began to fear that because of the warning, the illusion had no power over him, he realized he was utterly alone. Elda, Jannus, the Valde, the meandering Teks in their various beastforms, had all been blanked out, erased.

It was all right, then.

He turned toward the door of Downbase and found, instead, a ramp sloping into a roughly-carved pit like a quarry, stretching out along the rim of the lake dome as far as he could see. Nothing, he reflected, could be more unroofed than that. The Shai was taking great pains to reassure him, as well it might: since, through the projector, it could scan his rede directly, it would know one of them would be ended before morning.

Lur moved toward the head of the ramp, which had sprouted a railing since he'd last looked—in answer, he thought, to his doubt that the lamed cat could walk such a narrow way. And the pain of his leg was being adjusted, diminished. This tinkering with his perceptions made him all the more conscious of the unreality, of the fact that Downbase was *not* open, that tons and tons of rock roofed it—

He was partway down the ramp, although the second before, he hadn't set foot on it. The tinkering was still going on. That began to frighten him. It should have stopped at his first unease. Maybe the Shai planned to get him well underground, and then let him know it—become aware of all the solid stifling earth above him—and then hold him there, or drive him mindless into some surface illusion that would hold him, until he died of thirst or sunstroke and woke in some base at the other end of the plateau while the Shai dealt with Elda and Jannus, depriving him of allies—

There was a Valde walking the ramp before him, taking short steps because of her old-style gown that ended in a hobbling hoop around her ankles. The gown was iridescent green: he could see colors again. More tinkering. But it was proper to have Valde with oneself on such an occasion, though the usual number was twenty. The company reassured him slightly though he knew it was illusory; he was able to stop glancing to gauge the height of the sky.

The Valde looked back over her shoulder; she wore Poli's face. She said, "Your death was never withheld from you purposely, Teklord. It merely took time to secure the hands to make that death available."

Lur complained, "You could have told me in Lisle what you intended."

"Why?" rejoined the Shai, through the Valde's mouth. "Nothing but the accomplishment would turn you aside. Nor does the mobile know all my intentions or purposes. What a body can hold, a body can lose. Or it can be taken from him. He is more accessible to his enemies than I, to mine."

Lur could see the bottom of the pit now—a maze of roofless plarit walls, brightly lit, containing the diverse machineries of a base and other devices whose purposes he did not know. The space immediately before him at the bottom of the ramp held only a couch like a seamless green jewel, set off-center upon the rayed golden sun-circle that took up most of the floor. The spaces between the irregular spiraling rays were paved with obsidian, so that the sun disc seemed suspended in a void.

That was proper. That was how it was, except that the couch should have been a chair. The shape had been modified in consideration to his own.

Crossing the floor, the Valde took a place in the Witness Gallery under the shadow of a wall, so that her face was hidden. Her gown shone exactly the color of the couch, as was proper: *Something green,* the saying was, *in the place of death.* . . .

Lur stepped from the ramp onto the floor of Downbase and walked across the rayed sun to touch the couch in token of laying down on it: after all, it was really a high-backed chair. He didn't want to press the illusion too far.

The instant he touched the couch, thereby claiming the Rule of One, the Shai revealed itself to him without reservation. Layered like air, the information began to flow through him—status reports, complexities of plans and powers—bringing an intoxicating sense of expansion as the processes of the Shai linked with his own. A mutter of infinite information was proffered as a counterpoint to his every thought, enriching it in texture and depth, making connections where none had existed before for him. And as the inner wind blew, Lur shut doors against it, rejecting, denying, forbidding it to touch him. The swirl of contact diminished, faded, until he was briefly merely himself again in the silent dark. Then there was brightness too great to be felt as heat.

Jannus sat alone in the gelid moonlight before the blister that capped that tideless sea, the Lake of Down. Under the dome the liquid which was not water seemed a sheet of metal laid, rigid and smooth, over some abyss: it was so very much a surface that the sense of something even more vast beneath, as dark as the liquid was bright, was irresistible. Jannus was not perfectly certain he was awake.

Against that surface were silhouetted the small figures of Elda and Poli moving along that endless gradual curve. Elda was fishing for the boundary of what he called "the circle of dreams," fishing with Poli at the end of a long line. She'd be weaving in and out of the zone, pulled clear by Elda whenever she became confused or lost or trapped. Beyond the zone there'd be a place where the waterballs could be set right against the dome, to crack it and let the metal lake boil away into the sky. Elda had explained it all. But what Jannus saw were two blotches like mice against the base of the dome, creeping slowly from right to left.

He stayed level with them, moving when he had to, then relapsing into his insomniac contemplation of the lake and the dome. The dome sometimes seemed to him an immanent and gigantic moon poised in the act of emerging from the earth and sometimes a bubble whose iridescence was in twisting shades of grey. This, he thought, would have been the landscape Lur had seen, without colors, centered on one set of observing eyes. Jannus wondered if a Tek feared roofs as he now feared the circle of dreams.

The swirls of darkness on the dome became the flickering shapes of phantoms scampering along the inside of the zone. They reached with arms tenuous as smoke to snatch into strangeness anyone who ventured past the boundary. . . .

"Poli!" Frightened for her, he was waked to a sudden brittle alertness. He was too distant to be heard or answered. He forced himself nearer the dome until he'd acquired a second shadow and had reached the beginning of the strangeness, and called again, more sanely, "Elda—have you come to the end of it yet?"

"No," came Elda's reply faintly, reassuring merely because it was an answer. Jannus retreated again beyond the reach of the dome's glow on the ground, losing the malevolent second shadow into the general night.

It seemed to him presently that the dome wrenched free and floated, fully round—no longer like the moon but like the sun his eyes had been drawn toward more and more in past days, the sun which ruled the High Plain with heat and light too marvelously powerful to be borne and gave life and color to all lands beyond. The sun spoke to him. It asked why he was waiting.

"I don't dare do otherwise," he replied, watching in fascination as the disc became brighter still, so bright it was turning black. The whole plain and the sky darkened toward invisibility.

With the sun put out, only the dark would be left.

"Who are you," he protested, "to expect me to chance the dreams and the bases?"

"A mind," replied the sun's voice, "a body. A mind. . . ."

"You mind," called Elda's voice jarringly, "singing out, so's we can *find* you?"

Breathing unevenly, sweating in the chilly air, Jannus found their outlines against the pale dome. "I'm coming."

Poli leaned against him while she pressed the wadded safety line into his hands, her own fingers cold as bone, saying, "Come on. We can find the edge. We'll come back and tell him. He won't go on any more."

"That I won't." confirmed Elda, dumping down his pack. "An't rested nor eaten in six, seven hours. An't budging again till sunup. I don't care what a rush you're in. There's no more to be done now."

"We can go on," Poli was insisting, offering—shivering as she leaned against him, with four shadows rayed around them on the sands.

"An't what I'd like, it's what's necessary. You lose her into that dream circle and you'll never get her back, and that's bad enough; but the two of us couldn't find the end of the circle, or break the dome, without her. You won't go into the circle, which I don't blame you for. But I an't about to trust you on the safe end of that line and me on the other, you that had no more sense than to sit shadeless half the afternoon. Right now, I got as much claim on Poli as you do, for the sake of the tidestorm. Maybe that's too plain for you, but that's the way of it just the same."

Jannus twisted the tangled lump of cord until it was immovably taut. "You have to break the dome tonight."

"Can't. Make up your mind to it." Elda began cracking crusts of bread into his cup. "A while back I got to thinking about Solvig—how he'd come this way, wondering where he was now—and Poli all but pulled me past the circle before I knew it. I an't a safe anchor, nor won't be till I'm rested. And, at that, I'm twice as safe as you'd be."

Softly, Jannus stated, "I can't wait till morning. . . ."

"If you have to, then you will."

Jannus let the line fall. He helped Poli sit down and placed packs for her to lean against, then mixed a cup of bread, water, and bullion paste. He had to wake her to eat it. "What's it like," he asked her softly, "past the circle?"

"I tie a strip of cloth over my eyes so I don't forget and open them. Whenever I can see, I pull away. That's how I know I'm inside. Sometimes I turn the wrong way, but then he pulls me free."

"But what's it like?"

"It's different. Full of colors and smells. Once it smelled like evergreens, wet evergreens. I haven't seen any since my time of Choosing. And water, once—deep water, green, with bubbles streaming up. Flashes, bits of things. Then he draws me back."

Jannus did not ask her any more but made a meal for himself. When he'd eaten he occupied himself with filling the ten long waterbags they'd brought out from Ardun to use when the waterballs failed. He held each bag carefully between his knees, adjusting it as it filled, and touched his sore eyes with wet fingers from time to time. When all the bags were filled and stoppered he was the only one left awake. Poli was still shivering. Without rousing her he lifted her away from the packs, set his own shoulders there, and eased her back against his chest, his arms over hers. Eventually the shared warmth reached her and she slept quietly. He held her so, letting the irregular gusts of hallucination pass over him but remaining awake without need of real concentration, judging time by the falling of the moon.

When about three hours had passed and he'd begun seeing flashes of light whenever he blinked, he decided he'd waited as long as he could, and called her. "It's time to go."

She scrubbed slowly at her eyes with folded fingers. Then

they helped each other up. She nudged the packs inquiringly with her foot; Jannus had to concentrate to decide. After a minute he made a loose negative gesture. Casually soft-footed and without stealth, they walked away with the moon at their backs.

Poli's profile turned several times to the dome as they scuffed across the cold sand. "We came this way," she observed presently, a question in the tone.

"We're going into Downbase. I can't wait till morning. If I have to go into the dreams, I'd sooner have it be for something."

"Mm," she agreed without curiosity, and let something fall.

"What's that?"

"Just the line. But no." She turned back and bent to retrieve it. "I may not be able to see you. With the line, we won't get lost from each other."

That started Jannus recalling what had happened when they'd been in the circle together. "How are you armed?"

"Just darts. And a knife."

"Better leave them."

"I don't like that."

"You think I do? But I . . . turned on you once. Maybe I could be made to do it again."

"But there are Deathless there. . . ."

"They don't see each other." Jannus worked the slitted leather pad of darts off his belt and laid it on the ground. He added the Tek knife he'd been carrying and, with an effort, his own small sheath knife, the only remaining possession brought all the way from Newstock. Sighing, Poli tossed her darts and knife on the pile. Then, as an afterthought, she cut an arm's length off the line and left the rest.

A length of rope, Jannus was forced to realize, could be a weapon. But then there were hands, arms, fingers, teeth, knees, feet. . . .

He stared at the sky in almost physical pain at the awareness of how completely they'd be parted the instant they passed the margin of the circle. He'd have no protection, no company, no control. He could be made to do anything. His fear could be used against him, or his very need to keep her near him. He imagined himself tightening the cord of the Ardun rose around her throat under some persuasive delusion, believing it necessary, or harmless.

Poli began rubbing the back of his neck, as she had often

done when the nightmares ebbed into headaches. "What is it?"

"We can't go together. There's no use even trying. You stay with Elda and—"

"I won't," she rejoined, calm and absolute, without the slightest check in the rhythmic pressure of her fingers.

"We can't be together there. Better it should be some use."

"No."

"Poli, I'd do you some hurt. I know it. When the changes come I don't want you near enough to be hurt."

"No."

She was doubly immune to persuasion, being a Valde, and being isolate, hearing only her own feelings. Jannus rested numbly, unable to tolerate the consequences of either going on or turning back, with her. He could see no course not disastrous for everyone.

But all Poli cared for was that they be freed of his deathlessness, freed of the outgrown and repellently indifferent boy who would someday wake from his rede, having forgotten her and all the jeweled days and months together since Lisle and not *caring*. . . .

Jannus' mind looped back on that thought, touching its pieces like beads until he held the one that had resonated: Lisle.

Lisle, he thought, holding the name without asking questions, just waiting for it to answer him.

"Poli," he said slowly, "I claim my favor."

"No!" The reaction was immediate and frightened.

"It's the needful thing. This favor, and none other. Stay—"

"I won't."

"Stay with Elda, help him however he says. That's the one great favor that's needed. If you could hear me, you'd know. But you know anyhow. Don't you."

"Don't ask me. I won't. They go into the door, the Deathless, but none come out again. You could be dead, or lost, or waking somewhere and I'd never know. I could not—"

"Poli," he interrupted quietly, "if this promise is not kept, what other promises can stand?" He swung around until he could see her, dim against the chalky sand. He pulled her close, full of sadness for her sadness, trusting her to keep her word before her life, or his.

"I bound myself to this," she said presently in a muffled voice. "What comes of it, comes."

He went on along the dome's gradual curve for an hour or more, the night becoming darker and colder as the moon dropped. He felt no fear but only an enormous resignation, so that he had to concentrate at times to recall what it was he was doing. When he saw the mound housing the door of Downbase he drifted toward it simply because it was definite, because it was raised above the plain: a pile of rocks or a tree would have drawn him as easily. He never noticed when it was that he crossed the edge of the circle because fear of it was all that had been keeping him awake. Inner and outer dream became one.

He didn't have to do anything, there was nothing to be done. The realization was a great relief though he was sad about it too. He settled down on the sloping pier outside the granary and waited for the moon to rise. Either Poli would be killed or she wouldn't, and either way it was none of his concern. He was taking risk enough, just to come this far and watch. He thought about being caught and sent off to the farmsteads—where after ten or fifteen years he might be chosen as a factor, if he was lucky; where his scribe's training would make him the target of at least ridicule; where Valde never went. He didn't dare be caught here, or everything would collapse. He wasn't sure it was even safe to wait for the moon. Going on, to the window, just wasn't possible. If he went back now nobody would be the wiser and Lur would find no one to meet him and then Elda, too, would be safe.

If Sithstock's First Dancer killed her, though, he just didn't know what he'd do. Maybe just go off with Lur. He wondered what it'd feel like to wear a cat, the tan shoulders moving so beautifully under the sun—but Lur had said such things had to be set up specially and Jannus didn't know how. He'd just have to wait. There was nothing he could do.

Suddenly, for no reason, he felt scalding heat, pain in his hands, that as suddenly was gone.

Lethargically his mind turned back to the pain, puzzled, resolving it presently into just a splash of unexpected sunlight on the cobbled weed-clumped street. Morning came earlier in Lisle, he remembered now. He settled more comfortably on the riverwall, waiting for Poli to be brought out. He'd bought her, involving himself in whatever Lur hated and dreaded so, but that was all right since he now owned Poli and all he needed to do was wait for the shipment to be delivered to him. It would be even better if she could be deafened some-how, domesticated. . . .

Pain, heat, struck at him again—though he'd forgotten it had ever happened before—so fiercely that he doubled for-ward and fell, the pain transmuting itself into an overwhelm-ing sense of guilt and shame that racked him with weeping. He'd done something terrible, he didn't know what, but he'd rather die than live with it, and all the Valde would be hear-ing him and know all about it. He wished them all dead, in-stead—then he could stand it, if only he could come to terms with it gradually without his every fear and resentment being known, much less this scalding remorse for whatever it was he'd done. He didn't dare be caught here, it was too danger-ous even to wait, and there was still that guilt embedded in the day like a stone in a peach. The odd conviction grew in him that the sun was watching him in the intervals it shone through rifts in the passing clouds.

He wasn't jealous of the Valde, he decided, quite com-posed and deliberate. Not even Poli could write her name. He took off the Ardun rose and wrote his name on it in flow-ing well-shaped letters, then closed the trinket in his fist, feeling it was important. It reminded him of the bridestone, that was it. He watched Poli throwing it away—discarding all he had to bind her to him by the ways he understood or trusted. Of course he still had the promise to hold over her, but the promise was too precious for him ever to use because then it would be over and he'd have nothing. And what would he do if he called her to come out of the bow and she ignored him, with Perkalas and Orlengis up there watching? Better not to take the risk, but just wait until the sun came out of its own accord.

But maybe the sun didn't mean to come out. After all, there was Elda sitting in his barge holding up the sweep oar, to which was attached a long, long rope with a hook at the end. A green bird with silver wings was swooping with the hook, carrying it higher and higher. If the sun came out, Elda was going to drag it into the water and put it out because it was only the world's sun, not the true sun at all. Elda didn't care if the world went dark afterward and all green things died for lack of light. But Jannus was certain there was noth-ing he himself could do about it. He couldn't even give warn-ing. He could only wait because he would not go ahead.

It became cold, so cold his whole body was numb beyond shivering. He looked out across Erth-rimmon where frost was spreading like swift silver roots, the water jelling wherever the roots thrust. Sleet began to fall, changing to large hurtful hail that battered at him and shattered on the cobbles. A figure leaned from a near doorway and waved for him to come inside. For a second he thought it was Lur, under a roof, which was impossible. Then he saw it was Bluejay. "Quick," she called, "you can't stay out there—it's too dangerous."

"There's nothing I can do about it. I have to wait for Ashai."

"It's not my doing," she disclaimed impatiently. "I showed you all the protections."

"Bluejay, Crow's dead," he found himself telling her, forgetting his wariness of her in compassion for her loss. "He won't be coming home. Bremneri have no business on the High Plain."

"Nor do Valde," she snapped, "but what use is that now?"

The hail striking him in the face made him duck his head without answering. The stinging of the blows on his back was like heat, and he wondered why he was so reluctant to shelter in that doorway, why he felt it was so dangerous to go forward when it was so painful to remain where he was. Something cut into his hand, sharp as a flint. He opened his fist to discover the Ardun rose. He had to hold onto it: it was important.

He felt dizzy and stupid, and hoped the audiences wouldn't last too much longer. It was stifling in the Morn-hall, but there wasn't anything he could do about it but wait. The last factor went out finally and as Jannus began putting everything away, the bell rang peremptorily from behind the Stranger-screen. "Show me what you've written," his mother directed. Duty overcoming reluctance, he went toward the screen and entered an overpowering smell of roses. The odor made him somewhat lightheaded, with a hot, fevered feeling that gave a sheen of unreality to the Aihall Square before him.

They were walking down the Rose Way, the Thornwall at their backs. Poli strolled beside him, eating a sticky tart, while Lur, at leash's end, pulled her impatiently on. Jannus lagged behind, trying to concentrate. The last time, she'd said she wasn't really there at all. And she'd promised not to come. He'd called for the favor, and she'd promised. Therefore, she was *not* here. And he was *not* in Ardun either and Lur was dead in Downbase.

He stopped altogether and called out, "Shai, if you can hear me, stop this!"

A cloaked figure ahead turned and deliberately put back his hood: Ashai Rey, just as he'd appeared in Lisle. Ashai leaned on his stick, plainly waiting for Jannus to catch up, the indifferent strollers passing around him. Jannus went forward, the scene around him becoming firmer and more distinct with each step.

"I've been trying to rouse you for some time now," said Ashai. "But you refused to come near enough for me to edit your illusions with any precision. You're still on the fringe of my control. Come inside."

They turned toward the Aihall. Poli and Lur still accompanied them but Jannus ignored them because he knew they weren't there. Gradually he lost his immediate sense of their presence: they faded into strangers, into the anonymous crowd.

Jannus looked over toward the duelling pit where a match was in progress: a fish against a wheel, according to a notice board.

"A nice touch," remarked Ashai.

"Thank you," replied Jannus, since it seemed to have been a compliment.

"I like Ardun myself," commented Ashai, glancing up toward the arches and the railed galleries of the Aihall. "I would have sent the mobile there, but the Mastership is hereditary and there is too much assassination and thieving of children among the Andrans to make such a mobile practical."

That reminded Jannus that he was accompanied, not by Ashai himself, but by an image of the mobile that spoke directly with the Shai's own voice.

"Can you see my intention?" Jannus inquired, pausing before the central door of the Aihall, unwilling to go any deeper than he absolutely had to.

"Very little. The projector takes just enough to create this scene and adapt it to your responses. However, I deduce a great deal."

"Is it necessary for me to come in?"

"If you don't you'll collapse of sunstroke," stated Ashai's image curtly. "Nor can you safely retreat. If you try to go back, I'll be unable to reach you or help you in any way whatever."

Sunstroke? But he'd just left Poli. . . . That thought trailed off into uncertainty. "What time is it, then?"

"It's about an hour before noon."

Jannus recalled the sensations of heat and wondered whether they had been actual or the Shai's attempts to wake him or just more illusion spun from the threads of his own wishes. "Is this a matter in which you're constrained from lying?"

"I never lie. I merely do not always tell all the truth that I know. You must accept my word. You have no alternative."

Jannus could think of no argument to that. He went through the door.

They entered a broad straight hall carpeted with rush mats which gave the air a familiar smell. Shadowed half-seen figures like Valde stood in recessed niches, holding torches. Jannus was reminded of Northwing in his mother's household.

The cool hall led them to the arched opening of a brightly-lighted chamber with a black stone floor inlaid with a yellow circle surrounded by twisting fire-shapes. The whole inlay seemed to be metal—the largest amount Jannus had ever seen at one time. He wondered how so odd an image had been drawn from him.

In the chamber, as in a Bremneri audience room, there was only one chair. This one, green plarit not unlike the green-stone guest-seat in the Morn-hall, had unusual angles. It rose from a broad smooth legless base, curved in to form the seat, and curved again to a high pointed back topped with a small cross with equal arms. The effect of the chair was not square but triangular—three tall triangles, joined at the edges, with a seat cut into one side.

Ashai's image moved across the room and stood waiting for him.

Jannus paused in the door arch. "I don't know the Way of Downbase. I would like to know what any Tek would ordinarily know about the customs of this place."

"Very well. This is indeed Downbase, though what you see is an image of it. It is as you see it, except that no mobile is here. Through the sun image passes all the power collected by the lattice within the lake. By stepping onto it and touching the green seat, a Tek takes onto himself the Rule of One, claiming absolute control and absolute responsibility for everything done with that power. His redes are destroyed in that instant and no other is ever recorded. He has immediate access to all the information, patterns, and relationships I am aware of and he can direct me to pursue, expand, or apply my knowledge in any way that seems good to him. When he gives a command, one of two things happens: either the command is obeyed, or he is incinerated by the unshielded power. The restrictions that bind me also bind whoever holds the Rule of One; some matters must not be initiated or carried out without unanimous consent of that confederation of Teklords which is no longer available for consultation. . . . In practice, this means that some things cannot be commanded or done; instead, you would forfeit the Rule and its protections from the power. That is, I judge, as much as will be useful to you."

Jannus reviewed the summary as he would the terms of a contract proposed in his presence as Audience Scribe. He asked slowly, "Since there is so much of the High Plain I don't know, could I be warned before I commanded something forbidden, something not permitted to either you or the king?"

"No. Some allowances, I can make; but not that one."

"Then can this thing be settled from here, without my calling for the Rule of One?"

"Not by you. As I said, you cannot, now, go back through the field of the projector without my consent. And I will not shut down, stop, the projector except by command of the king. It is my only protection, and I am not permitted to fail to prevent my own destruction. Nor would I wish to. Immortality is natural to me."

Jannus considered the answer soberly and found it convincing. He stepped into the room, across the flame-shaped inlays and the disc, and settled into what he thought of as the guest-seat, conscious of its cold glass surface for an instant before ideas, concepts, information of all sorts burst upon him as though he were a funnel through which the sea was trying to pour itself. He was choked, blinded, overwhelmed by it, every thought rousing an infinitude of chaotic echoes so that the only thing left clear was the intensity of his desire that it *STOP*.

He sat panting, his face in his hands.

"This allowance," said the Shai's voice, both larger and more distinct than before, "I can make. You are not accustomed to handling information in this fashion. Were you a Tek, I would have killed you then."

Lifting his head, Jannus found himself alone. The chamber was full of golden light from no single source he could identify. He'd been exempted, he supposed, from the illusion. "If it is possible, I would have the image of Ashai back, to talk to."

Like a coin turning from side to face, Duke Ashai appeared, leaning on his staff before the chair, attentive. Jannus opened his hand, seeking the carved rose, and was surprised to find the cord still around his neck: so that had been a dream too. "If it is possible," he said carefully, "let all the redes that are left be scribed on some solid object. When that is done, let all the High Plain, and all its tools and bases, all die—excepting only Downbase and its lake, which shall continue as before, so long as the Shai consents to remain. Let it be done as quickly as possible. Is that a proper command?"

"You are still here," replied Ashai's image. "Therefore it is begun. When you go, the projector's field will not impede you: I will have no more need of it, either for protection or to allow the Teks to come in. Elda's tools will have no force, and no one will sit in that seat after you. You should know," Ashai continued calmly, "that the last king can command the service of the mobile called Ashai Rey, as a matter of right. But be careful how you command; don't interfere with his purposes for he will kill you if he must, as I would. You can also claim the friendship of the Master of Andras, during his life and yours—a less perilous bond. In token of that, go to the inner door and take what you find there."

On a small pedestal was a clear green oval jewel about the size of a plum, many-faceted. In one end was a small hole. Jannus took it carefully into his hand, guessing what it must be. On impulse he untied the knot of the cord he still held, removed the ivory rose, and strung the jewel in its place. The rose, he laid on the pedestal; the door folded inward like dark petals and was shut.

From the door of Downbase Jannus saw that the Teks had fallen on one another in fury when the illusion was ended. Only one still lived, one of the grey dragons, and it was stalking away, lurching heavily from side to side with each step. Jannus went cautiously from the door toward the lake dome, circling wide around each sprawled unhuman carcass. Though Downbase was roofed, these would not wake again: they had gotten what they had come for. He held them all, he thought, in the hollow of his hand.

He heard a cry like a gull's, far off and faint, and knew Poli had found the circle gone. She would come to him, or he to her, around the great opaque curve of the dome. Jannus went on, in the white sunshine, until he was overtaken by a vast quiet tiredness and had to rest and wait for Poli to come the rest of the distance.

Valde had been pets here on the High Plain for generations as numerous as the rain. From one Teklord's tinkering, he thought, had come all the Haffa, and all journies of all troopmaids to Bremner, and also the chance of children between Valde and folk of other nations.

Therefore Jannus felt it would be entirely suitable to gift Poli with the stone he'd brought from the sun chamber: his own jewel for her to wear, won by service of a sort; in script no eyes could see, much less decipher, it bore the redes of all the remaining Teks of the Empire of Kantmorie that at last was fallen and done.

DAW PRESENTS MARION ZIMMER BRADLEY

"A writer of absolute competency . . ."—Theodore Sturgeon

☐ **STORMQUEEN!**
The first novel to describe the Ages of Chaos and the original misuse of Darkover's matrix science . . . a brilliant new novel. (#UJ1381—$1.95)

☐ **THE FORBIDDEN TOWER**
"Blood feuds, medieval pageantry, treachery, tyranny, and true love combine to make another colorful swatch in the compelling continuing tapestry of Darkover."—Publishers Weekly. (#UJ1323—$1.95)

☐ **THE HERITAGE OF HASTUR**
"A rich and highly colorful tale of politics and magic, courage and pressure . . . Topflight adventure in every way."—Analog. "May well be Bradley's masterpiece."—Newsday. "It's a triumph."—Science Fiction Review.
(#UJ1307—$1.95)

☐ **DARKOVER LANDFALL**
"Both literate and exciting, with much of that searching fable quality that made Lord of the Flies so provocative."—New York Times. The novel of Darkover's origin.
(#UY1256—$1.25)

☐ **THE SHATTERED CHAIN**
"Primarily concerned with the role of women in the Darkover society . . . Bradley's gift is provocative, a top-notch blend of sword-and-sorcery and the finest speculative fiction."—Wilson Library Bulletin.
(#UJ1327—$1.95)
